CONSEQUENCES

A 2040 Scenario

Vaughan Whitlock

NATIONAL
LIBRARY
OF AUSTRALIA

A catalogue record for this
book is available from the
National Library of Australia

Publisher:
ASPG (Australian Self Publishing Group)
P.O. Box 159, Calwell, ACT Australia 2905
Email: publishaspg@gmail.com
http://www.inspiringpublishers.com

National Library of Australia Cataloguing-in-Publication entry

Author: Whitlock, Vaughan

Title: **CONSEQUENCES: A 2040 Scenario**/Vaughan Whitlock

ISBN: 978-0-6450559-5-5 (pbk)

Prologue

Elected in 2024, the Coalition of Independents was a revolutionary government, its makeup unprecedented in Australian political history. After decades of disillusionment over two major parties dominated by factional in-fighting and the peddling of power, a fed-up voting public finally pushed the trend towards Independents to a stunning Federal election majority in both Lower House and Senate. A dramatic shift in political culture.

The shift was fundamental. High achieving candidates running for causes, motivated by the disillusionment. Challenging a system that attracted too many salesmen-like fast talkers, often drawn from non-creative professions, selected by outdated party machinery for their ability to convince people and garner votes. Now the convincing would be policy based.

A constitutional crisis threatened, the Independents having a majority but no party structure or leadership. The two previously dominant parties each tried to form government by courting them individually. But that was against the people's mandate. Instead, all Independents joined a loose coalition. Consensus would be a prominent feature, each member required to seek, demonstrate then follow the will of their electorate on major social issues. Lightning fast electronic media would play its part. A Leader and Deputy were selected by majority vote of members, portfolios allocated by a consultative process based on preferred areas of interest and expertise each member submitted.

Two crucial factors, largely absent under previous politics, made for success and an amazing turnaround in respect from the people nationwide. Consensus in such pure form on issues socially significant meant a direct link to people power influencing government action. And the calibre of person in government was widely different. Creative people, with expertise in technical and developmental industries, specialists experienced in a particular sector of productive worth. Reflecting a culture of achievement, not just to have a political career or indulge in powerbroking. In the absence of boys club-type party machinations, women made up by far the highest proportion of members ever in an Australian government.

When the Coln government came to power, the world was struggling with the aftermath of a global health pandemic giving rise to deep economic recession. War had followed, centred in the Middle East. Pressures too great. It was swift, a culmination of perennial conflict in the region. Severe disruption to oil supplies exacerbated the sluggish recovery of an already decimated world economy, worst in the Middle East where recovery from military action would take much longer. Acts of terror, for years a blight on world peace, were further proliferating. Australia suffered two, resulting in loss of life and iconic infrastructure, several other attempts thwarted by vigilant police detection.

Climate Change was a critical issue. The world's oceans warming and acidifying, ice caps melting, sea levels rising, extreme weather events more commonplace. Australia, becoming a hotter drier continent, was foremost in the rapid depletion of biodiversity, affecting the food chain. Of great concern was a hot area off the coast of Japan, radiation spewing from a nuclear facility destroyed by tsunami over a decade ago. No known technology was available to contain the effects of meltdown, considered as potential ultimately for life extinction on the planet if unresolved. Scientists were working frantically on a solution.

Emissions to the atmosphere, largely from coal-burning power stations and fossil-fuel driven transportation, long highlighted by scientists as the principle cause of global warming and Climate Change, were not reducing despite intense pressure on international politics. Too much scepticism in quarters of power more concerned with economic ramifications.

Balance of power in the world was changing. The United States of America, weighed down by war and adverse economics, embracing nationalistic policies focussed on their own greatness, self-victimised by obsession with guns and socially imploding, was less influential, becoming isolated. Their unmatched military might, however, had the world on edge. Space travel ambitions, return to the Moon and beyond, were on hold.

China, neither weighed down by wars nor constrained by socially or morally demanding doctrine, was establishing a domineering influence, for many years having patiently and systematically pushed their tentacles into every corner of the world. Although powerful militarily, they preferred to wage war through economics. Quickest to recover from recession, they exploited a world economy in disarray to run alternative systems that were simpler, in line with their own direct ideology. Money only real and transactable if representing solid assets, of which they held huge reserves. Not money printed to chase or rollover indulgent debt and deficit, or floating in cyberspace under virtual transacting, like an elaborate pyramid scheme. That ever-expanding bubble, pricked by the pandemic, had exploded in a puff of virtuality. Opening the way for manipulating cyber activity to suit.

India, beginning from a far lower base, was also on a steeply rising curve of influence in the world. Along with China, future powerhouses through sheer weight of population numbers. Chinese and Indian presence in Australia was substantial and growing rapidly.

Such was the scene when Coln took office. Gelling with State politics loomed as a major obstacle. Every State and Territory government feared a similar outcome at their next election. In Queensland, where the trend to Independents first escalated to serious levels and continued strongest, incumbent State Labour took the pragmatic approach of full cooperation. They would be rewarded with holding on to office, albeit narrowly, the electorate favouring maintaining a power balance. Wisely, other States and Territories followed suit, giving Coln unprecedented freedom to implement their visionary agenda. Traditional blame game between State and Federal, while not completely eliminated, was largely superseded by Coln's determination to push through reforms they believed in, whether or not overlapping State responsibility. The public in general loved what they were seeing, the silent majority aroused and highly supportive.

Coln set out to tackle major issues of the day with immediacy. Many for years festering unresolved or stymied by political gamesmanship. Massive funding was channelled into Research & Development, recognised as fundamental in developing civilisation from the stone age through industrialisation to today's world of computer-dominated technology. A determined commitment to draw the nation's highly capable but hitherto under-utilised expertise and brain-power together, seeking to put the nation at the leading edge internationally of future advancement. Problems of the world beckoned.

The commitment covered a wide scope. Technical, Scientific, Medical, and by association universities, colleges, hospitals, the manufacturing sector all benefited and blossomed. The eternally ongoing quest for remedies to fight superbugs and viruses, of high priority worldwide following the disastrous pandemic all too recent in memory, was strongly supported by Coln. Antibiotics becoming increasingly ineffective was a widening void.

Breakthroughs soon followed. Discovering a use for carbon capture, capping off fossil-fuel power station releases, meant emissions polluting the atmosphere reduced to zero. The resultant economic windfall skyrocketed as all nations of the world took it up, alleviating Energy sector and Climate Change concerns. The demand for Australia's mining products boomed.

Renewable energy resources such as solar, wind and others also boomed. Coln fuelled competition by injecting even more funding into R & D. The effect was exponential, undreamed of in times gone by. Targets, an obsession of previous politics, were irrelevant as progress maximised. Unemployment plummeted, further feeding the economic blast-off. Coln's forward-thinking blueprint to embrace a big picture future was paying off handsomely, soon to wipe out the enormous debt the crippling recession had imposed. Reward from the bold, positive mentality of Coln members, supporting progress not politics.

Then another huge breakthrough. Nanotechnology. Research had begun many years earlier, but lack of political interest and minimal funding left it meandering to a near halt. Now, it was different. Working at the molecular level had enormous potential. A major advance was batteries small in physical size but of vastly greater storage capacity. Immensely significant. Nanotechnology, set to rival the wheel or computer in its profound influence on future life.

Such a versatile power source of light weight, no Climate Change worries led to the advent of hover vehicles, replacing fossil-fuel driven. Moving low over any kind of terrain in a state of least resistance represented the ulti-mate efficiency in land travel. An adaptation from drone technology, also advancing in sophistication. The demand for oil crashed.

Nano batteries were of great benefit to solar and wind energy production, elevating storage capability to the promise of future base-load power supply for domestic and industrial usage. Burgeoning energy farms would soon alter the landscape, increasingly competitive with back in favour clean coal. The effects were world-changing, countries relegating to obsolescence nuclear power with its intrinsic dangers.

Also beneficial to the Artificial Intelligence industry. Power supply, along with programming, was a limiting factor, but with an implanted nano power pack supplying energy near indefinitely, a robot would sustain itself without external source. Robotics, substituting for humans in menial repetitive and dangerous tasks, was greatly impacting the Manufacturing and Health sectors. Coln was intent on Australia's AI industry becoming world leaders, plying their unprecedented doctrine of value-adding wherever possible.

The visionary thinking of Coln manifested in many areas of practical and social significance. Past water resources studies gathering dust were revisited, with intent to alleviate drought-stricken inland areas and over-exploited river systems. Land once fertile now marginal, once marginal now unviable was a worsening trend affecting food supply. For too long blamed on Climate Change, but politics was no saviour. Severity deemed feasible the long distance delivery of water from regularly flood-stricken North Queensland, feeding into major river systems to the south. Coln seized on a scheme, fast-tracking it to completion of dams, catchments, long pipelines and tunnels within ten years. They slashed water allocations exploited by overseas big business and dealt harshly with callous uncaring over-users, those who'd been corruptly contemptuous of water agreements enabled by incompetent or complicit bureaucracy.

Water infrastructure enhancement led a boost to forestry, tree plantations, farming. Hence climate! Better able to deal with the menace of bushfires regularly plundering large tracts of land and communities. Again, Climate Change blamed, obscuring past failings. Coln set out to mitigate the effects, funding a huge lift in firefighting capability, maximising readiness. Playing catchup no longer the norm in times of crisis. Homesteads and settlements, people determined to live in bushfire-prone areas, required to take responsibility for themselves. Failure to comply with or maintain stringent protection measures would void their insurance. Coln left little to chance, focussed on adjustment and sustainability of life, not dwelling on appeasing dogmatic expectations of arresting let alone reversing Climate Change.

A wonderfully successful project was the Very Fast Train between Canberra and Sydney. Also completed inside ten years. Running express from upgraded Canberra airport to Sydney Central took an hour, less time than conventional transport would take from long-mooted but now discarded second Sydney airport out west. Or stopping at regional centres between, as well as branch route around western Sydney. Incentivised by Coln, businesses decentralised, serviced by the VFT. Movement of people followed, heralding a boom in regional town real estate that helped alleviate housing affordability crisis. Planning began for the same between Canberra and Melbourne.

A socially sensitive issue festering for decades was asylum seekers attempting to enter the country by boat. Coln slammed successive past governments for their morally bankrupt ineptitude. Some had drowned at sea under one regime that failed to control the numbers. But under the next, the methods had been worse than draconian, preferring the cynical debasement of people, including children, held in third country hell-hole detention centres for years. Or turning boats back, forcing them to be at sea longer, causing further drownings on one infamous occasion. Finally, remaining numbers were repatriated, offshore centres closed keeping open one only on Christmas Island, an Australian protectorate to the north west. Australia's human rights record had taken a battering internationally. Consequences.

Coln took a totally different approach when the first boat appeared on their watch. The toughest policy yet. Interdicted and towed to Christmas Island, would-be asylum seekers were taken ashore, boat burned on the beach. Two days were enough to confirm they were not genuine refugees, having paid big money for a people smuggler to carry them past other countries, as opposed to someone fleeing across the nearest border with the shirt on their back. All were sent back to country of origin. No hassle, no negotiating, no legal challenges, no leniency. Simply applying long-established international law that no one try to enter a country without proper paperwork. The effect was dramatic, killing off the supply and demand people smuggling business overnight. No demand for being immediately returned, a waste of time and money. No more boats after that.

Indigenous Affairs was another area Coln cited for past mismanagement. Endless talk about disadvantage, unemployment, health and education, alcohol and substance abuse, domestic violence and child abuse, incarceration, suicide, all the problems but no solutions. Former governments had thrown money at the issue, intent on favourable comparison politically. Or contrived gestures, symbolic apologies for historical abuse offering momentary appeasement but changed nothing.

Coln, again with a different approach, recognised a fundamental principle. Any human being needs something worthwhile to do in their life, a reason to get up in the morning with positive anticipation. Projects and programmes, run by professionally qualified engineers, managers, logistics experts, transportation and the like, being offered incentives to experience the outback, encouraged initiative and enterprise while training indigenous workers. Similar to overseas aid programmes of the past, why not within Australia?

Cleaning up outback settlements, building projects, assisting forestry, maintaining tree plantations, clearing scrub from around homesteads and settlements prone to bushfire. All useful to the nation's needs. Gelling also with wider vision in water resources, conservation, health of river systems. Study courses and apprenticeships abounded. A dramatic change in attitude swept indigenous communities, a shift forward from wallowing in the past, seeking more apologies, peddling guilt. Real change in living standards would take longer, but amazingly the entrenched problems of health, abuse, violence began improving, enabled through properly targeted funding. Natural consequences.

Communications overlaid everything. The dominating power of computer and mobile-based social media had become endemic in controlling people's lives. Speed of interaction between electronic devices meant time only to address superficial imagery and surface-deep impressions, increasingly substituting for in-depth human interaction. Social adjustment unable to keep up with technological advance. Confusion inevitable, especially in impressionable young people. And disrespect for authority, notably in schools. Privacy a major issue, personal information, hostile and intrusive contact inadequately controlled.

Breaking news anywhere, beaming worldwide at speed, had forced the more formal outlets of television, radio, newspapers and magazines to be involved. Invasion of privacy affecting all walks of life, changing behaviour. No one immune from exposure of their actions. Prominent public figures, personalities, celebrities, politicians all obsessed with avoiding the prejudice or discrimination label, terrified the rapid often superficial reporting of any utterance or stance taken could jeopardise their career. Or identified for past misdemeanours, sexual harassment and deviancy, in some cases going back thirty, forty years, bad ones proven going to jail. Deep questions being asked. Who was above the law? Powerful leaders? The most wealthy? Long-standing religious institutions? Royalty?

Safest was to slip behind the cloak of political correctness. Further blurring the boundaries between real and virtual. Confused consequences.

Behavioural change had given rise to the age of individualism. People focussed on self as protection from the exploitative speed and social maladjustment. Inevitably, it all hurtled towards crisis. The trigger pushing beyond tipping point of tolerance was when Faketing took hold. Ultimately scandalising. The ability to substitute fake images and actions in part of real ones, seamlessly, utterly demonised the internet, corrupting evidence, falsifying authenticity, turning virtual into artificial. Synchronised, of course, with the same ability as to voice and sound recordings. Social media platforms were decimated, until unprecedented new filters could be created to detect Faketing. Frantic global cooperation led to draconian legislation and huge penalties, jail and monetary, for platform operators and offending subscribers. Under the very tight restrictions, internet and social media evolution plateaued, still powerfully influential but no longer galloping wildly out of control.

Through it all, Coln members were smart, realising the all-pervasive use of social media was insurmountable. Yet while it helped with their consensus doctrine, they would not be dominated by it, ensuring the best filters sifted out scammers, crank and malicious contact. Practical action and achievement prevailed, let the media circus play out in whatever way its participants chose. Coln used all media as an open platform to inform and explain. Over ensuing years, their philosophy worked. No need for pondering over political poll results, their popularity clearly evident. Opposition politicians and media barons, often resembling automatons with no empathy for people, blitzed every available space to attack and denigrate. But the public at large appreciated the purest manifestation of democracy yet perpetrated. Reinforced by projects underway, resolution of long-running issues, a booming economy. People power, the non-violence of it not going unnoticed by the rest of the world.

A particularly proactive initiative by Coln was to set up Rehabilitation Centres for drug users. Acknowledging a worsening crisis decimating the nation's youth. Rejecting populist social theories such as safe injecting rooms, pill testing and the like, which they saw as copping out from a problem too difficult, Coln adopted the straightforward approach that drug-taking was destructive to the health no matter how it was done or in what environment. No such thing as "safe", there was only addiction, brain damage, hopelessness.

Draconian measures created a special arm of police, the DP or Drugs Police. Their task, helped by use of drones, was to pick up serious drug users and deliver them to a Rehabilitation Centre, no choice. With next of kin or guardian consent, the only concession to human rights advocates, treatment would follow. Centres were supplied with the best equipment and personnel, top specialists in psychology, neurology, physiology, skills assessment and other relevant disciplines. Only when fully cured, over months if necessary, would a detainee be released, to join a programme of placement in study, training or a job. Consistent with Coln's vision of full employment to promote growth and development. And to better prepare the nation's next generation workforce.

Cooperation of State and Territory Administrations was necessary. Faced with Coln receiving strong consensus support from the public, they reluctantly acquiesced. Human rights groups and Opposition parties were fiercely critical. But after a few years, initially overcrowded Centres were receiving more modest numbers, fewer addicts on the streets, the drugs trade less lucrative. An aggressive anti-drugs education programme had a major impact.

Education featured in the CoIn revolution. Using the political pull they'd established over the States, they put woefully deficient school curricula to the sword, replacing the socially trendy with a return to fundamentals and old-world values. Mobiles were banned during class. Naturally, every student worked with a computer, but to access relevant material only, all social media blocked. Ending the social experimentation. A determined effort to regain lost ground in education outcomes compared to countries hitherto more disciplined. Universities and colleges flourished, enjoying closer relations with professional and technical workforces, all boosted by the big push in Research and Development.

As an all-encompassing philosophy, CoIn dedicated itself to transcending the incessant preoccupation with inward-looking issues of discrimination, prejudice, racism, human rights, perceived threats to freedoms and other debilitatingly divisive obsessions promoted by the self-serving social do-gooders of Australian society and exacerbated by ambitious but nervous media pundits and petrified politicians. Instead, they focussed on positive thinking, achieving what was available to be achieved, enabling and encouraging all Australians, able and disabled alike, to maximise whatever they were capable of doing. No more legislating convoluted laws attempting to regulate people's behaviour. Rather, they relied on education and leading by example with forward progressive attitude, projects and programmes. The philosophy embraced all ethnic groups, helping to de-radicalise terrorist elements in some as moderate elements responded to better control their own. Gradually the heightened terror alert eased, nevertheless without fully dissipating.

Coln would not, however, repeal existing laws the people had voted for and were irreversible, such as same-sex marriage, an area where problems were developing. Respecting the people's wishes, consistent with consensus. Evolution decides consequences.

So successful was the Coln phenomenon, they were re-elected for a remarkable fifth term in 2036. But all was not so rosy by that time. After euphoric record majorities in their second and third terms, cracks in the never perfect consensus system began to widen during the third. Their majority was severely cut in winning their fourth, along with loss of Senate control for the first time. They won their fifth term with a paper-thin result and continuing hostile Senate.

Growing dissent from within, relentless pressure from Opposition parties and State Labour or Lib/Nat governments never relinquishing allegiance from their Federal counterparts were behind the decline in Coln's fortunes. Consensus by electorate had, early on, been a brilliantly successful example of democracy at work, but a little idealistic. Sustaining it consistently over time had become laborious, often unwieldy and not strictly adhered to. Even when done properly, it rarely produced a unanimous decision. Usually there was a member or electorate left dissatisfied, sometimes several.

The historical divide between rural, regional and urban priorities was mostly kept under wraps by Coln's progressive projects, but ultimately the forces were too powerful to resist. Some members felt they'd been made to compromise too much too often. Factions began to form, a return to old-style discredited politics imminent. Within an original structure loosely formed and spectacular for its absence of factions, a dramatic reversion was underway. Clash of egos and powerbroking followed as sure as night follows day.

The Opposition took full advantage, intensifying their opportunistic attacks, sensing an end to their long exile in the political wilderness. Throughout Coln's tenure, they never relented from politicising perceived abuse of human rights, portraying Coln's consensus system and control of the Senate as a blight on democracy, denigrating progressive achievement as discriminatory or prejudiced against freedom of speech, expression, religion or choice. Anything to dent Coln's popularity. Invasive media scrutiny and the time factor contributed, longevity equating to tiredness in the eyes of many.

A scandal broke early 2039, bad timing for Coln in election year. Exposed, as scandals often are, when a grubby scheme thought by its perpetrators to be foolproof went awry through a relatively simple miscalculation. A baby was born to a female same-sex marriage, deformed and in near vegetable state. It died soon after birth. An autopsy revealed the influence of drugs as high probability of culpable cause.

The parents, certain the pre-agreement screening and assessment of sperm donor and surrogate mother had been less than it should be, engaged a private detective. Quickly he found that a prominent drugs Rehabilitation Centre was involved. Detainees at the Centre had been used, in fact were still there and far from completing their rehab. Before the detective could take it further, he met with a myste-rious accident and was killed.

The involvement of a Rehab Centre, significant in the Coln doctrine, caught the attention of politicians. Suspicious, the Opposition delved deeper. A stunning revelation followed. The Centre had been receiving additional government funding, considerably higher than any other in the country. Then the truth came out. Coln's Deputy Leader, a gay woman instrumental in the drugs clean-up programme, and a male colleague backbencher also gay were running a secret racket in cahoots with Centre management. Drug detainees used to supply same-sex marriages with babies, without payment for their service. Examples were uncov-ered of rehab delayed, extended, or worse even reversed, if causing any trouble. A highly profitable scam.

Heads rolled within Coln, including the Leader. A reserved and highly intelligent family man with wife and two teenage children, always the quiet strength behind Coln's success. But he took the fall along with his callously crim-inal colleagues, accepting responsibility despite insufficient evidence implicating him directly. The furore accelerated the political trend, the damage terminal and Coln was deci-mated at the election later in the year.

The new Labour government came to power at a time when military conflict in the world was at a low ebb. Countries of the Middle East had been slow to recover from major war of the early 2020s, the region's influence on world affairs greatly diminished, demand for oil a fraction of its former due to technological advance. Terrorist acts and subversive reprisals were the preferred means of hitting back, however would-be attacks were largely thwarted as enhanced surveillance, intelligence and response capability worldwide became dominant.

Technology was the great focus now, controlling every facet of life. Artificial Intelligence, a major participant in industry, was verging on introduction to communities for domestic application. Set to match if not surpass the impact of computer and mobile communication. Social media advancement had levelled out, under strict control after a worldwide re-think over corrupting influences.

But the big worries were still Health and Climate Change. Vaccines to combat mutating superbugs and viruses came on stream regularly, but as yet no blanket protection such as antibiotics had provided. And despite technology having brought renewable energy and clean coal on stream, making full political will easier, more than a decade of zero emissions to the atmosphere had made no difference to global warming. Deforestation had come into greater focus, historically an unpalatable issue politically. Citing less wealthy countries cutting down their rainforests for economic gain was problematical. But the planet must breathe. Science was unequivocal about the vital role of rainforests. The practice had finally ended. But again, making no difference to global warming a decade later.

Depletion of Earth's ice caps continued unrelenting, North-west passage open to shipping year round, Greenland glaciers severely diminished. The Gulf stream drastically slowing caused Northern Europe and Scandinavia to become frozen like the northern parts of Canada, near uninhabitable. But the potential for worse was elsewhere. The great engine-room of world climate, Antarctica, was changing rapidly. Ice shelves being undermined, large chunks regularly breaking off to float north and melt. Several years back, a major shelf broke away and slumped into the sea. A small but significant rise in global sea levels resulted from the melt. An outcome ongoing, inexorable, inevitable.

Many questioned the science. Was warming simply a natural phenomenon irrespective of mankind's actions? Scientists were adamant politics had delayed solutions too long, making Climate Change irreversible. But the trend was not slowing even slightly, lending weight to sceptics' arguments. The focus gradually shifted from blame to adjustment, accepting that permanent change was happening, the sustainability of life paramount.

Balance of power in the world had continued to shift. The United States, devastated by mountainous debt, war engagement and destructive politics, was no longer supreme, despite their military strength still putting them above laws or meaningful influence from other nations. But choked by social decay within. No power on earth could cause their decline, they could only do that to themselves.

China had taken a defining step, further promoting their alternative version of capitalism by transacting only through their own currency. The yuan took over from the US dollar as the world's premier currency in trade, commodities and economic activity generally. A relatively simple act, cementing their superpower status while savaging the already depleted United States. World war was looming as an ever more likely consequence.

But China was afflicted with burgeoning social problems of its own. Many Chinese, no longer tolerant of a one-party system, wanted the freedoms enjoyed under western democracies. A dawning realisation as affluence abounded, more of their enormous population lifting from peasant to middle-class and beyond, everyone with a mobile connecting to instant social media that portrayed the world on screen. An unstoppable dynamic. Political unrest, steadily growing over years, was accelerating at a torrid rate in a strident push for democracy. Hong Kong had been through it years earlier, but swallowed up, no longer a major business and financial centre, becoming China's deep sea port most strategic as gateway to South China Sea operations.

India was following up fast. Along with China, some forty per cent of the world's population. World order, an inexorable process of evolution.

Such was the environment facing new Labour. In keeping with entrenched tactics, they focussed on distancing themselves from the Coln legacy. Not easy, with so many initiatives in progress, unwise if not impossible to denigrate. To chart a different course, they maintained concerns about discrimination and prejudice so effective in blunting Coln popularity to deliver electoral success. Hardly a practical action plan, at best a debate driver. Inevitably, combative politics and ego-driven power struggles resurfaced. Social do-gooders again to the fore, political correctness on a comeback, the news media back in the big-time.

An issue historically controversial challenged new Labour early, testing the genuineness of their freedoms and human rights focus. A boat of asylum seekers arrived in Australian waters, the first for fifteen years since Coln's tough uncompromising policy had cut dead the people smuggling business overnight. Only Pacific-based environmental refugees displaced by sea level rise had been accepted, but processed and transferred in an orderly fashion. Now, long memories of inept policy when Labour was last in power was prompting a new test of resolve.

Normal practice was followed initially, asylum seekers to Christmas Island, boat burned on the beach. Then everyone waited while a furious debate broke out. The government was intent on imposing new standards to claim the moral high ground as champions of human rights. Before the week was out, another boat arrived, then another. Coln and the Lib/Nat Opposition party combined their numbers in the Lower House and looked likely to top the government's slim majority as several Labour members threatened to cross the floor. With no alternative solution and fearing an early political crisis with more boats on the horizon, the government relented and adopted the Coln policy.

A humiliating defeat. The first seeds of disunity sown. Factional differences re-born. Would lessons of the past be heeded? Were there enough members left from that darker time to remember the destructive power of disunity deciding political fortunes?

Another issue arising early concerned drugs rehabilitation. The government chose to view forced detention of drug users at Rehab Centres as attacking their human rights, deprivation of liberty. The DP had become a well-knit, highly efficient arm of police in tracking and picking up drug users. In order to not lose that expertise, the government changed their duties. Still to be known as the DP, but no longer the Drugs Police, instead now the Discrimination Police. Set to identify and expose instances of discrimination and prejudice in the community, able to issue citations to offenders. Drone surveillance, with its ever-improving sophistication, would continue as an invaluable asset.

Rehab Centres began running down. No longer required, professional personnel and medical staff departed. Some Centres switched allegiance, facilitating drug users in the name of 'safe houses' or 'injecting rooms'. Others simply closed down.

Such was the new pattern of government. How would the radical change of political focus affect people in their day to day lives? Consequences.

Chapter 1

Jude sat staring out across the water, glad the bench seat had a canopy roof offering shelter from the direct sun. Jet skiers skimming over the gentle surf, a scattering of people on the sand, but he barely took it in, his mind preoccupied as usual with home.

"Why?" he murmured to himself, shaking his head worriedly. "Why don't I feel the way they do?" No one, including the school counsellor, was able to tell him anything that made sense. Only, it seems, what made sense to them. His own parents the worst, inflaming his frustration like nothing else.

The thought jolted him. Time! Anxious, he reached for his mobile to check. No mobile. Of course, it was confiscated today. Absent-mindedly, he'd forgotten to put it on silent mode at the start of class, the first time to slip up in more than eleven school years. At least he left it in a locker at the front, unlike some of his classmates deliberately or inadvertently defying the long standing restrictions. He was aware of a shift in attitude since the new Labour government came in last year. Pre-empting a likely easing due to policies more socially trendy than those of the former Coalition of Independents, which had successfully addressed the crisis in declining education outcomes nationwide. He smiled to himself, inwardly gratified at his small measure of defiance, even though unintended and it meant being without his mobile until tomorrow.

Feeling better, he returned to his hoverbike at the nearby stands. He took a long drink from his water-bottle, helping to alleviate the effects of oppressive afternoon heat. Heading away from the beach, he was resigned to whatever mood might prevail at home tonight. He passed an example of the DP, a special arm of police, interrogating someone by the side of the road. Not an unusual sight in the new political climate with its refocus on discrimination issues. A drone hovered overhead, instrumental in detecting the misdemeanour.

Dad was waiting on the front steps as he turned into the driveway. His fathers were always home before him, having arranged their work hours to suit. The hard-set thin lips and slightly bulging eyes was a familiar look. "What time is this!" Dad chastised accusingly. The reprimand was typical, no leniency for even small margins of error. "Dado wants to talk to you." He indicated inside. "You can explain to him why you're late."

Dado was slowly pacing the lounge floor, agitated. He looked up quickly as Jude entered. "Ah." He gave an insipid smile, running a hand over his short stubble haircut then rubbing a one-day unshaven chin. "How was school today?" A calculated opening.

Jude knew it was hardly where his father's concern lay. No mention of being late. "Okay," he replied carefully. "Except I had my mobile confiscated. Forgot to turn it off."

Dado gave a short grunt, Jude's admission barely registering. "Someone told me you're interested in a girl." He paused, giving Jude a sharp look.

A familiar tension gripped Jude's insides. His head dropped, his feet shifting nervously. "I'm not sure," he murmured, without looking at his father. His tongue stuck for anything further to say.

Dado suddenly flashed a smile. "That's good. Good." He emphasised the word, but it came over as strained.

An awkward silence followed. After a few seconds, Dado moved closer and put an arm around Jude's shoulders. "Son, we want what's best for you." Another pause. "You understand that, don't you?" His tone stopped short of demanding a correct response, but was condescending. "You're sixteen now. Past the age of consent. It's right that you form proper relations with others. We'll help you with that." He glanced away.

Feeling stifled, Jude followed his glance. Dad was leaning against the door jamb, having listened to their conversation. He moved closer, joining side by side with Dado. The two together could almost be taken as twins, both with shaven head appearance and medium build, Dad a little shorter in stature. Their sexuality was clearly evident, a partnership unremarkable now over twenty years since the advent of same-sex marriage.

They constantly pressured but stopped short of enforcing the shaven head look on Jude, who steadfastly refused to give up his full crop of wavy dark hair. Of similar height to Dado but slimmer, Jude was searching for his own identity, aware that having facial features similar to both obscured who was his real father. The identity question was not helped by having to call them Dado and Dad, no reference to their real names, Brett and Chas.

Dad's light blue bulging eyes continued to stare penetratingly at Jude. His body tensed as usual, he was as determined as his partner to impress himself on family dynamics. "As Dado says, we want the best for you." He glanced furtively at Dado, then back to Jude. "You know we're joining our friends tomorrow evening, at their place this time. Remember their son Josh? He's looking forward to seeing you again."

Jude felt sick, his mouth dry. Devoid of a response, he said nothing.

"Dinner will be ready soon." Dado stepped back a pace.

In his room, Jude sat on the edge of the bed, staring at the wall. His mind was abuzz, pulled every which way. He knew what they wanted for him, despite the show of favour for meeting a girl. But there was no girl. Pointedly, Dado had asked nothing further about that. No further information sought? Jude's lip curled and he snorted knowingly, realising it was just a ploy to test his reaction. Typical. Over the years, he'd grown to recognise the manipulative innuendo and subtle pressure. The only positive was the greater insight into human behaviour he'd acquired, a result of bad example they unwittingly provided.

He wished there was a girl. But he had no idea how he'd get to know one or what things to say. Through the social media his classmates used incessantly? He was afflicted with a strong aversion to its superficiality, the shallow imagery that was unreliable, often not genuine or authentic, detracting from more in-depth relations between people. Too much akin to the machinations of his fathers.

Jude was as proficient as anyone in using the internet systems necessary for day to day life, including schoolwork, as well as invaluable access to news and current affairs. But his aversion, never trusting it for social interaction, contributed to a feeling of isolation. Particularly at school from the other kids, even though he knew they were no better or worse than him. His existence was solitary, feeling close only to his mother. Unlike the obscurity over fatherhood, no crisis of identity existed concerning his real biological mother.

"Damn!" He really needed his mobile right now. Although Dado had installed a block on it to any communication with his mother, plus an encrypted link to his father's own phone for monitoring purposes, he'd met an electronics expert who disabled that abomination for him in a way undetectable.

A locks expert as well, the man was at orienteering one Saturday, engaged to set the checkpoints each competitor had to unlock and punch their card as proof of reaching there. He could pick any lock, even electronic. Taking a liking to Jude, he showed him how to do it, even obtaining another set of the special wires and equipment needed. Jude practised the skill in secret whenever opportunity presented. Certain it would be useful one day, he kept the gear well hidden from his fathers.

Without his phone until tomorrow, even just to access latest news, the heightened sense of loneliness and confusion churned inside him. He lay back on his bed and stared at the ceiling.

Lara arrived home a little later than normal after talking to her friend. She stowed her hoverbike, then found MumG in the kitchen.

"Hi, L," her mum greeted warmly. "How's your day been?"

"Yeah, good." Lara lightly kissed MumG on the cheek. Glenice responded with the same. Their usual exchange. Lara began helping with dinner preparations.

"I was talking to Jodie," she mentioned, breaking their comfortable silence.

"Oh yes?" MumG was genuinely interested.

"Yeah. She said her dad's away. His job again, happens a lot."

"Well, as a government agent for immigration, I suppose that's not surprising."

"Jodie talks about him a lot. Really misses him when he goes away. She loves her father." Lara went a little pensive. A long-time issue she'd generally become reconciled to had lately begun niggling at her again. "At least she's got a father."

Glenice looked quickly at her with concern. She was well aware, although Lara was very much an open-hearted outgoing girl largely without hang-ups, there was the one area representing something of a void in her life. "But you have two mothers," she replied, trying to make light of it. "What's wrong with that?"

Lara smiled brightly. "Nothing. Nothing at all." She gave MumG another kiss on the cheek. "Where's D?"

"Oh, out the back, I think. In the garden, probably."

Lara sauntered out, finding MumD tending the garden as she often did late afternoon once the heat of day eased a little. "Hi, D."

Doris straightened. "Hi, L. Hope you've got dinner on the way there." They exchanged an embrace of similar warmth as with MumG. Lara had to stoop slightly, Doris a little shorter in stature than Glenice. Both were of solid build, Doris with fair hair nearer shoulder length than darker Glenice. Lara loved her two mums equally. But one significant difference defined them. Doris was her biological mother.

Lara's normally cheerful disposition was still faltering, as the one issue wouldn't go away. She found either mum good to approach about anything, but her blood tie with MumD was a poignant factor. "Can I ask you something?"

"Of course, L. You don't need permission. Just ask."

Lara loved her uncomplicated way. "Well," she hesitated, "do you ever feel sad about not seeing my father?"

MumD's mouth dropped open in surprise. The first time Lara had asked such a question, even though the issue had always simmered as an undercurrent in their lives. "No, I don't," she replied firmly. "He was only the sperm donor. Nothing more."

Now Lara's turn to be surprised. Quite unexpected her father be depicted in such a lowly diminished role. For the first time ever, she felt a discord with MumD. She herself felt diminished, as the product of apparently a loveless arrangement of convenience.

"I'll see if dinner's ready." Forcing the cheerfulness back, she headed inside.

Later, in the confines of her room, Lara stood naked in front of the mirror. Self-examination was not usually her way, but tonight the simple structure of her life she'd always cherished seemed like a burden. At fifteen and nearing the age of consent, she sensed that her two mums were preparing her for adult life. Where would she fit in? Like MumG and MumD? Or like Jodie's parents, man and woman? Her first stirrings of sexuality a couple of years ago had been growing steadily stronger lately. Seemingly in tandem with a growing focus on the void that was her father.

She looked closer at her body. A young woman's body, not too thin or overly solid, just well-shaped with already firm good-size breasts at her still developing age. She liked what she saw. Would someone else like it? The stirrings of sexuality were there again. Somewhat different to how her mums described, whose teachings did not really resonate with her. But she had no idea in what way different. She ran fingers through her shoulder-length blonde hair, taking up a favourable pose.

A knock on the door. "Can I come in?" MumG's voice.

"Just a minute." Lara grabbed her dressing gown and hurriedly threw it on. "Yes, come in."

MumG entered, seating herself on the edge of the bed. She was concerned. "D said you asked her a question this afternoon. Is something troubling you?" She looked at Lara anxiously.

"Oh, I asked her about my father." Lara tried to keep it light and breezy, but without feeling that way. "D said he was nothing more than a sperm donor."

"Well, that's right." MumG turned away, herself vaguely troubled.

Lara picked up on it, always sensitive to the feelings of either mum. "Is there more to it?" Curious, she sat next to her.

MumG was silent for some moments. Her head dropped as past memories came flooding back. "Both of us were served by him." She lifted her head and stared directly at Lara, eyes moist with emotion. "We wanted it that way, equal opportunity. His sperm took with D and she got pregnant. But it didn't happen for me."

Lara nodded in comprehension. "That must have been disappointing for you."

"Oh no. We talked about it beforehand, agreed we'd accept whatever way it went. We just wanted a child, however it might happen."

Lara smiled, feeling buoyed. She had always felt loved by both her mums.

MumG glanced away, suddenly distant. Further emotion gripped her and she began sobbing, hands to her face as an unaccountable anguish took hold.

"There's something more?" Lara put an arm around her in comfort, alarmed.

Struggling to regain control, MumG nodded. The sobbing subsided a little. "He came back. One day when D wasn't there." A further pause. "He raped me."

She broke down again, her emotions more intense. Lara was stunned. Never until now had she any inkling of such a devastating event in their lives. She held MumG close. "What did D do when she found out?"

MumG shook her head. "She doesn't know. Not to this day. Please, you mustn't tell her." She was anxious now. "Promise me you won't tell her!"

"I promise." Lara didn't know what else to say.

Relieved, MumG continued. "It's a long time ago, happened when D was still pregnant. Best forgotten now, so long after."

"Why would he do something like that?"

A lengthy silence before answering, "You see, Lara, sex is not always about love. Often it is about power. His sperm didn't take with me. I don't know why. He was not a nice man. We thought he was to start with, when he first presented at assessment." She let out a deep sigh, becoming philosophical, eyes glazed as her mind went back to the early years. "When same-sex marriage was voted in, the Yes campaign was ecstatic, reward after fighting for decades to change society values. D and I were already together, and we were very happy. Straightaway, we got married, could at last feel equal with heterosexual couples. We looked for a sperm donor. And here we are, still very happy, the three of us together." She leaned against Lara, responding to her warmth.

Lara listened intently, captivated by MumG's reference to earlier times. "I remember you showed me photos and a video. Your marriage was like ---," she paused, "--- made in heaven." Smiling, she added, "Are all same-sex marriages like that?"

MumG gave a short laugh. "We all thought so. The Yes campaign depicted it that way. Deliberately, to win the vote. Glossy advertisements, focus on discrimination and equality, it all worked very well." She hesitated, shaking her head imperceptibly. "But now, years later, I'm not so sure."

"Why? What's different now?"

"Nothing," MumG answered quickly, anxious for Lara not to feel hurt. "But not all marriages are like ours, same-sex or heterosexual. Separation and divorce, adultery, domestic violence, child abuse, broken homes, drugs, the statistics are no different. Maybe worse for same-sex, because the pressures are greater. We've seen a lot over the years, D and I, working at the Rehabilitation Centre."

Lara nodded respectfully, appreciating the efforts and experience of her mothers. "You say the pressures are greater for same-sex. Why is that?"

"Because of having children. Same-sex marriages can't have a child other than by introducing a third party to the marriage."

"Oh yes, of course." An obvious reality, Lara realised. Sperm donor, egg donor, surrogate mother, every same-sex family involved at least a threesome of parents, not just a couple.

"A recipe for vastly more complex inter-relations and conflict." MumG paused, again thinking back to the early years. "We thought the No campaign would hammer that aspect leading up to the vote. Having children was always going to be a natural progression after legalising marriage. But the No people hardly mentioned it. More interested in freedom of speech and religion, all that kind of stuff. Self-interest, I suppose. We were amazed."

"I guess there was a lot of political pressure. It was always going to happen."

"Right, very much so. Pressure straight after as well. Legislation soon passed removing confidentiality around sperm donorship and adoption, legalising surro-gate motherhood. There was a boom in those industries, agencies springing up and flourishing. But they attracted every type of person, good and bad, interested in taking advantage and making money." MumG took a long pause, pensive. Wistfully, she continued, "Our sperm donor came through one of those agencies." She looked ador-ingly at Lara, understanding the problems yet thankful her own family was stable. Lara was a good girl in a loving environment. "But it doesn't matter about him," she said finally. "D has no interest in him. We just wanted you, not him."

Again Lara felt the warmth of their relationship, yet disturbed by the dismissal of her father as worthless apart from the donorship of his sperm. It made her feel of less worth also. She was created from him, just as much as from MumD.

Another question occurred to her. "You said you and D wanted equal chance with his sperm. Why not be egg donor for each other? Then whoever gets pregnant, the other is egg donor and you're both part of it."

MumG gave Lara a respectful look, appreciating her thoughtful insight. "Actually, we were keen to do that. But medical advice recommended a woman should be egg donor for her own surrogacy if possible. Much bigger chance of success, less likelihood of rejection." She hesi-tated, apprehensive. "Most follow that advice, and so did we, to maximise our chances. Of course, we might both have got pregnant. Not as it turned out though."

With an air of resigned acceptance, she stood and made towards the door. "We don't need to trouble D with all this." She wanted Lara to feel reassured. "I'm glad we had this talk. We should do it more often." She departed.

Chapter 2

Today was an important day for the factory. Testing about to start on the latest prototype. They'd been improving it for years since first trialled, promoted as the most advanced robot yet devised in the world. The former Coln government, as part of their popular election mandate, had funded a great push in Research & Development. Favouring Queensland, the State most instrumental in the rise of Independents to power, they moved the AI factory there from a southern State soon after taking office. The new Labour government, despite their more social agenda, were keen to reap political benefit by supporting the rapid advance of Artificial Intelligence. The Science Minister was often seen visiting the factory.

The Minister was not coming today, but the place was abuzz with anticipation. Three groups of technicians hovered at the edge of an arena, waiting. Each technician wore white one-piece overalls and held a handset. At the top of the arena, the head technician stood behind a bench on which sat a computer, about to control the action. Also mounted on the bench was a camera ready to record proceedings. Surrounding the arena were many workers from the factory floor, office and supporting facilities, allowed a break from duties to attend the occasion. An eerie quiet descended over them, a start imminent.

Robin3 was a further advancement from its two predecessors. The name Robin, equally male or female, championed to appease social commentators determined to emphasise its sexual neutrality. Robin3 stood at the centre of the arena, its appearance as humanlike as achievable under state-of-the-art technology. Future prototypes in the Robin series were planned, to introduce facial expression, body language and voice, just like humans. But the main focus in Robin3 was enhancement afforded by sight, hearing and touch senses.

The humanlike duplication was portrayed by a typical average height medium build fit-looking body shape and pale skin colour, overlain dark brown below waist, lighter brown above to the neck, resembling clothing. No hair on top, giving it a slightly confronting skinhead look, not unlike that popular with some people nowadays. The head technician had indulged his sense of humour by putting a pair of white sneaker shoes on its feet.

The entire body, including feet and hands, fingers and thumbs, had touch sense capability. Eyes coloured dark brown and ears housed sight and hearing senses. The nose and mouth, added to complete aesthetics, had no smell or taste sense.

The technicians, three in each group, were ready. A faint ripple pulsed through Robin3 as the head technician activated it from his computer. The dark eyes had greater depth, alive. They could swivel, with peripheral vision, able to take in a horizontal and vertical panorama similar to human capability.

Several workers chosen from the floor emerged, two unarmed, one with a stick, another a heavier club, someone with a wicked-looking knife, another with a long two-edge sword. Starting with the unarmed, each had a turn engaging Robin3, ranging from friendly non-threatening through various stages of intimidatory to aggressive and threatening. The mix was diverse, each worker performing across the full range. Robin3 reacted with speed and efficiency, body movements synchronised with well-coordinated arms and legs. It moved freely around the arena as required to meet every challenge. Response was commensurate with degree of threat, noticeably heightened in speed and focus when faced with the more dangerous weaponry.

The action ramped up as the challengers joined in together, until all six were engaged simultaneously. Some moved out of sight behind to test awareness. Robin3's hearing sense factored into sounds made. A degree of physical contact was necessary to test touch sense, stopping short of all-out attack with intent to injure, testing its reaction to the threat considered sufficient at this stage. Robin3 dealt with it all, impressive. Again, its speed and focus increased when the threat increased.

The final test involved the factory's strongest worker, a powerfully-built man, strengthened by regular training. Muscles rippling, he stepped into the arena, his task to wrestle Robin3. The contest was short-lived. Robin3 seemed to pre-empt every move the wrestler tried to make, thwarting him with speed and guile. Bemused, the wrestler departed. Testing over, the head technician deactivated the creature.

Throughout, the technicians with their handsets monitored and recorded data. One group of three for sight sense, one for hearing, one for touch. The head technician with computer and camera monitored action from an overall perspective.

The crowd of workers dispersed, back to their daily tasks. The test technicians headed for the main laboratory, hours of work ahead to collate and assess data.

Robin3 was developed after the failings of Robin2. Heralded in its day as a sea-change breakthrough in the dynamic world of Artificial Intelligence, Robin2 was the first serious attempt to link sight, hearing and touch senses as direct input to the software. The three senses had been developed in Robin1, storing in memory what it sees, hears and touches, but output reaction depended on programming relevant to set performance tasks reading that input. The Robin2 creation intended the reverse, input stored but directly feeding into the programming to seek an appropriate output. This would lead to greater autonomy, the ability to decide for itself appropriate output as input comes in. Similar to how a human learns from birth using the senses gifted by nature.

The testing of Robin2 had been progressing well, but one day it suddenly went haywire. Its behaviour departed dramatically from anything it was programmed to do. No longer controllable, it was de-commissioned. A reassessment followed, resulting in Robin3.

One of the technicians in the touch group was Brett. His partner Chas was the knife-wielding challenger at the arena. They had met at the factory, working there since its inception and transferring with it to Queensland. Their unwavering love and single-minded dedication to their work, together with bringing up son Jude, accounted for the sum total of their interests in life.

The day's events dominated their talk after work and at home.

"What about when I lunged at him from behind?" crowed Chas, flushed with a sense of importance over his role.

"He knew you had the knife," Brett replied, slightly amused. "His reaction was much quicker. I think you even touched him with it. I'll check sync with the hearing boys."

"Yeah, I thought I was in trouble. Had to back off."

Jude sat quietly at the kitchen table, forced to endure their self-congratulations. He knew enough to have questions. Struck by their male gender bias in describing a sexually neutral entity, he found such affection off-putting, Dado and Dad focussed on themselves. When they showed affection towards him, it felt artificial and too deliberate. But he had to sit there dutifully.

"We'll be late." Dado stood, suddenly conscious of time.

At their new-found friends' place, they were greeted cordially by Jeremy and Chongwe. The two families had met only recently, despite Chongwe working for years at the factory. In his capacity as world-renowned programmer, he was cloistered in the Computer Centre and rarely saw the factory floor, encountering Brett and Chas purely by chance. Common circumstances of same-sex marriage was a magnetic drawcard.

"Come in, come in." Jeremy led them inside, sporting a broad welcoming smile. His Caucasian looks mirrored Brett and Chas, a little more hair on top but similarly keen on the one-day unshaven appearance. Partner Chongwe was somewhat in contrast with his Chinese looks, slimmer build and straight black hair going a little grey.

Their son Josh was waiting at the dinner table. A good-looking boy, slim build, medium-length blonde hair. He said nothing, but eyed Jude curiously. Jude looked away, feeling ill-at-ease. The first time they all met, a brief introduction a week ago, he had quickly felt out of place, wishing he was somewhere else. It was the same now.

Dinner was uneventful as they enjoyed the food prepared by Chongwe, conversation dominated by small-talk or the factory. Jeremy took little part, the factory not within his sphere. Dinner over, they retired to the lounge.

Brett was curious. "What work do you do, Jeremy?" The question had been on his lips since they arrived.

"I'm in Child Protection Services." Jeremy gave a quick smile. "My life's work."

A silence fell, as if the announcement needed digesting. Brett and Chas shared a heightened sense of intrigue. Jude, for the first time, felt a spark of interest.

Chas took it up. "What area are you in?" Child Protection Services, under State government, covered a wide scope. He glanced at Brett, who gave a slight nod of approval.

"We identify children who need help, then guide them on the right path." Jeremy looked pleased with himself.

"Do you talk to their parents?" Brett countered.

Jeremy hesitated. "It depends. Often troubled children are out at night, roaming the streets, even homeless." Again, hesitation. "We use drones, but we're not going around door-knocking for cases, if that's what you're suggesting." He finished with a short laugh. His attempt to make fun of it fell flat.

Jude listened intently, wondering why Jeremy would feel the need to say such a thing. Sounded like a recruitment exercise.

Chas glanced at Chongwe, who'd been conspicuously silent since talk shifted from the factory. "Do you help with this work?"

Chongwe met his glance with steady eyes that bulged slightly wider than normal. "No. I too busy with my work." A momentary pause. "Well, when we take in someone."

"Take in?" Chas replied, further intrigued. "What does that involve?"

"We look after. To make better life."

"When there is no better option," Jeremy chimed in quickly, aware the conversation was taking a slightly undesirable turn. He was cautious, not knowing the other couple well as yet. Being same-sex, however, should probably ensure their support. Maybe even join the cause. He noticed the furtive looks turning in Josh's direction. "Yes, Josh here is a good example. We've had him about six years now."

Josh gave a faint smile. Aware of being suddenly the centre of attention, his head dropped and he stared at the coffee table, saying nothing.

"How did you find him?" Brett asked. He cast a curious glance at Jeremy.

"He's from a broken family. His father is alcoholic and violent, his mother has affairs with other men. We found Josh on the street one night. He needed help. Before getting into drugs."

"Was he on drugs?" A favourite concern of Chas.

"A little, but not in deep, yet." Jeremy was thoughtful. "When we first started helping druggies, it was easy. Then DP got underway, picking up and sending them to a Rehab Centre. We'd try to get them first. Show them a better way." He spoke with arrogance, expecting to exercise control. "It's changed again since the new Federals came in."

"Didn't his parents want him back? How old was he when you found him?"

"He was thirteen. Of course they want him back." Jeremy hesitated, careful choosing his words. "Child Protection Services have strong powers." Again he said it with arrogance, an insidious smile on his face.

To Jude, it presented like a business with a bad smell about it, Jeremy's body language evidence enough of something not right. The rather derogatory term used to describe someone on drugs seemed hardly consistent with a genuine conviction for helping. Warning bells sounded in Jude's head. Instinctively, he felt distrustful of Jeremy. After a lifetime of his own fathers' manipulations, he was sensitised well beyond his years to detecting character quirks.

He noticed Josh had barely moved. Still staring at the coffee table, but hands trembling, body rigid with tension. No one else seemed to notice.

Brett was next to speak. "So, how often have you done this?"

"Oh, many times. As I said, my life's work." Jeremy took a cursory look around the faces. The two fathers seemed supportive. "It is destiny. Identify someone in need, put them on the right course, find a partner and send them out again. Better off than they were." He paused, gratified. "Chongwe and I have taken in many over the years. But nowadays, we only want one at a time."

A stunned silence followed. But Jeremy was into his stride, buoyed by his own rhetoric. "I learned from my father. He was gay. Oh sure, he did enough to have me, and I'm grateful to my mother. But she couldn't stand it. She left when I was young and I've never seen her since." He shrugged, dismissive of it. "I'm fifty years old now." Another pause, momentary only. "My father was part of the Gay Liberation Movement back then. He campaigned for gay rights. Some say it was a political movement, and probably they're right. But it doesn't matter. It's the end result that counts. The momentum was unstoppable. When same-sex marriage came in, everything was possible. I met Chongwe around that time and we never looked back." Filled with self-gratification, he again looked around the faces. Satisfied with what he saw, he fell silent.

Chongwe spoke again, addressing Brett and Chas. "Maybe we retire to other room. Let Josh talk to your boy." He stood. The fathers and Jeremy followed him out.

Left alone with the main subject of the evening, Jude felt a familiar sense of confusion. And of being trapped, as if this was the reason for the evening all along. That his fathers would be complicit was hardly a surprise. Typical of the agenda they had for him. The covert way they operated didn't fool him.

"Sorry to hear about your family," he offered Josh, feeling a genuine concern for him. But he was wary, unsure what Josh expected. Or what the others expected of him.

Josh lifted his head, surprised at the show of kindness. "Thanks." He turned away uncertainly. "Are you gay?"

It was Jude's turn to be surprised, the directness of the question unnerving. But at the same time, it was honest. He appreciated that. "I'm not sure what I am. But I know I don't feel the way they do. How about you?"

"I think I'm gay." Josh spoke quietly, in a resigned tone. "Well, that's what they want me to be."

Jude nodded slowly, very much aware of the pressures. "How about your parents? Either of them gay?" He wondered if there were genetic or hereditary factors in the condition.

"No." Josh spoke with certainty for the first time. "And they're not as bad as Jeremy said just now."

"Why were you taken in here then?"

"Why do you think? In the wrong place at the wrong time." He looked away, suddenly distant again. "My parents fight a lot, no doubt about it. I just want to get away on my own. Try and find myself, who I am. J spotted me. He was full of kind words, especially that I'm good-looking, strong, physical stuff like that. It made me feel better. So I came with him here." A short pause, then he added, "I was not on drugs."

"But why couldn't you just leave anytime you feel like? Go back home. Or your parents find you?"

"I did, and still do. J and C don't try to stop me. You see, it's the kindness that gets you. When it's bad at home, I want to come back."

"Yeah, I see what you mean." Jude nodded in comprehension. But still something seemed not right. If Josh was happy going back and forth, then why the nervous tension? Hands trembling, obviously uptight in their company. Away from them now, he was much more relaxed.

Something else came into Jude's mind. "I remember Jeremy said Child Protection Services have strong powers. That was when he talked about your parents wanting you back. What's that about?"

Josh let out a snort of derision. "He works there. He always arranges a Restraining Order, to prevent parents coming anywhere near here. It's okay to go back home, but he doesn't want anyone knowing what goes on here."

Jude already suspected what goes on, struggling to get his head around it. "How many others?"

"Oh, others like me coming and going, plenty in my time but I think lots more over the years."

"Any girls?"

"No, never." Another derisive snort. "They don't want boy and girl getting together."

Their eyes met and they held each other's gaze in mutual recognition of a telling point. Looking away, Jude felt sick to the stomach at the further confirmation of why he was brought here tonight. But Josh wasn't pushing it, despite being self-proclaimed gay. Was he gay for real? Or converted? Did the latter explain Josh's nervous state?

Vulnerability exploited. And he was only thirteen when it started!

"There's something else they do too," Josh resumed. "Adoption."

"What! They adopt kids as well?"

"No, J and C don't adopt them. They arrange it for other same-sex couples. Male couples of course. I think they make money from it."

Jude's mouth dropped open at the further revelation. "Is that ones they can't find a partner for?"

"Right. Some families are so bad it's like they've lost their kid already. Makes it easy." Josh stared at the far wall, momentarily mesmerised. "I hear J and C talk about it all the time. Different ones, what to do. Part of the Child Protection service." He spoke the last words with a good deal of cynicism.

"It can't be that easy."

"It is. J is always harking back to when same-sex marriage came in. You heard him. Everything opened up after that. Sperm donors, surrogate mothers, adoption. Laws changed, nothing illegal anymore."

Before Jude could answer, the others were returning.

"Hope you two had a good get-together," Jeremy quipped, eyeing Josh.

No one else spoke.

After polite goodbyes, Brett, Chas and Jude departed for home.

Chapter 3

The large office area had a welcoming feel about it. Walls painted a light pastel colour, floor covered in plush carpet. Behind a long bench, evenly spaced cubicles provided work stations for officers. An information kiosk with computers for public use and rows of easy chairs for customers completed the main features.

Lara sat clutching her ticket, waiting for her number to come up on screen. Several others were before her, all seemingly of similar age to herself, male and female. One caught her eye, not immediately obvious which gender.

At last, her number came up. Lara went to the officer whose light was flashing on the bench.

"How can I help you?" the officer asked.

Lara noticed her name tag; Namjit. "I want to find my father."

"Name?" Namjit sat half-turned towards her computer screen, ready to input information.

"I don't know his name."

"No, your name."

"Oh, sorry. Lara. Lara Premble." She felt a little embarrassed, but comfortable in Namjit's presence.

"Your date of birth? And address, phone number?" Namjit spoke quickly, but her manner was pleasant. These were questions she asked frequently in the course of a day.

"Seventeenth of May, Twenty Twenty Four." Lara gave the other information and watched as Namjit entered it to her computer.

"When was the last time you saw your father?"

"Never. I've never known him. He was sperm donor." Lara felt a twinge of humiliation as she said it.

Namjit showed no reaction, the case so far still of common frequency. "Do you have one or more guardians? Age, phone numbers?"

Lara gave MumG's and MumD's details.

"Is one of them your biological mother? And do you all live at the same address?"

"Yes. Doris. And yes, we do."

"They should have a record of who your father is. Have you asked them? Do they have any contact with him?"

"I haven't asked them. And no, never any contact."

Namjit kept inputting Lara's answers. "Is there anything further you can tell me that might help us research who your father is? Anyone else who might help?"

Lara thought for a moment. Perhaps Jodie's father, who was part of State government. Probably unlikely. "No, I don't think so."

Namjit turned to face Lara more directly. "The first step is to ask your mothers. Give them this form to complete, then bring it back here." She printed the form and passed it over the bench.

Lara departed. She glanced at the form, headed 'Department of Family and Child Protection Services'. All the information she gave Namjit was there. Also space for MumG and MumD to write in further information. And, a requirement for one or both to sign giving their permission to proceed with the enquiry. Lara's heart sank, far from sure they would give permission. The rest of the form contained various disclaimers, terms and conditions.

In the heat of early afternoon, she stood on the pavement outside, unsure what to do. Lunchtime at school now. Having taken the decision to skip the morning, she had no desire to return for the afternoon. Keyed up and buoyed by her actions, she headed for the beach a couple of streets away.

Favourite spot for jet skiers, a couple scooting across the water. Watching their efforts emboldened her. "Yes, why not." She clicked Jodie's number on her mobile.

Jodie answered immediately. "Lara, where are you? Why aren't you at school?"

"Remember I told you I want to find my father?"

"Oh, yes?"

"Well, I've just been to the Department. They gave me a form. But I have to get my mothers to sign giving permission. I don't think they'll do that. I was wondering if your father might help. He's involved in that kind of thing, isn't he?"

Jodie didn't answer straightaway. When she did, it was with uncertainty. "Well, not exactly. I think his work is sort of related, though."

"Can I see him this afternoon?" Lara felt suddenly excited. "I remember you said he was back from overseas. Can you call him?"

A brief pause, then Jodie replied, "Tell you what, where are you now? I'll come there. He always sees me if he's not in a meeting."

"Great. I'm at the beach, near the government buildings." Filled with hope, she settled on a bench seat to wait, welcoming the roof that offered shelter from the direct sun.

Jodie arrived and they went to the Department offices where her father worked. He was available. His secretary knew Jodie well and ushered the girls to his office. He greeted his daughter with a warm hug, bringing a pang of emotion to Lara's eyes as the significance of having a father struck home.

"You must be Lara," he welcomed with an approving smile. "Jodie has talked a lot about you. I'm glad she has a friend at school." He indicated a set of lounge chairs around a marble-top coffee table. They sat.

"Thank you, Mr Thornton. I really appreciate you seeing me." Lara felt at ease, taking a liking to him.

"Jodie says you're trying to track down your father."

"Yes." Lara pulled out the form and handed it to him. "I don't think my parents will agree." She looked at him with hope.

He went to the photocopier, taking two copies. "It's not really in my area." He handed the form back to Lara. "I'll see what I can do. Maybe next week, before I go away again. Jodie can let you know."

"You're going away again?" Jodie couldn't hide her disappointment. "How long this time?"

"About a week. Another South Pacific forum. To decide the next movement of environmental refugees." He shrugged his shoulders helplessly. "A regular event, I'm afraid. Until all nations affected by sea level rise are taken care of. Worldwide phenomenon. Queensland takes its share."

Like everyone, the girls were aware of a changing world. The heat every day, especially into afternoon, was a constant reminder. After exchanging further pleasantries, they left.

Outside on the pavement again, plenty of afternoon to go.

"What shall we do now?" Jodie gave Lara an impish look. Neither felt like returning to school.

"I don't know." Lara glanced up the road. "Let's take a look around. I've never been here before."

They wandered past more Departmental offices. Coming to an intersection, they turned up a lesser road. The traffic was light, restricted to people with specific government business, accessing a two-tier carpark. Pedestrians were few. The road was a cul-de-sac.

At the far end, two rows of red and purple alternate flashing lights caught their attention. "Come on, let's see what that is." Lara urged Jodie forward.

Reaching a shop entrance, Jodie started giggling. A sex shop. Lara joined her laughing. They did a fancy dance together, overcome with hilarity at what they'd found.

"Shall we?" Jodie swept her arm towards the entrance in mock invitation. Lara was already heading inside, past the display of sex toys and paraphernalia in the shop window.

Several people were inside, browsing the stands carrying sexually explicit clothing and apparatus, every item imaginable to titillate and stimulate. Walls adorned the same, one taken over purely with videos. Screens were mounted in each corner of the shop at ceiling height. Four screens showing four different acts of sex, each with muted sound effects to match the activity. Surveillance cameras were mounted beside each screen. At the far end of the shop was a service counter, male attendant behind.

Lara could not take her eyes off the screens. One depicted a male and female fornicating, another of two males in similar position, two women together on another, the fourth not immediately clear what act was being performed.

"Stop looking at the screens," Jodie chided, giggling and giving Lara a nudge.

Lara burst out laughing, giving vent to a rising sense of awe at the screen images. Her mothers had never shown her material of this kind. They talked informatively about sexual matters, but coloured very much by their own experience and preference. Part of school education also, but nothing like this. Now she was finding out for herself.

Others in the shop were watching them disapprovingly. The shop attendant intercepted, attracted by the disturbance they were causing. "Can I help you?" he asked politely but slightly irritated. His voice was high-pitched, his appearance a little confronting with slicked-back blonde-dyed hair, earrings and dark floral shirt open to below chest level.

Lara was in ebullient mood now, her natural cheerfulness heightened by the crazy situation. She couldn't stop laughing, infecting Jodie the same. Together, they further irritated the attendant, customers becoming annoyed.

"What's this?" Jodie asked, trying to divert attention by pointing at an unusual shaped object hanging on an adjacent stand. Still she struggled to control the giggling.

"Excuse me?" The attendant had been put off his sales pitch. But it quickly returned. "I can show you a video, then you'll see."

"A video. Like those videos?" Jodie indicated one of the screens at ceiling level.

"Which one do you like best?" Lara asked him cheekily, also indicating the screens.

The attendant looked at her disdainfully, unsure whether to be offended or still might be a genuine sale prospect. For the moment, he decided on the latter. "You're the customer. Which one do you like?"

Lara was laughing again, but eager to respond. "Not that one, or that one." She indicated the screen with activity unclear and the one depicting two women. "Or that one. Yuk!" She indicated the one with two males together.

Now the attendant was offended. "What are you saying? That men should not love each other?" His tone was sharp, making obvious his own sexual preference.

"Not like that!" Lara could not hide her disgust.

"You're prejudiced." His tone turned harsh, threatening. "Why do people like you hate us? We fought for years to be recognised, for equality. Marriage was legalised for us many years ago, but still you discriminate." He thrust his face forward barely inches from Lara's, unable to contain his anger.

Startled, Lara staggered back a step, not meaning to rouse his sensitivities. "I'm sorry," she murmured.

"You will be!" Furious, he moved back, arm outstretched pointing his finger at Lara menacingly. Then he had his mobile out, making a call.

"Let's go." Jodie took Lara's arm. Subdued, they headed for the exit.

Before clearing the cul-de-sac, another surprise was approaching. Two uniformed officers turned the corner and walked towards them. Immediately recognisable in their grey and pink quartered jackets, grey trousers, the letters DP emblazoned large on jacket fronts. A drone overhead was guiding them, ready to record pending action. As the officers drew near, one of them spoke.

"We just received a complaint about you two." He eyed Jodie and Lara in turn, then inclined his head towards the sex shop. "From the shop proprietor." His manner was calm, expecting to be in control.

Lara and Jodie looked at each other nervously. The DP was an arm of police not to be trifled with. "Yes, sorry," Lara offered, anticipating the incident wouldn't be seen as too serious. "We were laughing at some of the things they've got there. It's quiet in the shop, maybe we were a bit noisy."

"That's not what the complaint is about." He gave a quick nod to his fellow officer, who was holding a handset. She pressed the 'On' button, ready to accept data. "ID please."

Both girls produced their ID cards. The officer processed, cards were handed back and the male officer was speaking again.

"It is an offence to express prejudice or discriminate against any section of the community. We will interview the shop proprietor and any witnesses. If a charge is warranted, you will be notified, and of the penalty." The officers moved away, angling towards the sex shop.

Shadowed by the drone, the girls continued back, in sombre mood as each contemplated likely further trouble and the reaction of their parents. The afternoon was wearing on, time to go home. At the bike stands, Jodie gave Lara a quick hug. "See you tomorrow." They rode off, going different directions.

Alone with her thoughts, Lara could not get the sex shop out of her mind. A first time experience to see such a place, a forbidden place her mums would condemn. Yet she could not deny feeling excited and stimulated. She could feel the stirrings in her body. The screen images of a man and woman together kept repeating in her mind, dominating over the other images. Suddenly, in one captivating moment, she knew she was not like MumG and MumD.

With the revelation came an enormous sense of relief, a huge burden lifted from her, freeing her mind. She thought about the other screen images. The two women together had little effect on her, consistent with what she'd gleaned from her mums. But the two men together, that was something she'd been vaguely aware of, but never had the actuality of what gay men do been so startlingly demonstrated in the raw. She knew it had health implications far more significant than for women. And yet, the only talk in public forums was about prejudice, equality, discrimination, words the shop proprietor had used in his angry outburst. As she neared home, Lara felt remarkably enlightened, the insight a defining experience.

MumG and MumD were waiting for her as she turned into the driveway. They knew something, that much was immediately obvious.

Inside, MumD faced Lara, with a stern look as never seen before. "You weren't at school today."

Lara said nothing, expecting MumD to continue.

"We know you went into town. What was that for?"

Lara hesitated, aware someone must have contacted them. Surely not Jodie's father! But suddenly, it did not matter. She had always been open and honest with her mums, not about to change now and they would have to know anyway.

"I went to the government offices. To enquire about my father." She pulled out the form and handed it to MumD.

"Oh no, really." It was MumG speaking, despondent and visibly upset.

"Your father!" MumD also was upset, a little shocked. She looked at the form. "We can't give permission for this, here on the form." She thrust the form back in Lara's hands.

Lara glared at her, feeling alienated from them for the first time ever. A sick sensation, her mind in a whirl. Yet she also felt strong, boosted by the day's events, flushed with a sense of entitlement over finding her father.

MumD spoke again, in a more conciliatory tone. "Lara, we've given you a loving home, brought you up to be a good girl. Why is that not enough for you? What is so important about your father?" Almost she was pleading, deeply worried.

"Because he's half of who I am," Lara blurted out. A natural answer requiring no thought.

"Oh!" MumG cried out. "I can't listen to this." She stormed off, on the point of breaking down.

MumD spread her hands in exasperation. "There, see? Is that what you want? To put stress on our family?" Her voice quivered with emotion. But she was a little sturdier than MumG, smitten by a rising anger. "Your father is a bad man. If you involve him in our family, there will be serious repercussions. That will be on your head."

Lara was taken aback, unprepared for MumD landing such a threat and blame on her. It seemed extreme. MumG had said no one knew about him raping her. Did MumD secretly know and kept it to herself all these years? If that came out, it would certainly cause stress.

"One more thing," MumD went on, as Lara turned to walk away. "A DP officer was here just before you got home. Do you want to tell me about that?"

Lara's heart gave a flutter. She was hoping to avoid further confrontation on that front. "I was given a citation," she replied truthfully. "For expressing prejudice." No point in denying it.

"Yes, so he told me. At a sex shop!?"

Lara burst out laughing, unable to help herself. A release of nervous tension, along with sudden flashback.

MumD gave a glimmer of a smile. Unimpressed but not overly concerned. "The officer said a charge has been confirmed. You'll be notified of the penalty."

"Oh, great." Lara nodded in resigned acceptance. "What's the penalty do you think?"

"It's usually a period of community service, in an area relevant to the offence." MumD was familiar with procedure, which overlapped with her former work at the Rehabilitation Centre.

"Charming. Just what I need." Lara gave a pout of disdain, not relishing the prospect.

"Maybe it is what you need. I don't recall we ever included sex shops as part of your education." She gave another half-smile, comfortable in the knowledge their solid upbringing of Lara stood her in good stead. They had never believed in overbearing dictatorship or suppressing her natural spirit.

"No, true." Lara was pensive, appreciating how well MumD was taking it. She made to move away.

"Wait a minute." MumD was serious again. "The officer said Jodie was with you. Why is that? You said you went there to enquire about your father. What's that got to do with Jodie?"

Lara looked away, avoiding eye contact. "Oh, she just came for moral support, that's all." She felt tense, not given to being anything but truthful.

"I see." MumD was unconvinced, but decided not to pursue it further. She gave Lara a quick hug, a little reserved without quite the usual warmth.

Lara went to her room, bemused. What stood out was the stark difference between MumD's relatively mild non-judge-mental reaction to the sex shop issue and how seriously condemning she was of seeking to find her father. Plenty to ponder.

Chapter 4

The next competitor was being sent on his way, two-minute intervals between. Jude returned to where the bikes were parked, having doubled back after his start. Doing enough to establish his presence in case Dad or Dado called the organiser to check. His fathers were keen on orienteering as a suitable activity for him on Saturdays, physically demanding in keeping with appropriate family image. Jude enjoyed it for its solitude, alone several hours running through bushland from checkpoint to checkpoint, only occasionally crossing paths with other competitors. The heat of day made it more strenuous, but so it was with any outdoor activity. Today, he had something more important in mind. Collecting his bike, he left quickly before someone spotted him.

When he arrived at his mother's place, she rushed out to greet him. "Jude!" She gave him a big hug. "I haven't heard from you for ages. What's been happening?"

He'd seen her in person on very few occasions, by stealth only. His fathers' fierce opposition to any contact had been lifelong, regarding her as no more than a vehicle to have their child. Once achieved, they had no interest in three-way parenthood, which would entail male-female relations. Jude often wondered what if he'd been a she? He heard a whisper that a foetal scan revealing a girl would have given rise to an abortion. Apparently in the pre-conceptual agreement. Post-conception a fifty-fifty chance of life! He was lucky to exist!

"Nothing much different." He returned her warm embrace. "I couldn't call. I think Dado has reinstated the block on my mobile. Can we talk?"

"Sure. I'm going out shortly, but we have time."

She led him inside. A modest home, basic furniture with a sprinkling of personal items, nothing of great value. Financially, she was comfortable but not well off. They sat at the coffee table.

Jude had many unanswered questions. Most related to his struggle for identity. He was hoping his mother might help.

"Who would you say is my real father?" he began. "Brett or Chas?"

Dulcie smiled, wishing she knew the answer. "There's no way of knowing. Both their sperms were used. Deliberately, so they could both claim to be father. They don't want to know which sperm was successful."

"Yes, I know. But there must be signs. To do with looks or mannerisms or whatever." Jude was happy about his looks, which he credited greatly to his mother. Her flowing black shoulder-length hair and classical facial features, although lined by difficult life experiences, together with a slim but well-shaped figure made her an attractive woman.

"That's true. In some cases, it's easy to tell. But Brett and Chas look quite similar. It's not obvious who you're closer to in looks." She smiled again, feeling great warmth and love for her son, her only child. "I don't know about mannerisms. They are gay, of course." She leaned forward, more intense. "How do you feel? Like them? Or different?"

Jude felt the intensity of her question. It mirrored his daily struggle for identity. The emotion welled up in his eyes. Dulcie moved closer, putting her hand to his face, sharing emotion of the moment. Each felt their precious bond growing stronger.

"I don't know," Jude responded eventually. "They want me to be like them. But I don't feel the same." He went on to describe the evening with Jeremy, Chongwe and Josh, sparing no detail. "Josh thinks he's gay, but I think it's because of the pressure."

Dulcie listened intently, nodding slowly in empathy. "Remember one thing, Jude. Just because one of their sperm made you does not mean you are the same sexually. There is no biological link that way."

Jude felt lifted by her words, filling him with new determination. "Yes, thank you. I will remember that." A defining moment, moving him forward.

They were silent for some moments as the impact sank in. Then Jude spoke again, curious. "Why did you want to be a surrogate mother?"

Dulcie hesitated, not expecting such a question. But she wanted to answer. "It was difficult times for me, financially."

"Is that all? Just for the money?" Jude didn't believe it was so.

"No, no. Well, to begin with." Again she hesitated, a little upset at revisiting past memories. "All surrogate mothers do it for the money. What other reason is there? Knowing you're doing it for someone else, someone you've only met for the purpose. After giving birth, you're flicked off, not wanted anymore. You're supposed to have no emotions. It is very tough." A tear rolled down her cheek. She wiped it away quickly.

Jude was shocked, aware for the first time of the pain she'd been through. "But it can be between people who know and trust each other too, can't it?"

"That happens. But not often. And always, to continue their relationships means a triangle of parents, not just a couple. Very rarely does that work out."

"So someone has to miss out."

"Of course. Obviously the one who's not part of the marriage, is only the supplier. Surrogate mother or sperm donor."

A sobering conclusion. To Jude, it represented further confusion in his quest for identity. "I can't believe you had me just for the money." He almost choked on the last words as a lump in his throat took effect. "What about your parents? Couldn't they help you with money?"

"Oh Jude, don't get me wrong," she implored, wiping away more tears. "That was in the beginning. This is why it's so tough. You were growing inside me!" She broke down, sobbing.

Jude went to her and they hugged, their emotions flowing freely. When it subsided, Dulcie continued, "My parents died in a car accident. They had no assets, bankrupt after a failed business venture. I was alone then, no brothers or sisters, no money. Only my grandmother was still alive. I'm so grateful she left me her house, this house, when she died. About ten years ago." Recovering, she gave Jude a loving smile. "I'm one of the lucky ones. Many never see their child ever. We've managed it a couple of times, in spite of your fathers. I love you, Jude. More than you know. I want you to always remember that."

They held each other longer. Jude's heart swelled with a sense of belonging. A foundation from which he could go forward with more confidence.

Suddenly, Dulcie realised the time. "Oh, I'm due at the forum. Better go." She paused a moment. "You can come, if you like?"

Jude considered how long before he'd be expected home. "Yes, I've got time. What's the forum about?"

"It's a support group for surrogate mothers. Every Saturday morning."

They arrived at a small hall. Some twenty women of various ages sat in a circle, awaiting an opening address. The organiser was seated beside a mounted microphone at the edge of the circle. Dulcie and Jude found two seats together. Looking around, he noticed two other women with a child, one a teenage girl the other a boy under ten years old. Another male presence made Jude feel more comfortable.

The organiser was a middle-aged woman, clearly with an upbeat disposition as she stood and adjusted the microphone.

"Hi, everyone, welcome to our gathering. I hope you've had a good week." She gave a sweeping look around the group, offering a broad smile. "I see we have two new ladies with us today. For their benefit, my name is Tara and I've been a surrogate mother twice. The first was a good experience with people I know well, the second not so good." She paused, surveying the group again. "But you've not come to hear my story. Everyone here has a story to tell, I'm sure more interesting than mine. Who would like to begin?"

A brief silence, then a woman from the far side stood.

"Yes, Marjorie. Would you like to take the microphone?"

Marjorie was already striding around the circle, soon standing next to Tara. A slight reaction from the group suggested she was well known for her input.

"I'm Marjorie. Most of you know me. I've spoken before about my girl and her fathers. For the new ladies here, I'll go over my situation again." She spoke in an abrasive tone, hardened by her experiences. It showed in her face, etched with lines of worry. "My girl Krissy is eight years old. Her fathers, John and Gary, were married ten years ago. John had been a drug addict before that. He was detained at a Rehab Centre and they got him off drugs. When he met Gary, they wanted a child, didn't care boy or girl." She paused, gratified to see everyone's attention riveted on her.

"It wasn't great but okay, up till last year. I was able to see Krissy on occasions, and she was fine, happy. Then last year, when the government changed and so did priorities, John went back to drugs. The Rehab Centre he'd been to before was converted back to safe injecting rooms." Again she paused as an angry frustration took hold. When she continued, her voice was shaking, nervous. "Everything changed with Krissy then. She withdrew into herself, depressed. I couldn't get her to talk, but I'm sure she was being abused. Then they barred me from seeing her anymore." Breaking down, she let out a cry of anguish. It was the only sound in the room, everyone listening spell-bound. Eventually, she resumed.

"Now I can tell you the latest. Last week, I was desperate. I went to the authorities about it. They spoke to John and Gary and found nothing wrong, or so they told me. I have no evidence. Yesterday, the DP charged me with prejudice. Now I have to do community service at the safe injecting rooms." She broke down again. Unable to talk anymore, she returned to her seat.

The next woman to speak was Shelley. Her surrogacy had produced a boy for a female same-sex marriage. The mothers were both wealthy professional career women who wanted a child to carry on their future legacy, but without the burden of pregnancy and giving birth to interfere with their careers. Money no object, they chose a sperm donor and Shelley. A nanny was engaged to bring him up, Shelley rejected for that role as being too close and likely to develop a rival bond with him. Shelley was cut completely from their lives. Having four parents plus nanny, sperm donor the only male influence but barely with a passing interest, the boy was confused. Pressured exclusively by female influence, he began developing feminine traits. Now, twelve years old, he wanted a sex change.

Jude was aghast as he listened to Shelley's story. His own identity crisis paled into insignificance compared to this boy.

The next two speakers each had a better story to tell. Relations with male same-sex marriages were relatively peaceful and cooperative, the fathers recognising the need for balance and some measure of female influence in their child's life. Consultation was frequent over decision-making in the child's interests, one of the speakers even saying she lived in with the family part-time. Of course, not everything was perfect. Invariably, as with any family, disagreements occurred.

"Even in the most perfect of arrangements," the second speaker observed, "three-way consultation naturally, by definition, is vastly more complex in problem-solving than for a couple. I've spoken to other surrogate mothers in similar position. They all confirm being compromised and subordinated, the marriage partners dominant. One told me a partner did side with her, and it caused a split in the marriage. I believe triangular contortions, if I can put it that way, must inevitably cause such splits. I think statistics on separation, divorce, broken homes are bearing this out. Domestic violence as well."

Glancing at his mother, Jude was again struck by the parallel to his own family dynamic. He was not alone. A common syndrome, it seemed. Consequences.

The next speaker was one of the new ladies. Diffident and shy to take part at first, she was encouraged by the last reference to domestic violence. As she moved nervously to the microphone, head down and hand up to hide her face, her low self-esteem and impression of a defeated woman was evident for all to see. Facing the group, she dropped her hand to reveal the side of her face. Swollen red with a cut by her mouth, blackened purple around the eye socket. A shocked gasp sounded around the circle.

She tried to speak, but no words came out. Tara stood and put an arm around her shoulders. "What's your name, love?" Tara spoke with a kind voice, genuinely concerned for her. "We're all on your side here. But it's okay, you don't have to say anything. We understand what you've been through."

"Sorry --- I --- I'm ---," the woman stammered in a broken voice. Too distraught, she shook her head and moved away, retiring to her seat.

Tara addressed the group. "We can all see the suffering of this good woman. I think she has shown great courage in coming here today and revealing herself to us." She looked across at the woman. "Congratulations to you for that. Anytime you want to talk, we will be listening." A few moments of silence, then Tara went on, "Is there anyone else with a domestic violence situation they wish to share with us?"

The second woman attending for the first time rose and made her way to the microphone. She was slim and attractive, with flowing auburn hair. No outward signs of injury from violence, but the hard lines to her face gave a clue as to circumstances.

"Hello everyone, my name's Gloria." Her voice had a sharp edge to it, but controlled and without rancour. "I've been a surrogate mother once. Like everyone, I did it for the money. My girl is five years old. I see her regularly, twice a week by arrangement. No problem with that." She gave a deep sigh, as if to ease the path of disclosure. "The fathers are Bobby and Nick. Both wanted to be sperm donor, so they mixed their sperm and agreed to accept whatever outcome. DNA testing proved Bobby's sperm was successful. Nick seemed happy enough about it, but underneath he was jealous. He came on to me one day, to prove some point, I thought. But actually, he's bisexual. Bobby didn't know that when they got married." She paused, reflecting for a moment. "Nick kept on with it, getting worse. One time, I gave in to him." Her lips trembled and she bowed her head as the emotion of it took hold.

After a lengthy pause, she collected herself and resumed. "I thought that would appease him, even things up with Bobby. Big mistake. It was more like a rape." She choked on the last word, but managed to continue. "That's when the violence set in. He beat me regularly, some excuse every time. Bobby was weak, turned a blind eye. But Nick was having affairs with other women. He and Bobby had a bust-up and they're separated now. Bobby's with a new partner, but Nick's jealous about that too, keeps going there causing trouble." Again she stopped, affected.

"My big worry is for my daughter. She's only five. I don't know what will happen to her in that environment. Violence has no boundaries. Going to the authorities is a waste of time when a same-sex marriage is involved. Identifying prejudice and discrimination is more important." Frustrated, she let out a deep sigh, casting a tired look around the circle. "Thank you everybody, for listening to my story." She returned to her seat.

A deathly hush descended on the group, collectively stunned by what they'd heard. Jude's head was buzzing. Another parallel to his own fathers, mixing sperm a shock as to potential repercussions.

Another woman strode forward. She exuded aggression, a hard-bitten look about her. "I don't know what's wrong with you women! You have to take your power back! I did. The sperm donor, he's in jail now." With a snarl, she let out a derisive snort of contempt. "What a weasel! And I told him so. Small man, in the places that matter. He hated it and we fought. The neighbours saw, great witnesses!" She laughed scornfully, as if in triumph. "Forget the DP and Police, they're useless! Go straight to the Family Court with a suitable lawyer, they support women." She turned on Tara, forthright. "You should be helping these women do the same!" Gratified, she strode back to her seat. The circle stared after her, numbed.

Two women came to the microphone together. Both were surrogate mother to the same male same-sex marriage, satisfying each partner wanting to be sperm donor and biological father. One had a girl, one a boy, happening a few months apart. Thirteen year-olds now. The household largely operated harmoniously, the two mothers allowed restricted access. But inevitably, distortions concerning role and identity had set in. The children were confused heading into puberty and adolescence, the fathers suspicious of them together. Incongruously, although raised as brother and sister, no biological link meant it was not incest. A host of other same-sex or heterosexual possibilities were looming, however.

The next speaker appeared calm and untroubled. She addressed the group with confidence, as if motivated by wider issues than her own plight.

"Hi, I'm Pamela. And I'm very pleased to be here today, listening to your experiences. I too have a story to tell."

She came across as a warm-hearted, giving person. "You may recall, a few years back a medic involved in genetic engineering research at a major hospital was exposed for manipulating the genome of an unborn foetus. Quite a scandal at the time." She took a moment to reflect. "I was the surrogate carrying that foetus."

"The fathers only wanted a son. A condition written into the agreement. But when a scan revealed a girl, instead of invoking the abortion clause, they arranged with their friend the research medic to engineer female into male through genetics. Faced otherwise with an abortion, I had little option but to consent." Again she paused, offering a quick smile to all the faces watching her enthralled.

"It was ground-breaking. Exciting for the medic, who actually is a brilliant well-renowned scientist. Subsequent scans showed up some problems, but the change to male was done, so we carried on through. I gave birth to a hermaphrodite. A person with both female and male sex organs, as further tests revealed." Her mouth quivered as the emotion of it caught up with her momentarily.

"Today, Jamie is five years old. We're not sure what to do. A few years on, when suitably developed physically, Jamie may have a sex-change operation. Returning to female would be the more complete option. But the fathers might be a problem there. Who I do get on well with, by the way." She stopped, taking a deep breath, gratified by the support she sensed coming across from the group.

"We get plenty of advice and assistance from the LGBT society. Some of it is a little overbearing, I might say, especially from Trans people who tend to push their own barrow somewhat selfishly, I find. But anyway, that's life. Everyone has their own issues." She gave a quick chuckle, slightly sceptical. "Oh, and just to mention, the scandal didn't seem to have a lasting effect. That particular research medic is still working at the hospital."

Pamela was the last to speak, the group stunned into silence by her revelations. That signalled the end of proceedings. Tara thanked everyone for coming. Refreshments were served, then people began dispersing.

On the way back, Dulcie wanted to stop at a store. She bought a mobile. "Use your phone for everything you normally use it for," she advised Jude. "So they see nothing is different. When you want to call me, use this one, and use it for nothing else. Make sure you keep it well hidden." She handed him the new phone. "I'll never call you, in case you're in wrong company."

Jude felt hugely buoyed. A perfect end to the stolen hours with his mother. The new phone would alleviate that lonely sense of isolation and disconnect at home. At his mother's place, they shared a final hug and he departed.

He arrived home mid-afternoon, around the time he usually got home from orienteering. No reason for Dad and Dado to have suspicions. But no chance to find out, as they had visitors.

"Ah, here he is," Dad exclaimed as Jude rode in. "Just about on time." He seemed in an upbeat mood, easier than usual over punctuality.

Jeremy and Chongwe were standing nearby. No Josh, but another boy of similar age was with them. All hovering outside, waiting for Jude to turn up.

"Hello, Jude," Jeremy greeted, stepping forward. "This is Cameron." He signalled the boy to move closer.

Jude offered a polite reply. Cameron had a strange look about him, with bushy blondish hair atop a thin craggy face, sunken slightly red-rimmed eyes as if he'd not slept a night or two. His mouth was fixed in a crooked half-grin. Slim of build, he hardly looked an athletic figure. He gave no response to Jude's greeting.

They moved inside to the lounge room.

"Josh went back to his family," Jeremy explained, expecting Jude to be curious. "I'm sure we'll see him again soon. But you weren't getting on well with him, so he told us." He gave a quick smile, intending to reassure but it came over as contrived.

To Jude, the obvious misrepresentation only deepened the distrust he already felt about Jeremy. But what of his own parents? Sitting there quietly, saying nothing, pretending to protect him through their suffocating control, but in reality complicit with the agenda. He glanced at Cameron. A new recruit? He had not long to find out.

Jeremy was speaking again. "We found Cameron a couple of nights ago. His parents have abandoned him. We told him about you and he said he'd like to meet you. So here we are." He spread his arms in a mock show of being fatalistic, as if some other force was responsible.

The thinly disguised confirmation of another match-making exercise made Jude feel like a prisoner in his own home. He sensed no worthwhile vibes coming over from Cameron. Was he on drugs? His spaced-out appearance and demeanour certainly suggested so. Why would Dad and

Dado be complicit with that!? Jude felt not only a prisoner but abandoned in his own home. A sudden panic gripped him. Nowhere to run! Thoughts of his mother swept in, rescuing him. He calmed. Suddenly feeling very tired, he slumped back in his chair and rubbed his eyes.

"Jude has had a big day today." It was Dado speaking for the first time. "Orienteering is a tiring activity. Maybe we can continue this another time." His apparent concern for Jude was a surprise. Did he have another angle?

Chongwe chimed in. "We go now. Let Jude rest."

The visitors departed.

"Wait a minute," Dado called as Jude started towards his room. "How was orienteering today?" He flashed the characteristic smile, his tone condescending.

Jude instantly recognised the signs. Only a few words, but dripping with innuendo. "Fine," he mumbled uncertainly.

"Fine?" Dado let the word hang in the air. He flashed the smile again. "We know you weren't at orienteering today."

"Oh." Jude's heart sank. But he would not divulge being with his mother. Did they know already? He waited.

"Yes. Dad rang the organiser. It seems you left at some stage, didn't complete the course."

Jude nodded confirmation. But Dado's knowledge seemed sketchy, unaware he had barely even begun the course. He decided to play innocent. "I didn't feel good out there, too tired. So I went to the beach instead."

"I see. So why didn't you let us know? Why did you say fine when I asked you just now?" Agitated, he paced the floor for some moments, then stopped to stand close in front of Jude threateningly. "You've been deceitful. That's not the way we've taught you." He produced an object from his pocket, holding up a small black box. "See this? It's a tracker. We'll put it on your bike. I've also arranged similar means on your phone. It seems more measures are necessary, until you prove you can be trusted again." He turned and walked away.

Jude went to his room, feeling further demeaned and frustrated, yet happy avoiding any reference to his mother.

Chapter 5

The crowd hushed as the official party and dignitaries entered the arena and took up a row of seats behind a podium temporarily set up in the centre. The news media were present in numbers, cameras pointed at the podium where a row of microphones awaited the first speaker. A long anticipated announcement was about to commence.

The Prime Minister rose and mounted the podium. He adjusted his coat lapels and tie. Clearing his throat, he addressed the crowd.

"First of all, I'd like to thank the directors and workers of the factory for showing us around today and demonstrating the latest in Artificial Intelligence technology. My Science Minister and the State Premier have been here numerous times. For me, I am most impressed at the advancement since my visit during the election campaign last year." He half-turned to acknowledge his State and Federal colleagues seated behind.

"Today, we are here to announce a major step forward in the application of AI technology. As you know, with increased funding since we came to office, the AI industry has pushed ahead, leading the world in new innovation.

The Robin series of robot design and development has been foremost and now at a stage where we are ready to trial it in the community at large. Initially, one hundred commercial and industrial premises and private households have been chosen from a group of volunteers. Each will trial one Robin. If the trial proves successful, the path will be open to commercialising the product on a wider scale." He paused as a cheer broke out from the factory floor, followed by a resounding round of applause. This was the announcement they'd been working towards for a long time.

Gratified, the PM continued. "The AI industry worldwide has been steadily growing and expanding in recent years. No, decades, in fact. Some countries have been commercialising robots for years, assimilating them into society for all those tasks people find menial, repetitive, for protection, security, whatever. Here in Australia, we decided to go high-tech. And we are leaders, no doubt about that. But others have taken practical benefit from our innovations, while we lag behind in that regard. Now, with today's announcement, we set out on a new path. We will commercialise at a higher level using Robin's capability than others have done. Then we will truly be world leaders." The PM's voice was rising in excitement, gripped by the occasion. As he paused to take stock, the crowd erupted again in cheering and clapping.

Not going unnoticed was his veiled criticism of the previous Coln government. He made no mention of the Robin2 disaster being a major setback for Coln just when commercialisation was about to flourish. Nor did he give any credit to Coln for bringing nanotechnology on stream, an enormous advancement not only giving AI robots an independent power source but in many walks of life.

"Thank you, thank you." Raising one hand in acknowledgement, he waited for the applause to subside. "I will now ask the Science Minister to talk about some of the more technical aspects of Robin." He stepped down from the podium and returned to his seat.

The Science Minister took centre stage, his enthusiasm for the portfolio well-known and clearly evident today. He began by reiterating much of what the PM had said. Then he moved on to describing Robin's history and the advanced level at which commercial production would proceed. Robin1 had signalled a quantum leap in the world of AI, introducing self-regulating sight, hearing and touch senses. Robin2 was another giant leap from there, facilitating direct access from input through programming to output. The government faced a tough choice, torn between the highest level possible and safety, given the problems with Robin2 previously.

"After due consideration by Cabinet," the Minister proclaimed, "the government has decided to use Robin1, with the capability of Robin2 incorporated but lying dormant until activated should it be considered safe to do so. In the meantime, Robin3 will continue undergoing tests and when ready, will be brought into the mix." He drew a deep breath, pleased with the positive response emanating from the people before him. "This is a great moment in time, folks. The roll-out of Robin will begin immediately. Congratulations to all those who have been involved in this wonderful development, and especially to those taking part in the trial, some of you here today. We look forward to the results. Continue the great work, everyone!"

The State Premier was next to speak. She heaped praise on the AI industry and its workforce, thanked the government for its support of jobs in Queensland, lauded her State as the most progressive in attracting investment, projects, employment opportunities and having vision for the future. Although Labour, she strongly endorsed the former Coln government, with which her State had enjoyed the most cooperative of relationships.

The formalities over, a lavish buffet lunch was served. It was the opportunity for the Prime Minister and his party to mingle informally with workers of the factory. Keen to be amongst it were Brett and Chas, one of the households chosen to trial a Robin. Brett managed to manoeuvre close to the Prime Minister, feeling bold enough to engage him in conversation. He introduced himself, adding, "I'm one of the technicians working on touch sense with Robin3."

"Really?" The PM sounded interested. "I'm fascinated by how that works. How does Robin recognise a touch?"

Brett was flushed with a sense of importance. "Tiny sensors close together, impregnated just under the surface of his skin, all over. Simulating how human skin works."

"Oh, I see. You mean like nerve-ends?"

"Yes, sort of. Took many years to perfect. Especially the hands, fingers. Synchronising with movement was hardest. And it must be robust, not easily damaged by an impact, for instance."

Chas had moved alongside, keen not to be left out. Brett introduced him. "This is my partner. We're one of the trial households."

The PM was about to break off, but with renewed interest he asked what tasks they're expecting Robin to perform for them.

"I like the security," Chas responded immediately. "Robin will protect us."

"And surveillance," Brett added thoughtfully.

Several of the PM's colleagues were gathering around, giving the PM a chance to move on. One overheard Brett's last comment.

"Did you say surveillance?" he queried. "How does that work?" He was sharp, involved in technical aspects of the portfolio. "I understand Robin inputs to memory what its senses detect, then outputs because its programming reads that. But if you want surveillance, how does it report back to you?"

Brett relished the chance to expound his knowledge. "Ah well, we can read his memory too. That's just normal computer capability from way back, nowadays far more sophisticated. Every Robin has its own individual code. We give him a signal and he transmits what's in his memory, for whatever time period or set task we ask for." He paused, a little surprised at the attention from a growing group of dignitaries.

Another spoke. "Can we call it mind-reading?" A quick chuckle of amusement accompanied the comment.

The earlier speaker took it up. "That's a lot of input coming in from its senses, every second of every day! Much of it superfluous or unimportant. How do you control or decipher all that?"

"No, no," Brett responded. "Robin only stores in memory if it's identifiable in his programming. Otherwise, we'd get a lot of junk, that's for sure. And we can specify a particular area of interest we want to read as well, to further narrow it down."

A woman in the group spoke up. "Why do you always refer to Robin as 'he' or 'his'? Aren't they supposed to be gender neutral?" A ripple of laughter went through the group.

Another, well known as a political head-kicker, chimed in. "Yeah, I hope there's no DP officer here. You'll be in trouble." His laughter was loud, with arrogance.

Chas felt the sting of it. Clutching Brett's arm possessively, he replied, "We don't mean anything by it. Just makes it feel more personal, that's all." His tone was defensive.

The antagonist eyed them both, his laugh turning to an insipid smile. "Oh, you two will be okay. No problems with DP, I'm sure."

Brett took it as a back-down. Chas, more sensitive, thought it might be a prejudiced snipe at same-sex partnerships. Always he was aware not everyone shared the same degree of acceptance.

The small gathering, including news and cameraman, lost interest and dispersed away to mingle with others. Soon after, the Prime Minister and his party departed, the event over. Factory workers were given the rest of the afternoon off.

That evening, television news showed the event as a major item of the day. Ending the coverage was the exchange of views with Brett and Chas. Jude watched with his fathers at home, gaining significant insight beyond disclosed by his dads. He knew a Robin was soon joining their household, but the point about surveillance was disturbing.

"When is Robin coming?" Jude asked.

"Tomorrow," Dado replied, then hesitated. "That is, if I can get our computer set-up ready. I'll be home tomorrow doing that."

Jude's heart sank. He had in mind something he wanted to do tomorrow, risky as it already was. But impossible if Dado was home.

Next day, when Jude arrived home from school, Robin was there with his fathers. It stared at him as he entered the lounge, unnerving him. Jude had seen Robins before, when visiting the factory under guidance of his fathers, who expected he would follow in their career footsteps. Nevertheless, its appearance was confronting. The skin-head look and thin line of mouth with slightly pinkish lips were complemented by two-tone body colouring to simulate clothing. But it was the eyes that stood out. Dark, staring wells, unblinking, penetrating, epitomising a cold emotionless entity. Jude shivered, affected by those eyes. In the centre of the forehead was branded its ID; R1 – H17.

Having processed Jude's entry, Robin turned away to resume household set tasks activated by its masters. Jude took in the additional equipment on the computer desk in the far corner. A green blinking light indicated activation.

"You'll get used to him," Dad proclaimed enthusiastically, noticing Jude's reaction. "He'll be a big help to us."

Dado nodded his agreement. "And to the programme." Interested in the longer term.

Jude wasn't sure, further alarmed when Robin suddenly appeared at the bathroom doorway as he was preparing for bed. Checking on him? Would it be checking all his movements?

Next morning, Jude was in a quandary as he rode to school. He'd made up his mind after the day with his mother and the eye-opening revelations of the surrogate mother's forum. But the advent of Robin was untimely. How capable was it? Suddenly, he didn't care. Feeling bold and committed, he turned his bike around and returned home. Why be worried about an unfeeling robot?

Robin was nowhere to be seen at home. Had Dad and Dado taken it with them to work? Problem solved, he went straight to his fathers' bedroom, determined to proceed.

He had no idea what he was looking for. Something, anything to shed light on his family and the meaning of his existence. Each side of the king-size bed were identical sets of cupboard and drawers, where he knew each father kept separately their documents and anything of importance. He went to Dado's side first. Locked, naturally. He'd come prepared, ready to use the special skill he'd honed and knew would be useful some day. Congratulating himself on his foresight, he pulled the specially shaped wires from his pocket and soon had the cupboard unlocked.

Two large boxes were stacked inside. He lifted out the first and opened the lid. Folders filled with papers and documents. A sheet on top was a line by line summary of contents. All about the factory, terms of employment, step

by step promotion through the ranks, pay slips, other corre-
spondence. He studied a pay slip. Dado was well paid. And
obviously highly regarded in the hierarchy and by management. Impressed, Jude turned to the second box.

The contents were similar, but pre-dating the factory.
Family history, Dado's upbringing including photos, education, university graduation in science, post-grad training
leading to employment in 2022 at the newly opened AI
factory. Birth certificate was in a folder. Born early 2000, to
mother and father married a year earlier. Happily married by
all accounts, no evidence of a separation or divorce. Well-
educated people. Jude wondered at what stage Dado's
sexual preference had emerged. His parents' reaction was
not apparent, but indications suggested acceptance.

Jude returned the boxes and opened the top drawer,
not locked. More papers, of regular day to day activity.
Purchase invoices, bank statements and the like. Nothing
of real interest, except to note all, including the bank statements, were in Dado's sole name. No joint account with
Dad?

The bottom drawer was locked. Again Jude had no
problem picking it open. One folder inside. Exactly what he
was looking for. A dossier on his conception and life, starting
with assessment of potential surrogate mothers. Quite a few
prospects were considered, including several high quality
hard to fault, it would seem. But one after another, they
were rejected. One reason was clearly apparent. A document, several pages long, requiring the surrogate mother's
agreement to hand over the baby immediately at birth and
never at any time or under any circumstances attempt to

contact the child or fathers. Long-winded and detailed, it covered every remote possibility imaginable that might otherwise justify contact, even major illness. Yet the fathers had the right to make contact if they chose, such as the need for genetic or hereditary information. Also a clause by which the fathers could force an abortion if a girl was conceived. The document was in convoluted language, obviously concocted by a lawyer.

Astounded at the severity of it, Jude looked further. The name Dulcie came to light. A news item with photos of an horrific car accident struck him in the eye. Dulcie's mother and father died instantly when their vehicle plunged over a cliff and exploded on impact. Dad and Dado ploughed into a bank, sustaining non-life threatening injuries, but the car was a write-off.

Jude caught his breath in shock, remembering what his mother told him. He read on. Police investigations found Dulcie's father to be at fault, inattentive driving. They had just purchased the vehicle, not yet completed insurance formalities. Dulcie, an only child, was left having to compensate Dad and Dado for the loss of their modern, expensive car. But she had few assets, personal or inherited, unable to meet the demand cost. Again Jude recalled her words, visualising the chronic circumstances.

Next document was the agreement. Dulcie would be surrogate mother, no payment, the legal waiving of rights to contact signed, in exchange for waiving the car compensation.

Jude stared at the papers, his heart bleeding for his mother. What she had been through! But it only strengthened the bond he felt. Her tragedy, the pain and cynical exploitation, it had given him life! Suddenly, for the first time, he felt there was meaning to his life. He resolved to do everything he could for his mother.

There were other papers in the dossier. An agreement between Dad and Dado, signed by both, resolving to use their sperm simultaneously and never seek to know who was the real father. Confirming what Jude already knew, but interesting to see it formalised.

Further on, another caught his attention. It was on the letterhead of a medical laboratory. Intrigued, he looked closer. DNA test results. Dado was confirmed to be his biological father!

"Wow!" he uttered, stunned. He sat on the edge of the bed, his head buzzing with the implications. Foremost was the fact itself. Dado his father! A huge revelation, dramatically altering his perspective. For the second time in minutes, he felt he knew himself better. Just realising Dado had wanted to know, that he cared that much, was amazingly liberating. He suddenly felt a warmth for Dado he'd never felt before.

Awareness of other implications kicked in. The date of the test was barely a year after his birth. Did Dad know? The deliberate breaking of their signed agreement strongly suggested not, with no further evidence on file to the contrary. It raised more issues. Dado, happily secure in the knowledge, had cynically kept it secret all their years together, pretending to honour the dual fatherhood concept.

"Wow! That is cynical!" Jude muttered, incredulous. It gave a distorted, contrived twist to his fathers' relationship. And yet, it must have an effect, psychologically, on behaviour, attitude. Perhaps explaining why Dado always seemed the stronger one, in control. Jude slowly shook his head, dumbfounded.

He thumbed through the rest of the dossier, finding material concerning his upbringing, schooling, decision-making, but nothing further of dramatic impact. Returning the dossier, he clicked the drawer shut. Everything back as he'd found it.

After moments of reflection, he crossed to Dad's side of the bed. The setup of cupboard and drawers was the same, locks again easily picked. Similar material in folders, much of it duplicating or overlapping with Dado's. There were significant differences, however. Several run-ins with factory management had dampened promotion prospects, particularly one where over-zealous actions at the test arena resulted in injury to a fellow technician. His education and training mirrored that of Dado, he was just one month younger, all indicators of equal opportunity for the pair. Except for one difference, a telling factor. His mother and father were of similar station in life to Dado's, but they rejected outright his sexual preference, evidenced by numerous file notes he'd written. Jude wondered if the lack of parental support was behind Dad's frequent state of nervous tension, possessive following of his partner, poorer work performance and lower pay.

Noteworthy once more was Dad's sole name bank account, no joint account. Further confirming an obsessive insistence, despite being married, on keeping their private affairs separate.

The locked bottom drawer contained another dossier on his creation and life, near duplicate to Dado's. The assessment and rejection of potential surrogate mothers, legal document about no contact and abortion provision, car accident that killed his mother's parents, engagement of his mother for surrogacy, signed agreement between his fathers about dual fatherhood, all were there. And again, DNA test results on medical laboratory letterhead! But it was not the same laboratory as that of Dado's test. And performed several months later. The test proved Dad was not the biological father.

Jude stared at the page, once more dumbfounded at the secrecy and psychology at play. He turned the page. Another DNA test sheet, at the same laboratory but a month later struck a further blow. It proved Dado to be the biological father. Jude caught his breath in shock. Dad had certainly been thorough and determined in his quest to know.

The implications were mind-boggling. Both fathers secretly sabotaging their signed agreement, each hiding their knowledge behind a façade of pretence. And maintaining it intact for so many years! A damning indictment of the close partnership they purported to uphold. Surely each must suspect the other. Yet an unspoken barrier seemed impregnable and neither would ever cross the line. Dado was confident, Dad for sure must be harbouring an underlying resentment.

Jude felt a sense of empowerment over his new-found awareness. He was sure, at some future stage, their deceptions would blow apart. But for now, he would keep his own secrecy. Let the repercussions evolve naturally.

He checked the remaining items in the dossier. Nothing further of much interest. He returned it to the drawer, ensured all was back as before, then turned to walk away.

Suddenly, a shock. Robin was standing in the doorway! Jude's heart leapt in fright, then started pounding in his chest as a nervous fear took hold. He stood rigid, nowhere to run. What would Robin do?

Robin stood passive, its dark eyes boring into him. Data inputting, but as yet no programmed output. Was this the surveillance Dado had alluded to?

Jude moved forward cautiously. Robin stepped aside, allowing him to pass. Still no action taken. Relieved, Jude left the house, found his bike untouched where he'd parked it and departed for school.

Chapter 6

"Please sign this consent form. You agree to our privacy policy." The attendant, Macey according to the nameplate on her desk, pushed the form across to Lara. "You must maintain confidentiality. Do not disclose to anyone what or who you see here."

Lara looked over the form, then signed where indicated. She handed it back to Macey.

"The DP advice is for you to do one hundred hours community service," Macey continued. "As penalty for a discrimination offence." Cold and formal, a middle-aged woman with seemingly little empathy. Surprising in a person running an ex-Rehabilitation Centre turned safe house for those in need.

Unimpressed, Lara waited for further instructions. Macey wasted no time in delivering.

"Because you're only coming Saturdays, this will take several weeks to complete. You will assist at our medical unit and the cafeteria, cleaning and other general duties as required." She gave Lara a hard look, expecting her to be recalcitrant as was usually the case with someone sent by DP. "Here, we cater for the gay community, same-sex couples and affiliates. I imagine the nature of your offence is why DP have sent you to us. Perhaps you will learn something in your time here."

Lara felt a little insulted by the presumption of character flaw. But she'd come with a humble attitude, prepared to accept her punishment without rancour. Macey seemed not to appreciate that. Instead, she stood abruptly and headed for the door, signalling Lara to follow.

Down a hallway, noticeably dingy, painted walls fading and a lack of décor giving the impression of maintenance no longer a priority. Part way along, they entered a large room. Lara was directed to the far side, passing several people seated on wooden chairs against one wall. Some kind of medical facility, evidenced by a white-padded bench-like table in the centre, a long bench on the far side carrying medical items and apparatus, two white-coated personnel in attendance. A computer, activated, was at one end of the bench. Along a side wall were two closed doors and an alcove leading to toilet/rest room. Lack of general maintenance was again apparent, faded paintwork, chipped and cracked floor tiling, rough water-damaged edges to bench and cupboards beneath.

The two medics each greeted Lara with a smile, the first sign of any friendliness in the place.

"Hello, you must be Lara. We've been expecting you. I'm Barbara." The woman was older than Lara expected, but with a bright, positive disposition.

"Gidday, Lara," the other followed, also in a positive tone. "I'm Tony." He looked of similar age to Barbara.

"We understand you've been sent here by DP," Barbara went on, used to overseeing assigned placements from that source. "You will see things here you're probably not expecting, maybe find confronting. But that's what DP sent you for, what they want you to see. So we won't hide anything, okay?" She made a sweeping gesture around the room, presenting the workplace as is. "There are cleaning duties, in between patients and when we've finished. But you can talk to anyone you want, no problem. All part of the exercise."

Lara thanked her, then followed her to the rest room. A white coat hanging on a locker door was for Lara's use. She put it on and re-joined the others, standing to one side.

The next patient came forward. A male of around thirty years, with the one-day unshaven look favoured by many gay men. Tony received him. "Hello, Padraig. Is it the same problem?" A repeat patient.

Padraig nodded glumly. In silence, he undid then stepped out of his trousers, followed by underpants. Tony obtained a folded plastic sheet from a stack by the bench and spread it over the padded table. He pulled on a pair of disposable gloves. Knowing the routine, Padraig lay on the table, taking up the foetal position.

Padraig's rectum was torn and bleeding. A cursory examination by Tony was sufficient on this occasion. Straightening, he pulled off the gloves and tossed them in a nearby trash can. "That's worse than last time. Can't you and your partner restrain yourselves for a while?" He handed Padraig a tube of special cream, obtained from a tall cabinet carrying a large store of tubes and bottles. Then to the computer, recording the consultation. Padraig, fully dressed, departed, morose and silent.

Barbara stepped forward, signalling Lara. Together, they folded the four corners of the plastic sheet into a bundle and Barbara took it to an adjacent room for disposal. Lara winced as an unpleasant smell struck her nostrils.

"We get a lot of those," Barbara commented nonchalantly, her bright disposition unaffected. "Not something you'd generally know about." She gave a chuckle of amusement. "You won't see that in the same-sex promos."

"You ain't seen nothing yet," Tony added, also with a chuckle.

The next consultation was a male couple, here for the first time. Looking forlorn and unhappy, they presented with STD problems. Tony took their personal details, then gave each a rectal examination, having to penetrate deeper this time. Then the penis, each with a discharge. He took swab samples, handing them to Barbara for testing. Discarding a third set of gloves, he turned to the couple, needing information.

"How long have you had this condition?"

"A few days," one of them answered.

"Has either of you had another partner recently?"

Both hesitated, neither keen to answer. "He's bisexual," revealed the one who'd spoken before, glancing at his partner. He didn't seem perturbed about it.

The other spoke. "I was with a woman, a week ago. A couple of days later, I noticed the discharge."

Barbara appeared beside Tony, handing him the test results. Tony only needed a brief moment to assess. He looked hard at the two men.

"One of you is not being truthful." He allowed the comment to sink in. "The test results show you both have the latest strain of chlamydia. That has an incubation period of seven to ten days. Which means one of you must have contracted the infection at least that long before noticing the discharge. And passed it on to the other, of course."

A tense silence followed. The bisexual partner, suddenly comprehending, snapped his head around to glare at the other. "It must be you, Tommy. I've not been with any others."

Tommy dropped his head. Moments passed, everyone waiting for an answer. "Yes, I was with someone," he admitted eventually, feeling humiliated. "Someone I knew years back. I met him again by chance at the LGBT club."

"Okay, this is what you must do," Tony butted in, before the growing angst escalated. "You must immediately contact each person you've been with, the man at the club, the woman, tell them they must contact anyone else they've been with. They all must come here for treatment without delay. They must have no sexual contact with anyone until treatment has eradicated the infection, or if they do then that person must also come for treatment. Do you understand what I'm saying?"

Tommy and his partner nodded meekly. Barbara handed two syringes to Tony. He injected the treatment to the buttocks of each patient.

"What I just said of course applies to you two as well. It may take a couple of days to clear up. If symptoms persist, then you'll need to return for another dose." Tony left them, moving to the computer.

Barbara gave Lara another nonchalant look. "Probably unlikely they'll follow Tony's instructions. I expect we'll see them again. That's the usual way." Another chuckle of amusement. "It's probably spread already before they even speak to others involved, that is if they do speak to them. Like a stack of dominoes."

Her nonchalance seemed like a kind of protective shield, necessary to maintain sanity in this depressing environment. Already Lara could feel herself beginning to adopt the same mindset. Certainly a different scene to anything her mums had divulged, keeping quiet despite their long working stint at a Rehab Centre.

Someone else had just entered the room. An agitated young woman looking for immediate attention. She stumbled forward, propping against the centre table, in a dishevelled state and sweating profusely.

"Can you help me?" she stammered, out of breath.

Barbara rushed over. "Are you injured? Let me examine you."

A large bruise to the side of her face and torn clothing with blood stains were obvious signs of violence. "I'm pregnant. Two months."

"Oh, I see." Barbara tended to her injuries, then asked her to lie on the table. After an examination, she declared, "Your baby is fine. Is it boy or girl?"

"Girl. That's the problem. The fathers only want a boy. They told me to get an abortion, but I refused."

"So they beat you. Have you reported it to the police?"

The woman pouted, scornful. "Why would I bother. I've been there before. They don't do anything."

Barbara took her details and entered to the computer. The woman left.

Several more consultations kept them busy as the morning wore on. Barbara treated a female couple. One had endometriosis, a condition occurring naturally in some women but hers was particularly severe, likely exacerbated by female sexual activity. Her partner was suffering a chronic case of thrush, confirmation of sexual cause.

A male couple presented with genital herpes. As Tony finished treating them, another man entered. An obviously sick individual, sunken eyes peering out from a thin emaciated face, skinny body, his clothes hanging loose. Tony did what he could, gave him medicine and the man went on his way.

"He has AIDS," Tony explained to Lara. "At an advanced stage. Nothing we can do."

"He looked awful," Lara replied, shaken. "How many people are like him?"

"Well, years back AIDS was nearly eradicated. Advancement in medical treatment and better drugs kept HIV sufferers under control, rarely progressing to full-blown AIDS. But in recent years, HIV has mutated into new strains. We don't have the drugs now to prevent HIV becoming AIDS. New AIDS, we call it." Tony looked grim, no sign of the amusement shown other consultations. "You'll see plenty of people like him coming here. It's getting worse. The regular hospitals are struggling to cope with them. Not enough beds."

Lara was aghast. Another problem known but not greatly revealed in the wider community. "Sounds like an epidemic! Is this because there's more same-sex activity these days?"

"You mean since same-sex marriage came in? Could be, I'm not sure. This began more recently. Not yet an epidemic, but it's a worry. Original AIDS started from same-sex activity, although that wasn't the only cause. There was beastiality, drugs use, needle sharing, contact with contaminated blood, extending to all sex if one partner was infected. New AIDS doesn't have those other causes. Only from same-sex activity, according to recent studies."

"Really!" Again, Lara was stunned by the further revelation. "Why should that be?"

"Nature's call." He took a long pause. "Always there are consequences."

Barbara joined them, pointing to a clock on the wall. "Nearly lunchtime. I was told you're helping out in the cafeteria."

"Oh yes. Where do I go?"

Barbara gave directions. "See you back here after lunch."

Lara exited to the hallway. At the end was a T-junction. She was about to swing left when a figure scurried alongside, stopping briefly to stare wide-eyed at her. A moment only, but enough to portray a young man desperate, his craggy face contorted in an ugly grimace and bathed in sweat. His body shaking, the wild eyes haunting, his entire demeanour spaced-out. He swung right, then quickly disappeared through a door part-way along the corridor.

Reaching the cafeteria, Lara found the manageress in the kitchen. A kindly woman, who greeted her warmly.

"You have lunch first. Then you can help clean the tables."

Lara sat alone at a table with her food. The place hosted a scattering of people. Mostly of the type witnessed through the morning. The young man encountered in the hallway came in and took a table. His demeanour was different, no longer with the shakes or sweating, a much calmer almost serene look about him. Lara stared in surprise, wondering what he'd done to manage such a dramatic change. He glanced at her, a dispassionate look displaying no interest. Just sitting there alone, no food to eat, nothing to do.

Her mobile sounded, jolting her back to reality. Jodie's number showing, giving her a much-needed lift in spirits. "Hi, Jodie, how's yours going?"

"It's okay," Jodie replied, upbeat. "I'm at the LGBT Centre. Lots of people meeting each other, socialising. I don't mind doing my hundred hours here. Not my kind of people though, if you know what I mean."

"Of course. I think you got the better deal." Lara described the events of her morning.

"Maybe we can ask to swap for some of the time," Jodie offered.

"Ha, I doubt they'd agree to that. I was the one making those comments at the sex shop, remember?" Lara laughed, glad of some light relief.

"Oh well, not to worry. Do the time and move on. Hey listen, Dad's got some news about your father. He's home today. Do you want to come by after?"

"Really? Great, yes I will. Late afternoon, I guess." Further uplifted, she felt a buzz of anticipation.

"See you then. Enjoy the afternoon." Jodie gave a quick chuckle and signed off.

On the way back after fulfilling her cleaning duties, Lara stopped at the T-junction, smitten with curiosity. She could talk to anyone, according to Barbara. Feeling bold, she moved to the door she'd seen the young man go through, entering the room beyond.

The purpose of the facility was immediately apparent. Safe injecting room. Several open cubicles down the side walls, each with standing room at a small bench on which sat appropriate equipment. Two cubicles were occupied by users. A supervisor sat behind a desk at the far end. Having seen enough, Lara exited, comprehending the dramatic change in the young man she'd met briefly.

A man passed as she started back. Not the typical type she was seeing in this place. He appeared in good health, well-dressed and in control of himself. But he flung Lara a shifty look. Immediately, she had an impression of someone she wouldn't trust. He moved further down the corridor, stopping at another door. Using an electronic key, he unlocked the door and disappeared inside. The significance of a locked room was not lost on Lara.

Back with Barbara and Tony, the afternoon went by similar to the morning. One young man presented with a diseased penis. Scabby sores partly healed and oozing infection, eating away at the flesh. Tony gave him an injection, handed him a tube of cream and sent him on his way.

"We get plenty of those too," quipped Tony, with character-istic chuckle of amusement. "As many as damaged rectums."

A mother came with her twelve year-old son. Both looked unhappy, the boy withdrawn. His affliction was typical of male patients Tony had treated already today. As the boy pulled his underpants and trousers back on, Tony turned to the mother.

"This is serious child abuse. Do you know who's responsible for doing this to him?"

The woman nodded, forlorn, wiping away tears. "Yes, I do."

"This is a reportable offence," Tony went on. "I'm obliged to notify the authorities. You should report it to police as well."

"Oh!" The woman was scared. "What will they do? I'm his mother. Will they charge me? Duty of care?" She gripped Tony's arm, pleading. "Please, I'll make sure it doesn't happen again."

"Sorry, I have no choice." Tony went to the computer and completed details. Mother and son departed.

"What do you think she'll do?" Lara asked, worried for the boy.

Tony gave a snort of disgust. His first sign of anger over any of the patients treated. "She won't do anything. More concerned about herself than her son's welfare. The offender has probably threatened her. Makes it hard. The authorities won't act without her evidence."

Barbara joined in. "The boy is depressed, traumatised. You could see it in his eyes." She was grimly serious, upset for the first time over any patient. "We see these cases all too often. Sometimes younger than this boy. You'd be shocked at how young, actually."

"Our pet hate," Tony added. "Paedophiles." He spat out the word as if it was poison.

The afternoon passed with a steady trickle of consultations keeping them busy. Lara felt glad when it was time to leave, mentally exhausted by all she'd seen. She checked out with Macey at front reception then headed away.

Arriving at Jodie's place late afternoon, she felt the excitement mounting. A warm greeting with Jodie and her parents, then they were sitting around the lounge coffee table. Lara could not help marvel at the plush living standards Jodie enjoyed. The advantage of having a father. Desperately, she hoped her own father would be as capable as Jodie's. She was about to find out.

Jodie's father leaned forward, looking serious as he appreciated the importance of the moment. "I assume Jodie has told you I have news about your father," he began tactfully. After a lengthy pause, he went on, "I have to say it is not the best news you would like to hear. Are you sure you want to know?"

Lara felt her excitement beginning to deflate. "Yes, I need to know."

"Right." Another pause. "His name is Brent and he is forty seven years old. He lives alone, not far from here. But I can't give you his address." He allowed time for the facts to sink in.

Lara sensed a reluctance to reveal more. "Please, Mr Thornton, I want to know everything."

"Okay. Well, he's been in jail. He was released about a year ago, after serving a fifteen year sentence. Parole was denied several times."

Lara slumped back in her chair, the shock of crushing news putting her head in a spin. Utterly deflated now, she made no response as a numbness took over.

"Sorry, Lara. I know it's not what you wanted to hear."

"But he's still your father," Jodie observed, trying to be positive. "No matter what he's done wrong."

"Yes, that's right," Lara responded, thankful to Jodie for snapping her back to reality. "What crime did he commit?"

Jodie's father was again hesitant. But the whole truth had to come out. "He was convicted of sex offences, with violence. Two charges were proven, one of rape, the other having sex with an under-age girl. There were other charges too, molesting under-age children with violence, but insufficient evidence to convict."

"Oh, no no, it can't be," Lara murmured, breaking into a sob. "Surely that's not my father." She put hands over her eyes, shaking her head in anguish.

Jodie moved closer, putting her arms around her in comfort. A deathly hush fell over them, Lara's sobbing the only sound.

Jodie's mother was next to speak. An intelligent woman with strong family values, she was usually adept at charting a path through adversity. "I think you need time to digest all this, Lara. Don't make any decisions now, not until you have a clearer picture of how you feel."

"Very good advice," her husband agreed.

Lara nodded, gaining some measure of control over her emotions. She thanked Jodie's father for his efforts and stood to leave.

"See you Monday," she farewelled Jodie, then headed homewards on her bike.

Chapter 7

The atmosphere was near intolerable. Mealtimes worst, when the three of them sat around the kitchen table at closer quarters than any other time. Long silences commonplace, the pretence steadfastly maintained.

Jude felt the deepening tension acutely, however on another plane was not unhappy with it, accustomed to the murky undercurrents his fathers created incessantly. But a shift had occurred, family dynamics taking a subtle turn in his favour. A bizarre result out of their major row a couple of days ago.

Dado and Dad had learned of Jude infiltrating their private documents, through the surveillance provided by Robin. Initially, they reacted with fury and threats. Imposing heavy restrictions would stifle whatever independence he still enjoyed. But then, each father suddenly and simultaneously seemed to comprehend wider implications. Underneath, it was all about the DNA testing. Jude could see the wheels turning in both their heads, yet amazed they couldn't read each other. Or could they? Was confession untenable? So an unspoken pact reaffirming the pretence fell back in place.

Jude was the beneficiary. Each father would rely on him not divulging to the other the DNA testing he'd seen on file. That gave Jude a measure of power he'd never had before. Chas in particular was distraught and uptight, taking Jude aside in private to attempt a reconciliation of convenience.

"I know you've seen the DNA tests in my file," he began testily. "I want you to promise you'll never under any circumstances tell Dado. Even that you've seen the tests done at all." He grew more nervous as he spoke.

Jude knew instinctively he had the inside running. Dad would do anything to maintain the fantasy of fatherhood, achievable as long as he was sure Dado knew no better. Their agreed equal opportunity doctrine must hold. Denial of psychopathic, pathological proportions.

"What will you do for me in return?" Jude retorted boldly.

Dad was taken aback, never before faced with such a stance from Jude. "What do you want me to do?"

"Two things." He needed no time to think about it. "I want to see my mother. Regularly. And I want to find out for myself about my sexuality. Not have boys pushed on me all the time."

Again Dad was left floundering. "I see." He took a long pause. "Why is your mother so important?"

"Because she's my mother."

Another long pause. "Have you spoken to Dado about this?"

"No. Why don't you speak to him?"

Dad nodded imperceptibly, but the nervous tension was rising again. "I'll see what I can do."

Jude felt a great surge of confidence. Just talking about things was to break through a barrier for the first time.

Brett also took Jude aside for a conversation in private. His concern was the same, to maintain confidentiality over the DNA test on his file. But his motive was different. Safe in the knowledge of real fatherhood, he wanted to continue a sense of superiority long established by keeping Chas ignorant. All about power, perpetuated at a psychological level with a self-serving smugness that Jude found nauseating.

Again Jude used his position to advantage, although extracting concessions from Dado was tougher. When he put forward his two conditions, Dado laughed. A rarely seen reaction, out of character for a serious person.

"Why would I agree to that?" The nauseating smugness was there. "You overplay your hand. I'm sure we taught you never to do that."

It was the closest Jude would get to satisfaction. Dado had less incentive than Dad to maintain the pretence, underpinned by the fall-back position of real fatherhood should their secret scam blow apart. Jude could only rely on Dado's desire to perpetuate the status quo and not risk probably irreparable damage to a comfortable life. A very uncertain dynamic.

He had another avenue to explore. Happy to have broken the ice with both fathers, he would proceed without fear of the tracking and surveillance measures threatening to control his every move. More time off school was needed, a minor problem only.

Aware, from their time with Jeremy, that Child Protection Services supposedly helped children with family issues, he left school early afternoon and made his way to the Department offices. He sat in the waiting area, clutching his ticket and information he held on his mother. The place had a welcoming feel, pleasant surrounds. Customers were at a long bench, served by officers in cubicles behind. Two more sat patiently waiting for their number to come up on screen.

Another entered, taking the next ticket then sat two seats removed from Jude. An attractive girl, with shoulder-length blonde hair, shapely figure, appealing facial features. Jude stole a second look, impressed, but glimpsing a line of strain on her face. He glanced away quickly, embarrassed as she turned her head to meet his gaze.

The news about her father was a devastating setback for Lara, throwing her into confusion over what to do next. But not for long. She had embarked on an irreversible course in her quest to know him. While the revelations about his sex crimes filled her with fear, the clamour inside her head 'he's my father, he's my father ---' would not go away. She decided on a return visit to the Department where she'd first enquired, hoping to obtain an address or contact details from the information she now possessed. This despite being unable to convince either mum to sign the form giving their permission.

She entered the Department building, took the next ticket then a seat in the waiting area. Three others waiting, she noted, anxious to get on with it. She sensed someone two seats away looking at her. A glance in that direction was enough to put him off staring. What was his problem? Yet there was a certain appeal about him. Dark wavy hair, athletic build, a kind face of some depth. He looked determined. She glanced away.

The two before him were served and Jude's number came up. He strode to the available officer; Prudeep, by her name tag.

"How can I help you?" Prudeep asked.

"I'd like to arrange an order authorising that I can see my mother." He pushed across the papers showing Dulcie's details.

"What's your name? And your date of birth, address, phone number?" Prudeep inputted to her computer as Jude supplied the information.

"Why do you need an order to see your mother?"

Jude described the circumstances, the long-time opposition of his fathers to any contact. "But I think they might be more generous if I have a Department order." He was pensive, the reason sounding a little weak as he said it.

Prudeep was somewhat bemused. An unusual request, which seemed a little ambiguous. "We can't force someone to allow contact. If your fathers are likely to be more generous, then you wouldn't need an order, would you?" When Jude made no reply, she went on, "We can offer you mediation. A session where the two parties talk to each other under controlled conditions. Try to work out a plan that suits everyone. Would you be interested in that?"

Jude gave a sickly smile, knowing there was no chance whatsoever of mediation. He had avoided telling her of the DNA tests and entrenched pretence. "I'm not sure," he replied, his hopes of achieving anything here quickly fading.

Prudeep completed computer input, then printed out a form. She handed it to Jude. "Sometimes in a marriage there is a legal agreement in place defining issues such as access and contact. For this reason, you must obtain your fathers' signatures agreeing to mediation. Where shown on the form, then bring it back here." She offered a parting smile, the interview over.

Jude departed, irritated he'd wasted his time. He left the building, jumped on his bike and headed for the beach. Settling at his favourite bench seat sheltered from the hot sun, he stared out across the water, trying to reconcile his next move. It seemed every time he came here, it was out of frustration, struggling to find a way forward.

A movement close to his right interrupted his thoughts. He looked up quickly. The blonde girl he'd seen at the Department waiting area was standing a few meters away. Surprised, his heart leapt, his head instantly abuzz. As before, she impressed as an attractive figure, stirring a strange feeling inside him. Should he say something to her?

Lara moved to the end of the bench seat. "Can I sit here?" She cast a quick look in his direction, again sensing a certain appeal about him.

"Yes, sure." Jude shifted position, giving her space. He tried to think of something more to say, but his tongue seemed stuck in his mouth.

Lara sat. A few moments of silence, then she turned towards him and said, "I saw you at the Family Services office." Her outgoing nature to the fore.

A thrill of excitement coursed through Jude, that she would bother speaking to him. "Yes, I saw you there." He needed to say more. "Did you get what you want?"

"No. They won't help me unless my parents sign a form. But they won't sign it." The expression on her face hardened momentarily.

"Yeah? Same with me." Suddenly, he felt comfortable with her. She was confiding in him!

"Really? Are your parents strict?" She felt a surge of interest. Someone else with family issues.

Jude nodded vehemently. "Very. They won't let me see my mother." He blurted it out without thinking. Immediately, he felt foolish. Now she would know he came from a same-sex marriage and think he was gay. Inwardly, he cursed himself. The first girl he'd ever got talking to, especially one so attractive, and he'd blown it! He stared at the ground in self-recrimination.

Lara was intrigued. "Do you have a stepmother? Or two fathers?"

An escape route. He could pretend to have a stepmother. "Two fathers," he replied, being stupidly honest. Again he cursed himself. He half-turned away to stare out over the water, expecting to be rejected now.

To Lara, it was a positive. She felt more drawn to him, stirrings of affection. He had issues troubling him, that much was obvious. But that only intrigued her more. Coming from a same-sex marriage, was he gay? She sensed not, going by the vibes, body language and appeal. Suddenly, inexplicably, she wanted to know.

"I have two mothers," she responded. "No father." Every day, she felt increasingly confident her own sexuality was different from her mums. Why not for him, different from his fathers? She found herself hoping so.

Her admission galvanised Jude. He snapped his head around and their eyes met. An incredible moment. A sensation pulsed through his body, uplifting him as he'd never experienced before.

Lara felt the sensation of the moment also. She wanted to know him better, to share their stories. "I don't feel the same way as my mums. I think I'm different to them." She hesitated, but held his gaze. "How about you? Are you the same as your fathers?"

A crucial moment. Jude broke from her gaze, staring out to sea again. "I don't think I am. But my fathers want me to be like them. They keep trying to set me up with other boys my age. I feel nothing. Just want to get away." The words of his mother came into his mind, 'just because one of their sperm made you does not mean you are the same sexually'. Words he would always remember, helping to overcome a lifetime of pressure from his fathers.

Lara listened intently. Almost certainly he was not gay, she decided. She was about to respond when her phone sounded, breaking the spell.

"Hi, Jodie," she answered. A short pause. "No, they won't help me. I have to find out for myself." A longer pause. "Right. See you tomorrow."

"That's my friend at school," she explained, turning back to her new friend. "Ashley Girls. Year eleven. My name's Lara. I'll be sixteen in two months." She smiled and looked at him enquiringly.

Jude was taken with her smile, white even teeth adding to her attractiveness. "I'm Jude. Ashley Boys, year twelve. I'll be seventeen next month." Having heard her brief phone conversation, he was curious. "You said you have to find out about something. Is that about your mothers not signing the form?"

Lara nodded, a little pensive. "Yes. I'm trying to contact my father. I've never known him. He was sperm donor." She bowed her head and looked away, eyes moistening and lips quivering as the emotion welled up. Learning of his criminal past was a major blow to reconciling the worthlessness depicted by her mums.

Jude saw her emotion and it touched him. He wanted to give her a hug, but refrained, instead asking, "What's his name? You might be able to trawl online."

"Brent. But I don't know his surname." She lifted her head and wiped her eyes. "Or his address, except he lives alone not far from here. He's forty seven." She felt too humiliated to mention his crimes or time in prison.

"Could you find out if he belongs to any organisation or group you can look up online?"

Her head dropped again and she broke into a sob, starkly aware of what organisation that would be. She stood, whispering, "I have to go now," in a choking voice. Distraught, she ran off without a further glance in Jude's direction.

Jude stared after her, aghast. Disappointment quickly hit hard, a lump in his throat replacing the emotional high. He cursed, blaming himself. His last question had gone too far, with someone he'd only just met! How he wished he could have it back. Then she'd still be here, with him, the first time he'd ever related to a girl. He was alone again, back to the feeling of desolation he knew so well. Only worse now, having blown his opportunity. He didn't even know how to contact her, no arrangement to meet again. Despairing, he returned to his bike and made his way home.

Before reaching home, Lara was already regretting her actions. She'd just met someone unlike anyone of the male sex she'd met before. Yet she flounced off, unable to control her emotions over an issue not of his making. She was disappointed in herself. He had impressed on two fronts. A physical attraction, helping to dispel any lingering self-doubt about her own sexuality. And he had empathy. Whether that was natural or because seeking his mother was a similar circumstance to her own, didn't matter. It was there.

She'd met boys before, plenty chasing her because of her good looks. But no one of any depth. Her disinterest in them had created a reputation for herself, especially when they learned of her female same-sex family background. Not helping her self-doubt. Jude was different. Suddenly, she realised she'd left without arranging to meet him again, or get his contact details. "Damn! Stupid!" she admonished herself.

That evening, her mums detected something different about her. MumD commented.

"You seem preoccupied, L. Did something happen at school today?"

Lara was thankful they'd not been informed of her afternoon absence. Best not tell them about revisiting Family Services. But the other event should be safe enough.

"I met someone today. After school. He's really nice."

"Well, that's great, L. Do you want to bring him to meet us?" MumD was genuinely pleased. MumG also.

Lara hesitated. "I only just met him. See how it goes."

After dinner, she retired quickly to her room. She sat at her computer. Jude's suggestion was repeating in her mind. Upset when he said it, but now it appealed as an avenue to explore. Where to start?

She searched 'Prison Records'. Too wide a scope. A sub-search 'Sentences over Ten Years'. Still too wide. She sat back, realising she was hedging. Must face the truth. Taking a deep breath, she searched 'Sex Crimes'. Wide also. But a sub-search caught her eye. Of course, that's it! The Sex Offenders Register.

She searched and it came up. Anyone convicted of a sex offence was here, for public access to know where they are after release from jail. The Home page was a line-by-line summary, easy to use. Excited, she scrolled down, looking for any name Brent. There's one. Brent Schumaker, D.O.B July 2005. No. Scrolling further. Then suddenly, Brent Chester, D.O.B. August 1992. He was 47!

Lara slumped back in the chair, her mouth dropping open in mild shock. Leaning forward, she clicked on the line, feeling nervous. It was all there, his entire details and record, including photos.

With mounting trepidation, she zoomed in on a head-and-shoulders mug shot of the offender. A finely-chiselled face, clean shaven, short-cropped hair slightly greying with receding forehead. Nothing outstanding there. But the eyes and mouth gave him away. The brown eyes were cold, slightly dilated as if startled or aggressive response to an affront. His mouth, thin-lipped and crooked, unsmiling except the upper lip curling one side in the merest hint of an arrogant smirk. A shiver went down Lara's spine. She was far from sure she wanted to meet this person. Was he really her father?

She checked the details. His current address, just two suburbs away. Almost walking distance! Two convictions, one of rape, the other violating a minor. The prison sentence, fifteen years, released early last year after serving full term.

Parole denied several times due to lack of remorse and violent behaviour against fellow inmates. All consistent with the advice from Jodie's father. Lara stared at the screen, shocked as confirmation of who was her father struck to the core.

Each conviction was further detailed, with description and graphic photos. The rape of a nineteen year-old woman was particularly heinous. The photos of her battered body, bruised and bloodied, portrayed her desperate struggle to fight him off. But unsuccessfully. She recovered from near death but with permanent disability. The other conviction involved no obvious signs of violence, prompting defence counsel to argue the act was consensual. This was inconclusive, however the girl was just fourteen years of age, violation of a minor the clear verdict.

Two other charges were laid and included in the class action bringing all charges into one trial. Violating under-age boys, one just ten years old the other fifteen, both with violence causing moderate injury. There were allegations of others similar, but insufficient evidence culminated in deferral to possible further trial at a later date. Lara took another deep breath, trying to calm the nervous reaction worsening as each revelation presented. But she was determined to follow up. What happened to those two other charges? Why no convictions?

Suddenly, she realised the dates didn't fit. A fifteen year prison term meant he'd been jailed early 2024. But the charges dated back to 2017. Why the gap? She read on. Another man was implicated along with her father in the offences against boys. Alarmed, Lara read the profile on

Gordon Pascalladis. He was a prominent figure in the 2017 'Yes' campaign to legalise same-sex marriage. It seems he was close to politicians as well. Mysteriously, the charges against him and Brent Chester were suddenly dropped. Lara was aghast. The clear implication was of sweeping away a pending scandal linking paedophile behaviour to the same-sex debate raging at the time.

Years later, Brent was charged again, this time just for the two offences against women that did not involve Gordon Pascalladis. The trial was late 2023, his sentence beginning early the next year.

Coming to the end of the descriptive text, Lara sat back to contemplate the ramifications. Her own situation was playing in her mind. All evidence pointed to a man who was sex-crazed or power-driven or both, not only committing horrific crimes but also active as a sperm donor! How shonky was the screening and assessment of potential sperm donors!? How many others besides her mums impregnated with his sperm? How many unknown brothers and sisters are out there? Dismayed as the full picture unravelled, she could only wonder what the relevant authorities had been doing.

The timing was an incredible twist of fate. Her father should have been convicted in 2017, jailed straightaway, no sperm donorship, no Lara. As that ludicrous scenario dawned on her, she could only burst out laughing, kicking up her feet under the table in a mock show of defiance. She had cheated the odds! Just like her father for a time at least. Was it a hereditary factor passed on? "No, no, cut it out!" she admonished. Imagination running wild.

Another piece of timing occurred to her. From her birthday, she calculated back to August 2023 when MumD fell pregnant with his sperm. Only just before he went on trial. A close call. Again, she was lucky to exist! Then a chilling thought. There was still time after that for him to return and rape MumG. Sex offending right to the end, unremorseful for previous crimes. Also undetected, not reported by MumG, or even divulged to MumD. How many others? What chance for her father ever to be rehabilitated?

Having learned all she could about her father, she ran off a hard copy of the page containing his details, crimes and photo. She folded the page and slipped it into her ID pouch. Evidence available for an appropriate occasion. She closed down the computer and lay on the bed. Her thoughts turned to Jude. Somehow, she would meet him again. Probably at the beach. A warm feeling coursed through her body in anticipation.

Chapter 8

Workers again congregated around the arena, another round of testing imminent. The previous had been appraised exhaustively, aspects of the software rewritten, Robin3 further enhanced. It stood passive in the centre of the arena as the three groups of technicians with their handsets, and six challengers, gathered. The head technician took his place behind the computer/camera setup.

Appraisal had largely focussed on Robin3's memory. The central reservoir from which programming exercised decision-making and output. With input from the three senses, first mooted in Robin1, an ability fully proven through consistent performance, testing was at a stage to ascertain whether output reaction would build on the stored memory from previous testing. Proving whether Robin3 could learn, making the most effective use of its programming. The aim beyond Robin1 capability, paralleling human development. Additional safety features were now incorporated in the software, ever mindful of the disastrous Robin2 phase.

Colby, the head technician, activated Robin3. The intention was to repeat the same set routines as last time. From unarmed through various stages of weaponry, from one to all six challengers, interest would centre on detecting signs of Robin3 predicting pending action or aware of how challengers' movements and body language signalled intent. Possibly pre-empting the routines. This would reveal whether knowledge stored in memory from previous testing was helping to decide output, confirming if the concept of learning was feasible. Perhaps the beginnings of lateral thinking. But always within the safe confines of its programming.

Early indications were encouraging. Then it was the club-wielding challenger's turn. He barely entered the arena before Robin3 moved swiftly to snatch the club from his grasp, clearly recognising it as a danger. A collective gasp of surprise went up from the watching crowd. The first time for Robin3 to output pre-emptive aggression.

Colby called a lull in proceedings. He moved to a quick conference with the sight, hearing and touch technicians. Of concern was the next routine, Chas wielding a knife.

"After seeing what just happened, I'm not comfortable with Chas and the knife," Colby told them. "Chas is a problem sometimes, as we all know. He gets too excited. If something goes wrong here, it could be dangerous, with a knife involved."

Brett stepped forward, feeling he should support Chas. "How about we call Chas over and you can speak to him."

"Yes, okay."

Anticipating being the next to perform, Chas was keyed up. A common state for him anyway, more so lately with the unusual tensions and shift in family dynamics at home.

Summoned to join the technicians, he asked, "Is there a problem?"

Colby responded. "We're concerned about the knife. After what we just saw with the club." He eyed Chas with suspicion, tolerating him in the team largely out of respect for his longevity at the factory.

Chas was determined not to miss his turn. "What if I hide the knife behind my back? In its pouch, like this." He relocated the pouch on his belt.

A little dubious, but satisfied the knife was invisible from in front, Colby nodded his approval. "Don't bring it out unless you're certain it's safe."

Chas returned to his position beside the sword-wielding challenger due to follow after him. Keen to impress, he stepped into the arena.

It all happened quickly. A brief skirmish, Robin3 seeming to recognise Chas and alerted to danger with heightened movements, Chas unable to control his exuberance and pulling the knife from its pouch. The challenger with sword leapt forward to restrain Chas. But too late. With unmatched speed, Robin3 grabbed the knife, computed the swordsman as greater danger and plunged the knife into his chest.

The sword clattered to the floor, the man clutching at the knife handle protruding from his chest. His eyes rolled back. With a gargled cough, he collapsed to the floor. Screams filled the air from the crowd of onlookers. A rapid exodus turned mayhem as they backed off in fear. Chas yelled an obscenity and staggered back, a gash across his left forearm streaming blood. Brett quickly wrapped a towel around his arm, then led him away to the factory's medical bay. Colby deactivated Robin3.

Medical staff rushed in to attend the fallen swordsman. An official from management appeared, microphone in hand. "Please, everyone, remain calm. The danger is over. Please return to your work stations. You will be advised further in due course."

Gradually people calmed, control restored to the factory floor. The swordsman was carried by stretcher to the medical bay. Shortly after, he was pronounced dead.

An inquest was immediately underway. Factory management grilled the team of technicians, the Head put on notice for failure to exercise sound judgement. The lead-up incident involving the club was reviewed, then attention turned to Chas. He took the brunt of the blame, having disobeyed specific instructions to keep the knife hidden. Given his record of previous misdemeanours and managerial reprimands, he was suspended from duties without pay until further notice.

A wider enquiry expected to be commissioned by government would no doubt reassess the Robin programme and direction of AI development generally. In the meantime, the factory's internal inquest began addressing what went wrong with Robin3, the practices and procedures leading to tragedy, the loss of control Robin3 had so easily exploited. Systemic failure was evident, coming on the back of Robin2.

The two arms of factory hierarchy, policy-making and implementation, were immediately at loggerheads. The Policy gurus, charged with a higher calling conjoined with government policy, held the ascendancy. They argued that

Robin3, contrary to the instant outcry of disastrous failure, had actually worked brilliantly well. Too well. Clearly, Robin3 had exhibited a high degree of learning. But Implementation had not installed adequate safeguards, checks and balances.

Implementation chiefs grudgingly conceded the point about Robin3 working too well. But they argued vehemently that the policy direction was synonymous with freedom for Robin3 to express itself. Learn, react, whenever it encounters a situation again.

"Checks and balances are not possible," remarked the Chief Officer of Implementation, as all parties sat around the conference table. "That would be self-defeating. How can we have a policy allowing Robin freedom to react, then put a stop to it when it does so? By then, it's too late. Either Robin reacts or it doesn't react, nothing in between."

"Why isn't there?" the Chief Officer of Policy retorted. "Francis, you can programme anything into its software. Stop its reaction as soon as it shows rogue signs."

"What signs, Bernard? You see, what we must understand here is that Robin is not like a human being. Much as we're trying to give it human capability, capacity to learn and so on. Input to output can happen without warning signs. Cold." Francis sat back, genuinely troubled by the trend of Robin3's behaviour. Before he could continue, Bernard cut in.

"I do understand that. But it doesn't matter. Robin is still limited by the programming we give it, is it not?"

Francis was silent. Part of the trend troubling him. Judith, his deputy and a woman highly qualified in this area, spoke. "That's something we're looking at very closely. There are indications that Robin exceeded its programming."

A murmur of surprise sounded around the table. "How can that be?" It was Bernard's deputy, Catherine, speaking. Like Judith, she too was highly qualified in her field. "The programming decides everything, surely." All eyes turned to Chongwe, the factory's leading programmer.

Chongwe sat upright, alert and confident his knowledge of software creation was greater than anyone else's. "Robin reaction not exceed programming," he declared boldly. "Many element in software. We programme many situation. Robin have much option to choose output. Some for defence, security have element of violence, necessary for provide protection. Input from senses link any element it find suitable. Input store in memory, use next time when same situation come."

Everyone in the room listened intently. "So what you're saying in effect is that Robin can enhance its own programming?" Catherine pursued. "From input it sees, hears and touches? That's the learning we talk about."

"Maybe." Chongwe seemed less assured, his eyes shifting away uncertainly. "Maybe exaggerate element it find in software." Still unwilling to concede Robin3 could exceed the programming.

A stunned silence descended on the room. Someone else spoke. "What if it sees something really violent?"

All sat spellbound, horrified by the ramifications. No one spoke for some time. Then Francis took it up again. "We've given Robin the capacity to learn. I think we all see that now. But as I was saying before, Robin is not human. In us humans, we have moral standards, feelings and emotions, a sense of right and wrong. A person might want to take certain action against someone, out of jealousy or whatever, but most of the time refrain from doing so because of society's values we follow. These are the checks and balances. But not so in a robot. Robin is a cold entity, no chemical processes, no feelings, purely input and output." An unusual stance for someone so deeply embroiled in creating Robin.

Bernard responded. "Sounds like you have serious reservations about the project, Francis. I'm surprised. You've been dedicated to it for a long time."

"Yes, it's been worrying me for a while," Francis admitted, giving his colleague a concerned look. "Ever since Robin2, really. And now? Well, obviously we can't ignore what just happened on the shop floor. A man is dead."

"Yes, agreed." Bernard returned his look, appreciating the gravity of the situation. "We're due to meet government shortly. I think they might want to suspend the project. Or at least any more testing until an in-depth review is done." He hesitated, thoughtful. "Do you think we should recall the hundred Robins sent out for trial?"

After a few moments of consideration, Francis replied, "No, I don't think so. They only have Robin1 capability. Can only perform set tasks controlled by the programming."

"Robin2 capability was installed too, wasn't it?"

"Yes, but dormant, not activated. We were hoping to supersede with Robin3 if all went well, but obviously that won't happen now." In a more upbeat tone, he added, "There's a lot we can learn from the Robin1 trial, a lot of data to collect."

With the conference finishing on a positive note, the participants dispersed to their stations.

Suspension from duties hit Chas hard. Factory and family were the two areas of his life that dominated over all else. Both now crashing around him. Even before the factory disaster, tensions at home had further ramped up. A blazing row when Jude got home.

The tracker on Jude's bike had alerted his fathers to unusual and suspicious movements. Missing school again, visiting the Family Services office, then a long time at the beach. But they backed off before the demanding of explanations went too in-depth. Jude knew why. After the conditions he'd laid down, each must surely suspect attempted contact with his mother. They couldn't join forces to expose it, the secrets and pretence might also be exposed.

Brett put in place a stringent measure, setting Robin to tighter surveillance. Robin would shadow Jude, ensuring he went nowhere but where he was supposed to be. Jude was afraid to test it, knowing Robin could be physical. When he heard what happened at the factory, that quickly turned to a deeper fear.

Jude did extract a minor concession from his fathers. He could address them as Brett and Chas, discarding the childlike Dado and Dad. Soon to turn seventeen, he felt he'd outgrown the latter.

The all too obvious heightened tension in Chas was becoming entrenched as a permanent state of mind and body. Communication in the household was at an all-time low, meaningful conversation rare. When it did happen, it was negative and carping. Jude didn't mind the silence, but the Chas mood was hard to tolerate.

It was at the dinner table when Chas finally snapped. "So many years of my life I've given them," he suddenly burst out, slamming the table-top with his fist. The crockery jumped, a glass fell over spilling contents across the table. "How was I to know what Robin would do? I was only doing my job!"

The suddenness of his outburst startled Brett and Jude. Brett glared at him with disdain. "You were told not to show him the knife," he countered, devoid of sympathy. He grabbed some napkins to mop up the spilled drink. Jude assisted.

"So it's my fault the man's dead!" Chas was shouting, his voice quivering precariously, body shaking alarmingly as all the pent-up emotion erupted. "That's what you're saying, isn't it? Why don't you just say it!" His voice rose to a high-pitched scream. He flung his chair back violently and stood, banging into the table. More spillage, plates and glasses crashing to the floor, splintering into pieces to scatter food and drink everywhere.

He stormed away, then turned back, arm outstretched pointing directly at Brett. "I've been there as long as you. But you're Mister Perfect, aren't you! Yes sir, No sir, all's good sir. Never a problem with Brett, he's our boy!" He finished with a gasping yelp, hyperventilating. Stumbling away, he threw open the front door with a bang and disappeared outside.

Jude stared after him, flabbergasted. Never before had Chas lost control of himself in such a way. Instinctively he knew, whatever Chas did now, family relations had changed irrevocably.

"Let him go," Brett responded finally. "Let's clean up this mess."

Next day, Chas caused another scene at the factory. Turning up soon after opening time, he strode straight to the conference room. A further meeting was underway, between the chiefs, senior personnel and government officials. Gate-crashing the party, he stood staring at them, brimming with aggression.

"You people want to blame me for everything," he stated threateningly. He moved closer, fixing a steely gaze at the Chief of Implementation seated halfway along the far side of the table. "What about the programmer!? What about the policy decisions!? I didn't do that! You all did!" His shaking voice lifted to fever pitch, shouting his last words as his outstretched arm made a sweeping gesture along the table.

A deathly hush descended on the group. "Where's security?" Francis called out, looking to the entrance door. "Get him out of here."

Someone had already called security. Two officers appeared, moving to restrain Chas. "Don't touch me!" Chas shrugged them off, stepping closer to the table, again eyeing up Francis. "Yeah, you don't like hearing the truth, do you!? Well, I'll tell everyone the truth. About Robin2, what people don't know. Then you'll see!" He glared at the Chief, unflinching, all inhibitions discarded.

Francis stood abruptly. "I remind you about the oath of allegiance you took when signing up to work here. You are bound by privacy law and the Secrets Act not to divulge information to anyone. Any breach of your oath and we will prosecute."

Chas yelled something unintelligible. Before he could take it further, the security officers each took an arm, marching him towards the door. "Leave me alone! Leave me alone!" Struggling furiously, he continued yelling obscenities as the officers forcibly dragged him from the room.

Outside, two DP officers, never far from the action, had arrived. They arrested Chas, taking him to the police cells, where he would remain for the rest of the day and overnight.

At the conference room, one of the government officials turned to Francis and asked, "What did he mean by 'Robin2, what people don't know'? If there is anything you need to tell us, now would be a good time." He gave Bernard a hard look also.

"No, he just wants to hit out after we suspended him. Create a scandal. There's nothing in it." Francis looked a shade flustered, casting a quick glance at Bernard.

Aware of potential trouble, Bernard quickly nodded agreement. "That's right. He's caused problems before, has he not, Francis? We might have to let him go altogether."

The government official spoke again. "He questioned the programmer and policy-makers too. What's that about?"

"Same thing," Bernard replied. He gave Chongwe a side-long glance. "But that's what we're here for, isn't it? To work through these issues."

With that, the conference returned to business.

Chapter 9

The morning was busy, many cases similar in nature to the first Saturday. Tony attended to most of the consultations, men with disease or injury from same-sex activity. With fewer cases involving women, Barbara busied herself unpacking recently delivered supplies, preparing medicine, injections and other consumables, cleaning and sterilising equipment. Several swabs required testing. Lara assisted her, learning quickly. With many hours of community service still to serve, she decided to embrace the duties and learn as much as she could about a seldom revealed side of life.

During a brief lull, Lara's growing curiosity compelled her to ask Barbara, "What made you decide to do this kind of work?"

Barbara gave a friendly smile. "Tony and I started here when this place opened as a Rehabilitation Centre for drug users. That was about fifteen years ago, soon after the Coln government came in. Their policies worked well. Centres like this really helped people. In a genuine way, not just talk. We had the best doctors and facilities available."

"Sounds like it was quite a calling for you and Tony." Lara was again impressed by their dedication.

"Well yes, you could say that." Barbara hesitated, looking sad as past memories returned. "Our son died of a drug overdose. Before the Rehab Centres were started."

"Oh, I'm sorry."

"No no, nothing to be sorry about. He made his choice. What I'm sorry about is how this place has gone now, under the present government. The safe injecting room is back, and whatever else in other parts of the building, not sure. Nothing of medical benefit though, I am sure of that." She gave a grimace of disapproval.

Wondering what she could be referring to, Lara asked, "What about Mental Health? Must be part of it too?"

Barbara gave her a sharp glance, impressed by her insight. "That was huge when we were a Rehab Centre. Not anymore. Tony and I do what we can, but we're not qualified for it really. We've heard the Mental institutions have many more cases these days."

Tony was just finishing with the last patient when another entered, a man accompanied by two DP officers. The man was hyped up, in a frenzied state requiring the officers to restrain him.

"Can you do something to calm him down?" one of the officers asked.

"What's the problem?" Tony responded, moving forward for closer inspection.

"He was held in custody last night after causing a disturbance at the AI factory. But he's no better this morning, still going off his head."

"I don't have a problem!" Chas was furiously indignant. He strained to break free, but the officers held a vice-like grip on each arm. "You have no respect! Don't you know I'm the longest serving worker at the factory? Take me back! I have to tell them!" He was shouting, unable to fathom his change of fortune.

The officers twisted his arms back. "Do you want the handcuffs again? Or are you going to cooperate?" The second officer spoke in a harsher tone.

Chas struggled. His feet slid forward and his backside hit the floor with a thud. He yelped as a stab of pain shot through his body, momentarily dazing him. Tony took the opportunity, moving in quickly to administer an injection. In moments, Chas succumbed to the tranquiliser.

"That'll keep him quiet for a while." Tony shifted to the computer. "What's his name? And age? For the records."

One officer provided the details. "Will he fall asleep now?"

"No, it's only to relax him and calm the nerves. I'd suggest taking him along to the cafeteria. They'll be serving lunch there now. See how he is after that."

"Good idea." The officers led out a much subdued Chas.

Lara, having watched with a mixture of alarm and amusement, was also ready for lunch. "Keep an eye on him," Barbara suggested.

At the cafeteria, Lara received her food then took a table adjacent to Chas and the two officers. She stole a glance at Chas. Short in stature, one-day unshaven head and face, the mannerisms, not hard to pick his sexuality. But he was not at peace with himself. Despite the tranquiliser, he was fidgeting nervously, picking at his plate of food, silent and sulky. The impression was of a person with more issues in his life than the trouble for which he'd been detained.

Two men entered the cafeteria. One Lara recognised as the man she saw briefly last Saturday heading for the locked door past the safe injecting room. Well-dressed in a slightly crumpled suit no tie, short dark but greying hair with receding forehead. The other man was of similarly average height and build, also well-dressed but more casual, fair hair greying and balding, another with the one-day unshaven look. Both exuded a sense of authority, but with a shifty aura about them. Formidable people not to be trusted, Lara decided instinctively.

As they drew near, the fair-haired man broke stride. "G'day, Chas. What brings you here?"

With a jerk of his head, Chas looked up in surprise. "Oh hello, Jeremy." He blinked his eyes, trying to clear his mind and present himself better to someone of personal importance.

Always astute, Jeremy turned to the DP officers, one of whom he knew. "Hi, Gary. Is Chas here in some kind of trouble?" He flashed his characteristic broad smile. "Perhaps I can help? Chas is a good friend of mine."

"Yes, I am." Chas felt a spark of pride returning.

"He spent last night in custody," Gary responded. "He's had something to calm him down, so we can release him now." He stood, then turned to Chas. "Stay away from the AI factory, or next time you'll face charges." The two officers departed.

Jeremy took one of the vacated chairs. With an insipid smile, he gave Chas a long hard look, sizing him up. "I saw the news reports. It seems you're copping the blame for what happened at the factory." Always he was intent on exploring the opportunity to manipulate a situation.

"That's right." Chas perked up, easily taking the bait. "It's not fair. I was only doing my job."

"Right, right. I understand." The smile broadened. "What does Brett think about it?"

"Oh, he doesn't care. He's on their side." Chas was gaining in confidence. "Brett's always like that. He's their golden boy. Gets all the favours." He paused, a more sensitive concern rearing up. "At home too. He wants to control everything to do with our son."

Even Jeremy was surprised at the embittered response. It portrayed an alarming depth of feeling. Their exchange was interrupted as his colleague returned with two plate-fuls of food. He handed one to Jeremy and took his seat on the other side of Chas.

"Thanks." Jeremy introduced him. "Chas, this is Gordon Pascalladis. He and I work together. We can help you."

Chas' eyebrows lifted involuntarily as he recognised the name. "Weren't you heading the Yes campaign years back? For same-sex marriage?"

Gordon flashed a broad smile, similar to Jeremy's in its ostentatious effect. "That was over twenty years ago. You have a good memory. Or maybe you were involved yourself?"

"I certainly was." Chas was excited now, courting the attention of two important people.

Jeremy proceeded to inform Gordon of how he met Chas, partner Brett and son Jude, their links to the AI factory and recent tragedy there. He intimated how mutual interests in same-sex matters, particularly relating to Jude and other boys of similar age, was fostering a growing friendship. "Jude is nearly seventeen," he added. "You know, that age when boys are questioning everything? Often confused?"

"Indeed, indeed." Gordon nodded wisely, listening attentively, maintaining a knowing half-smile. He and Jeremy were usually on the same wavelength, after many years of association.

"Yes. He wants to contact his mother," Chas remarked, pleased to confirm Jeremy's contention. "We've never allowed that."

"Very wise," Gordon agreed. "It only causes trouble."

Jeremy was looking thoughtful. "I'm curious about what you said before. Brett being controlling. What's that about?" Another opportunity to manipulate was on offer.

"Oh, he is." Chas was further buoyed. "He acts like Jude belongs to him. He cuts me out. He knows I hate it. He does it deliberately. But when we're with others, he acts all good and proper. Like the perfect father." His voice became more strident as the words tumbled out uncontrollably.

Again the depth of feeling was a surprise. Jeremy and Gordon exchanged a quick glance, enough to be of one mind in recognising the opening for exploitation. "Tell me something," Jeremy took it up, "is it you or Brett the biological father of Jude?"

Chas dropped his head and looked away, suddenly deflated. The crunch issue he always hated having to face. But he didn't want his present companions to know it was a problem. With a big effort, he tried to look confident, replying, "We don't know. We mixed our sperm, so it could be either and we agreed not to find out."

Jeremy gave another quick smile, again glancing at Gordon, both picking up on Chas' negative body language. Instinctively, each sensed the real truth. "Wouldn't you like to find out?" Jeremy suggested, still maintaining his insidious smile. When Chas didn't immediately reply, he continued, "We have access to a laboratory. We have DNA testing done there sometimes."

"Really?" Chas was stuck for further words, his mind buzzing with confusion. Loyalties trapped in an emotional no-mans-land.

"We can obtain whatever results you want," Jeremy went on. "All you have to do is bring the right samples."

The idea hit Chas like a thunderbolt. His eyes widened as a shock rush of adrenalin suddenly cleared his mind. He could see the way forward, how to get back on top, to wrest the ascendancy off Brett. Deception was no hindrance in the wider scheme of things. "I'll bring the samples," he heard himself say, trance-like.

His reaction was precisely as Jeremy expected. A nod of approval from Gordon. Chas was ripe for the picking. "There's something we'd like to show you," Gordon coaxed. "But we can't talk here." He was aware others in the cafeteria may be hearing their conversation, particularly the blonde girl at the adjacent table.

He and Jeremy stood, beckoning Chas to follow. They left the cafeteria.

Lara had overheard all their conversation. The mention of Jude's name was startling, and exciting. A stunning insight into his family situation. One father before her eyes a mental case, the other seemingly a control freak. After her enticing encounter with Jude at the beach, she'd returned a couple of times, but disappointingly he wasn't there on either occasion. Now, she was even more keen to know him.

Gordon's name mentioned was just as startling. A vivid image of her computer screen depicting him in cahoots with her criminal father flashed through her mind. To see him here in person was a shocking revelation. He and his fair-haired colleague called Jeremy, cynically grooming Jude's naïve susceptible father, nefarious intent obvious. The shifty aura she initially sensed around them had deepened to something more evil. Was her father involved too?

With troubled mind, she cleared the table and went to assist the cafeteria hostess. That duty done, she returned to the clinic, pausing to stare down the corridor. The locked door posed new questions of iniquitous intrigue.

Inside the locked room, Gordon made a sweeping gesture. "We call this the Cave," he informed Chas.

Several computers were spaced along a bench down a side wall. Seated at one near the end was another presence, a man too engrossed to greet them. On a bench along the opposite side wall, a line-up of drones with associated equipment sat ready to deploy.

At the far end of the spacious area was the standout feature. A large double bed adorned with rich red-coloured cover and pillows, housed beneath a light blue and pink four-poster canopy. Obviously crafted to create a sexual backdrop of maximum sensuality. Hanging from the ceiling above the foot of the bed was a trapeze, adjustable in height, bonding rope loosely draped around. A nearby stand carried various paraphernalia. To one side, a camera atop a wheeled tripod stood poised to record action.

Gordon and Jeremy led Chas to a computer at the near end. They sat and Gordon hit the start button. Images quickly came on screen. Sexual activity, explicit, depicting male involvement with young boys. Gordon brought images up one by one. Acts of sodomy, masturbation, fellatio, leaving nothing to the imagination. Couples, threesomes, groupies. "What about this one," he crowed, putting on an excited air for Chas' benefit. An adult male with two boys, contorted in simultaneous sex acts. The boys looked young, barely teenage.

Eventually, he brought the extensive viewing session to a close. "We have lots more. But you get the idea." He and Jeremy were watching Chas closely throughout. "We have whatever anyone wants." Gratified, Gordon leaned back in his chair, still focussed on Chas.

"There's a big demand for this," Jeremy proclaimed. "Someone will always supply a demand. So why not us?"

Chas reacted with a jumbled mixture of shock at the raw nature of the material and feeling stimulated by it. Never had he been involved with an under-age boy, let alone as young as some of these boys. Yet he couldn't help being aroused by images consistent with his sexuality. A pang of guilt gripped him. Others of his sexuality indulged in it, he knew. But today's society reviled paedophiles like never before. Was that an incongruous anomaly? Even hypocrisy? In the modern world, same-sex activity and marriage was never more greatly embraced. He felt confused. But of course, it was merely a matter of age. Sixteen, the age of consent. A day under reviled, a day over revered. Many of the boys were considerably younger. How much below sixteen was too young?

Although afflicted with confusion, he felt a greater motivation. Acceptance. He was desperate to impress his new friends, to prove himself worthy of their attention. After the recent upheavals, fear of rejection dominated. "Wow!" he exclaimed, cracking a grin and punching the air for greater effect. It helped to clear the nervous fog. "Where did you find all this?"

"We don't find it, we create it," Jeremy admonished mildly, waving an arm towards the setup at the far end. "I can see it excites you." He placed a hand on Chas' thigh, moving it up to feel his arousal.

What followed was mind-blowing for Chas, culminating in a whirlwind sexual release. When it was over, Jeremy led him to an ensuite adjacent the drones, where they cleaned up. They re-joined Gordon.

"You can help us," Gordon stated, as Chas re-took his seat. "We need someone to make deliveries." His broad smile was again on show. "Then we can help you too."

"Oh yes?" Chas felt calm and positive now. His fear about acceptance had suddenly dissipated.

"Great. Well, this is how it works." Gordon leaned forward, giving Chas an intense look. "We make videos and deliver them to clients. You do the delivering, by hand. It's just as simple as that. Strict confidentiality is paramount, of course."

"I see. That sounds easy enough." Chas nodded in agreement. "What if I get caught? By the DP? They already know me." A stab of fear returning, recent events still fresh in his mind.

"You won't be." Gordon placed a hand on his shoulder. His infectious smile broadened again. "Don't worry, we have contacts in all the right places. Some DP officers are even our clients." He gave a self-gratifying chuckle.

Jeremy chimed in. "Videos are not all you'll be delivering. Some clients want the real thing. So we deliver partners, boys of suitable age, whatever the client requests." He spoke with a brazen arrogance that seemed a regular Jeremy characteristic.

It irked Chas a little, shocked at the stark nature of the operation. The supply of boys as partners mirrored the activities promoted during their recent family get-togethers. But this was much deeper and darker than merely picking up troubled children off the streets, giving them shelter, placing with genuine partners, adoption and the like. This was cynical, systematic abuse and exploitation, with no age limit. He felt a little sickened, but was committed now.

Jeremy was speaking again. "If you do good, you might progress to other tasks. We often make videos with clients, if they have that wish and their facilities are suitable." Again the arrogance.

"You can be involved in whatever takes your fancy. Every job has its perks." Gordon flashed the smile again, chuckling. "But be careful. It's all about the client, what he's happy with. You upset a client and you're out. No second chance." The smile vanished as he spoke the last words, grimly serious.

"There's good money in it," Jeremy continued. "The clients pay us. You'll be paid well for what you do. Better than you were getting at the factory." He detected Chas' uncertainty. Anything but total commitment and trust meant potential trouble. More pressure needed. "You're in a lot of strife at the factory. They blame you for the death of that technician. You might be charged with murder or manslaughter." He paused, allowing his words to take effect. "We can make sure that doesn't happen. And we can get you the DNA test results you want, just bring us appropriate samples." He sat back, satisfied they had Chas hooked.

The lingering doubts in Chas quickly dissolved, his untenable position clear. And the chance to reign supreme over Brett was overwhelmingly an irresistible temptation. "Okay, that's fine. I'm in."

There were handshakes and smiles all round. "Welcome aboard," Gordon heralded.

Chas looked at the computer screen again, curious. "Tell me, why do we have to deliver videos by hand when you can do it electronically?"

"Ah well," Gordon replied, "some clients are afraid of being traced. Actually, with the systems we use, electronic transmissions are untraceable and we do most that way. But for clients who are nervous, we deliver by hand and install for them. Or if they're not computer wise, we can install on their TV, video player or whatever device they like to use."

"I thought anything by computer can be traced. Or hacked." Chas felt confident enough now to ask more in-depth questions.

"Have you heard of the Dark Web?"

"Yes, I have. But so have lots of people. I've heard it's not as inaccessible as it's supposed to be."

"You heard exactly right. Which is why we don't use it." Gordon was enjoying testing Chas' knowledge. "Have you heard of the Darker Web?"

"No. What's that?"

"Ah." Gordon paused to lay a hand lovingly on the computer. "Very few people know about the Darker Web. You wouldn't even know how to obtain a Username. Access is by personal one-off Password generation plus Eye Recognition. There is no advertising or promotion, purely interaction between Users or sending material to clients. The encryption and eradication techniques are the most sophisticated known, impossible for a source to be traced or hacked. All traces of a transmission are eradicated on exiting. This is how we operate, worldwide. No hacker or rogue user has ever infiltrated the Darker Web. It is impossible. Eye Recognition is continuous throughout a use, access cut if any irregularity."

"Wow! That's incredible." Chas stared wide-eyed at Gordon, in awe of the forces at play and with some trepidation over having a role.

Gordon continued. "You might wonder how we gain clients without advertising or promotion. It is not needed. Word of mouth is the greatest advertiser. Anywhere in the world. Every User controls their local area, then we interact and exchange over the Darker Web."

"There is great cooperation between Users," Jeremy added. "Naturally, because that's how we all flourish."

"Too true," Gordon agreed. "Any material a User sends to other Users must include a short excerpt, just enough to titillate clients. A Flasher, we call it. Price must be shown with a

Flasher. Automatically, the software adds it to a video of all Flashers, for presenting to clients locally. There's a sophisticated system of bank transacting, using ID and client codes, for whatever a client chooses to purchase. If a transaction is for another User's material, we get a percentage cut. A transaction has no link to the material and is completely separate from the Darker Web."

"Yes," Jeremy emphasised. "The whole operation is tight and foolproof. Material a User receives cannot be varied, edited, corrupted or omitted." He placed a hand on Chas' shoulder. Subtle pressure through physical familiarity. "A Flasher video is always hand delivered, never sent via the Darker Web. You'll be delivering them a lot. Often to repeat clients. We have one now for delivery." He indicated a small memory stick sitting on the bench.

"It is read and choose only, cannot be installed on a client device. You wait. Each choice the client makes is red-flagged and payment options appear on screen. He completes payment for each, can be one or more. When all payments are complete, only then do you leave and return the video stick here. When his payments come through, we check them against the red flags on stick. If in order, full video delivery can proceed, usually through the Darker Web. Or can hand deliver, as Gordon was saying."

Gordon leaned forward, capturing Chas with an intense look. "Under no circumstances, whether a client chooses or not, do you ever leave the video stick with him. Clients will often try this on, saying they need time to decide or whatever. But there is no exception. The client chooses and purchases while you wait or not at all. If you leave or lose a video stick, you'll be out, no second chances. That applies to any stick, Flasher or full video."

Chas met his look nervously, fully aware how this deeply secret dire operation could impose harsh punishment if he messed up. But he was desperate to be worthy. To demonstrate he was switched on, he asked, "What happens if a client causes trouble? Maybe aggressive?"

"You mean tries to snatch the stick off you, for instance?" Jeremy suggested. "First of all, you never give him the stick. If he doesn't accept you working with his device, then you leave. No compromising. Some clients can be difficult. If you need help, use this." He reached inside a drawer and produced a small black box gadget. "Press the button and someone will be there in short time. The client will never cause trouble again. Maybe never be capable of anything again." He finished with an amused chortle.

"We assume you are computer capable," Gordon went on. "In a minute, we'll give you a demo of how to use a stick on a device. Any questions?"

Chas was thoughtful. "What if a spy poses as a client, an impostor? Or a User goes rogue?"

Gordon's demeanour quickly changed, the short laugh and broad smile again. "That has happened. But the impostor is only a problem for the local User, can't access the Darker Web without the User's assistance. A rogue User? That's different. And very unlikely. We heard of one who suddenly disappeared. Later, there was a tip-off and his body was found at the bottom of the harbour, hands and feet bound and a set of dumb-bells tied to his ankles." He gave another short laugh. "No User has turned rogue since."

Jeremy joined him in laughter. "That should answer any other questions you have too."

They proceeded to give Chas a demonstration of video stick use. When finished, Gordon turned to indicate the man further along the bench. "Come, I'll introduce you."

The man was engrossed in similar type images on his own screen. He looked up as Gordon and Chas approached. Immediately, Chas was struck by the impression of a hard-bitten individual. A sleek, clean shaven face, finely etched with faint lines depicting toughness. Strong jawline, slightly greying short-cropped hair with receding forehead. His brown eyes held Chas in a steady gaze, cold and unblinking. The hard set to his thin-lipped, slightly crooked mouth was unnerving.

"Chas, this is Brent." Gordon spread his arms in a welcoming gesture, as if to draw them together. He turned to Brent. "Chas is joining us. He'll be doing deliveries." Then to Chas. "If you have trouble with a client and press the button for help, it'll probably be Brent here who comes to sort him out." Gordon's characteristic smile contrasted Brent's stoicism, highlighting their differing roles.

Brent stood, offering to shake hands. His unwavering eyes held Chas captive, the hard-set mouth unchanged. He said nothing.

Chas felt daunted. The man towered over him with a powerful physical presence that left no doubt as to his main role in the hierarchy. Chas shook a hand that nearly swallowed his with a latent strength unused on this occasion. Brent was a man not to be physically challenged.

Introductions over, Brent returned to his screen. Chas eyed the bed setting, unambiguous in its function and a further source of stimulation. Another Gordon laugh sounded. "As I said, you can be more involved if you prove yourself. We do everything here. Sometimes girls too, same-sex or with male partner. But I know you are not interested in that." He led Chas back to re-join Jeremy.

"Come back Monday morning and you can start with your first delivery," Jeremy advised, laying a hand on Chas' shoulder again.

Full of positive anticipation, Chas departed the Cave.

Chapter 10

Straight after Chas was ejected from the conference room, the meeting fell apart. Dissatisfied with the response to Chas' threats and suggestion of corrupt practices, the government officials suspended the Robin programme on the spot, and indefinitely pending an outcome of enquiry. Factory management immediately moved to temporarily reduce staff and downsize the workforce. Some shifted to other projects, planning priorities revised, a change in emphasis important to maintain the flow of Research & Development funding. It all happened fast, same day.

The development of drone technology had been a steady if unspectacular achiever for the factory over the years. Privacy concerns had always held it back, even under Coln but more so since last year's change of government. Always in second place behind Robin. Now it would take centre stage, at least until the enquiry gave Robin a green light again.

Brett was excited to be one of several technicians switched to the drone programme. A new focus. Working more closely with Chongwe, at the forefront of computer technology rivalling space travel as the most advanced of the times. To date, application for military use had taken it farthest. But future vision saw air travel by drone one day supplanting land travel in the regular day to day transportation of people and goods. Powered by nanotechnology, the drones of tomorrow would be any size, carry vastly greater payloads, offer wider diversity and sophistication than the surveillance and messenger services of today's non-military drones still in relative infancy. Hover vehicles had been a wonderful adaptation, but land based only, reliant on roading networks and associated infrastructure. To further adapt for air travel was an ambitious leap forward.

The limiting factor was not the drones, it was infrastructure. If as many drones were airborne as vehicles on the road, traffic control would be disastrously chaotic. A comprehensive system of levels and corridors dividing the sky into trafficable lanes at stacked altitudes was the only feasible solution. Entry and exit, changing lanes and levels, avoidance of aircraft flight paths, speed control, poor weather, night vision, all were problematic issues. The computer system required to define virtual lines and levels then maintain order and control would be horrendously complex. Drones self-driven was essential, any computer glitch potentially catastrophic, back-up system hard to envisage. Every drone carrying a crude parachute?

Already connected personally, Brett and Chongwe gravitated to each other when the changes to work arrangements were announced. By afternoon, both were in ecstatic mood.

"This very good for my career," Chongwe confided gleefully. "I make programme no one do before." Never short of confidence in his ability, self-motivation often set the agenda but not always in harmony with management. Sometimes seen as a loose cannon, but his supreme skills were invaluable and carried him through.

Brett saw him as his best opportunity to enhance standing and move up in the hierarchy. "And I'll be testing the first prototype," he responded enthusiastically.

"I make you number one technician," Chongwe proclaimed. "I talk to Francis. He like you. Head technician gone. His fault to let Chas have knife."

That evening, with Chas held in custody, Brett and Jude were home alone. Chas' demise was no surprise to Jude, coming the morning after his mental capitulation at the dinner table. Would Chas be a permanent mental case now? Hard to imagine any circumstance that could reverse his fortunes.

Brett did not really care. Disinterested in talking about it, he was instead full of his new role on drone technology and likely promotion in association with Chongwe. "He will be a great man one day, when his computer skills create a new era of drones, changing the world," he heralded, obsessed with lauding Chongwe's praises. "And I'll be right there with him, as leading technician." He stared wide-eyed straight ahead, consumed with passion for his own vision of fame.

Jude only half listened, hearing merely a further example of narcissistic focus on self. A little insight told him a deeper motivation drove the self-promotion, given the clue from reading Brett's dossier the other day. Despite being blessed with understanding parents, Brett had joined the quest for wider acceptance before society's values changed to embrace same-sex unions. But once achieved, entrenched mindset only demanded more, to prove himself of higher worth than the average. Over-compensation? Probably Chongwe was the same. Perhaps with parents who didn't care, so he went his own way?

The focus on self was with both fathers, despite moving in opposite directions of success and failure. After a lifetime of their selfishness, Jude could feel himself going the same way, at least over family issues. Yet he always felt more compassion towards people than they ever showed, and he didn't want to lose that. He was more confident than ever of being fundamentally different from them in his sexuality.

The last thought returned his mind to the girl Lara at the beach. He desperately wanted to go there, to see her again, to rectify his dumb comment causing her to abruptly run off. Still the self-recrimination was hurting. But the overbearing shadow of Robin stifling his life was a crippling barrier, greatly exacerbating the frustration.

He decided to test Brett again for leniency, while his father was in an upbeat mood and Chas absent. "I want more freedom, without Robin hounding me all the time," he stated boldly. Time to follow a more selfish path, regardless. But it would be easier if his father agreed.

Jolted from his self-aggrandising reverie, Brett eyed Jude disdainfully. "Or what will you do? Tell Chas about the DNA test? That I'm your real father? Tell you what, I might tell him myself. It doesn't matter now." Quickly settling back into characteristic smugness.

Jude was taken aback, comprehending the damage done to his fathers' marriage, maybe irreversible. But to help himself, he was determined to take a stand. "Okay, tell him. Who cares? I'm going to do more things I like to do, that's all. And you can make your robot friend back off!" He shouted the last words, surprising himself as the long-held frustration suddenly released.

His vehemence startled Brett, unused to such a show of defiance. "Tomorrow, you go orienteering. What's wrong with that?"

"And see the same people I see every Saturday. I have no other activity. School, home, orienteering. Every week. Or you push me into meeting boys of your choice, not people I choose to meet. You think that gives me a well-rounded upbringing?" Again he surprised himself, but proud to be upfront, at last tackling his father's narrow prejudice for the first time.

A stony silence followed. "I suppose you'll talk about your mother next." Brett still holding firm, but a small chink in his dogmatic rigidness was evident.

Jude seized on it. "Yes, why not? What's wrong with that? She's my mother! Why are you afraid of her? You should be pleased to involve her in my life!" He'd managed to call her secretly a couple of times on the phone she'd given him, but the incessant presence of Robin generally prevented it.

A snort of derision from Brett. He was intransigent. "What are you thinking? She can take the place of Chas now?" He broke into a rare laugh, mocking the concept. "Maybe you've been listening to someone about the old times. When same-sex people were hated by heterosexuals. If that's what you're learning, then maybe you have too much freedom!"

Jude felt sick, defeated by the futility of trying to convince a closed mind. It dawned on him where the problem really lay. The over-compensation. It actually steeped Brett in reverse prejudice. Was this a common trait in the same-sex community? Disgusted, he stood and left without another word.

Next day, he went to orienteering as usual. On the way home, he diverted to the beach. Compliance then defiance. Lara was not at the beach. But he felt good just being there, giving himself the chance. Probably she came after school, if she came at all. Disappointment set in. With a lump in his throat, he left, arriving home late afternoon. Robin had shadowed him all day, in the background observing his every move. Nothing changed.

Chas arrived back at the same time. After a couple of days without him, Jude anticipated the home front returning to a tense battleground. Surprisingly, Chas was calm, a little distant, almost spaced out in the way he barely acknowledged his partner and son. At the dinner table, despite the debilitating issues hanging in the air screaming for resolution, no one spoke a word. Jude was curious, detecting a strange preoccupation in Chas, the usual nervous tension absent. What could have happened? Such a dramatic change.

Brett didn't care. He ignored Chas. Jude waited for him to follow through on his DNA test and fatherhood threat. But Brett kept it under wraps. Instead, with dinner over, he addressed Jude.

"I've been considering the talk we had yesterday," he began, serious, for now without the smugness. "You said you want to meet people of your choice. I've arranged for you to attend a group around your age. You can talk to whoever you want there."

Jude stared at him in mild disbelief. What's he pushing me into now, was his first thought. But then, perhaps an opportunity? "Okay, sounds interesting." He hesitated, again wondering what's the catch. "What sort of people are they?"

"They are children of same-sex marriages, just like you. Some are themselves married, some not. All sorts. It's a social gathering, nothing more than that. They may have activities there, music, whatever, I'm not sure."

That was the catch. A forum of his father's choosing, of his type of people and sexuality. Nevertheless, it was a concession, which he wanted to believe he'd extracted by taking a bold stance. "When is it?"

"Tomorrow afternoon. I'll drop you there and pick you up at an agreed time. Or you can call me if you want to come home earlier." He offered the slightest hint of a conciliatory smile. "And I'll keep Robin back here."

Another concession. Jude felt a big lift in spirits, appreciating Brett had taken on board a couple of his complaints at least. Perhaps some of the motivation was to further subordinate Chas, who was silent throughout, taking no part. Yet Chas seemed not fazed by it, watching without rancour or tension. Strange.

As promised, Brett took Jude to the gathering early afternoon next day. At the LGBT Centre. They agreed a pick-up time and Brett left.

Jude joined a trickle of people entering the building. Already he felt a little out of place, if only for the conservative clothes he wore and lack of jewellery commonly favoured by the younger same-sex sect nowadays. Inside, that reality was further confirmed. Once through a reception area where event organisers and a couple of tough-looking bouncers were checking and monitoring patrons, the space opened out into a large hall where a sea of multi-coloured figures milled about. Music was playing, a light variety not too loud. A low hubbub of conversation added to the noise level. Jude moved uncertainly into the fray, looking for a spot where he wouldn't be conspicuous.

He found space against the wall, a suitable position from where to observe. Further along was a kiosk, light refreshments being served. A stage at the far end hosted people dancing to the music. All as expected, everyone seemingly adhering to an acceptable mode of behaviour.

Screens mounted in each corner of the hall at ceiling level plus midway along the longer walls were showing images of same-sex intimacy. Stopping short of raw sexual acts, but enough to be titillating. Jude found them vaguely off-putting, not stimulating anything in him other than a further sense of being out of place.

His attention turned to the people. All around his age, it seemed, as his father had said. An array of colourful garb, jewellery, trinkets worn as body enhancement, exotic hairstyles. Like several he knew at school, probably exaggerated for a social occasion. Conforming in their quest to be society's non-conformists.

As he watched, he began seeing a different dynamic. Someone on his own, then another, a girl, another, more and more he picked out individual figures standing around or against a wall, seemingly no partner or anyone interested in them. Several were difficult to pick whether boy or girl. With mild shock, he suddenly realised they were the same as him. Others out there solitary or feeling lonely, just like him. A bizarre conundrum, in a place bristling with many couples and groups enjoying themselves.

He wondered if they were all same-sex. Was he the only one from a same-sex marriage who felt different? Whether groups or couples, boys and girls were intermingling. A mixture, same-sex or not? No obvious pattern to it. Even within a group, the odd individual seemed detached or uninvolved, solitary. Jude kept observing, fascinated.

Nearest to him was a boy on his own. Jude searched for a smart thing to say, to be involved. "Seems like the place to be today," he blurted out, catching the boy's attention.

The boy stared at him uncomprehending, making Jude feel he'd said something dumb. Then he broke into a grin, but was silent.

A girl close by, colourfully dressed and sporting blue-dyed spiky hair, saw the exchange and moved closer. "He's my brother," she announced nonchalantly. "He doesn't talk much but he's okay."

"Oh, right." Jude felt an immediate lift just to meet someone willing to communicate. "I'm Jude."

"Hi, Jude. I'm Clancy. That's Bryce." She flung an off-handed gesture towards her brother.

"I can tell him," Bryce suddenly retorted in a whining voice, at the same time punching his sister on the arm. He was slight of build, no bigger than her, but the punch carried some force.

Clancy reacted swiftly, punching him back with equal force. Then a flurry of arms before they settled back as they were, giving the impression this was their regular routine.

"How old are you?" Clancy asked Jude, as if nothing had happened.

"Nearly seventeen. How about you?"

"Same as me. He's fifteen." Again Bryce objected to being spoken for and a flurry of violence followed.

"What are your parents like?" she persisted. Her forthright manner was a little irksome.

"I have two fathers." Jude paused, considering what more to say.

Before he could continue, Clancy butted in. "We have two mothers. I don't know my father. His father comes around a lot. We don't like him. He fights with our mums." She barely paused before asking, "Are you going to get married?"

Jude was flummoxed, the relief of talking to someone beginning to wear off. Again he was given no chance to reply.

"I'm not," Clancy went on. "I'll be a surrogate. I don't even know if I'm same-sex. Maybe I will. Yes, I will get married. Then I'll find out." Her casual nonchalance bordered on uncaring, arms waving about randomly.

To Jude, it was an eye-opening example of dysfunctional family. With four parents responsible, how would confusion not happen? Violence a factor also. He knew all about identity confusion, the struggle to reconcile sexuality. And his family was simpler than theirs. The examples revealed at the surrogate mothers' group came to mind. Plenty of problems there. The common denominator was three or more parents involved.

What if Clancy did get married? Same-sex or heterosexual, what chance for success? What if she had children? What role or influence from the grandparents? Mind boggling.

Shaking his head in amazement, Jude moved away from Clancy and Bryce, finding another spot further along the wall. He resumed observing, wondering how many others had circumstances like them.

A couple nearby caught his attention. Two boys, flamboyant in their dress and adorning paraphernalia. They saw Jude watching them and sidled over.

"Hello," one of them greeted in a husky, somewhat effeminate voice. "Are you enjoying the view?"

Jude felt embarrassed, not wishing to offend anyone. "I like your bangles," he remarked, thinking quickly.

"Oh, thank you." He held out his arm, wrist limp, offering a closer look. "Are you with a partner?"

"No. Just me."

"My name's Carlo. I'm trans. In case you're wondering." He turned to the boy next to him. "This is Andy. We are partners. He's not trans though." Carlo spoke confidently, as if to pre-empt any opinion someone might have.

"Oh, right." Jude searched for something more to say, beginning to feel out of place again, aware he might appear boring to these more colourful characters.

Andy spoke, conscious of Carlo taking a shine to Jude. A syndrome Carlo had a propensity for. "We're having a baby," he announced proudly, placing a hand possessively against Carlo's slightly bulging belly. His voice was deeper than Carlo's, his sexuality only made obvious by who he was with, to a lesser extent his dress makeup.

"What?" Jude exclaimed, unable to hide his surprise. "How can that happen?"

"Ooh, you are naughty," Carlo responded amusedly, waving the limp wrist towards Jude again.

"He still has a woman's body inside," Andy explained.

Jude struggled to get his mind around the concept. He refrained from questioning the mechanics, instead asking, "What do your parents think about that?"

"Oh, my fathers were disappointed when I was born a girl. They only wanted a boy." Carlo for the first time was less amused, but quickly reverted to the care-free façade. "That's okay, I'm happy with who I am now." He nudged Andy playfully.

"What are you having? Boy or girl?" A question Jude couldn't help asking.

"It's a girl." Again Carlo seemed slightly concerned, but momentary only.

Andy quickly stepped in. "My mothers are happy. As long as I'm happy, they're happy." He was upbeat, sliding an arm around Carlo fondly. "Happy, happy, happy. All is good."

Jude kept staring at them in amazement, his mind grappling with the implications. What if the new-born, a perfectly normal innocent girl, were to suffer the same pressures from Carlo's fathers? Similar indoctrination imposed!? Sex-change was a drastic solution. How did the fathers get on with the other budding grandparents, Andy's mothers? The family dynamics were impossible to fathom. Jude felt sorry in advance for the unborn girl.

Detecting that Jude failed to share their joy, Carlo and Andy moved away. Jude went back to observing, looking for anyone resembling a more normal scenario. Or was this the accepted normality?

Others he met as the afternoon wore on were mostly brief superficial encounters. One boy depicted his family of two fathers, married, and one mother broad-minded enough to all live together in the one house, putting his interests first. A stable, secure foundation for his upbringing, except there were endless squabbles about money and demarcating responsibilities. Also regular friction over his mother pursuing an independent life that often impacted the home.

Another boy, with two fathers and two mothers, was continually used as a pawn in the never-ending struggle for power and advantage within family dynamics. Dating back to early pregnancy when problems first showed up then persisted through birth and early childhood. Medical expenses much greater than defined by their agreement issued in the blame game, implicating the egg donor, the surrogate or both, or one father the sperm donor. Both fathers refused to pay for everything or, after birth, to honour a substantial portion of the agreed payment to the mothers. That set the pattern of family life, blame kicking in whenever an issue involving him arose. Never shielded from their conflict, he developed a doctrine of guilt at even being born, resulting in several suicide attempts.

Jude was reticent to approach any girl, for fear of rejection. He spoke to none in any depth after Clancy. However, with just as many at the gathering as boys, he'd seen and heard enough to realise girls had just as many problems.

A stark reality emerging was that very few same-sex marriages had more than one child. Too many hassles and convoluted outcomes? Minimum three parents to have a child, very likely a different sperm donor, egg donor and/ or surrogate to have another. A multiple child family might have any number of parents! Not surprising most settled for one child. Jude knew well, as an only child himself and no brother or sister to bounce around with, the difficulties he faced adjusting and relating to others. Many here seemed the same, confused behaviour very evident. How would an only-child trend manifest in future society? Consequences.

Jude met two boys about the same age as him, in love and planning to marry when of legal age next year. They intended creating their own family. One was the only child of two fathers, who were both wealthy successful lawyers. A major concern of the biological father was the fate of his legacy. Who ultimately would inherit his wealth?

"No problem giving it to me," Clive claimed. "I'm his blood-related son. But after that, he has no guarantee I'll be the sperm donor for a grandchild." He spoke in an off-handed way, giving a quick smirk, obviously without sympathy for his father's position.

Jude could see clearly the father's dilemma. Potential loss of bloodline, his life's work and wealth disappearing to others unrelated, anything possible.

"Of course, being a lawyer, he's made up a legal document he wants us all to sign," Clive went on, undeterred. "Covering every contingency, even allowing for our marriage to fail. I won't be signing it." He turned to his partner, who responded with an amused grunt in support. "I don't think my other father will sign it either," Clive continued. "He's not my real father anyway. He's got his own money and law practice, probably making other arrangements, who knows?"

Jude nodded in comprehension, trying to envisage a family with two lawyers going at each other. What about the mother? Clive had not mentioned her. Jude refrained from asking, instead turning to the other boy, Steven. "How about your parents?"

Steven described his family. Mother and father, two sisters one older one younger and each with a boyfriend. His sexual preference was a disappointment to his parents, causing disunity amongst family members, but eventually acceptance prevailed. Except this also was a well-off family, the father a prominent accountant and just as concerned as Clive's biological dad about who might inherit family money and assets. The two real fathers were at loggerheads.

"If we marry and have a child," Steven revealed, "dad wants me to be the sperm donor. But Clive's dad wants Clive to be sperm donor." He gave a quick chuckle. "My dad hasn't said so, but mum warned me on the quiet he was thinking they'd favour my sisters if I mess up. But I don't care. They can do what they want with their money. I'll do what I want with my life." He gave Clive a nudge and they clasped each other in a reassuring hug.

Jude was agog. Yet another scenario possible with his type of family! The undeniable truths were stacking up. Same-sex marriages, without exception, necessitated third party involvement to have a child. But also, only one partner could be the biological parent. Sperm donor if males, egg donor if females. Irrefutably, only heterosexual marriages could accommodate both partners to be biological parents, naturally. He'd not yet come across an egg donor with surrogate partnership, but was sure that example would be out there, coming closest but not quite, still requiring a sperm donor.

Despite being a child of same-sex marriage himself and amongst supposedly like folk, Jude felt more isolated and out of place than ever. But he trusted his propensity for rationalising all that he saw and heard. Some scenarios were fiendishly complex, outcomes dramatic. Confused children with identity crisis about to have children? How would the next generation evolve? He slowly shook his head, incredulous, unable to imagine it.

Clive and Steven moved away, leaving Jude on his own again. He noticed a group in front of the stage being organised for some kind of game. Someone announced it in rousing tones over the speaker system. Feeling thirsty, he weaved his way along to the kiosk. A girl behind the counter finished serving a customer, then looked at him enquiringly.

Jude was immediately impressed. A girl unlike the others he was seeing in this place. No fancy clothes, no trinkets or ornaments, no attempt to over-state herself. Yet she was attractive, shoulder-length dark hair and appealing facial features. He felt a little nervous, but managed to ask, "What drinks do you have?"

With the glimmer of a smile, she indicated a cooling cabinet to one side offering an array of drinks. "Or tea and coffee."

"How much?" Jude responded. He had his ID card ready to make a purchase.

"No no, it's free. This afternoon is put on by the LGBT society, especially for their children. Didn't you know?"

Her smile broadened. She'd already picked him as somewhat disconnected, by the unremarkable clothes he wore. Unbefitting the flamboyance widely on show, but he came across as sincere. And with natural good looks. Someone more her own type.

"Oh, right." He felt flattered by her friendly smile. And her manner was non-judgemental, despite his ignorance. He pointed to a drink in the cabinet.

She handed him the drink. "Is this your first time here?" She paused, then offered, "I'm Jodie, by the way."

Jude sensed a connection, sure he'd heard the name before but couldn't remember where. "I'm Jude. Yeah, it's my first time." Becoming more comfortable in her presence, he felt confident enough to ask, "How long have you been working here?"

"I'm still at school, don't work here normally. I'm doing community service. My friend and I were caught by the DP, for committing a discrimination offence." Then suddenly, his name registered. And his looks fitted a description. "Wait a minute, you might know my friend. Her name's Lara. She told me she met someone called Jude at the beach recently."

Jude's heart leapt, his breath catching in a gasp of euphoric reaction, thrilled that Lara would think further about him. A stunning reversal from the relentless blame over lost opportunity. Was this a chance to see her again? To make amends for his dumb comment at the beach that still haunted him? "Is she here?" he blurted out excitedly. His eyes darted, looking behind Jodie then around the immediate vicinity.

"No." Jodie was intrigued by the depth of feeling in his reaction. "She's doing hers at the medical clinic for same-sex. You know, that place behind the government buildings? Used to be a Rehab Centre. She got a worse penalty, I think. The DP thought she offended worse than me. She only goes there Saturdays, not doing Sundays."

The news was a further revelation. Jude felt captivated. Lara copping a penalty suggested defiance he found exciting, her struggles similar to his own. Sharing common ground. "She told me she's looking for her father. She's never known him." He looked at Jodie keenly, eager for their conversation not to end.

"Yes, that's right. She's found out about him now. But I don't know if she wants to meet him. There are issues." Jodie hesitated. "Excuse me, I have other customers." She turned away to serve someone.

More customers were coming to the kiosk. The group by the stage had finished their game. Jude found himself eased to one side as a boy pushed in wanting a drink. He lost contact with Jodie. But he felt greatly uplifted by what she'd told him. Now he knew where to find Lara!

His mind preoccupied, he had no further interest in talking to anyone. The gathering was showing signs of breaking up, people leaving. Time to call his father and go home.

Chapter 11

The start of a new working week did nothing to improve matters at home. Brett delighted in self-promoting, using every opportunity to rub Chas the wrong way with grandiose talk about the factory and his new position working on drone technology. Bringing him closer to Chongwe provided fuel, often using snide innuendo to needle Chas at a more personal level.

Chas was remarkably restrained in response. Mostly he walked away whenever his partner started up, preferring to be on his own and refusing to be baited. The psychological warfare was hardly a new phenomenon, except for Chas' behaviour. Uncharacteristically calm, without the familiar nervous tension, preoccupied. Jude couldn't understand it. What had happened to change him so drastically?

Brett poured on the pressure, dimly aware of a different Chas and a little irked by it. To complete the shroud of domination, he focussed on Jude, asserting parental control and relegating Chas to spectator.

"I want to talk to you about your future," Brett announced, signalling Jude to the lounge after dinner.

Comfortably seated, Brett went on, "We've talked before about a future career, after you finish school this year. What are your thoughts about that?"

Jude was mildly surprised, allowed the opportunity to express himself instead of the usual being told what to do. Along with promoting his attendance at yesterday's LGBT gathering, it indicated a conscious deliberate change of approach. Or a cynical ploy to further subordinate Chas. Setting out to supplant Chas in the family pecking order? Regardless of the psychology at play, Jude felt encouraged. But wary, doubting it was for real or permanent.

"I'm not sure," he responded, aware it was unwise to disagree with Brett's vision for him. A tense silence followed.

Brett took it up. "The subjects you've been doing are more on the science side," he observed correctly. "Which you seem better suited to. You could carry this on to university, a science degree. And I can get you a position at the factory."

Jude nodded. Hardly unexpected. The path always intended for him. Certainly, he was doing well at science and enjoyed it. But following too closely in his father's footsteps did not appeal. He had a penchant for something more people-oriented, giving vent to the keen interest he'd developed in human behaviour and psychology. At odds with where his fathers were at, but in a cynical moment he thought of thanking Brett for being an unwitting catalyst. A positive outcome from their devious, manipulative conduct over the years. What a sick irony!

His silence encouraged Brett to continue. "School holidays start next week. I'll talk to factory management and find you a training spot for the two weeks. Get your toe in for the future."

With mixed emotions but no better alternative to suggest, Jude agreed. Cynical again, he saw it as another ploy, sticking it to Chas no longer working at the factory. But on balance, he was not against the idea. A good beginning.

In a strange way, he felt closer to Brett after recent events. Almost as though he had only one father now, his biological father. It helped his growing confidence over identity issues. Plus a feeling of greater freedom. Chas fading into the background with a diminished role he seemed to accept was commensurate with the self-inflicted damage. He'd disappeared after dinner. Only Robin was present, always hovering, its senses constantly taking in and inputting to memory.

Next day, Brett confirmed the arrangement for Jude to work at the factory over school holidays. Chas barely registered awareness. Incongruously, his closing off made for a more peaceful atmosphere. In the absence of any reaction, Brett desisted from needling him, merely reverting to ignoring him.

Arriving home from school next day, Jude knew something was wrong the instant he turned into the driveway. Yelling and shouting emanated from the house, loud enough to indicate more than a mild altercation. Alarmed, he quickly stowed his bike and hurried inside.

More alarmingly, it was Brett doing the shouting. Wild, unlike any state seen in him before, his face thrust forward to be inches from Chas'. "What's this piece of crap!? Where did you get this!? Who do you think you are!" He was sweating heavily, quivering with rage, hyper-stressed like a coiled spring wound to maximum.

Chas stood his ground, tense and worked up also. Bulging dilated eyes and an insidious half-grin was of a man verging on madness, consumed by malicious intent. He was holding up a sheet of paper for Brett to see. "Who do I think I am? I'm Jude's father!" His voice rose to a high-pitched squeal, exaggerating the picture of near-madness. "His real father! This proves it!" He shook the paper violently in Brett's face.

Brett took a step back. "Wait there! I'll show you something!" Incensed but gaining some measure of control on himself, he stormed off towards the bedroom.

Jude moved forward, his head buzzing with confused impressions. "What's going on? What's this about?"

Chas thrust the paper at him, transfixing him with a wide-eyed stare that only confirmed an unhinged state of mind. Fearful of him, Jude stepped back as he took the paper. DNA test results on laboratory letterhead! Dated yesterday, stating Chas was his biological father!

Dumbfounded, Jude stared at the evidence, his mind spinning in a crazy whirl. Before he could react, Brett returned. Striding up to Chas menacingly, he shoved his own sheet of paper in his partner's face. Recovering from initial shock, his fury was easing to a cold anger as he strove to reassert control.

Instinctively, Jude knew what the paper was. Chas snatched it from Brett's grasp. "What's this!?" Moments later, he erupted. With a blood-curdling scream, he flew at Brett, striking him in the chest with clenched fists. Caught unawares, the force of it threw Brett backwards to crash against the dining room wall, the air expending from his lungs in an explosive grunt.

Jude leapt forward. "Stop!" he cried. "Stop! Stop!" But to no effect.

Chas kept screaming, his mind snapped beyond the point of sanity. He flew at Brett again, they careered backwards, into the kitchen to slam against the bench. Items scattered, a shower of plates and cutlery flying. Then, the unthinkable. Crazed beyond reason, Chas clasped a large knife and plunged it into Brett. Twice more he plunged the knife in, then swung away, banged into Jude, dropped the knife and ran off.

With a spluttering moan, Brett slumped to the floor. No movement. An edge of blood slowly seeped from under his body, gradually spreading across the kitchen tiles. In a state of shock, Jude stood rooted to the spot, unable to respond. A cut across his left wrist was dripping blood. It galvanised him. He grabbed a kitchen towel and wrapped it around. What to do!? Robin was nearby, taking it all in but useless for contributory action not programmed. Jude bent to examine Brett, then straightened and backed away. Nothing he could do. His mind began working again. Call emergency!

Just then, the police arrived, summoned by a neighbour. The paramedics rushed in, straight to Brett. Still in shock, Jude shuffled back. He picked up Brett's sheet of paper from the floor, a quick glance enough to confirm the early DNA test performed.

"Please don't touch anything," a police officer shadowing him ordered. He took the paper from Jude. "You can go with the medics, to treat that injury. Then we'll need to ask you some questions, when you feel up to it."

The paramedics carried Brett out on a stretcher. Jude couldn't see if there were signs of life. He was escorted to the ambulance cab, past a gathering crowd of ogling onlookers. The ambulance departed.

Brett died before they reached hospital. One stab wound had punctured a lung, another partially severing an important artery and internal bleeding could not be contained.

Chas was quickly rounded up and arrested. He faced court next day, charged with murder and incarcerated pending trial. The finality of events hit Jude with traumatic effect. Impacted by direct involvement, he was unable to face police questioning immediately. It was postponed for a day. With the house cordoned off as a crime scene, he went to stay with his mother. Technicians from the AI factory were called to repossess Robin.

Police interrogation the following day was harrowing, but released Jude from blame. Once through it, his nerves began to settle and he started gaining some perspective on what had happened. Chas would pay a heavy price and rightly so. The price paid by Brett was far heavier. But fault was never all one-sided. The angst building over years to finally explode so savagely had been a ticking time-bomb. The DNA testing created the trigger. Chas' latest had to be shonky. The early tests done, including by Chas himself, proved Brett to be his biological father. How had Chas obtained this one!? Jude vowed to find out.

Strangely, he felt no sense of grief. Perhaps that would come later. All his life, he'd felt alienated from both fathers, the late concessions from Brett insignificant to overturn entrenched dogma. Now, even while numbed by lingering shock, he couldn't help feeling liberated. Shameful under the circumstances and he felt guilty, but it was there and he couldn't deny it. Moving in with his mother was huge. No barriers anymore. Dulcie was thrilled, only distantly connected to his fathers and largely free from the trauma surrounding their demise. For Jude, a new future beckoned. Too soon to embrace it, the heinous event no doubt over-shadowing the longer term for a while. But temporary only.

Next day, Saturday, offered choices. Orienteering as usual? Didn't appeal. Dulcie's surrogate mother group? Of some interest, but he'd done that, knew what to expect. To pursue answers concerning Chas was highly motivating, but he didn't feel ready for that yet. He had a vague idea where to start and would be a challenge.

Mid-morning, Dulcie was ready to leave. "I'm off to the forum now. What are you doing today?" She was happy, basking in the delight of having him there.

"Not sure. I'll go out for a while." They hugged, a warmly felt embrace. Dulcie departed.

Jude rode to the beach. He sat on his favourite bench seat, watching action on the water, trying to clear his mind. An idea was firming. Yes, why not? Just as early in the week after meeting Lara's friend Jodie last Sunday, Lara was again returning strongly in his thoughts.

Lara was giving the centre table a clean, after Tony's last consultation with a male couple left it a little soiled. Unusually, she was preoccupied this morning, returning to the place she was certain harboured big issues. Questions about her father dominated. Closely followed, after last Saturday at the cafeteria, by Jude's father, his dodgy asso-ciation with the man named Jeremy, and of course Gordon Pascalladis. Almost certainly, her father was involved, partners in crime with Gordon from way back. More and more, her mind was focussed on the locked room so tantalisingly close down the next corridor. How she'd love to see what's going on there!

"You can go to lunch now, if you like," Barbara interrupted.

"Is it that time already?" Lara was roused from her thoughts. "Okay, see you after lunch." She finished off then headed out the door.

Entering the cafeteria, her step faltered at the sight of two figures seated at a table. Jude's father Chas with that Jeremy again. No Gordon this time. Intrigued but wary, she moved on quickly, not wishing to attract their attention. After obtaining her food, she took a table not too close as to arouse suspicion but close enough to perhaps overhear.

The two men were sitting in silence, a sombre air about them. Like an established couple, not just a casual meeting. Yet, as Lara knew from previous, they were not partners, Jeremy was not Jude's other father. Strange. Neither had a plate of food in front of them. Chas looked particularly glum, head bowed staring at the table-top. His companion was making no effort to lift Chas' spirits. Their association together looked decidedly unhealthy.

Jeremy was aware of her presence, had noticed her interest in them. He looked directly at her, cracking a quick smile. "How are you today?" he greeted. A smooth, steady opening, confident.

Lara felt a little nervous. "I'm okay, thank you." She turned away, disconcerted as he continued to stare at her.

"Are you enjoying our company?" Again he flashed the smile. "You were here last Saturday, enjoying our company then too. Is there something that interests you?"

The insinuation was obvious, threatening. Caught eaves-dropping, Lara stood to leave, regretting her mistake.

He was quickly on his feet, moving to Lara's table. "Please, don't run away. If you want something, just ask. We are reasonable people." His tone started condescending, then turned conciliatory as he plied his renowned manipulative expertise. Another smile, broader this time. "My name's Jeremy. That's Chas." He indicated their table, where Chas was still self-absorbed, not watching. "And you are --- Lara," he added, noting the name tag on her lab coat. "You must be working at the clinic."

She made to move away, acutely distrustful of him and his slick manner. Not to mention the nefarious activities. But then, another thought. He was an avenue to her father. 'Only the sperm donor', the words of her mums, were repeating incessantly in her head, making her feel of less worth. She loved her mums, but couldn't forgive them for that. A conflict was raging inside her. The need to know versus the danger in finding out.

While she was distracted, Jeremy took the opportunity to run his eyes over her. An attractive girl, shapely body with full breasts, well-formed facial features enhanced by shoulder-length wavy blonde hair. Always looking for potential, he whetted his lips in anticipation. "There is something concerning you," he cajoled, feeding off her hesitation.

Lara glared at him long and hard, wrestling with which way to jump. Finally, she decided. From her ID pouch, she extri-cated and unfolded the page she'd gleaned online, handing it to Jeremy. "This is my father." She waited for a response, which was slow in coming. Suddenly emboldened, she added, "I think you know him. He knows Gordon Pascalladis, and I saw Gordon here with you last week."

A glance at the page was enough. Jeremy's eyes widened in genuine surprise. "Where did you get this?" Gone was the smile and desire to humour her, replaced by a grim-faced steadfastness. "Brent doesn't have any children. This proves nothing. Why do you say he's your father?" Jeremy could see trouble looming, of an unexpected kind.

"He was sperm donor. I've never seen him or known him. I found out from the authorities. Then looked him up online." Sure of her ground, she took a deep breath to steady her nerves.

Jeremy's mind was ever-calculating. He paused for a long moment. Fixing on a new perspective, he refocussed. "Do you want to see him?" A glimmer of a smile returned, but insidious. "He's coming here. Should be here very soon."

Lara's heart gave a flutter, her nerves jangling. She held herself steady. "Yes, I can wait."

"Well, not here. He won't come to the cafeteria. We have an office in the building." The smile deepened, momentary only, conscious not to overdo it. He wanted to stay in favour with her.

The locked room! Lara's heart flutter took a leap. She'd been so curious to see inside there, but now the prospect scared her. What to do?

Jeremy sensed her fear. "Do you want to see him or not?" Then, returning to cajoling mode, "I'm sure Brent will be excited to meet his daughter for the first time."

That clinched it for Lara, the need to know winning out over the danger. "Okay," she heard herself say, unable to resist the temptation.

Jeremy nodded. "Let's go then." Pocketing the page about Brent, he summoned Chas and the three of them exited the cafeteria.

The door clicked shut behind them. Lara found herself escorted to the centre of a large room. Gordon was seated at one of several computers spaced along a bench down one side wall. No sign of her father. "Welcome to the Cave," Jeremy uttered, drooling with expectation.

Lara began looking around, anxiety mounting. Gordon's computer attracted her eye. Instantly, she regretted her decision to come here. "Oh!" A shocked reaction. On screen were images of a man with two young boys, all naked and performing sex acts of a nature unimaginable to her.

Horrified, she backed away. The activity going on was suddenly clear. She turned to flee. "Let me out of here!"

Jeremy blocked her path to the door. "Uh, uh. No, no." With an evil snarl, he grabbed her arm, twisting it violently behind her back.

"Let me go! Let me go!" Panic-stricken, Lara fought to free herself.

Gordon, quickly to his feet at the first sign of trouble, gripped her other arm, twisting it back. "Well, well. What do we have here? A feisty one. We love feisty ones." With a devilish grin, he held his face close to hers, invading her space.

"No-o-o-o! I want to go! Let me go!" Desperate, she strained to break free, legs kicking out wildly, her face contorting in rage.

"This is Lara," Jeremy announced, enjoying a rush of power-driven adrenalin. "I think she's going to scream. We can't have that. Disturbing the peace." The insidious smile was back.

Unable to tear herself free, she broke down, hyperventilating. A rag was shoved in her mouth, tied tightly around to affect a gag. She fought to breathe, her face bathed in sweat, hair dishevelled. Her eyes bulged in raw fear. She felt her wrists being tied.

"Well now, that's better," Gordon declared, leering into her face invasively.

The sound of the door opening caught everyone's attention. Brent entered. He came forward, eyeing Lara with mild interest. Expressionless, he hovered close by, looking at Gordon enquiringly, his assistance perhaps needed.

Lara reacted with renewed fervour, straining against her bonds, her muffled cries unintelligible. Her father was here! A real person! And she couldn't speak to him! Mind-blowing.

Jeremy moved swiftly to intervene, taking Lara's arm to push her away from Brent. Another agenda beckoned. Propelling her forward, they approached the far end of the room. With a shock, Lara comprehended the setup. Red-covered double bed, pink and blue adorned posts and canopy, supporting apparatus, camera. All for an obvious purpose. Her fear deepened, dilated eyes like saucers, gagged cries unheard. Desperately, she tried to wrench free.

"Oh yes, she's fiery all right," Jeremy acclaimed. "She's a good one."

Brent joined in, clamping his cavernous hands to each arm. He was emotionless, the thin crooked line of his mouth unchanging. Lara couldn't move. She felt the man's breath on her neck. Her own father! Why did Jeremy not tell him!?

Jeremy moved to face her. "Do you like videos?" With sinister intent, he indicated the bed. "You're going to make a video. All that fire, I think you'll make a great video." It was the ultimate in evil.

Gordon was there in support, impressed by Jeremy's find. "Yes, indeed. You can pick 'em." Sporting his characteristic grin, he took a step closer. His hands touched Lara's breasts, sliding down to feel her well-shaped body. "Do you prefer same-sex or with a man? Nod if you like same-sex." Terror-stricken, Lara made no response. "No? With a man then. Tell you what, we'll do both." He gave a quick chuckle. Then, indicating Brent behind her, "But not with him. He can't do anything. He's been chemically castrated."

"We have good partners for you," Jeremy added, relishing the pending episode. "We'll bring them tomorrow. Give you time to calm down. But not too much, keep that fire burning!" His voice rose, consumed with anticipation.

Lara kept kicking out but in a weakened state as they dragged her across the floor to a door adjacent the ensuite. The room was a bare four walls, no window, no furniture, no cupboards or wardrobe. Pushed inside, she slumped to a mattress lying on the cement floor. Exhausted and crying uncontrollably, she lay prone, quivering in fright. Her captors exited, Gordon locking the door, the room plunged into pitch darkness.

Throughout the drama, Chas remained uninvolved, preoccupied with his own troubles. Nevertheless, the harsh treatment of Lara was an eye-opener, resonating as to what his new colleagues were capable of. It made him nervous, fearful of messing up. And he owed Jeremy big-time for bailing him out of jail, even the promise of getting him off the murder charge. To justify it, he must perform.

With Chas and Brent engrossed in their computers at the far end of the bench, Jeremy pulled Lara's sheet of paper from his pocket. He spoke in low tones, for Gordon's ears only. "Take a look at this." He handed the page to Gordon. "Lara gave it to me in the cafeteria. She claims Brent is her father. From what she tells me, I think it might be true."

Gordon read it through. "Oh, my my." He shook his head, as worried as Jeremy had ever seen him. "I'm glad you didn't tell Brent. You know how hard it was settling him down on an even keel. And you know what he can do if he gets upset and goes off."

"I certainly do. Something like this would set him off for sure. Being his guarantors, we're in the gun too, as you know. He's okay here, but I don't fancy sharing a jail cell with him." He gave Gordon a look of deep concern. "That's why I had to get the gag on her quick smart. Before Brent arrived and she spilled her guts."

"Yes, good work. But what do we do with her now? We have to keep her gagged."

"Or worse?" Jeremy's words hung in the air. Both men were grim-faced.

"Better make sure Brent's not here tomorrow," Gordon observed. "We can't gag her for the video." He paused, his facial expression hardening further. "Maybe she keeps on making videos. Best way to control her. With the right drugs, of course. Otherwise, we make a different decision."

They fell silent, pondering the task at hand.

Jeremy was suddenly aware of the time. "I have to go. Meeting a new client. I'll take Chas with me. Set it up for a Flasher."

He went to Chas. With relevant items in a shoulder bag, they headed for the door.

At the beach, Jude rose from the bench seat, determined to act on the information Jodie had provided. Feeling bold, he recovered his bike and headed for the old rehab centre behind the nearby government buildings.

Arriving at the bike racks, he noted several bikes there, one no doubt Lara's. At the front entrance doors, he hesitated, suddenly far from sure Lara would welcome seeing him. Jodie had given no indication either way. At last contact, Lara could not have run faster from him. Suffering a heightened sense of vulnerability to any rejection, his earlier boldness abruptly evaporated. Feeling foolish, he turned to walk away.

A man was standing behind, waiting to enter. Jude bumped into him. "Sorry," he blurted, given a fright.

The man was tall and powerfully built. He gave no reaction, standing firm, glaring at Jude with cold unblinking eyes, a hard set to his slightly crooked mouth. Thinly disguised physical intimidation. Recoiling, Jude hurriedly turned back and pushed through the doors. The man followed, strode past him without a word, down a hallway, turning right at the end and disappeared.

Jude stood for several moments in the hallway, waiting for his heart to stop thumping. The place looked dingy, not helping his nervousness. Lara was working at a medical clinic, Jodie had said. Where would that be? He moved forward, coming opposite an open doorway.

"Can I help you?" a woman's voice sounded from inside the room.

Jude entered. "I'm looking for Lara. She works here."

"Next on the left." Macey indicated with outstretched arm.

He came to a closed door. No sign on it. Committed, he drew a deep breath and went on through.

A white-coated woman, Barbara by her name tag, was close by. "Please take a seat, we'll be with you shortly," she advised, noting his uncertainty.

"Is Lara here?" he replied quickly, to avoid patient status. "She's a friend of mine."

"Oh." Barbara gave him a welcoming smile. "She's gone to lunch. Should be back very soon, she's been gone a while. Or you can find her at the cafeteria. Turn left at the end of the hallway."

Jude followed her directions. Swinging left, he glanced to the right, wondering where the strongman he met earlier had gone. No one in sight. The cafeteria was nearly empty. No sign of Lara. A lady was cleaning the tables. He approached her.

"Hi. I was told Lara would be here," he enquired politely. "But I don't see her."

"No. She's supposed to be helping me clean up. She was with two men, talking for a while, then they left together. That was a while ago, and she hasn't come back." The lady spoke in a kindly way, but a little annoyed at Lara letting her down.

The beginnings of concern stirred inside him. "What did the men look like? Do you know them?"

"I know everyone here. I've been managing this café for fifteen years." She paused to further consider his question. "One I know well, comes here regularly. Fair haired going a bit bald, Jeremy's his name. The other one I've only seen a few times the last week or so. A bit shorter, with shaven head."

Jeremy! Alarm bells immediately rang in Jude's head. Lara talking to Jeremy! Was it the same Jeremy? The lady's description fitted. And the other man's description sounded like Chas! But how could that be? Chas was in jail.

"Thank you for your help." Jude left the cafeteria, perplexed.

At the T-junction, he stopped to reassess. His concern for Lara deepened, Jeremy's name reverberating in his brain. How many places could she be? He set out to survey the entire building. Down the right hand corridor, he came to a door. He entered. Open cubicles down each side wall evidenced safe injecting room. No one he knew there. Further down the corridor, another door. This one locked, electronically. Curious. So far, the only door preventing free entry. No other doors along there. He returned. Very soon, he realised he'd seen the sum total of the building interior. Reception, clinic, cafeteria, injecting room, locked door. That was it, nothing more.

Back to the cafeteria, he found the manageress in the rear kitchen area. She confirmed Lara had not returned.

"Is there any other exit to the building?" Jude asked her.

"There used to be, at the rear." She indicated beyond the kitchen. "But it's been boarded up the last year, since rehab closed. Front entrance is the only entry or exit now."

Another check at the clinic. Barbara was concerned. "Lara hasn't returned and lunch is well gone. That's very unusual. If you see her, please let us know."

Finally, to reception. Macey also had not seen Lara. "But anyone can come or go without me seeing them," she advised. "Except Lara should checkout with me on leaving, to record her hours. Usually she leaves four o'clock."

Dumbfounded and carrying major concern for Lara now, Jude exited the building. He sat at a seat by the bike racks, in full view of the front entrance. Only two possibilities remained. Most likely, Lara had left against her will, forcibly with Jeremy and the other man. Abduction? Or she was inside the locked room. The only place he'd been unable to check.

As he was considering the options, two men emerged. Jude leapt to his feet. Jeremy and Chas! Lara was not with them. Jeremy carried a shoulder bag and they appeared to move with purpose.

Chas stopped in his tracks on seeing Jude. "What are you doing here?" He pointed at Jude aggressively, attempting to assert himself.

Jude looked at him with disdain, devoid of any respect. It gave him the confidence to reply strongly. "More to the point, what are you doing here? Why aren't you in jail?" The reason was obvious, standing next to Chas in support.

As if to confirm, Jeremy stepped forward. "Jude, how are you? Haven't seen you for a while." The contrived smile was in place. "Now really, is that a way to talk to your father?"

"He's not my father."

Chas jumped forward to respond. But Jeremy was quicker, putting his arm out in restraint, silencing him. "The court will decide," he declared, arrogant. "DNA test results are available. Very unfortunate what happened. Brett was so angry, Chas here forced to act in self-defence." He paused, enjoying himself. "You will be called to testify, of course. I'm sure Chas can depend on you to be a reliable witness." He signalled Chas and they moved on, disappearing around the corner of the building.

Jude was seething. He stared after them, incredulous. Why would Jeremy bail him out and support him? Now he knew where the shonky DNA test had come from. But a person like Jeremy always takes more than he gives. What did he expect from Chas?

The more important question resurfaced. Nowhere inside had he seen Jeremy or Chas, or them entering the building. He knew where they came from. The locked room. That gave it far more significance, a connection directly to Lara! A horrible sensation gripped him. What had become of her?

Still he was uncertain. They could have abducted her from the building then returned unseen. He decided to wait, at least until after four o'clock, Lara's finishing time.

People were entering and leaving sporadically. He monitored it. Four o'clock came and went. No Lara. He waited longer. Barbara, her colleague, the receptionist, the cafeteria lady all departed. Only one bike apart from his own left in the racks. Surely Lara's.

Two men exited. Jude instantly recognised the strongman he'd bumped into on arrival. That was around lunchtime, a fair while ago. Certainly an imposing individual, physical monster with a cruel disposition. He had turned right, towards the locked room. The man with him was different. Well-dressed, exuding authority. He looked a bit shifty.

Together, a fearsome duo. Apart from the strongman arriving, he'd not seen them at all inside. The locked room again! It had to be. And another connection to Jeremy and Chas. What a combination!

The locked room loomed huge in Jude's mind. Heart in his mouth, an awful fear for Lara overwhelmed him, a sickness in the pit of his stomach. He knew what he must do. But he had to go home first. Quickly, he jumped on his bike and left.

Dulcie was concerned but didn't question why he had to leave again at a late hour. Or why he changed into dark clothing, soft shoes and carried a small bag. "Please be careful, Jude," she implored. "I couldn't bear to see you hurt." They hugged and he departed the house.

To be sure, although itching to act, he'd felt it safest to wait a few hours. Arriving back, he was pleasantly surprised the entrance doors had not been locked. The hallway and corridor lights were on. Turning right at the T-junction, he comprehended why as a boy emerged from the safe injecting room and hastened past. The facility available around the clock.

The building was otherwise deserted. He went to the locked door. The corridor lighting helped, his torch not needed yet. Electronic locks were hardest, but he had the right gear. First, the detector. No alarm connected. Gratified, he chose the two thinnest wires from his bag. His acquired skill to the fore now. It took a while. At last, the wires were inserted correctly. The electronic black box next. Touching across the wires sent a pulse. The lock gave up a faint click. A push on the handle and the door swung open. He was in.

Heart pounding in his chest, he closed the door behind him, then flicked on his torch. Through the dark, the beam picked out a long bench down one side wall, idle computers spaced along. Deeper in, a larger square shape emerged. Tensed, he crept closer. A bed! With posts and canopy. All adorned for sensual effect. More equipment, a camera! He caught his breath in shock, his fear for Lara extreme now. What had Jeremy and his evil cohorts done to her!? Where was she?

He swung the torch around, up the other side. Another bench, several drones sitting there. An opening adjacent, to an ensuite, unoccupied. Back out, further along to a door. It was locked. His heart leapt. He delved in his bag. This lock was easy. The door pushed open. With trepidation, he entered.

Pitch black inside. He groped for a light switch, finding it, bathing the room in light. "Lara!"

She was lying shivering on the mattress, wild eyes fear-struck as the door opened, someone entering. Suddenly, light. Then she saw him. Jude! Her eyes blazed, a euphoric surge of adrenalin replacing the fear. Muffled cries of joy, scrambling to sit up, desperate to be free.

Jude rushed to her, horrified. She was a mess, dishevelled hair and clothes, her breathing a shallow wheeze. Quickly, he untied the cruel gag. Relieved, she gulped in the air. He undid the bonds. Released, she flew into his arms, clinging to him desperately, her body shaking with fright.

"Lara, Lara. What have they done to you!" Jude held her tight, engulfed by the moment, sharing her trauma.

Still gasping for air, she crushed herself to him, frantic, burying her face against his neck. Her breathing gradually eased. She whispered, "How did you find me?" Her voice quivered with emotion.

Jude became aware of their circumstances. "Come on, let's get out of here." Suddenly, the place had a morbid feel about it, the den of evil. Releasing Lara, he collected his torch and bag of tools, took her hand and they headed for the exit.

Once in the corridor, they ran. Meeting no one, they crashed through the entrance doors and reached the bike racks. Lara was in no state to ride. On Jude's bike, she straddled the pillion seat, her arms holding him close. Jude accelerated away.

Chapter 12

The first glimmer of morning light was filtering through the blinds, the room's contents faintly emerging through the dark. Lying on his back wide awake, Jude watched it gradually strengthen. He'd slept only fitfully. Partly due to residual adrenalin from the night's drama, but more engaging was that every time he moved, Lara would press closer in an instinctive reaction. One arm slung over, she lay half across his chest, her face firmly nestled against his neck. Her regular breathing played warmly on his skin, a pleasant sensation he wished not to interrupt.

The bedsheet was again slipping a little. With his free hand, he gently pulled it up to keep her covered. More light in the room revealed her ample blonde hair scattered across him, partly hiding her face. He was captivated by it. Seeing her at peace now, so different from last night. The stakes had been high, the danger real. Only on reaching home did he feel safe. For Lara, the trauma lasted well beyond a hot shower and change into bedclothes Dulcie provided, eventually dissipating only after hours holding Jude close, refusing to be separated. Finally, feeling secure in his arms, she had drifted to sleep.

For Jude, sleep was more elusive. The night's events, following several momentous days of life-changing proportions, had culminated in an outcome he could only dream of. Here she was, in his arms. An incredible reversal from the relentless self-doubting that had dominated his life. Maturing a lifetime in a few days. Sad the death of his father was part of it, yet he didn't feel sad. He felt only the warmth of Lara's body.

She stirred, lifting her head. Her eyelids flickered then opened. Light blue eyes looked into his face an inch away. "Hi," she whispered. Her impish smile was there. She felt a contentment at odds with events of the night. "You're awake already." Propping on one elbow, she surveyed the outline of his face, enchanted. "Have you been watching over me?"

"I have. All night." He gave an amused chuckle. "I thought you'd never sleep. Then I thought you'd never wake up."

The light was strong now. They emerged from the bedroom and looked for Dulcie. She'd risen early, to wash and dry Lara's clothes. Breakfast was on the way. Dulcie was very happy, her long-held yearning to know her son and be a genuine mother to him being realised. And thrilled Jude was finding himself, his sexuality no longer a cause for confusion. Wonderfully evident by Lara's presence, despite the traumatised state she'd arrived in last night. Dulcie waited patiently, hoping they would confide in her.

Over breakfast, they told Dulcie everything. And a chance for Lara and Jude to fill in the gaps, unaware of each other's lives since first encounter at the beach. Lara described how she'd been enticed to the locked room by Jeremy and the treatment meted out to her there.

"They call it the Cave." She grimaced. "I looked up my father online, like you suggested." She went on to detail his crimes, time in jail and association with Gordon Pascalladis. "I'm cured now, never want to see him again." She barely took her eyes off Jude as she spoke, placing a hand on his forearm affectionately. No sign of lingering trauma from her ordeal.

Jude nodded solemnly, returning her look and putting his hand over hers. "I bumped into him at the entrance. The way he looks, I'm sure glad he didn't take it personally. Not much sense of humour." Then, on further reflection, "I saw this Gordon with him too, when they left. Not someone I'd trust." On a lighter note, he added, "Don't know if my suggestion at the beach was good or not. At the time, I thought I'd lost you when you ran off." He felt embarrassed by his over-sensitivity, a crippling inhibitor.

Lara responded with an enchanting smile. "I upset myself doing that. But I reckon it was a good suggestion. Now I'm purged of my father, don't have it eating me up anymore."

Her strength was inspiring to Jude. Accepting treatment suffered as fair exchange for resolving the father dilemma. Only something extreme could rid her of that lifetime burden.

"What happened to your hand?" She gently touched the bandage still covering his left wrist.

With mild surprise, he suddenly realised she didn't know. Of course, how would she know? He told her then, describing the murderous scene at home between his fathers. "Brett didn't make it." He bowed his head, revisiting his own trauma.

"Oh no, was that your ---?" She caught her breath in shock, having heard on local news but only now making the connection. Shifting her chair closer, she put her arm around him in comfort.

"Yep. But I'm okay." His moment of sorrow passed quickly. He planted a kiss on Lara's cheek. "I'm like you, needed something terrible to happen to put me in a better place." And here he was with his mother, representing the better place. Amazing.

Dulcie listened intently. One concern worried her. "You have to watch Chas. We don't know what he might do now."

"Yes." Jude was thoughtful, her words striking a strong note. "He's been charged with murder. Jeremy bailed him out of jail. He wants to argue self-defence." He let out a hiss of anger, then recounted the relationship his fathers had forged with Jeremy and Chongwe, their efforts to set him up with other boys, Jeremy's position in Child Protection Services and other subversive activities. And Chas responsible for the death of a fellow factory worker, also involving a knife, his suspension, mental state after and arrest.

"That's a lot of pressure," Lara lamented with growing dismay. "How could you live with all that?"

Jude tried to shrug it off. "No choice. Brett and Chas were always at war psychologically, manipulating. I hate it, never want to be like that." He paused in reflection. "It was bad at the end, but goes way back, right from the start." He divulged the early deception by both fathers having DNA tests done, the insane pretence poisoning family life, the recent shonky test that backfired. "Chas is not my real father. Brett was. I can't understand why Jeremy had that

190

test done for him and supports him. What's Chas doing in return?"

"I know why," Lara replied. "I overheard them talking in the cafeteria. Chas was a mental wreck. Jeremy and Gordon were twisting him up, some kind of deal. There was talk about DNA tests, your name mentioned a lot. That was the week before, when the DP brought him in." She paused, affected by other images.

"They're doing paedophile stuff in that Cave place. I saw it on Gordon's computer. And they were going to force me into making sex videos. Starting today." Her lips quivered, eyes stinging with emotion as the remnants of trauma regurgitated briefly. She laid her head on Jude's shoulder, safe now.

Jude held her close. "I saw the bed, camera and other gear. They are evil people." He'd suspected Gordon and Brent at first sight. Jeremy also coming across as devious early on, but this seemed extreme even for him.

Dulcie wiped away tears, sharing their emotion. And learning, after so many years, which sperm had conceived Jude. But for that, she felt only indifference, even towards the death of Brett the real father. Remote process, remote feelings. Only Jude mattered. "You must be very careful. They might feel you're a threat, now you've seen their operation from the inside. And Chas carrying a grudge as well."

A sombre silence fell. Lara broke from it, her naturally bright disposition resurfacing. She talked about her mums, their open-hearted mindset, a happy family life with freedom, the only discord her father. Their unprecedented intransigence regarding him she now clearly understood.

"Of course," she surmised, "rapes, violence, under-age children, he's a predator, a paedophile. My mums must know all about it." She was settling on a fate-driven honesty. Then a further thought. "Not any more though. Gordon let it slip he's been chemically castrated. Can't do anything now."

"Really! Wow!" Jude's imagination ran wild. "He acts like something's missing. No wonder."

"Oh!" Dulcie reacted, shocked. "They only do that to the very worst of them!"

Lara was determined to remain positive, refusing to feel affinity for a man she'd never known. "I want you to meet my mums." She looked at Jude purposefully.

"Yes. They'll be worried why you didn't come home last night. Let's go."

They returned to the scene of last night's drama, thankful Lara's bike was still in the racks. Not wishing to linger there, Jude followed Lara to her home.

MumG was in the kitchen. "Hi, G," Lara greeted brightly. She planted a big kiss on MumG's cheek. "This is Jude." She grabbed his arm, pulling him forward.

"Oh --- well --- hello, Jude. I'm Glenice." Surprised, she gave him a welcoming smile. First impression was favourable. Then to Lara, "Take Jude into the lounge, L. I'll get D. I'm sure she'd like to meet Jude too."

Soon they were sitting around the coffee table. Doris also gave Jude a warm welcome. "Well, does this mean we don't have to ask where you were last night?" She aimed a knowing half-smile at Lara.

"Right." Lara let out an enticing giggle. "Remember I said I met someone recently? This is him. Jude lives with his mother. She's really nice. You'll like her."

Glenice and Doris were keen to know more about him. Jude answered their questions carefully, avoiding mention of dramatic issues, just as Lara had omitted.

Doris responded when he told them his age. "Lara has a few weeks till her sixteenth birthday. Not quite of age yet." She eyed them both with another half-smile.

That set Lara off giggling again. "We haven't done anything yet." She leaned closer to Jude, hand on his knee. Stirrings of excitement coursed through her body.

Jude's heart swelled with the thrill of anticipation. Something he'd only imagined was an exhilarating reality.

"Let's go to the beach." Full of enthusiasm, she jumped up and headed for her room to change clothes.

As they were leaving, Lara addressed her mums. "By the way, I'm not trying to contact my father anymore. I don't need to now." Lying by omission, normally unthinkable, but she felt it best under the circumstances. Permanent closure, hopefully.

After Jude changed into beachwear at home, they rode to their favourite spot. A healthy Sunday crowd had flocked to the beach, creating a sea of umbrellas. Necessary protection nowadays, in a climate too hot to withstand direct sun for long. Jude and Lara set up their umbrella. They spent the day having fun, swimming in the surf, laughing and playing, hired a jet ski, taking turns in front skimming the waves and beyond. Then lying on the sand side by side, kissing, enjoying the closeness, the stimulation of mutual attraction. A glorious day, experiencing each other with unequalled joy.

As the sun sank slowly below the horizon, they returned to Jude's place. After dinner, in Jude's room, they came together, kissing fervently. They shed their clothes, lay on the bed and were as one. Their first sexual experience. Building through the day, the fire was intense, the unspoken promise of fulfilling their desire satisfied. The physical act lasted not long, but the afterglow continued as they lay clasped together beneath the bedsheet, enjoying the sight and feel of each other's bodies.

The fire re-intensified and they made love again. Lasting longer this time, a culmination of shared recent trauma fuelling their passion with raw emotion. And so it continued through the night.

As first morning light filtered through the blinds, both slept peacefully. Lara lay across Jude's chest, arms flayed each side, face nestled against his, tufts of blonde hair strewn about. Their legs were entwined, Jude's arms loosely wrapped around her. Easy breathing, shallow and rhythmic, were the only sounds.

Lara was first to stir. Rolling to one side, she rose from the bed and headed for the bathroom. Jude woke in time to marvel at her magnificent form as she crossed the floor. He joined her in the shower and they possessed each other once more, engulfed in the splashing water.

By the time they reached the breakfast table, sexual appetite satiated, they were ready to face the day. Dulcie could hardly miss noticing the glow they exuded.

"You two look great this morning," she exulted, very happy they felt safe in her home, consummating their relationship. "I know it's the start of school holidays today. What are your plans?"

"I don't have any plans," Lara murmured, unconcerned about anything as she looked at Jude dreamily.

"School holidays, right." Jude was suddenly reminded. "I'm supposed to start at the AI factory today. Brett organised it for me. Practical experience for two weeks." He returned Lara's look, resting a hand on her shoulder. "But I'm not sure I want to go now." Partly he wanted just to be with her, partly events of the week were off-putting.

Lara perked up. "Oh, you should go. It's okay. I'll call Jodie. See what she's up to."

"Are you sure?"

"Yes." She gave him a big kiss. "It'll be good for you. Don't worry. I'll be fine. And I'll see you when you get back." She wanted him to feel free, her natural belief she'd always followed for herself.

Breakfast over, Jude left for the factory.

Management was keen to have Jude join the workforce. The trial of a hundred Robins in the community was ongoing, but further time needed before an in-depth assessment. However, the forced return of Robin from the defunct Brett/Chas household offered the opportunity for an interim appraisal. Of great interest was how the violent drama unfolding there had impacted Robin. A unique windfall for the project coming out of tragedy. Jude was a vital factor, not only part of input detected by Robin's three senses, but also available to test subsequent interaction with Robin.

Chongwe was assigned. Not a willing participant after transferring to drone technology with its promise of fame and notoriety. Devising new ground-breaking computer systems was far more motivating than reassessing old ones. Nevertheless, he accepted the management directive, realising the future of Robin was at stake.

Knowing he'll be working with Chongwe made Jude nervous. Too close to Jeremy and a scene he wished to distance himself from as far as possible. Chongwe was disinterested in discussing anything personal, but did confirm Chas had been taken in to live with him and Jeremy. Jude couldn't help an amused chuckle, trying to envisage the three males together in the same house, sure to be different from that scenario as he knew it. The irony of supplanting Chas as a factory worker was not lost on Jude either. He considered himself as representing Brett and his legacy. Would it cause further angst with Chas?

As a tribute to Brett, who'd been highly regarded by all factory personnel, the repossessed Robin was named RobinB. A name tag was affixed over the ID branded on its forehead.

Being of Robin1 vintage, its output in performing a set task was expected to remain consistent, enabled by input from its senses but not altered by it as had happened with Robin2 and Robin3. If input received is incompatible with the task, a Robin1 should merely ignore it and seek something more suitable from which to produce output. Pivotal in the appraisal would be to ascertain exactly what RobinB did consider relevant enough to store in memory not ignore. Knowledge in this area was very uncertain at this stage.

Brett and Chas had activated three of the set tasks available in Robin's programming. Housekeeping, Security, Surveillance. At the arena, new head technician Marcel signalled RobinB's individual code from his computer and received transmission of contents under 'Housekeeping' from stored memory. Technicians and computer staff began assessing the images coming onto the large screen. A mixture of still shots and video clips, accompanied by associated sound recordings. Input from touch sense was demonstrable in sync with sight and hearing evidence. Jude watched awestruck, not keen to revisit some of the scenes likely to come up.

Images included household kitchen, bench and sink, cleaning implements, the dishwashing process, followed by lounge room, vacuum cleaner, others relevant to house-keeping. The full period from Robin's deployment to repossession was run, a multitude of images and sounds. Gratifyingly, no repeats. A particular point of interest in the assessment process. Once memorised, input was re-used for repeat output. Only if significantly different from previous input would it be added to memory. Evidence of a crude learning ability even at Robin1 stage, without altering performance of the set task.

To test sustainability, duplicate settings were recon-structed in the arena and RobinB asked to re-perform. Jude was introduced, not required to do anything, just part of duplicating the scene. RobinB's performance remained consistent, unaffected by whatever else it had witnessed. A technician unknown to RobinB was substituted for Jude and the creature signalled to re-perform once more. Again, it was consistent. Pleasing to the assessment team.

'Security' was next. Again Jude waited with heart in his mouth for confronting images to appear. More so knowing this set task, unlike 'Housekeeping', directly involved people. Initial images were of the house, inside and outside, fixing the parameters of the place to be secured. Then of people entering the property. The number was relatively few. Incredibly, none were of Brett, Chas or Jude unless by chance inclusion while focussed on a visitor. No record of domestic disturbances or violence leading to Brett's murder, surely qualifying under 'Security' by any reasonable assumption. Jude was relieved, not having to re-live that torment. Others in attendance were amazed, all aware and anticipating a viewing of the recent big news as it had happened.

Chongwe provided the explanation. "We make programme identify security threat to household from outside person. Programme exclude inside. Everyone have domestic problem sometime. Robin not take action for that."

The dearth of images reflected the family entertaining few visitors. Brett and Chas had always been single-minded in their interests. The factory and their son, little else. And Jude had nobody at school he called a friend.

Mildly surprising was an almost total absence of physical enforcement by RobinB, seemingly at odds with a security-type discipline. On one occasion, a salesman coming to the front door was persistent when Brett told him to use a website like everyone else. RobinB shunted him away with enough force to scare him off.

Chongwe again offered an explanation. "We make programme two part. Robin identify possible threat. Part two if threat need action. Most time threat go away." Authoritative, he enjoyed being the team's kingpin, confident in his superior knowledge.

Jeremy and Chongwe had visited one evening, bringing Cameron to meet Jude a second time. Jude again endured the invasive challenge to his sexuality, unchallenged now yet it irritated him to watch the images. Hovering menacingly, RobinB appeared on the brink of crossing the threshold to action. That didn't eventuate, but evidence suggested it was close, as if RobinB sensed Jude felt threatened but the subtleness of it without being physical was confusing. A void in the programming? He glanced at Chongwe, amused.

Chongwe felt distinctly uncomfortable at being personally involved in a real scenario. He expected to be the controlling force, not a near victim. A bad look in front of the team. "Programme need adjustment," he announced animatedly, but with a twinge of uncertainty. "I speak to Bernard. Let me work on Robin again."

Unable to fathom the concern, Jude took it as somewhat over-bloated. Another side of Chongwe? He'd seen the ruthless streak in him, but what if something didn't go his way? He could easily fall apart, Jude realised.

Reinforcing the impression he was rattled, Chongwe pushed the session quickly past 'Security', foregoing the phase requiring RobinB to re-perform. Touch sense, needing assessment on the arena floor, went largely untested.

On to 'Surveillance'. Jude felt his nerves calm a little. Surveillance was a passive activity for RobinB, not programmed to follow up with physical actions.

As expected, it was predominantly about Jude, particularly after Brett took a tough stance to monitor his every move. The images were numerous, RobinB following him everywhere on a daily basis. But selective, not storing repeat activity or regular routines such as attending school. Again pleasing to the assessment team. Out of some respect, Brett had chosen to give RobinB a judgement call under a 'keeping distance' option, therefore it was not always close enough for meaningful sound recordings. Due to the passive role, touch sense was irrelevant.

Images of Jude infiltrating his fathers' records revealed RobinB inputting the entire scene, Jude too engrossed to notice the spy at the bedroom door until finished and ready to leave. Embarrassing to see it played out on screen.

Further images featured Chas' outburst at home after the factory incident, Jude tackling Brett to demand more freedom, Saturday orienteering and the beach after, Brett offering Jude attendance at the LGBT gathering, their discussion about working at the factory over school holidays. All stored in RobinB's memory as non-routine one-off events. None of it surprised Jude.

Then suddenly, it began. The images he did not want to see. Sounds of Brett shouting opened the sequence, Jude arriving home, the entire interaction with Chas and murder of Brett, injury to Jude, Chas escaping the scene, the police and ambulance. Nothing missing, a continuous video clip complete with sound effects, talk and yelling all clearly audible.

A collective gasp went up from the team, the chilling evidence giving vision and voice to speculation. Sickened, Jude turned away, unable to watch as the emotion of it surged through his brain. The sounds were inescapable. He thought he'd moved beyond it, a new life, but the aftereffects of trauma still lingered.

Chongwe reacted swiftly as the sequence ended. "We see too much. No more now." Grim-faced, he signalled to Marcel, who deactivated RobinB. Chongwe uplifted the stiffened figure and carried it to a small storeroom adjacent the arena. He stood it inside, next to two similarly inert figures, the prototypes Robin2 and Robin3 banished to exile after their disastrous performances. Name tags affixed to forehead portrayed their unique IDs. Chongwe locked the door and re-joined the team.

Homicide police were called, quickly on the scene. They cordoned off the storeroom, out of bounds to protect evidence. At a more convenient time, they would review the damning video clip, in preparation for Chas' upcoming murder trial.

Calm again, Jude watched Chongwe dictating to the factory team. Instinctively, he didn't trust him. Altogether too clinical, steeped in self-interest. Chas staying with him and Jeremy! How would Chongwe's personal involvement play out? Not to mention the influence of Jeremy! Jude shuddered, unaccountably struck by an unnerving premonition of more trouble. He resolved to observe Chongwe closely.

With little of the working day left, he was given free rein to wander through the factory and familiarise. At closing time, he left happily, putting all behind him as he anticipated getting home and Lara.

Chapter 13

Not yet a year and already rumblings of discontent were plaguing the new Labour government. Their focus on human rights and discrimination issues, the platform largely responsible for reversing political fortune, was becoming a stumbling block to achievement. People remembered the Coln government and its impressive array of successful projects, moving the country forward throughout their fifteen year tenure. Now, a revival of old-style political conflict in pursuit of self-interest and a populist vision was threatening a return to stagnation. Less than a year for it to happen.

The government's first Budget was looming. Certain to reflect a radical departure from the Coln doctrine and last Budget, conjecture was attracting unprecedented scrutiny and debate. Just what did new Labour actually believe in? Plenty of talk in Opposition about what they were against, but their inability to transition from a negative denigrating formula to offering a positive progressive agenda was already obvious. A return to traditional failing, typical of incoming regimes pre-Coln when lack of genuine leadership equated to lack of a visionary blueprint for the country's future.

The Energy sector represented enormous potential. Paramount through the Coln years, when massive funding for Research and Development had elevated Australia to leading edge status in technological advance. Truly clean coal, renewable energy, nanotechnology, hover vehicles and AI, all initiated or embraced by Coln. Would the momentum continue? Climate Change concerns had driven much of it. Still a major worry in the world. Despite carbon emissions and deforestation eliminated more than a decade ago, global warming was continuing unabated.

The AI factory was coming under increasing scrutiny. First the Robin2 debacle, then Robin3 going the same way, suggesting an endemic problem. The enquiry was ongoing, but technically complex issues deemed definitive conclusions or recommendations unlikely. And now, another Robin complicit in a violent murder, again involving a knife. All a bad look politically. And socially a crisis, with the hundred-Robin trial underway in the community.

Privacy issues resurgent in the public forum were clearly linked to the human rights and discrimination obsessions of new Labour. Relevance to the surveillance capability of Robin and refocussed drone development threatened to further impact the factory.

Regular interviews keenly sought by an aggressive media kept the pressure on State and Federal ministers. Opposition shadow ministers were more willing, Coln focussed on promoting their proven philosophy and policies of the recent past. As always, social media overlaid everything, the instant beaming to electronic devices with frenetic response time a major influence on conduct at interviews.

The Prime Minister and Coln Leader were often on prime time as pressure ramped up towards the Budget. One evening a week was set aside for a head-to-head session. All topics on the table.

Midweek following the latest Robin furore, they sat opposite each other at the national broadcaster studio. Already, social media postings had begun, lighting up a large screen at the head of the table in full view of interview participants and cameras.

The interviewer, Sharon, opened proceedings. "Prime Minister, can I begin by reminding you of your undertaking last week to report further on asylum seekers currently held at Christmas Island? As we all know, two more boats were sighted entering Australian waters just two days ago. The Immigration Minister has been vague in disclosing what action was taken. Also with those already in detention. Can you please clarify for us?"

The Prime Minister cleared his throat, prepared for stiff questioning and exposure to instant often fiery public response, inescapable. "I'm not sure what you mean by vague. The Minister has ---"

"Excuse me, Prime Minister, what I mean is we have reliable reports of the boats being turned back. The Minister refused to confirm or deny the reports. Remembering of course, this practice was discredited when lives were lost due to leaking boats being forced to remain at sea longer. We know turn backs were only ever shadowed until gone from Australian waters." Sharon spoke confidently, sure of herself having done her research. Young, ambitious and attractive, she was on a rapid rise in the cut-throat media world.

"If you let me finish," the PM retorted, with slightly amused politeness, "the Minister confirmed the two boats were interdicted then towed to Christmas Island and burned on the beach, as is normal practice. I don't know where you get your information from. The people will be processed along with others already on the island." Middle-aged and balding, he was an experienced career politician with some charisma. A wily operator.

"We have our drones in the air," Sharon responded quickly. "We can release the evidence, if you like."

"Drones, yes, I believe that's another topic for discussion this evening." Regularly seeking to gauge public reaction, he glanced at the screen. Several hostile postings coming through.

"It is." Sharon paused, checking the screen also. "It appears your answers are not too popular so far. Let's hope for some improvement." With a cheeky smile, she turned to the other participant. "Shadow Prime Minister, I'd like to bring you in at this point. How would you respond to what the Prime Minister tells us?"

The Shadow PM leaned forward, keen to contribute after waiting patiently. "You know, these boats keep coming because the government is not taking strong action. Detainees have been on the island for weeks and not processed. Under our government, a few days maximum. They are not genuine refugees. It's not rocket science. Send them back. No need to complicate the issue." Leading Coln by example, he was a fierce advocate of positive action. A younger man than the PM, but with much longer experience in power. He'd inherited the Coln leadership late, when the long-serving incumbent took the fall for a scandal that helped ruin Coln's election chances. He was far less sensitive to the screen postings than the PM.

"These people have rights," the PM hit back, indignant. "You cannot ---"

"What rights? They try to enter our country illegally. You are ---"

"Illegally you say? Are you the judge and ---"

"Exactly what I mean by not complicating the issue. You pander to ---"

"Gentlemen, please," Sharon cut in, before the exchange escalated out of control. "I want to move on. We have a lot to get through." She focussed on the PM again. "Prime Minister, a report just out highlights recent statistics that show a spike in drug use and drug-related crime. Would you consider reopening Rehabilitation Centres for drug users? Since your government took office, every State has closed their Centres."

"Well again, I've no idea where people get their statistics," the PM chided, unimpressed. "Our figures show there is no spike." He paused, giving Sharon a condescending smile. "Theories abound with this kind of thing. One theory I hold dear is that results are always better when someone does something willingly or voluntarily rather than forced into it."

"Oh really!" the Coln Leader castigated in dismay. "I can't believe what I just heard. That demonstrates a total ignorance about drugs. A drug-affected person is incapable of rational decision-making. So the decision must be made for them." He shook his head, frustrated. "I must say I'm very disturbed we now have a leader of this country unable to appreciate such a basic principle."

"And I'm disturbed we have an Opposition leader with so little respect for basic human rights," the PM fired back.

"Please, please." Sharon held up her hands to arrest further deterioration. A flurry of postings critical of the PM had come through. She highlighted two of them on screen: 'Has the PM ever taken the time to meet a drug addict?' and 'Did the PM ever visit a Rehab Centre?' Sharon addressed him again. "How do you respond to the postings I've highlighted, Prime Minister?"

The PM shifted in his seat, tested by pertinent questions. "Yes, I have met drug addicts and visited Centres. And on each occasion, I was thanked for respecting their rights."

"I take it you will not reopen even just one or two Centres, then?" Sharon persisted. "And see how they go?"

"No," replied the PM firmly. "Those Centres soaked up major funding handed the States under the previous government. We intend to make better use of those funds."

Sharon looked perplexed, but was anxious to move on. "Okay, that brings us to some important questions concerning the upcoming Budget. It's no secret you intend to boost funding for the DP. Can you explain what that's about?"

"Yes, thank you, Sharon. We believe there's a need to strengthen DP powers. Our statistics show instances of discrimination and prejudice in this country increasing at an alarming rate. We are determined to stamp it out wherever it occurs." The PM sat back, confident he was appealing to a popular social opinion.

"What sort of discrimination and prejudice are you refer-ring to?" Sharon pursued, purporting to be curious but expecting a familiar predictable answer. "Some examples?"

"Well, sure. Some is racist, or against women, or against same-sex marriage and the LGBT community, the disabled, the disadvantaged. You name it and there's probably discrimination happening."

The Coln Leader gave a short chuckle, displaying a degree of scepticism. "How about against indigenous people? Or country folk? Plenty of discrimination there."

"Well yes, exactly. I'm glad we have consensus on this." The PM looked pleased with himself. "We need to protect anyone who might have a reason to be discriminated against."

"Quite right. And there are so many examples, in all walks of life." The Shadow PM gave another chuckle, also begin-ning to enjoy himself. "Like someone with a funny walk. Or with blue eyes. What about people with a loud voice who talk too much? Challenge for the DP, don't you think?" His voice dripping with sarcasm. "Of course, anyone discrimi-nated against should go on a Social Security benefit. You know, the one that compensates victims?"

The PM bristled with anger, not appreciating being depicted in a humiliating light. "You mock the process. I'm sure we'll see how our viewers react to you demeaning their concerns." He took a hard look at the screen.

Postings were coming in fast and furious. Sharon allowed a short break for everyone to study them. A mixture across a wide spectrum of opinion, from one extreme to another. Confused public? Sharon looked for one or two of more sensational quality, finding plenty but with no definitive pattern, decided to forego entering that minefield. All beaming back out there to people's devices perpetuated the continuous merry-go-round.

"Very interesting. I don't see much support for your ideas," the Shadow PM observed, maintaining a sceptical tone. He held the PM in a steady gaze. "If discrimination and prejudice is increasing, at an alarming rate according to your statistics, it's because the DP are out there picking up on any minor misdemeanour they can find. Of course, what else but for statistics to blow out?"

A stony silence was deafening for a moment. The PM arrested it before damage took hold. "I see plenty of support." He continually glanced at the screen, the confusion offering protection, relief. "No, the statistics are a measure of how poorly you addressed these matters during your time in office."

The Shadow PM let out a laugh of derision. "The Prime Minister would have us return to a bygone age. Sixteen years ago, the Australian electorate voted Coln in because they were fed-up with this kind of rubbish. The country paralysed by over-analysis, stifled in the punitive clutches of social do-gooders. But creative industry achieved great progress developing our nation, without any discrimination watchdog. That is the Coln legacy, and I sense already a yearning in the community for a return to it." He kept a steady gaze on the PM, barely interested in the frenetic postings coming on screen.

The PM stiffened as the pressure ramped up. But he was of tough resolve, not elected leader for nothing. "The

Opposition leader would have us disband the DP, I'm sure. Such good work they do. But their expertise is not respected by our friend here." He returned his opponent's gaze with equal intensity.

The Shadow PM laughed once more. "Your memory is a little selective, Prime Minister. We created the DP. Their expertise was developed by Coln, as the Drugs Police. That capability has been callously disbanded by your government. Perhaps you wish not to discriminate against drug pushers too?"

"Sharon, can you ask our friend to keep his personal prejudices and insults to himself?" The PM was undeterred, always seeking to claim the moral high ground. "I think we're here to give viewers something informative, are we not?"

A further amused chuckle from the Shadow PM, sensing he'd struck a telling blow. Pointedly, he inclined his head towards the screen. Postings swinging in his favour.

"Gentlemen," Sharon intervened. "Let's not get bogged down here. Please put your point of view then respect the other's right of reply."

"Very good, Sharon," the Shadow PM agreed, in jocular mood now. "You'll get the political correctness prize. Unless the DP find something, of course. Which I'm sure they could." He broke into a laugh. The subject matter was right up his alley. For years, he'd waged a crusade against political correctness choking progress, obsessive discrimination debate stifling freedom.

Sharon took it in good heart. But the session was getting off-track. "Prime Minister, can you outline the measures you intend taking to strengthen DP powers?"

"Thank you, Sharon." The PM cleared his throat, glad a more formal stance beckoned. "First, we will put more DP officers on the streets. I'd like to put one on every street corner, but of course that's not possible. We can, however, increase the numbers and we'll do that."

"Second, we will update the technology DP officers use. New surveillance capability, in line with the latest electronic advancements. Their mobile devices will be able to monitor communications within a certain radius, to detect activity of a nature the DP is assigned to police. The ability to intercept will greatly reduce response times, going a long way towards eradicating the scourge of discrimination from our society. Prevention better than cure is a proven principle I have always held dear. This is another area in which we can lead the world by example."

A deathly hush fell over the studio. Even the postings were markedly fewer for the moment, evidence of a shocked public out there.

The Shadow PM was first to break the spell. "I've been expecting this." He was solemn, more serious than at any other stage of the interview. "The government has kept it under wraps, but we've heard rumours. Although none of us expected anything as heinous as this." He hesitated, searching for the right words. "We will fight this blight on our freedoms to the death. I believe, Prime Minister, if you wish to impose such deeply draconian measures on the Australian people, you must take it to them in a general election."

The PM had not finished. "Third, we will increase the number of drones in the air. It is well proven how invaluable the use of drones is in assisting the DP. Naturally, we will give drones the same technological upgrade as for officers' devices. As good as having an officer on every street corner. The upgrade will include more effective remote control." He paused, gratified to be guiding proceedings now.

"Fourth and finally, of course it would be negligent of us not to address the penalties and correctional responses in line with improved capability. An offender may be immediately placed in detention if an officer considers the offence serious enough or unduly threatening to a victim. Mandatory jail terms will be introduced for serious cases, replacing community service as currently the usual penalty. We envisage a three-tier graded scale, with a grade three offence attracting the jail term." Satisfied, the PM leaned back in his chair, prepared for whatever reaction ensued.

Postings were picking up again on screen. Sharon allowed time to study them. A wide variety. Some hysterical in nature, but surprisingly, as many in favour as against. Unwilling to pick out any and jeopardise her position of perceived neutrality, she refocussed on interviewing.

"Prime Minister, how do you respond to the Shadow Prime Minister's call for a general election? Do you agree to seek the people's mandate for these measures?"

The PM leaned forward, intense once more. "No, that will not happen. We have a mandate. The election was less than a year ago. If you remember, we were relentless in Opposition highlighting the contempt Coln held for issues of discrimination and prejudice. This was the main driving force behind their defeat and our election. Decided by the people. We are giving due reverence to their wishes."

Certain he was on safe ground, he glared at the Shadow PM, challenging him directly.

The Shadow PM returned the challenge, unperturbed. He also was sure of his ground. "We'll see." He remained calm, seeing no future in arguing the merits at this forum. "There's a lot of water to go under the bridge before this has any chance of happening. Try getting the legislation through Parliament!"

"The only legislation required will be to tighten penalties," the PM contended. A touch of arrogance now. "The rest is changing nothing of the powers the DP possess already, just improving operational matters."

"Gentlemen, please," Sharon cut in, a little frustrated. "We must move on. A lot still to talk about." She drew a deep breath. "Perhaps we could take a short break at this point. Time for refreshments, anyone?" A trolley was being wheeled out.

Ten minutes later, they were seated again and Sharon resumed proceedings. "Thank you, Prime Minister, Shadow Prime Minister. I'd like to move on and talk about other Budget-related issues. We understand there will be funding cuts in some areas. Prime Minister?"

"Yes, Sharon, that's correct." The PM took a cursory glance at the screen. A few postings but nothing of particular concern. "We're looking at Research and Development. This has received major funding in recent times. Climate Change is still happening, we know, but with global emissions already zero, there's not a lot more we can do in the Energy sector to further alleviate this painful phenomenon. So R and D is less of a priority."

"Shadow Prime Minister, Climate Change is an issue of great concern we need to discuss," Sharon concurred. "Would you like to respond?"

"Yes, I would." The Shadow PM struggled to contain a rising anger, seeing another Coln success story about to be unpicked by inward-looking new Labour. "Perhaps we can come back to Climate Change. Research and Development is about more than that. Coln's far-sighted Energy initiatives made this country a leading player in the world. We discovered the ultimate clean coal solution, by R and D finding a use for carbon capture. Revolutionary, rewarding us with a huge economic boom. Our renewable resources, abundant compared to most other countries, the AI factory in Queensland, nanotechnology, hover vehicles, all wonderful Coln achievements. And now, you want to drop the ball and let it all slide. Developed nations of the world are moving fast, advancement is never static. We'll lose the edge, just like that!" Angrily, he snapped his fingers, aimed at the PM's face.

The PM was unmoved. "There are more sensitive and important social issues now that have been neglected and require our attention," he countered, remaining adamant. "Such as boosting the DP we've talked about. But I'm glad you mentioned the AI factory. Recent problems there indicate a lack of proper checks and balances on how funding is being utilised. Another tragedy involving a Robin robot even since we set up an enquiry! Too much ambition, not enough accountability. So we will reduce their funding, have put the factory on a holding pattern until the enquiry is complete and we find out what's really been going on there."

The Shadow PM's anger was escalating. Still he managed to hold himself together. "I wonder how your Science Minister feels about that. He's been very supportive of the AI factory." The prospect of promoting disunity in the government spurred him on. "The factory has brought forward its drone programme. I assume you'll support that? Since you're boosting drone capability for the DP?"

"No, we'll not support that." Determined to follow their chosen course, the PM was unflinching. "Drones are as advanced as we need them to be. The boost is from new software, not drones themselves. For the DP is for the public good. As I understand it, the factory's programme has a vision for as yet unheard-of private use. Quite frankly, I don't trust the AI factory to do that responsibly." Gratified, he sat back and gave the screen a long hard look. Postings a mixture as always, but several highly encouraging.

The Shadow PM also noticed a measure of public sympathy for the PM's contentions. Best let it rest for now. One further technological prospect was worthy of mention. "What about nanotechnology? Enormous potential there. We've hardly scratched the surface yet."

The PM paused, giving it serious thought. "We can look at that. It is very futuristic. But I'm not convinced the AI factory should be involved."

A brief lull followed. Sharon moved to keep the session flowing. "Prime Minister, you said there are sensitive social issues that require your attention. Can you elaborate on this and how the Budget will be impacted?"

"Thank you, Sharon." Shifting to preferred territory again. "We've covered the DP and enhanced surveillance.

Of course, this means additional costs to the Budget. More officers, upgrading infrastructure, social security payments, correctional services. But this is only one area needing our attention. The Social Security network has been systematically neglected for many years. Contrary to the former government's focus of peddling in international prestige, we are focussed on our people, those disadvantaged, discriminated against, discarded and dumped in the poor basket. We must protect their human rights. And their privacy, another reason why we reject the AI factory's drone programme that would invade everyone's privacy. The Robin robots too, privacy issues there." The PM became steadily more animated as he expounded his agenda.

To the Shadow PM, it was symptomatic of the struggle to transition from long-term Opposition. And perhaps appeasing resurrected factional power bases within Labour? Experienced in the political arena at the young age of forty-three, he saw through the PM's façade as if it was a pane of glass. A different agenda and strategy, ideologically based from further back, had eventually wrested power from Coln, but now must be justified. Credibility was at stake.

While the others perused screen postings again, his mind wandered. In reality, he realised with amusement, Coln's support of the Social Security system was not greatly different from new Labour. Almost bipartisan. But they came to it from totally opposite perspectives. Much Coln had tolerated rather than believed in, accepting it was entrenched, an egg diabolically too daunting to unscramble. With money rolling into the coffers from economic boom, the Social Security tab had been easily managed and Coln let it be. But they refrained from deliberately adding to it, preferring people to work and have enterprise not hand-outs. Coln being a fresh political phenomenon meant no pre-conceived dogma.

Whereas new Labour were steeped in ideology evolving from decades back, courting political popularism. Had some enjoyed too soft living for too long? Creating contrived issues like discrimination, political correctness, privacy to fill a void that struggle for survival would otherwise occupy? And so, new Labour were tied to their doctrine, believed in a burgeoning Social Security network, determined to main-tain populist do-goodism. How long before public rejection of political power plays repeated? The signs were there.

He refocussed, glancing at the screen. The postings were varied as usual. Not overly concerned, he reverted to assessing the PM's rhetoric, feeling obliged to tackle him on the anomalies and hypocrisy abounding out of dogma not fundamental conviction.

Having allowed enough of a break, Sharon resumed, "Shadow Prime Minister, have you a response to the Prime Minister's comments?"

"I do." The Shadow PM offered a knowing smile, shaking his head slowly in rebuttal as he looked the PM directly in the eye. "Your fine talk is so full of contradictions, I hardly know where to begin. You talk of protecting privacy, yet you boost the DP, converted by you into the greatest invasion of privacy ever devised. You wish to upgrade drone surveil-lance for DP use, yet you intend closing down the AI facto-ry's drone programme that will benefit everyone, handing leading edge advantage to our overseas competitors. You talk of focussing on the disadvantaged, yet you suspend the AI factory's Robin programme designed to massively advantage every household and industry when comes on stream. Again, we'll fall behind international norms." He paused, letting his words resonate. Postings were coming in at a furious rate. But he kept his gaze steadfastly on the PM.

"You talk of protecting human rights, yet detention of asylum seekers on Christmas Island is blowing out while you vacillate. More boats coming and you have resumed perilous turn backs. Where are the human rights of someone drowning at sea? You talk of helping people discarded or dumped, yet you close down Rehab Centres for drug users. What price for their so-called human rights? You talk of stamping out discrimination, as if to do so is even feasible, yet you plan to increase Social Security handouts, discriminating against hard-working enterprising people who provide that funding. You ride on the back of overflowing coffers and a large Budget surplus Coln handed over, yet you scornfully denigrate Coln as peddling in international prestige. Your doctrine is so confused, even the hypocrisy is anomalous." He laughed briefly, then took a deep breath. More to come.

Before he could resume, the PM cut in. "Sharon, our friend has his personal prejudices on display again. Can you please rein him in?"

Sharon held up both hands to call a halt, seeking some balance. "Okay, Prime Minister. You have the opportunity to respond." She continued signalling restraint on the Shadow PM.

"Thank you, Sharon." The PM cleared his throat, determined to prevail. "It is a fact, and statistics prove, Social Security payments at best flatlined through the Coln years, in some areas declining. I think that tells us a lot about Coln's attitude towards the welfare of our people. One sector increased, and substantially too, which I concede is a surprise. Family and Child Protection Services. We are assessing the reasons, however we strongly support this sector and continue to provide whatever additional funding the States need."

"I know the reasons," the Shadow PM interrupted. "Sharon, if I may?" When Sharon nodded, he continued, "We came to office just a short time after the advent of same-sex marriage. We soon copped a sudden explosion in the number of Social Security benefits approved. You know, for the usual reasons same as heterosexual unions, except of course every same-sex union having a child involves three parents or more not two. It's a whole new benefit area, not existing before same-sex marriage came in. If we are to follow your precious statistics, they show same-sex breakups, divorce, violence, abuse and so on at best on par with heterosexual if not a little worse. So, the Social Security cost is far bigger now, and we expect will continue to rise."

The PM took it up. "What would you have us do? Remove their entitlement? These people have as much right to a benefit as anyone. The way you talk is precisely the kind of discrimination we've been discussing. But maybe that's the Coln way." His tone scornful now, unable to contain himself. "I believe you voted No in the 2017 same-sex ballot."

"Well, well, well," the Shadow PM replied, sitting back happily, gifted an opportunity. "The Prime Minister cannot help himself. At last he shows his own prejudice. I did vote No. That's no secret. But Coln always respected and honoured the people's decision. Did I say we refused to pay any Social Security benefits? I don't believe I did. Why do you think those payments blew out? What's your explanation?"

Momentarily, the PM was unusually lost for words, regretting his ill-advised last remark, now like a noose around his neck. All eyed the screen with more than usual interest. A flurry of postings indicated strong endorsement for the Shadow PM's stance and against the PM.

"Perhaps we should discuss some of these postings," the Coln Leader quipped, feeling the PM deserved to be needled. "But anyway, about declining Social Security payments under Coln the Prime Minister accuses us for, was that not a good thing? Rather than lack of care on our part he would have you believe, in fact the opposite is true. Less dependency, more enterprise." He paused, again encouraged by the display of positive postings in support.

"One decline we are very proud of was the cost of Unemployment benefits. In our time, everyone able to work was working. The disabled too, as far as their capability, bringing about a decline in that benefit area also. Very interesting to see how it all pans out under this backward-looking government, with its focus on closing down factories and enterprise, its preference for identifying discrimination and moving people to victim status. Let's see how long the healthy Budget surplus we handed them lasts."

"Sharon, how long will you allow our friend to spout his prejudices?" the PM retorted, unimpressed with the free run afforded. He felt on a knife-edge as adverse postings continued to trend the wrong way.

A little anxious, Sharon was aware she must enable equal time. To avoid becoming bogged down, a new focus needed. "Okay, Prime Minister. Let's move on. I wonder if you could expand on your earlier comments about Climate Change. The effects of this worsening crisis on daily life are greatly worrying everyone."

"Quite right, Sharon. Thank you." An issue the PM was more comfortable with. "My earlier comments were in relation to funding priorities. I think we all understand it is not possible to stop Climate Change from happening. Therefore, it would be irresponsible to sink money into hypothetical ideas or research we imagine might arrest what we now know to be part of our planet's natural cycle. Coln contributed to achieving zero global emissions, and well done for that, but subsequently it made no difference to global warming. That is proof of what I'm saying. Same goes for deforestation ceasing worldwide." He gave the Shadow PM a nod of acknowledgement as he spoke, happy to adopt a less combative stance over an issue that had been largely bipartisan.

"So instead, we will channel funds into what people need, bringing communities together to sustain our way of life in a world that's changing around us. This is what our social agenda supports, actually. Which we promised in our election pledge to the Australian people." Pointedly, he avoided further including the Coln Leader in togetherness.

"We will continue to assist those in low-lying coastal areas needing to relocate due to sea level rise. Not a big demand at present, but we fully expect it will grow over time. Planning for alternative urban centres and cities inland is ongoing. Of course, we can't do much about the higher temperatures we endure every day, or the greater intensity storms and cyclones that come our way, or loss of biodiversity. Current infrastructure spending is adequate to deal with it as best we can. And we will continue to meet our international obligations in accepting environmental refugees from South Pacific nations, our designated region." He sat back, satisfied, expecting an improvement in postings now.

"Shadow Prime Minister, your comments?" Sharon prompted, after a brief look at the screen. Again, public reaction too varied to pick out anything specific.

"Thanks, Sharon." The Coin Leader leaned forward, keen to take it up. "And thank you, Prime Minister, for recognising our efforts regarding emissions, and Climate Change reality. You were not always so accepting. But then, before we came to office, all the clamour from pundits and popular scientists worldwide was about blame. Politicians too. Everyone in conflict, emotional over the problems not solutions. And an arrogant assumption that we control the planet's environment instead of the planet controlling us. As if Climate Change would be decided by one single factor like emissions. So simplistic. I think we know our planet is vastly more complex than that." He paused, giving the PM a half-smile, depicting a fatalistic belief in destiny. Without bothering to survey the postings, he continued.

"We in government followed the prevailing science also. And I'm glad we did, if only for reasons of public health, to help rid major cities of choking pollution. But later, when evidence started showing no improvement in global warming from zero emissions, the serious questions began. Other scientists who'd been silent came forward. You know, ones not following politically correct dogma to ensure continuation of their funding. Genuine modelling of ----"

"Excuse me, do we have to listen to this? Can we be spared the history lesson?" the PM interrupted, irritated by his opponent's last comment. He had friends in the science fraternity. "Another set of prejudices coming on. We don't need that." He glanced strongly at Sharon.

"Yes, I think we should move forward," Sharon agreed. "Unless you have suggestions on measures that can be taken to alleviate the problem, Shadow Prime Minister."

The Coln Leader hesitated, itching to remind everyone of plain truths scientists he knew had put out in the public domain. That carbon dioxide was in fact a poor greenhouse gas contributing very little to warming, water vapour far more an impact. That to be credible, modelling of the planet's entire history, many millions of years, was necessary, not merely citing the last tiny sliver of mankind's existence. That such modelling evidenced a regular cycle between full ice melt and full ice age. Earth was emerging at the tail-end of an ice age. What other cause but astronomy? That cycles correlated with varying activity of the Sun and Earth's orbit moving a little closer or farther from it. Willing to concede human intervention may have a slight accelerating effect, but how miniscule by comparison? He decided to forego indulging himself, just as keen to take the opportunity Sharon was offering.

A quick check of the screen, plenty of postings in favour. Encouraged, he resumed, "Yes, I do have some suggestions. Prime Minister, the infrastructure spending you say is adequate, does that include the projects and enterprises you're closing down? Because to mitigate against the impact of Climate Change, they are what people need and bring communities together, to quote your fine words." Openly sceptical now. This was the moment to go on the offensive.

"The scheme we built transporting water from often flood-stricken North Queensland to previously drought-stricken areas south and feeding into river systems, stage three is ready for construction. Will you follow through? Abuse of water rights and allocations we had under strict control has started happening again. You need to be tough with that. This country has ample water for essential needs. We've been harnessing it, returning rivers to good health. But there's more to do. Forestry and tree plantations, with involvement of indigenous communities, pulling these people up. Will you follow through? Measures to control bushfires and enforce responsible upkeep of threatened land, requires continual enhancement. Will you keep it going? These initiatives, to name just a few, have delivered sustainability and secured our way of life in the face of a harsher climate. But will you follow through!?" Increasingly strident, he fixed a steely glare at the PM.

"Prime Minister, you say planning for alternative cities is ongoing, for when sea level rise demands relocation from coastal areas. We started that, but no further action since you came to office. Your words are empty unless we see progress. The Canberra to Melbourne Very Fast Train project was progressing well under Coln, on the back of the VFT Canberra to Sydney that's been such a boom for regional towns between. Will you follow through? This creates the future cities you talk about, serviced by the VFTs. There's a lot more, haven't even touched on Health with its R and D needs. But we probably don't have the time here this evening." He shifted attention to Sharon, gratified to be given enough opportunity to put forward this much of Coln's agenda.

"Unfortunately, we are out of time," Sharon confirmed reluctantly, receiving word from her director to wrap things up. "One last chance for you both in closing. Shadow Prime Minister, you first. But please be brief, we need to hear the Prime Minister's closing comments."

"Well, I think we need to hear from the Prime Minister what projects and programmes he will support, not just those he won't." The Coln Leader flung another pene-trating glare at the PM. "It's very interesting, Prime Minister, when asked to comment about Climate Change, how quickly you managed to divert onto this social agenda you keep claiming to have a mandate for. I'm wondering how the needs we've just been talking about will be met by boosting DP powers to invade privacy and detain social transgressors. Or how running down the AI factory will keep us ahead in the technology race. But never mind, I think we've heard enough on that already." He maintained his hard look at the PM.

"I'm more focussed on the numerous enterprises Coln had ongoing. Some I've mentioned already, but by no means all. Providing employment to the abled and disabled alike, to indigenous communities. Doing more socially than your so-called mandate could ever hope to match. And bringing about decline in Social Security entitlements in the process that we talked about earlier. Our much-needed reforms in Education brought us back to international standard. This was structural and socially based, nothing to do with funding. More to be done, but will you continue on the path we set? Social media, constantly under review for its impact on our society. I'm pleased you regard nano-technology with some favour. That's good." He hesitated, busting to say more on this enormously significant and far-sighted potential of the future. But satisfied for now, he shifted attention from the PM. "Thank you, Sharon. I have more, perhaps for another time."

"Yes, thank you, Shadow Prime Minister." Sharon turned to the PM. "Prime Minister, your closing comments?"

"Well, I'll be very brief," the PM responded, unimpressed with the free rein Sharon had allowed his adversary challenging on so many fronts. The postings supporting the Shadow PM were not helping. The sooner the better to end it now. "I'm not about to go through every issue that will make up the Budget, but our agenda is certainly different. Our friend here is concerned about his precious surplus, but we believe in times of affluence the people should share in the spoils. My government is focussed on socially sensitive areas neglected by the former regime, such as Health, Education and most importantly, the right for people to live without being victimised by the discriminatory, prejudiced actions of others. But you will have to wait for the Budget, when all will be revealed. That's all I have to say, Sharon. Thank you for giving me this time."

Sharon moved to wrap up proceedings, thanking both participants for their attendance and candour in presenting their views. The head-to-head interview over for another week.

Chapter 14

The next days at the factory hardly inspired Jude to imagine an exciting future career there. Head technician Marcel, hurriedly appointed following the recent upheavals, was not a particularly motivated character or seemingly interested in motivating Jude. The assessment of RobinB on Jude's first day had been less than adequately performed, few conclusions drawn. With the Robin programme officially on hold, no one took it any further. Only the hundred-Robin trial in the wider community would run its course.

Pleased to be released from further appraising, Chongwe returned to more appealing drone technology. Happily, Jude hardly saw him then. With the work low-key, Marcel dismissively put Jude to general duties helping anyone in the factory with a need. Transporting and delivering, clearing away rubbish, lending a hand with anything. Having regular use of a cart, he could roam the place at will. Hardly what he expected, not highly technical, but he was content being given free rein to observe and learn.

Several work bays were already closed, but a few Robins still on the production line were being finished. Enough for Jude to see how a Robin was put together. A skeletal metal frame with joints and extensions as closely resembling human equivalent as years of painstaking research and trial could devise, overlaid by a thick pliable skin also with characteristics close to human and even more years of effort in creating. Impregnated just under the surface all over, tiny sensors close together relayed touch sense via white transmission cords to input the black box. Black cords signalling output exited to all parts of the body. Particularly intricate to work the hands, fingers and thumbs. Similarly, different coloured cords to and from the black box enabled sight and hearing senses. The black box was embedded centre of the chest.

Unlike humans with organs, multi-systems and senses necessary to sustain breathing, food blood and oxygen supply, expel waste, reproduction, movement and awareness, a Robin needed only its black box and three senses to simulate humanlike existence. Simple input and output. The complexity, multitude of responses and capability controlled by its software was safely ensconced within the black box, along with the nano-power pack providing near limitless energy. And therefore, independence. Acceptable as long as humans retained the power to activate and deactivate it, Jude surmised thoughtfully.

He watched in fascination, moving bay to bay, following the step-by-step fabricating and installing procedures. Although humanlike, all systems were electrical and mechanical, no chemical processes. Therefore no emotion, no empathy, no moral compass. Consistent with Robin actions to date. Input and output, totally cold. He shivered. Despite having lived with a Robin, he was struck by the bizarre contrast between innocent-looking components and the confronting specimen emerging as end product from the last bay. Still he couldn't get used to the eyes. They epitomised the coldness, deep dark wells, windows to a soulless interior.

The final step was to brand its individual ID on the forehead. Having seen enough, Jude moved on, passing a large storage area full of completed Robins. Then to where other products were being manufactured. Mostly experimental, bringing new ideas together, nothing as yet with the prestige of Robin. Apart from several bays dedicated to drones. From small to large, the latest was here. All nano-powered hover vehicles, the largest capable of a sizeable payload, people and goods. Representing the vision Chongwe was so excited about.

At the factory's far end wall now, coming to a door. No nameplate. Curious, Jude pushed through, entering a modest-sized room. Two white-coated technicians stood at a bench along the far wall. A laboratory. Not large compared to the main laboratory, but significant work obviously in progress, evidenced by plenty of equipment and paraphernalia on the benchtop.

"Can I help you?" one of the technicians asked, disturbed by Jude's entry. A young man, fresh-faced and bespectacled, the look of an academic about him.

"I'm supposed to help anyone who needs assistance," Jude responded quickly, not wishing to be seen as an intruder. "Cleaning up, removing rubbish, anything. Part of my training. I just started here."

The other technician, a young woman, gave him a smile and pointed at an overflowing bin. "You can empty that for us, if you like?" Natasha, by her name tag. She spoke with a positive friendly air, obviously enjoying her work. "How's your training going?"

"It's a bit slow." Jude felt happy to be accepted. "I'm trying to learn everything I can. Looks interesting what you're doing here?"

"This is nanotechnology. Have you heard of it?"

Jude was suddenly excited. "Really? I've heard of it. I know it's the power source for Robin and other things, like drones. Apart from that, I don't know much." His attention was captured by a large structure taking up most of the far side wall.

"Would you like to see?" She invited him to look through an observation window protruding at the front. "This is a very special microscope. Tell me what you see."

He peered through the window, which sealed across his face to exclude external light. Viewing was of a glass slate covered in a close-knit mass of dark shimmering dots. "Are they molecules?" He knew nanotechnology penetrated to the most extreme boundaries of size.

"Certainly are." She cast him an amused glance, proud to display something of the vast potential in train. "We can make new products, mix and manipulate different elements with suitable properties. The possibilities are endless."

"Oh wow! You mean like new alloys?"

She laughed, taken with his naivety. "That's old science. Even the compounds produced at the international space station, using zero gravity, is old science now. Nanotechnology involves not just metals, but any and all elements of the periodic table. Countless permutations and combinations. We're only at the start of it. How good is your chemistry?" Again she laughed, enthusiastic.

Jude stared open-mouthed at her. "How many of these new products are coming on stream?"

"Not that many yet. Nanotechnology started over fifty years ago, when a physicist named Feynman created the first microscope powerful enough to see atoms and molecules. But no one took it seriously until the Coln government came in. Now? We're not sure what's going to happen."

"Same as everyone else here," Jude concurred, again made aware of the downward-spiralling dispirited atmosphere in the factory. So different from the odd occasion he'd visited when his fathers were here eagerly singing its praises. "Anyway, thanks for showing me. I thought nanotechnology was just about making more powerful batteries."

"Well, it's that too." Natasha looked away wistfully, reminded of past successes. "Even Coln were surprised how fast their support for R and D produced breakthroughs. Luke here can show you about batteries." She indicated her colleague further along the bench.

Luke signalled Jude closer. "Have a look at this." With a friendly smile, he held up a small glass vessel with screw top, three-quarters filled with a deep purplish-coloured liquid. "This is a very special liquid, with very special properties." Gleefully, he gave it a gentle shake.

Fascinated, Jude peered at it from close range. The liquid was free flowing, but viscous enough not to splash when shaken. Too dark to see through, the rich depth of colour created an intrigue of its own.

"We continue refining it, but basically this is the result of many years research," Luke heralded, talking fast, bubbling with excitement. "The most efficient substance ever known in holding electric charge. Makes your old conventional batteries like barely a pin prick by comparison. This is what we put in batteries now, to make nano-power packs. This amount could drive a Robin for months."

Awestruck, Jude ogled at the harmless-looking vessel, daunted by the latent power held within. "How can it do that?"

"Ah. How can I explain it better." Luke thought for a moment. "Maybe you learned in chemistry class how the amount of charge a battery cell can carry is a function of its surface area. Well, in a nano-battery, like this liquid, the whole mass carries charge, in the space around every molecule. As an analogy, think of a block of wood. It has surface area of six faces, right? Cut it in half and you have two extra faces, more surface area. Keep on cutting it over and over until you have a mass of molecules. That's your answer."

Jude listened intently. "I get it. So, what does the future hold?"

"Who knows? A breakthrough can happen anytime, can lead to anything." Luke indicated his colleague, who was engrossed once more in her work. "That microscope can see smaller than molecules. It can see to atomic level. The ability to manipulate at that level means the ability to change the structure of matter."

Dumbfounded, Jude stared at him, stunned by the immense implications. How would that ability be used? Would people misuse it? Inevitable. Was there any invention that had never been corrupted by someone? He shuddered. But nature always prevailed. Consequences.

"I'd better go. Thanks, I really appreciate you showing me." After emptying their bin at his cart, it was back to scouting around the factory. Becoming a routine, but with more to think about now.

Next day, the mood in the factory was even more morose. Last evening's weekly media spectacle had featured the Prime Minister further denouncing the AI and drone programmes, leaving little room for optimism. More redundancies looked certain. An already greatly depleted workforce milled about the arena, bringing on an impromptu gathering as management and computer staff joined in. Chief Officers Francis and Bernard were doing their best to answer questions, keeping it informal.

"We are seeking clarification from government on their intentions," Bernard advised, confronted by an irate woman who'd risen to senior foreperson on the floor after many years dedicated service.

"Do you have other work for us to go on with?" the woman fired back, struggling to deal with the shock of a seemingly secure future suddenly ripped out from under her. "It's not just me. All of us here love this place. And we all have families to support." Her work team was grouped around, of one mind.

Francis stepped in, determined to allay their fears. "We will do everything we can to keep the factory operating. Hell, I myself, my colleague and friend Bernard here, all the management team, have given our lives to building the high-tech expertise we have here, second to none in the world. We are desperate not to lose that." He choked back a moment of emotion, genuine in his conviction.

And so the exchanges continued as everyone crowded closer. Jude watched from the sidelines, sobered by how easily the political divide could impact people's lives. He felt fortunate himself, with only the school holidays to invest, unlike many pledging entire careers to a solid, once-assured future. Looking around the cross-section of people present, he saw a variety of backgrounds, race, religion, different private lives, sexual preference, but all of common purpose when they come here. No discrimination in this place. The populist catchcry making a comeback was at odds with reality, the threatened demise of the AI factory more like hypocrisy at work.

Chongwe was hovering at the fringes, listening to everyone giving voice to the common dilemma. Impatient, he suddenly stepped forward, taking centre stage.

"If no work, I leave. I go to Hong Kong." He spoke with confidence, arrogant. The news about drone development politically out of favour incensed him. Opportunity being squandered, his expertise unrecognised. "China lead world economy. I have many contact. Many time I get call to come back. They need high-tech skill." He aimed his tirade at Bernard, who he saw as the most influential.

Bernard reacted with concern. "We have meetings with government scheduled for later today and tomorrow. Please give us that time, don't make any hasty decisions until we have more certainty. We're hoping to gain some concessions, convince them about the amazing work we do here." He addressed his words to everyone.

Chongwe was quick to reply. "You let me work on Robin. Then I stay. I know Robin problem. I can fix." He half-turned away, looking for someone. His eyes picked out Jude. "I need him to help. He have special relation with trial Robin." He signalled Jude to join them.

Startled, Jude came forward hesitantly, not expecting to be a prominent player. Why would Chongwe choose him? Relations between them had been lukewarm at best. Jude felt uncomfortable, nonplussed to think he had any greater experience with RobinB than others with their Robins.

Bernard took it up. "We're not deciding anything right now. After we've met with government, then we'll know more." He glanced at Francis, who gave a nod of endorsement.

"Please, everyone, be patient," Francis reiterated in support of his colleague. "Management has decided to give you the rest of today and tomorrow off work, on full pay. If you all come back Monday morning, we'll have more to say then."

That signalled an end to the informal gathering. The people slowly dispersed. Chongwe strode away angrily, unimpressed his proposals had gone unheeded. Jude watched him leave, more convinced than ever he could not be trusted.

Temporary closure of the factory meant Jude and Lara could spend more time together. Straight to the beach, where they played in the surf, rode a jet ski and lay close side by side under their umbrella until nightfall. And always the promise of making love at night, finding new ways to enjoy each other's bodies, discovering the joy-filled depths of sexual pleasure. Lara as good as moved in to live with Jude and Dulcie. Her mums didn't object, as long as they saw her regularly. An agreed arrangement Lara respected. School holidays a time to relax, rejuvenate, no pressure.

Friday dawned as their first chance to sleep in together, no factory today. Lara propped on one elbow, ran her forefinger around the outline of his mouth then planted a loving kiss on his lips. Under the bedsheets, their naked bodies snuggled close, both feeling the warm afterglow of the night's energy-sapping sexual exertions.

"I'm not worried about the factory," she mused, her face an inch from his. "We're free today, let's enjoy it."

Jude appreciated her cheerfulness, slightly bemused she'd be thinking of the factory. A strand of blonde hair was falling across her face. He lightly brushed it back. "We'll find out Monday. It doesn't look good. Especially Chongwe." He tried to push the nagging distraction from his mind. "But I'm more concerned we have room for improvement on the jet ski." He gave a quick laugh.

Lara giggled in delight. Feeling positive, she rolled onto her back, swung her legs out of bed and headed for the bathroom.

A leisurely breakfast with Dulcie, then to the beach again. A simple, fun-loving agenda for the day.

Lying peacefully together on the sand, they didn't expect an interruption. It came as a light splash of sand at the front edge of the beach towel, landing just short of their faces. Both jerked their heads up, encountering at close range a pair of shoes and long trousers hardly befitting beachwear. They looked up. Jeremy!

"What a perfect day to enjoy the sand and surf," Jeremy began, displaying a familiar smirk to accompany the cynical tone of voice. "No, don't get up. I'll just park myself here." He plonked a small canvass folding chair on the sand close to the towel. Holding his umbrella aloft, he sat.

A stab of fear instantly gripped Lara. She grabbed her top and quickly pulled it on to cover herself. Jude was struck by a sick sensation in the pit of his stomach. "Are you looking for something?" He was barely able to stay polite. Sitting up, he steeled himself. Jeremy was alone. That eased the tension a little. Perhaps they could come to an understanding, put to rest the fear of reprisal he and Lara had been wrestling with since that fateful night.

Jeremy focussed on Lara. "No need to hide yourself," he chided condescendingly. The smirk deepened. "You're a beautiful girl. You should be proud, show it to the world. We gave you the opportunity to do that." He broke into an insidious laugh. Then suddenly, in a bizarre switch, he turned serious. "But it seems you're also a clever girl. We must be more thorough next time. Make sure the bonds are tied correctly. And you have nothing to pick a lock with. What did you use, a hairclip?"

Uptight, Lara said nothing, crouched behind Jude with an arm around his shoulders. Jude was gratified not to be implicated in Lara's escape. But he knew Jeremy well enough, careful to give him nothing. Jeremy unaware was no indemnity from danger. He'd know Lara would reveal everything about her traumatic experience and the place dubbed the Cave. Most concerning was the threat of repeat circumstance, if not worse. Jude realised he must try to settle the score if possible.

"We have no interest in your operation, whatever it is. Lara saw inside your place, that's true. But no one else knows she's seen it. So no one will ask her. And she won't tell anyone." He inclined his head towards Lara, who was pressing her face close. She nodded frantically. "We just want to be left alone, do our school work and move on, like nothing happened." His argument sounded weak and pleading, but they had no better one.

Jeremy laughed again, treating Jude's comments with disdain. "But she does know. She has seen what we do. And you know too, obviously. So we have a problem." He fell silent, allowing his words to hit home.

Lara stiffened in fright, letting out a strangled gasp. Jude felt a gut-wrenching sensation shoot through his body. "What do you suggest?" He could think of no worthwhile comeback to help their cause.

As if flicking a switch, Jeremy turned serious again. "I'm sure you're aware we can call on all types of people who work for us. You can be taken, just like that!" He snapped his fingers aggressively. "Whatever outcome we decide appropriate. And you'll never see it coming. Could have happened already, and Gordon wanted to do it. Why take the risk of having you running around like loose cannons?" He spread his hands in an expansive gesture, as if appealing to common sense, intent on striking maximum fear into their hearts.

When neither replied, Jeremy continued, enjoying the power he wielded. His eyes fixed on Lara's trembling face. "Gordon favours getting you back to finish what we started. Such potential. He says why let it go to waste? I have to agree about that." The insidious laugh was back, his cruel gaze holding Lara captive. "But I convinced him to hold off for now. We can have you picked up anytime. If another option doesn't work out."

Lara was becoming distressed. Jude could feel her body shaking as she clutched hold of him. He was far from calm himself, desperate to find solid ground. But there was nothing to relieve Lara's vulnerability. "What other option?"

Jeremy turned his attention to Jude. "You are willing to cooperate. That's good." The smile again, and return to cynical sarcasm. "It's so wonderful to see young love flourishing. Not exactly what your father expected from you, of course. But we can help Chas through that. As long as you help him, that is. Naturally, he is anxious, needs reassurance you will testify with the right evidence at his trial. So good we come to an understanding on that."

"Is that all? Just to help Chas?" Jude was sceptical. Hard to believe that's all this was about. But then, he realised the importance for Jeremy and Gordon to shore up anyone who knows about their operation. Chas could be a threat if left exposed to talking the wrong way in evidence. "Chas is not my father, by the way." The prospect of perjuring himself in court for someone he now despised, acquiescing to Jeremy's demand, did not appeal, only adding to Jude's stress level.

"Oh really. You're so unkind to your father. The DNA test is proof. That will be used in court." Jeremy paused, making sure the point was made. "But you ask is that all. No, Chas is a sidelight issue. There is something much more useful you can do." He leaned forward, switching to serious mode. "Chongwe needs your assistance. He has plans to improve Robin capabilities. In ways that will greatly benefit us."

Jude stared at him, disbelief mixed with a new fear. The first time for Jeremy to show any interest in his partner's work. Why now? "The factory has suspended any more work on Robin," he retorted, feeling he must tackle Jeremy on this one. "Chongwe has no authority to do anything. I was at the meeting when he asked. We'll know more on Monday. They might close the place. Why does he need me anyway? I don't have any special skills to do with Robin."

"I'm aware of all that," Jeremy responded dismissively. Another sinister grin. "When a door is closed, it opens a window. Why you? Think of it as an insurance policy. Protection for your love interest here." His eyes darted to Lara, rubbing in the pain. Then back to Jude. "Chongwe will meet you tonight at the factory, outside the side entrance. At eleven o'clock. Make sure you're there."

A gasp of shock from Lara sounded in Jude's ear. Stunned, Jude was lost for a reply. They were trapped! A clandestine late night meeting! Surely confirmation of subversive intent, obviously without the knowledge of factory management. Again he felt sick, with no choice but to cross the threshold onto the wrong side of the law. Never had he even remotely faced such a risk before. He could be framed! If caught, Chongwe would likely take off back to Hong Kong, his stated preference anyway. Entrapment! Jeremy and Gordon installing their own insurance policy. For Lara's sake, Jude was forced to comply.

He thought of a last chance. "Why don't you wait until after Monday? Management is meeting with government, funding might be agreed, the programme continue. Then Chongwe can do what he wants legally."

Jeremy was shaking his head in rebuttal before Jude had finished. "No. No more funding. We've heard already." He sat back, arrogant once more. "The new government is surprising us with their funding priorities, I must say. More money to Child Protection Services. They understand what great work we do, with our focus on troubled children and marriage breakdown. It is always good to be appreciated." He let out a roar of laughter, wallowing in the irony, indulging his penchant for self-aggrandisement.

Hardly noticing the reaction of disgust from Lara and Jude, he continued revelling in his own gratification. "More money for the DP also. Great to see support for these officers, many we know so well. Such wonderful allies since their duties changed, no longer rivals to pick up druggies. Once we re-educated them, of course." Another burst of laughter, his arrogance extreme, epitomising the cynical disdain he held towards any opposition. "Upgrading their technology will be so helpful. Yes, I am impressed with our new government." Oblivious to them, he descended into a trance-like self-serving reverie.

Lara eased back from gripping onto Jude. They exchanged looks beyond disgust, witnessing the extent by which evil could corrupt authority. Were DP officers even supplying subjects? Was the new government accommodating it? A systematic breakdown of values in those purporting to be leaders!

"Have you finished?" Jude asked.

Jeremy roused from his self-absorbed state. He stood and folded his chair, about to leave then hesitated. "One more thing." His attention returned to Lara. "About Brent, the man you claim to be your father. Do not speak to him about that. Do not even approach him or attempt to see him. If you do, there will be dire repercussions." He was totally focussed now, another dramatic switch. "I think you know what we can do." Then to Jude, "Don't forget. Eleven o'clock tonight. Chongwe will be waiting." He turned abruptly and strode away.

His last threat to Lara left them staring at each other in astonishment. "I don't want to know my father anymore," Lara bemoaned. "But why is Jeremy so concerned if I did? Even just to see him!"

"Very good question. He seemed afraid. First time I've seen Jeremy afraid of anything." Jude tried to imagine any reason for such a bizarre aversion. "It can only be because your father might say something they don't want you to hear. I wonder what that could be." He paused, his mind incisive. "When they had you in that room, was there any chance to speak to your father?"

Lara grimaced as the memory rekindled. "No, none. They had the gag on me very quickly, before my father arrived. Jeremy deliberately didn't tell him who I was."

"Right." Then another thought. "Jeremy was big on how easily they could pick you up if they wanted. So why haven't they? This might be a reason. Avoid any possible contact with your father. Interesting. Maybe we'll find out some day. But I don't mind if we don't. Best keep well clear of them."

"I have to do community service there tomorrow." The sudden realisation hit Lara with a bang. Then the whole episode with Jeremy hit her and she broke down. Crying, she clutched hold of Jude, quivering with fright as a delayed reaction set in.

Jude held her close, sharing her anguish. But they felt strong together, coming through much already in a short time. A powerful emotional and physical bond had taken root, growing rapidly out of adversity. It sustained them now, transcending the spectre of looming challenges.

"It's okay," Lara whispered, releasing her grasp. A quick smile, a loving kiss helping to ease the stress. "I can deal with it. We can deal with anything. Yours with Chongwe tonight too." She was resilient, her natural cheerfulness not far off resurfacing. Always she could draw on the solid upbringing her two mums had provided.

Jude stroked back a lock of her hair, loving her more. He felt nothing was unachievable. "Let's keep focussed on what we believe in."

The day was still young. As best they could under the circumstances, they went back to enjoying the sun and relaxed beach environment.

Chapter 15

L ight traffic gave way to a deserted minor road as Jude
made the turn. He cruised along slowly, cast into
shadow by the towering factory wall. A half-moon night
and sparsely spaced streetlights took the edge off darkness. The beam from his bike pierced the gloom, bringing
the truck bay into view as he reached the side entrance.
Double doors to facilitate delivery and despatch. He pulled
in, stowing his bike against the wall. A check of his mobile;
just coming up to eleven.

A dark figure emerged from the shadows. Chongwe
offered a muted greeting then moved to unlock the doors.
Inside, he worked a remote, bathing the arena in bright light.
He closed and locked the doors behind them. Jude's sense
of unease immediately heightened. Locked inside removed
the option of escape.

Chongwe carried his own computer. He set it down on the
head technician's bench next to the camera. Without a word
to Jude, he went to the small storeroom, soon returning with
a Robin. He stood it in the centre of the arena. Cautiously,
Jude moved closer, until able to read its ID tag. Robin3.

Still saying nothing, Chongwe started his computer
and connected the camera. He activated Robin3. The

characteristic faint ripple pulsed through its body. Watching with mounting trepidation, Jude recognised the readiness, the greater depth to its dark eyes.

"I improve Robin programme," Chongwe proclaimed proudly. "Now I install. Then we test." He worked his computer. A glow emanated from Robin3's chest, flashing intermittently. Transmission being accepted to the black box. When it stopped, Chongwe moved away from the bench, satisfied.

He joined Jude. Using a handset, he snapped Jude's photo from different angles, greatly exacerbating Jude's nervousness. What was the purpose!? "Maybe Robin need better recognition," Chongwe explained. "Now you go to corner. I test application." He pointed to the far corner of the arena, meters away.

Unconvinced and distrustful, Jude moved there. Chongwe aimed his handset, firing a green laser dot onto Jude's chest. Suddenly, with lightning speed, Robin3 dashed across, its hand gripping Jude's forearm, using enough force to not hurt but Jude knew he could not break from it. As Robin3 forced him back towards Chongwe, Jude resisted momentarily. A mistake. In a flash, his arm was twisted up behind his back, again with sufficient force to hurt just a little, the threat of worse very obvious. He gave a yelp, more from surprise than pain. Forcibly, Robin3 steered him to Chongwe, then released him.

"Very good." Chongwe was pleased. "Now we test night vision and heat sense. This new, no one do before." Excited, he indicated the dark bowels of factory floor stretching well beyond influence from the arena lights. "You find place to hide. Far from here. Try place Robin not find you. Stay still and quiet."

Jude stared at him, comprehending intent but perplexed as to ultimate purpose. Deeply suspicious but in no position to argue, he headed towards the blackened interior.

Groping his way along the aisles, he found a suitable place far from the arena, squeezing into a small space beneath a bench. Well hidden, he crouched into the corner and waited. The eerie quiet was nerve-racking, accentuating a fearful sense of being hunted.

It seemed an eternity passing. Disbelieving Robin3 could find him in the maze of bays and aisles, he was about to extricate himself when a shuffling of feet sounded close by. Jude's heart beat furiously. The noise stopped. Suddenly, a pair of glowing green eyes were peering at him hauntingly. A hand shot out, grabbing his arm. Busted, he let Robin3 escort him back, willingly to avoid rough treatment.

At the arena, Chongwe was ecstatic. "He find you?"

Jude nodded, calmer now. "How can it do that?" Putting aside the deeper questions, he was genuinely impressed. Not least, undeniably, with Chongwe's creative brilliance.

Chongwe couldn't contain his enthusiasm. "I give touch sense extra power. Heat sense too. Better than human. Fix on body warmth when in range to you. Then night vision. You see eyes go green?"

Jude nodded, the spectre of those haunting green eyes indelibly etched in his brain.

"One more test." Chongwe went to the storeroom. He emerged with a humanlike dummy, setting it down at the far corner of the arena. "I test 'Attack' application." He worked his handset, pointing it at the dummy. The green laser dot highlighted the target.

In a flash, Robin3 was there, wrapping both hands around chin and upper neck. A quick twist and backward jerk, the dummy's head snapped to a crazy angle, left flopping uselessly side to side.

Jude watched, horrified by the brutal finality of the act. No human could resist or withstand such a force.

"All work very good. Robin ready. Break new ground." Gratified, Chongwe deactivated the creature, using his handset this time. He carried the stiffened figure to the storeroom, threw the broken dummy in and locked all away. Then to his computer, disconnecting the camera and closing down. "All recorded," he declared. "But this control everything in field operation." Gleefully, he held up the handset in Jude's face.

Jude was torn between admiration for Chongwe's efforts and trepidation as to potential application in practice. Particularly with Jeremy involved. But for now, he just wanted to leave the place and get home. "Are we finished?"

"Wait." Chongwe fixed him a steely glare. "Message from Jeremy. He say you and lady friend quiet. Tell no one knowledge you have. Your image here." He shook the handset, invading Jude's space with it. "One signal and Robin pick you up. You in system. We can use much benefit anytime. You will be notify if we need you." Exuding self-importance, he held the hard look another moment then swung away quickly, satisfied he'd imparted the message effectively.

Jude felt sick as confirmation of entrapment set in. He'd been thrown over to the wrong side of the law, inside Jeremy

Gordon operations. The only positive was they'd likely leave Lara alone now. But not guaranteed, dependent on compliance per the Jeremy threats. Mutual deterrence at best. How might the images Chongwe had taken of him be used?

In sombre silence, he followed Chongwe to the exit. The arena was pitched into darkness once more and they left. Chongwe locked the double doors behind them, then departed into the night without another word. Jude retrieved his bike and headed home.

Next day, Lara attended the clinic for her community service, feeling more comfortable about it after Jude described his session with Chongwe. Being trapped was alarming, but seemingly in exchange for averting a repeat abduction. To avoid the cafeteria, Jude brought lunch and they went to the beach. Otherwise confined to the clinic, Lara was happy to finish the day and leave without encountering any of their adversaries.

That evening at home, their attention was riveted on the media bringing a news item relevant to the AI factory. After meetings between government and factory management, the drastic reduction in support for AI projects had been confirmed. The Science Minister was being interviewed. A young man with a bright political future, he'd always been staunchly in favour of continuing the Coln initiatives, a stance now putting him at odds with his Leader. The voracious media circus was on to it with typical invasive speed.

The interviewer, Wing Li, was experienced despite her youthful years, expert at maximising opportunity. "Minister, can you explain why the government is closing down projects that you personally have been so keen to support? With particular reference to the Robin and drone programmes at the AI factory."

The Minister cleared his throat, straightaway under pressure. He gave a quick laugh. "Well, you know how it is. In running a country, it is all about priorities, not always possible to get everything you want. Sometimes it is necessary to compromise. For the greater good."

"You sound disappointed," Wing Li countered, noting the potential for a rift. "Can you outline some aspects of the greater good?"

"Certainly." The Minister had his answers prepared, the questions not unexpected. "It is well known this government's priorities are to catch up on long-neglected social issues, at least to begin with. Further down the track, projects such as you mention will come back strongly, I have no doubt." He hesitated, struggling to find the middle ground, trying to justify all angles. "Technical problems at the AI factory are well documented. An enquiry is in progress. We must wait for the results of that, then decide further."

"It seems the enquiry has become rather a lame duck," Wing Li retorted incisively. "Since your government has already decided to close the factory down."

The Minister was quick to respond, in danger of being pushed out on a limb. "No, that's not true. Besides, there are many projects to consider, not just the AI factory."

"Can you name some of these other projects?" Wing Li was determined not to let him off lightly. "And isn't there a danger of losing high value technical personnel?"

"We are not closing down any projects, as you wrongly suggest. Just taking stock and reassessing. I think you should wait for the Budget. Not long to go now. Then all will be revealed." Back on safe ground again. Another hesitation, weighing up how much to divulge. "One thing I can tell you will be in the Budget. We believe the private use of drones has gone too far, too indiscriminate and intrusive on people's lives. So future funding will be public sector only, such as to enhance the DP for instance. We will not only cease giving funding assistance to private sector development, but also intend to curtail, even outlaw, the use of drones by individuals and private organisations." He gave Wing Li a sharp look. "That will impact the body you work for. All media outlets in fact."

Wing Li's eyes widened in surprise. Slightly flustered, she was unusually lost for a comeback. "Thank you, Minister. We appreciate your time."

As the interview concluded, Jude looked thoughtfully at Lara. "Well, he said not much there we didn't know already. Full of diplomatic double-talk. Except maybe taking the drones thing further."

"Yes, but it's mostly what he didn't say," Lara agreed.

"Right. He was probably scripted to talk about drones. Not much conviction coming across. Really he's worlds apart from the Prime Minister. No telling what might happen there."

The following day, they were lying on the beach amongst a large Sunday crowd when a breaking news item came through.

"This is interesting." Jude held his mobile closer for Lara to see. Heads together, they focussed on the screen.

A luxury launch, berthing at the far North Queensland port of Cairns, was under police guard, the crew of ten arrested, a large haul of amphetamine drugs confiscated. Exposure was by an Australian news media team, having covertly tracked the launch continuously for months. Highly secretive investigative journalism, using drone surveillance, study of social media and in conjunction with media counterparts in Hong Kong, from where shipments originated. A pattern established of regular cruising between the two destinations, calling in at exotic or receptive locations along the way. An elaborately devised hidden compartment in the bowels of the boat had apparently escaped detection, repeatedly, by Customs officials. Questions were being asked. Police only informed upon certainty of sufficient evidence gathered.

Usually, the voyages involved six crew. The boat's owner/captain, his offsider, their wives and a male married couple. All aged early to late thirties. On this occasion, two other couples had joined them. The investigative team had patiently waited for the opportune moment to nail not only the regular sea-goers but also the higher echelons of their drug-running operation. One of the additional couples was a Federal Labour MP and his wife, the other a senior DP officer and his wife.

"Wow!" Jude exclaimed, incredulous. "That's a full-blown scandal about to erupt."

Lara let out a low whistle, shaking her head slowly in dismay. "This goes right to the top. How many other MPs and DP involved?"

Another thought struck Jude. He pointed to the section of text describing the participants. "Same-sex male couple?" He gave Lara a worried look. "Guess who else might be involved?"

Lara's mouth dropped open in shocked realisation. "Drugs too?"

They peered closely at the screen as Jude scrolled slowly through the names and images of arrested persons, but neither recognised anyone they knew. He saved the information to file folder for future reference.

"There's more to come for sure," he concluded, then added, "I'm keen to watch the financial report on tonight too. You know, the money trail? Last one before the Budget. Could be revealing, after that Leaders' interview the other night."

At home that evening, they settled back to view the regular quarterly event on big screen. The national broadcaster, compered by Sharon, was presenting. Their chief economics analyst, Hangsu, outlined the general state of the economy, quoting up-to-date statistics and indicators, then focussed on the more contentious aspects.

"Balance of payments has worsened considerably, after a downward trend starting two quarters ago and seems to be accelerating. The upcoming Budget is expected to remain in surplus, but small only, greatly reduced from last year's final Coln Budget." He went on to detail the main contributing forces. Exports steadying, due to reduced demand for coal, an established trend over several years that Coln had factored in as renewable energy continued to overtake clean coal. But also due to lower Manufacturing productivity, a recent reversal under Labour and not expected. Imports higher to supply domestic consumption. Significant job losses featuring, tax receipts down, government spending up especially in Social Security, and the Health sector to complement State spending.

"Thank you, Hangsu, for your input," Sharon commended. "We'll come back to you if we need further clarification."

Next was an interview with the Treasurer, by video link. Faced with the poor economic figures, he went on the offensive. "The Coln surplus was built at great cost," he contended, unwilling to concede anything to his predecessor. "In pushing through their programmes, often ruthlessly, respected social conventions were corrupted, people's rights trampled on, privacy concerns treated with contempt. As the Prime Minister reiterated the other night, we believe the spoils of prosperity should be shared by all people of the nation. This is our intention, to restore the social balance, while we have the economic means to do so. And our upcoming Budget will still be in surplus, so really there is nothing to worry about."

Sharon interrogated him further, questioning the drastic downward slide and effects of losing technical expertise, however he remained intransigent in espousing new Labour's philosophy. Shifting tack, Sharon asked, "Okay Treasurer, since your government is focussed on promoting social and moral welfare, can you explain how one of your MPs was implicated today in a drug-smuggling operation?"

The Treasurer hesitated, but was expecting the issue to be raised. "Yes, we've heard the reports. We knew nothing of this and are waiting on further information. Until then, I can't comment, except to say if the allegations are proven, and I stress they are only allegations at present, that does not alter any of Labour's beliefs and principles. It only means one member who has failed to uphold Labour values, nothing more."

"I see." Sharon gave a knowing smile, his answer predictable. But another issue was relevant. "Treasurer, yesterday the Science Minister confirmed in an interview that you will no longer permit use of drones by the private sector, including by the media. Yet drone surveillance was instrumental in detecting, tracking and finally exposing the drug-runners captured today. Can you explain how removing this capability squares with your so-called restoring the social balance? Or do you consider drugs to not be a social problem in this country?"

Momentarily stung, he made no immediate reply, prompting Sharon to continue, "Treasurer, at the same time as removing a vital tool in the war against drug traffickers, you intend greatly increasing drone technology for the DP. Another of the drug-runners caught today was a senior DP officer. Can you explain the logic behind your reasoning? Do you think a reappraisal is warranted?" More damaging questions were on her lips, but Sharon restrained herself.

"No, the issues are unconnected," the Treasurer responded irritably, determined to regain the ascendency. "Quite frankly, Sharon, to suggest that somehow we are complicit with drug-smugglers is very offensive. I believe the Police were on the point of intercepting this boat anyway. It is not for the news media to do the work of the Police."

"Well, that's interesting, Treasurer. I never suggested you are complicit with drug-smugglers. I'm not sure where that comes from, why you ---" She stopped abruptly, putting a hand quickly to her earpiece. "Excuse me a moment ---" She paused, a message coming through. Looking a little startled, she returned attention to the Treasurer. "I just received some breaking news. Another of your Labour colleagues, a State Cabinet Minister this time, has been implicated in today's drug bust. Queensland's Minister of Family and Child Protection Services."

A crushing silence followed, as if time was suspended, awaiting response to a damning challenge. Eventually, the Treasurer replied, "Obviously, I cannot comment at this point, until we know more. But a State Minister, you said. That's a matter for the State Premier to address."

Sharon nodded imperceptibly. "Okay, but Federal and Queensland State government are very close, we know. I'm sure there's a lot more to come on this." She eyed him coolly. "Perhaps we can move on to something else. Treasurer, can you enlighten us on why the quarterly figures show such a spike in Social Security and Health spending?"

"Well, I wouldn't call it a spike," he refuted, glad of the shift to familiar territory. "These numbers can be quite volatile. No doubt it reflects the wonderful initiatives in the social arena we've been following through on, as promised. More spending on Health, yes. I'm sure all the viewers out there would be very happy to see us spending more in this vital sector, catching up."

Sharon questioned him on the particular areas of cost blow-out, but he continued to reply in general terms, intent on avoiding specifics. "All will be clear on Budget night," he concluded. That signalled the end of the interview, a some-what unfulfilling exercise.

Next to come on screen was Coln's Deputy Leader. Like the Shadow PM, Carmen had long experience through their years in power, reaching her leadership position at the time of late upheaval. She was well-versed in financial matters.

Offered the opportunity to comment on the latest quarterly figures, Carmen launched into a blistering attack on Labour policies. She cited projects and enterprises closing or downsizing, including the AI factory, highlighting the direct link to severely reduced R and D funding. In the process, she reiterated much of the well-known Coln doctrine. A series of questions and answers followed, a good rapport in evidence between the two women.

"Of course," Carmen emphasised, "with reduced activity comes reduced tax receipts, higher unemployment, a crash in Budget figures. That's basic economics. But this government has no understanding of that. Or any interest, it would seem."

Well into her stride, she required no further prompting to castigate Labour for their actions and inactions alike. "Sharon, I watched your last guest. What the Treasurer didn't say spoke volumes about their twisted priorities. On drones for instance, as confused and choked with hypocrisy as you could imagine." She paused, catching breath for a further assault.

Sharon took the opportunity to slip in a question. "Carmen, can you rule out any Coln members being involved in the drugs scandal breaking today, or any other matters of the sort? As you may have heard, two Labour MPs, one a Cabinet Minister, have been implicated."

"Sharon, we set up Rehabilitation Centres for drug users. I think that answers your question. This government has closed them down! How hypocritical is that!? Labour is not only incompetent and backward-looking, they are rotten on the inside. Let's see how many others are implicated in coming days."

"Okay, I'd like to move on," Sharon resumed, trying to keep a straight face. "The economic quarter shows the continuing trend of increased spending is particularly noticeable in the Social Security and Health sectors. Can you comment?"

"Thank you, Sharon. Yes, this is a worry." Carmen took a deep breath, ready to re-launch. "You know, from when we began years back achieving surpluses, the Federal Budget contributed a greater and greater share to Health, which pre-Coln was largely State responsibility. We kept a close watch on this ever-increasing demand. Now, I believe the Health figures are spiking in one or two specific areas. Perhaps you should talk to our Health spokesperson, she'll have a better perspective on this than me."

"As for Social Security, it is as we've talked about already. Unemployment, Disability Insurance, these have spiked, caused by massive job losses. Single-parent payments are way too high. The reversion to backward self-indulgent issues like discrimination and prejudice, enabled and encouraged by Labour, has many claiming victim status, easiest is to take a benefit handout." She paused, allowing her words to sink in. "When we were in office, we climbed beyond these attitudes. By and large, the people came with us. Not anymore, now it's all regressing back. And of course, the drugs problem, further adding to the spiking figures in both these sectors."

Sharon was giving Carmen's assessment considerable thought. "Do you see the figures as having a strong correlation to where we are as a nation?" she pursued. "In social terms, that is. If so, how much do you attribute this to changing values over the years?"

"Most certainly there's a correlation." Carmen gave a quick smile. "I'm no psychologist, Sharon, so I'll leave the social commentary to others more qualified. But changing values define us, I have no doubt about that. Often the winds of change are not felt until years later. The advent of same-sex marriage, for instance. Who was to know how that would manifest in today's world? Not only the impact on Social Security we've been discussing, with a whole new class of claimant created, but the effect of multi-parent relations, the confusing examples and expectations on children growing up in those situations. We in government presided over the period when this evolved through its infancy to where it is today, so we understand the issues." Another pause, again the smile. "Of course, if you ask Labour, they will only talk about discrimination and equality."

Sharon decided prudence was advisable, resisting the temptation to escalate a controversial topic. "Your comments will spark plenty of interest out there, I'm sure. Perhaps a debate for another day." With that, she ended the interview.

The broadcaster was trying unsuccessfully to contact a Health spokesperson from either side of politics, but did manage to locate the President of the National Medical Association. She came on-screen, keen to contribute.

"Thank you, Nadi, for joining us at short notice," Sharon began. "Nadi, we've just had the Coln Deputy Leader talking about blow-outs in Health spending. I wonder if you could shed some light on this?"

Nadi gave a general overview of where government funding had increased in line with rising costs and galloping technological advance. Administrative, operational, supply to public hospitals, research and Mental Health were areas of growing demand. The prolific use of robotics, leading to regular breakthroughs in non-invasive surgery and cancer treatment, keeping AI at the fore. And the quest for new drugs and vaccines, an ongoing race against treatment-resistant superbugs and viruses that often mutated to thwart success. Always at critical levels of urgency and a major cause of cost blow-out, hospital facilities becoming overloaded with cases of untreatable infections. Nadi pointed to one in particular.

"The biggest problem is New AIDS. We can't control the numbers of people presenting now with this horrible condition. Ever since the HIV virus that leads to AIDS mutated, known drugs became ineffective. Huge resources are going into research, desperate to find new treatment. But this is the worry with a virus, it can mutate further anytime." She ended with a look of great concern.

A little affected, Sharon moved quickly as a morbid silence ensued. "The Deputy Coln Leader mentioned same-sex marriage and the effects of changing values over time. Do you think this is behind the resurgence of HIV and New AIDS?"

"Yes well, I can't say really. I'll let others in the wider community talk about the social issues. I can only comment from a medical viewpoint. Certainly, it is true New AIDS has only been identified thus far out of same-sex activity. But this can easily change, as it did with original AIDS. The HIV virus is elusive."

Sharon nodded in solemn recognition of a looming crisis. "And you mentioned Mental Health. What's the situation there?"

"Yes. This is a major problem also." Nadi paused, concerned. "In our Mental institutions, suicide, self-harming, the numbers are higher than ever before. Especially in young people."

"Does this correlate in any way to the matters we were just discussing? Like New AIDS and so on?"

"Well, I don't want to point the finger at any one group, I'll leave that to the social commentators. Except to say children, especially teenage and even younger, are at greatest risk. The numbers have been trending the wrong way for years, and considerably higher than the same time last year. It's quite disturbing."

"Thank you, Nadi, for your input."

Sharon finished with a brief summary and thanks to all interview guests.

Having watched enthralled throughout, Jude and Lara shared a sense of bewilderment over the alarming forces at work. The exchanges focussing on same-sex marriage came close to home for both, bringing on uncomfortable questions.

"Gay activity has been around forever," Lara observed, uncomprehending. "Why has this New AIDS only happened since same-sex marriage came in?"

"Good question." Jude returned her a look encapsulating the confusion each felt. "Maybe it reflects the greater freedoms in society. More people of different types inter-acting. Or recruited." He thought of Jeremy's activities. "Higher level of sexual activity. And infidelity too no doubt, goes with the territory, just like heterosexual."

Lara gave him a hug and a kiss. "Not us. I'm with you, that's it." Then another thought. "My mums never talk about this kind of thing. I'm only finding out now."

Jude nodded knowingly. "My fathers the same. But no one talks about what same-sex people actually do, the sex acts they perform. It's not politically correct to talk about social and medical consequences."

Late that Sunday night, a secret meeting was taking place. A serious mood hung over the group. Six men hovering in the centre of the Cave, three of them having just arrived together. Jeremy pulled down a kitchen-style table hinged at the side wall. With fold-down seats, it doubled for meet-ings in their no-frills premises. They settled around the table. A seventh man, Brent, sat as usual at his computer, adrift from the others.

Gordon was first to speak. "We hope you made it here undetected, Karl. After today's revelations, they'll be tracking anyone involved."

Opposite him, Karl gave a nod in recognition. "Quite so. I think it's okay, I was very careful. The media are the problem, we can't control them. Drones can operate unnoticed from high altitude, as you know." A middle-aged man, paunchy and overweight, reddish flushed complexion from regular drinking, receding forehead. His long association with the

Prime Minister since their youthful days at law school had kept him in good stead politically, currently Minister of Family and Child Protection Services in Queensland State Parliament.

"How did the media manage to identify you today? We've always been so thorough in covering anything traceable." Highly concerned, Gordon glanced around the other faces. Signs of strain showing. Only Chas, seated next to Jeremy, was new to the powerful forces at play, but learning fast.

Karl shrugged his shoulders, aware of the heat being applied but not fazed by it, having for years sailed close to the wind successfully. "Kerry and his wife were caught on the boat, joining up for a holiday this time. It's no secret he and I are close, politically and personally. He's in Federal politics, but we work in the same sector. So I'm naturally in the spotlight, by association only at this stage. To keep it that way, I'll have to step back for a while. Until this all blows over."

"Yes, understood." Gordon was thoughtful. "In the meantime, our friends in the Police and DP will keep us safe. As you say, it's the media we have to worry about. How far away is removing drone capability from the media?"

"I've been expediting that, talking directly to the Prime Minister and Treasurer. They are onside with it. Suits the political climate at present." He gave a quick chuckle of amusement. "I think you should talk to the Federal Science Minister. He's not happy, for reasons that suit us very well. I can speak to him and set up a meeting."

"I know Science Minister." It was Chongwe contributing for the first time. "He come to AI factory many time. I talk to him about Robin and drones." He gave the man next to him a sidelong glance. His Chinese compatriot, Mingsu, was a regular traveller liaising to and from Hong Kong. He kept a deadpan expression, giving nothing away.

Jeremy was next to speak. "We need to review our priorities. With this happening today, we have to pull back on the shipments. Until it all blows over, as Karl said. Mingsu, how many shipments are in train at the moment?"

"We have two drug shipments coming, leave Hong Kong already. I will divert to other places. No more will come here for while." Mingsu spoke in a business-like monotone, his facial expression never changing. About the same age as Chongwe, with similar looks, difficult to read his thoughts or body language at any juncture. He went on, "Also I adjust movement of sex partner. You do local only for now." While not a triad boss, he was a senior figure in that hierarchy, his words commanding great respect, intent going unquestioned.

"Yes, very good," Jeremy agreed, remaining astute. "What about arms shipments?"

"No. But this only occasionally involve you."

"True." Jeremy paused, his thoughts turning to future action. "I think we bring forward Operation Robust. Top priority now. We've been planning this long enough and the final upgrade tested well the other night." He looked meaningfully at Chongwe, who nodded confirmation.

"I agree," Gordon responded. "As you say, Mingsu, we'll focus just on local until further notice. Easiest to keep safe where we have the strongest protective contacts. So it's the ideal time to introduce Robust in practice." Looking serious, he surveyed the faces before him, gratified by the unanimous support evident.

They went on to discuss logistical issues. Each participant with a specific role, but collectively the same goal. The way forward clear, the meeting dispersed.

"Any new material?" Karl asked Gordon, before heading for the exit.

"Yes, sure." Gordon produced the latest video stick from the drawer by his computer. He copied the contents to Karl's mobile. No payment. The price of having the right contacts.

Karl cracked a sleazy grin, his eyes bulging, body perspiring as he anticipated indulging himself. "How about a piece?"

"No problem. We're expecting Robust will net us good quality. When would you like?"

"One night next week. I'll let you know." Gratified, Karl departed.

Chapter 16

The second week of school holidays was shaping up similar to the first. Jude attended the Monday morning meeting at the factory, but it was no more than reaffirmation of a holding pattern for the two major projects. The greatly reduced workforce would keep the factory open for its other commitments, but these were of much less interest to Jude. His menial tasks boring, he found the time dragged, pleased to get home at day's end. He didn't see Chongwe at all, not even at the meeting.

More and more, he felt a burden of responsibility to act somehow on what he knew. The activities of Jeremy and Gordon were pure evil, but seemingly Lara and himself were the only people on the outside aware. Spilling knowledge to the authorities would only invite the drastic retribution Jeremy had threatened and could easily instigate. And he had no faith anyone he might tell was not themselves complicit. Nothing he could do.

"We could find out more," Lara suggested, when Jude put his concerns to her. "Very secretly of course." She hesitated, reconsidering. "No, it's too dangerous. Just let it go."

"I keep thinking about Chas. What have they got him doing?" He slowly shook his head, still struggling to reconcile the traumatic events engulfing his family. "I've lived in the same house with him all my life, but feel like I hardly know him."

"You've been to where he's living now with Jeremy and Chongwe. How about we watch from a safe distance and follow him when he goes out?" Lara gave an impish smile, the idea appealing despite the dangers.

Jude loved her positive intent. The prospect of meaningful action uplifted him. "You mean like private detectives do?" he commented with a laugh. "Yes, why not?"

"Let's go now. Late afternoon a good time."

For disguise, they changed into darker clothing and donned caps, then left home on Jude's bike.

Reaching their destination, a quiet suburban street, they parked at an old bus shelter conveniently located opposite and a short way past the house of interest. The shelter's side wall offered part concealment. They sat, prepared to wait indefinitely.

It was near dark when a vehicle approached then turned into the driveway. Jeremy and Chas alighted. And, surprisingly, a Robin! Activated, it followed the others to the house obediently.

Lara let out a gasp of dismay. "Didn't expect that! How come they've got a Robin?"

"No idea. I'm sure Jeremy and Chongwe weren't allocated one in the trial." Jude shook his head, perplexed. He caught a glimpse of its face. The ID was not branded, instead a tag. "See that? Only three Robins have a tag ID! Couldn't quite make it out, but I bet it's the one from the other night. Robin3. Chongwe's not with them, though." The late night session at the factory was vivid in his mind.

"Let's wait. Maybe they'll go out again."

Well into the evening, the same three figures emerged from the house. They clambered into the vehicle, Jeremy reversed out and they departed.

"Come on, let's follow them," Jude exclaimed excitedly. He retrieved his bike from behind the shelter and they headed after them, keeping a safe distance back.

Jeremy was making for the seedier side of town. They approached the 'Valley', notorious for its nightclubs, strip joints and sex shows of all variety. Home to or frequented by a wide range of character types exploiting for self-gratification or exploited in their vulnerability, and all shades between. A predator's playground.

The night was young, most entertainment outlets yet to open. Plenty of people were roaming the gloomily lit streets. Traffic was diverted away, leaving the central precincts free. Jeremy pulled into a parking area at the fringes. Careful to stay out of sight, Jude followed, finding a set of racks to stow the bike.

"They went that way," Lara indicated, hastening after the three figures.

Soon immersed in the crowd, Lara and Jude kept them in sight, watching their every move. Quickly apparent was the number of DP officers present, in pairs mingling freely amongst the people, on the lookout for misdemeanours. Several times, a pair stopped to greet Jeremy and chat briefly. Further evidence of the strong insider contacts he and Gordon had cultivated to advantage. Mild interest in Robin3 from passers-by signified its presence was unusual but not alarming. Most people had seen at least one on occasion in the course of the community-wide hundred-Robin trial.

An unshaven, haggard-looking youth barred Jude's way, begging for a handout. Disgusted, Jude refused and pushed past him. Lara also was held up on the busy walkway. She mouthed an oath, sidestepping around him. Impoverished druggies not uncommon in this part of town. His desperation was palpable. But unlikely anyone would supply a fix for free and few people carried cash these days in a world largely of card-only transactions.

"Damn!" Jude cursed. "Now we've lost them!" They shouldered their way through, anxiously searching for a glimpse of Jeremy, Chas or Robin3.

Suddenly, a disturbance further on. People were spreading away, leaving a small group on their own in the middle of the walkway. Shouting and yelling was from a young girl distraught, confronted by a pair of DP officers. Her partner, a clean-cut well-dressed teenage lad, was screaming obscenities, immobilised by Robin3 twisting his arm up behind his back. Jeremy and Chas stood close by. With control established, Jeremy stepped in. A quick word to the officers, then they departed back the way they'd come, Robin3 propelling the irate youngster forward. His girlfriend was left behind.

About to be exposed, Jude quickly backed into a darkened shop entrance recess, pulling Lara in with him. Spellbound, they cringed back in dread as Jeremy and the officers passed. Then Robin3, but it stopped abruptly, turning its head to them. Its eyes blazed green, directly at them! Momentary only but chilling, striking fear to the core. Robin3 proceeded on, shoving its captive ahead, Jeremy not alerted.

Trembling with fright, Lara clutched Jude's arm, frozen to immobility. Similarly gripped with inertia, Jude stared after the back of Chas disappearing into the crowd. Suddenly, he was galvanised. "Come on, we have to see where they're taking that boy." Incredibly, a sense of outrage surged inside him, replacing the fear. His own contribution, helping Chongwe test the creature's upgrade, was manifesting in practice.

They stepped out and tracked the party back to the parking area, able to witness Robin3 forcibly bundling the unfortunate victim into Jeremy's car. One DP officer climbed in with them. Jeremy drove away. Jude and Lara ran to the bike and were soon following, again at safe distance.

Travelling a considerable way through suburbs, Jeremy eventually reached an old industrial area at the edge of town. It was deserted, the streetlighting poor. At the end of a cul-de-sac lined with warehouses, Jeremy took the last driveway. The vehicle headlights illuminated a rough gravel roadway ahead, barely passable in its overgrown state. He stopped outside a derelict warehouse.

Jude and Lara pulled up short. Having switched off the bike's headlight several streets back, a hiding place was hard to find in near darkness. A stone wall fronted one property. They took station behind it. Peering over, they could make out figures moving in a pool of light, Robin3 marching the young captive inside the building. It was over quickly. Mindful of Robin3's enhanced night vision and heat sense capability, they ducked down as the vehicle turned, slowly moved out then sped away.

"Here we go again," Jude muttered. They pushed the bike out and started after them.

"Where to now?" Lara mused, holding tight around Jude's midriff.

Jeremy led them back to the Valley. The same scenario played out again. This time, Jude and Lara were able to witness use of the handset. The sequence was simple, irresistible. Cruise for prey, identify, green laser dot picking out target, Robin3 moving in to capture. Chas performed the task. Another respectable-looking male youth ripped from his girlfriend's side, kicking and screaming. Shrieks of terror burst forth, onlookers scattering, DP officers present and enabling it. Another victim snared, marched back to the vehicle. Again one officer accompanied them as Jeremy drove away, maintaining the appearance of action sanctioned and performed by the mandated DP.

Activity on the streets quickly returned to normal. But people were nervous, word spreading fast of the repercussions if caught contravening regulations policed by the DP. Fewer were roaming the walkway, everyone fearful. Also patronising the nightclubs, sex shows and discos well underway at the late night hour. A changed atmosphere, darker mood prevalent. Flanked by stoic hard-headed bouncers, flashy doormen plied their trade, cajoling passers-by inside, offering titillation, pleasure, prostitution. And the ever-present DP patrolling up and down.

Lara was mindful of another occasion. "That's how Jodie and I got caught, going to a sex shop," she whispered to Jude, as they took a final walk through. "I've learnt to be more careful what I say." Her interest was very different now.

"Same for everyone," Jude concurred, looking around furtively. "But with Jeremy and Robin3 lurking, you don't even have to do anything wrong. Can't trust any DP."

Passing a dingy side alley, they noticed a dishevelled individual slumped against a building wall. His gaunt sunken face with bloodshot eyes was upturned towards a man standing over him. An exchange taking place. The tough-minded drug pusher, unsmiling and looking only marginally of better station in life, dropped a small parcel in the other's lap then left quickly, brushing past Lara with oblivious impunity.

"That's stark!" Lara uttered, shocked.

"Where does he get the money to pay for it?" Jude murmured, keeping his voice low. "Social Security, I suppose."

Back at the parking area, the atmosphere less confronting, Jude paused to gather his thoughts. Affected by the night's revelations, Lara came to him and they hugged, drawing strength from each other. "Jeremy could do that to us!" she lamented. With plenty to ponder, they retrieved the bike and departed the Valley.

In the safe confines of home, Jude's mind was abuzz. "Did you notice the type of person Jeremy chose?" he considered reflectively. "Young and respectable, not low class. Plenty of druggies out there he could easily pick up and no one would care, they wouldn't be missed. But he's recruiting. We know what he and Gordon are capable of."

"Yes. And male only," Lara added, disgusted. "He didn't want the girl each time."

"Right. They're deliberately targeting heterosexual, aiming to convert them. Increase same-sex numbers." A familiar sick sensation struck his insides as he tried to comprehend the rationale. "Up till now, they've only targeted kids in trouble, loose on the streets, from broken homes. Vulnerable ones easiest to recruit. But this is a leap further, a higher ambition using Robin3."

Lara was unsure. "But how can they convert someone who's not really gay? I don't understand that."

"Good question." Jude shook his head slowly, bereft of a good answer. "They have their methods, we know that. I think we can assume they're into drugs. With the right drugs expertly administered, anyone can be indoctrinated. Drugs changes people."

Lara felt a cold shiver run down her spine. "That's really scary. It might have happened to me, if you hadn't saved me." She flung her arms around him again. "We know too much. What are we going to do?"

"Yep." Their options were few. "Let's hope the mutual deterrence holds up." He knew it was precarious at best. "Right now, what I think we should do is go to bed. And see what we can do there." He gave a quick chortle.

Lara responded in like kind, leaping to her feet, pulling Jude up by the hand and they headed for the bedroom.

Another day at the factory, another dose of boredom. The tedious tasks were of little worth in providing the technical training for which he'd been engaged. Jude seriously considered walking out and not coming back, but he'd made a commitment and would honour that. More importantly, if any further developments occurred, the factory was a likely place to pick up on it. Still he saw no sign of Chongwe, such a crucial figure. Chongwe's direct connection to Jeremy precluded any notion Jude had of informing factory management about the corrupted use of Robin3.

Marcel was organising a rearrangement of the factory floor to more efficiently support altered priorities. He wanted to relocate the small portable storeroom, enlisting a couple of technicians and Jude to help. Needing to first remove the items inside, he unlocked and opened the storeroom door. Immediately, a shock.

"Where are the Robins!?" He swung round, looking for someone to enlighten him.

Jude could see inside the storeroom. No Robins. All three gone! He took a step back, stunned. RobinB and Robin2 joining the Jeremy train? Very likely. Had Chongwe upgraded their software the same as for Robin3? Probably. What escalation now in Jeremy Gordon operations from a three times heightened Robin capability!? A wave of nausea swept through him as he envisaged potential ramifications. Surely they couldn't get away with this? The authorities must catch up with them. But he knew significant elements of the DP and Police, even politicians, were not only enabling it but actively involved. How extensive was the Jeremy Gordon network?

He backed away, conscious not to give an impression of knowing anything. Marcel was already on his way to inform management. Soon the factory was buzzing, a search conducted for the missing Robins, everyone questioned.

Jude also, but no one suspected him. And no one could shed light on the mystery. Chongwe appeared briefly, putting on a show of concern. Superficial. He gave Jude a sly look, obvious vibes coming over, then retreated quickly to the computer centre. Pointedly, he was quiet, no more aggressive threats about returning to Hong Kong, despite ostensibly dissatisfied with a greatly depleted workload. Jude knew why, and how dangerous he could be.

Later in the day, the Science Minister visited. Jude glimpsed him entering the main office. Hardly a surprise. A while elapsed before he emerged, then entered the computer centre. A little surprising. Not long there, he reappeared to straightaway leave the building. Very soon after, Chongwe appeared and hurried to the building exit. The distinct impression was of an association between them. Meeting elsewhere, leaving separately to allay suspicion?

Media outlets were reporting on use of a Robin robot by the DP to detain social behaviour offenders. A couple of eyewitnesses from the Valley gave accounts, raising concerns. Denied access to see their sons in detention, the parents were outraged. The Science Minister, on interview, when asked to elaborate confirmed the escalation in DP capability, to complement enhanced drone surveillance announced recently. He intimated the government may further review the Robin programme. Also stated that the detainees had been released after questioning and issuing of citations.

"Wow!" Jude stared at Lara in dismay as they caught up with the news that evening. "That's not what we saw.

Detainees released!? That's a straight out lie. He's involved too! I saw him today, meeting Chongwe on the sly."

"Three MPs involved now, two of them Cabinet Ministers!" Lara was equally astounded.

"That we know of. Maybe more!"

Next day, the factory was shrouded in an even more sombre mood, workers further dispirited following the actions of Robin. No one knew who was responsible. Jude stayed watchful, however the day wore on with no appearance or signs of intent by management or Chongwe. Into the afternoon, he began looking forward to viewing the regular weekly session between Prime Minister and Coln Leader tonight. Surely fireworks, the PM certain to take a roasting over intentions surrounding Robin. In cahoots with the devil? Jude was confident he and Lara would detect any indications.

Mid-afternoon, little left to do. He returned to the arena. Two Police officers had entered the building. Not DP, but they were purposeful, looking for someone. They spied Jude, immediately changed direction and headed towards him.

"Are you Jude?" one of them asked. Perplexed, Jude gave confirmation. The officer checked his ID, then continued, "You're under arrest. For murder." In a stunning condemnation, he formally read Jude his rights and detailed the charge. The other officer moved behind and applied handcuffs. They confiscated his mobile, then led him out past bemused workers.

Numbed with shock, Jude could only comply. Tongue tied, his head spun in a whirl of confusion. At police headquarters, he was taken to a secured interview room. A bare table in the middle with wooden chairs was the only furniture, large screen on one wall the outstanding feature. Seated to face the screen, Jude waited, tense and fearful. The interview officer set down his computer, sat and proceeded to play a video clip.

It was the scene of Brett's slaying at their home, extricated from RobinB memory. But instead of Chas carrying out the murderous rampage, Jude was doing it! All actions exactly replicated. Similarly, Chas images were in place of Jude wherever he appeared in the sequence. The audio also, Chas and Jude voice intonations seamlessly swapped.

Horrified, Jude jerked forward in his seat, spluttering, "That's ---- that's ----," choking on the words. His heart beat furiously. Desperately, he fought to control himself. "That's Faketing!" he eventually blurted out. "That's Faketing!"

The officer sat back, smiling condescendingly. "The video has been checked by experts and found to be authentic. No one does Faketing nowadays. It is detectable and the penalties are very severe."

Jude knew as much. Faketing had nearly ruined the internet years ago. Undoubtedly, this was the work of Chongwe, his brilliant expertise surpassing known detection techniques. Coupled with Jeremy Gordon stooges infiltrating everywhere, complicit. He felt overwhelmed by the devastating forces at play. With no expectation of impressing, he managed to ask, "Why would I want to kill my father? That's crazy." His quivering voice was beginning to return more even, heartbeat steadying.

"It is." The officer gave him a dispassionate look that lacked empathy. "Are you aware of DNA tests done recently that prove who your father is?" When Jude failed to respond, he went on, "How did you feel when you found out Brett was not your real father? Were you angry with him?"

"This is sick," Jude responded, overpowered by a sense of helplessness. "Chas was angry, not me. Because he'd just been given proof Brett WAS my father. Have you seen the other test results? Done when I was small?" A feeling of indignation and vague hope were kicking in, yet he knew his plight was hopeless.

"No, there are no other tests." The officer leant forward. He replayed the portion of clip showing Chas fleeing the scene. "You say he was angry. But you can see how terrified he is of you, running to get away."

Jude stared at the screen, dumbfounded. Incredibly, the Faketing ended at a point unseen. After RobinB viewed Brett prone on the floor, the Chas and Jude images reverted back true in time to square with what others arriving at the house or outside saw. His heart sank as he realised how clever Jeremy and Chongwe were, covering all bases, including control of whoever in authority was handling the DNA evidence.

The officer continued his interrogation. "How do you feel about same-sex people?"

A strange question. Jude sensed a trap. "I've been brought up in a same-sex family," he replied cautiously, deciding the less he said the better.

The officer seemed disinterested in his answer. "Your father Chas says you always resented being in a same-sex family. That you rejected contact with same-sex people. You have a girlfriend, not same-sex. Are you prejudiced? Maybe you harbour hatred towards same-sex, built up over years. Is this what came out in your actions against Brett?" He held Jude in a steady gaze, intent on nailing him to a preconceived portrayal.

Jude was seething, aware he was being railroaded. He knew the interrogation was recorded, anything he said able to be manipulated or re-constituted to suit a purpose. Bitterly resigned, he decided best to say nothing.

The interrogation over, he was led to the administration wing for processing. Then to the remand cells, where he would remain incarcerated pending a court hearing next day to decide bail.

Alone in his cell, Jude slumped to the narrow bed. He contemplated his fate. Nothing attributable to Jeremy, Gordon or Chongwe was a surprise anymore. Yet the thought of copping the demise meant for Chas was like poison gnawing at his guts. He could see no way out, nothing available to challenge their power. Nevertheless, he resolved to pursue every avenue possible for justice once released on bail. With that, he felt a little better.

His mind turned to Lara. How vulnerable she was! Would Jeremy and company, feeling threatened, target her too? Jude lay back on the bed and stared at the ceiling, gripped by an overwhelming dread over Lara's safety.

His was part-way along a row of cells separated by open bar walls. The adjacent on one side was vacant, on the other a rough-looking youth ignored him. That suited Jude. The light was gloomy from bare bulbs spaced along the access corridor ceiling. No windows in the block, no way of knowing the time without his mobile. He estimated early evening.

A warder came and escorted him to the visitors room. Dulcie and Lara were waiting on the other side of a thick glass partition at one in a row of cubicles. He sat opposite them and lifted the handset to communicate. Both women were clearly upset.

"Why are you here?" Lara lamented, bewildered. They'd not been told any details.

When Jude explained the murder charge, she gave a shocked gasp. Dulcie reacted with a whimpering cry. Trying to keep calm, he described the circumstances, the evidence of Faketing, the accusations of same-sex prejudice. Suddenly, communication was cut off. A moment later, the warder appeared at his shoulder, pulling him to his feet. Visitation, obviously monitored, was over. Jude caught a final glimpse of the two beloved women in his life standing distraught at the glass, before the warder whisked him away.

Back in his cell, Jude broke down crying, head in his hands as he slumped to the bed, the pressure of it all overbearing. He was interrupted by the warder bringing a bag of items and clothes Lara had left. And a meal. He picked at it, too churned up to eat. Nothing but his thoughts to occupy time. Soon it was lights out, the block plunged into semi-darkness, a dimmed light kept on at each end of the corridor.

His sleep was fitful. Time passing seemed interminable. Eventually, the lights came on. Breakfast delivered. The silence was deafening, the warder uncommunicative. Inmates of the other cells were quiet, a minor blessing at least. He ate a little. Nothing else to do. His mind was on the court hearing. Bail a formality, surely. The prospect of freedom perked him up. Soon he'll be back with Lara. He waited patiently.

The morning wore on. No summons yet. Lunch came and went. The afternoon was passing and he grew agitated. Pacing back and forth, anxious and frustrated, he sensed something was wrong.

At last, two warders appeared. This was it. They unlocked the cell gate and led him out in silence. But they were not going to the courtroom. Instead, it was back to the interview room. With heart in his mouth, he sat behind the table, facing the interrogation officer.

"Your court hearing has been delayed," the officer began. He maintained a hard look into Jude's face, trying to remain impersonal but unable to hide an air of dislike distinctly nastier than yesterday. "There are more charges pending. We are assessing evidence right now." His eyes continued to bore into Jude accusingly. "Yesterday, we talked about your resentment of same-sex people. Where were you three nights ago? Monday night."

Jude's mouth dropped open, his mind flying into a crazy spin. Another railroading on the way? He tried to stay calm, find a way out. "I was with my girlfriend," he replied, struggling to keep his voice steady. "We went into town for a while, to the Valley." Best to admit what was probably known already, he decided. In a flashback, he envisaged Robin3's green eyes briefly blazing as the creature spied them in the shop recess. No doubt enough to inform then galvanise Jeremy.

"Yes, we know that." The officer leaned forward, giving Jude a disdainful look. "In separate incidents that night, two teenage boys were detained by the DP for misbehaviour. The evidence we have is of you following them, then after their release from detention abducting them with the help of a Robin robot. We know you've had extensive access to a Robin, through the community trial programme."

"What!" Jude was horrified. Incensed, he jumped forward in his seat, banging into the table as all his pent-up frustration exploded. "What's this evidence!? Where is it? Show me!" he shouted.

In an instant, two security officers burst in, mobilised by Jude's outburst caught on monitor. The interrogator held a hand up in restraint and they took station each side of Jude as a protective force. Jude eased back, constrained to battling the boiling rage inside him.

"The evidence came through this morning and is being expert assessed," the interrogator resumed. "You will see it in due course. You will remain in custody under the current charge, with further charges likely. The nature of these will depend on what you've done with those boys. Your bail hearing is delayed for the same reason."

"I can show you what happened to the boys," Jude cut in, throwing caution to the winds. "I can take you there. Right now!" Desperate, he no longer cared about Jeremy reprisals. The derelict warehouse loomed huge.

A moment of hesitation from the interrogator was enough. Jude stared at him, incredulous. Why didn't he leap at the chance to find the missing boys? In that moment, Jude knew the officer was another cog in the Jeremy Gordon ring of evil. His spirit plummeted. What chance to combat this ever-widening web?

A response needed, the officer replied, "We'll get to that." But his focus was elsewhere. "Why did you target these boys? Is it your hatred of same-sex?"

Jude continued to stare at him, seeing the quick switch as further proof of complicity, but devastated by the futility of trying to fight it. The hatred label, backing him into a corner, really riled him. "Both those boys were with female partners before they were detained. Why do you accuse me about same-sex? Nothing to do with it!"

"The evidence doesn't show that. It starts with you hiding in a shop recess, waiting for opportunity. You will see once the clip is authenticated." The merest hint of a smirk belied the officer's supposed professional impartiality. "Your feelings against same-sex are renowned, confirmed by your father as lifelong. That's why you're here, already on a murder charge."

Jude felt utterly defeated, his hopes dashed. The setup was cleverly contrived, concocting a plausible motive, ticking all boxes for Jeremy and his cohorts, exonerating Chas. The as-yet unseen video clip another Faketing? Undoubtedly. Authenticated by who? Jeremy's experts? And now, he had only jail time ahead. A better insurance policy for Jeremy and Gordon. And a brilliant rationale for the continued disappearance of the boys ostensibly released from DP detention. Proving also the worth of Chongwe's Robin upgrade. Where was it all heading?

The interrogation was over. "Now you can show us what you did with the boys," the officer pursued.

283

Jude's last hope. Escorted under police guard, he took them to the derelict warehouse. But it was empty, unkempt and bereft, no residual signs of recent habitation. Another devastating reversal for Jude, yet hardly a surprise. Plenty of time for Jeremy to make alternative arrangements. Everything was well coordinated.

They arrived back at the police centre late afternoon, completing an exercise in maintaining appearances, the monitored interrogation likely to be reviewed by others. A show of force threatened Jude into revealing how and where he'd disposed of the boys or their bodies. But it was only a put-on, contrived for the records. He knew the main game was to keep him locked away, out of commission.

He was not long back in his cell when the warder came again, taking him to the visitors room. Dulcie was waiting, alone. She was highly distraught.

"Oh, Jude, Jude!" she cried, beating her hands against the glass partition. "Lara's gone! They took her! They took her!" The tears were streaming down her face.

"What!" Jude stumbled against the partition in a daze. "What happened!? Who took her!?" His voice was choking.

"The DP. They came this afternoon. Two officers." Wiping at the tears, she managed to gain some control of her emotions. "They didn't say why. Just took her. And they threatened me. Told me to tell you ---- oh!" Again she broke down. "They told me ---- if you make more trouble, then we will never see Lara again." She slipped into quiet sobbing.

Jude fell back into the chair, aghast. Struck by a debilitating fear for Lara, he was unable to comfort his mother. An officer appeared and led her away. The warder returned, taking Jude back to his cell.

Chapter 17

"Tell us exactly what happened. We need to be sure these people are sorted out and won't cause more trouble." Jeremy was grim-faced, ever vigilant in stamping on any threat that could expose their operations.

Chas was highly nervous, fidgeting in his seat and avoiding eye contact. "Brent sorted them out. Especially the woman." His voice was shaky. He shuddered, reminded of the brutal treatment Brent had handed out.

"We'll speak to him in a moment," Gordon responded, seriously concerned. He threw a quick glance at their trusty hitman engrossed as usual in his computer at the end of the bench. "Right now, we want to hear the story from you first."

"When you say the woman, I assume you mean the boy's mother," Jeremy added. He turned to Gordon. "Surrogate, using her own egg. The boy's thirteen." Then back to Chas. "So you arrived with the Flasher. What then? Why was the mother there?"

"Yes." Chas was calming. "The fathers said they allow her regular contact. But she turned up unexpected, while I was showing them. Bad timing." He drew a deep breath, relieved he could depict himself as blameless. "She saw the material. They told her it was to help educate their son, but she went crazy off her head, tried to snatch the video stick. That's when I hit the beeper and Brent came."

"Did you bring the stick back?" Gordon looked hard at him.

"Oh yes, no problem." Chas delved in his pocket. He put the stick on the bench.

Jeremy laid a hand on his shoulder. "Okay, you've done good." He caught Gordon's eye. Of one mind in their focus on security.

Gordon called Brent over and they heard his version.

"I took care of them, Boss." Brent's voice was soft and husky, at a light pitch anomalous with the powerful aura surrounding his fearsome physical presence. His facial expression was unchanging. "I put the girl in hospital. The men won't be a problem now either. Did I do good, Boss?" He looked directly at Gordon for validation.

Gordon gave him a light slap on the back. "You did good." Brent returned to his computer.

"We need to be careful here," Jeremy uttered. "I'll notify our DP friends to shore it up, but this is our third crisis in as many days. We can't have too many of these happening, too reliant on our political friends to dampen the media."

"Yes, very true. Especially now we've begun Robust." Gordon was thoughtful, glancing briefly at the three Robins standing deactivated in front of the drones. "We'll keep assessing it stage by stage."

"Chongwe's coming late tonight with Mingsu, to talk about Robust." Jeremy turned to Chas. "That means we've got plenty of time for this other one."

Chas looked puzzled. "What one's that?"

"Didn't I tell you?" Jeremy paused, reflective. "Oh, maybe not. A lot's been happening. There's a boy, been in foster homes all his life. We picked him up wandering around aimlessly on his own. Another lost soul ripe for the taking."

"How old is he?" Chas was learning to be nonchalant, how to let people's pain and distress wash over without touching the emotions.

"Early teenage. He's had health problems on and off all his life. A premature baby rejected by the clients. The surrogate was stuck with him, but she didn't get paid and not well off. No one wanted to adopt him. He's been in and out of a dozen different foster homes. Too hard to handle."

Chas' mouth dropped open, an involuntary reaction. "What about for us? What do we do with him if no one wants him?"

Jeremy spread his hands in an expansive gesture. "There's always a suitable client, for anyone. I have two in mind." He shrugged his shoulders. "If it doesn't work out, we use him for a video, the usual fall-back to plan B. Maybe include him with those two new boys we had Robin pick up the other night. We're working on that. Great video material."

Chas knew what 'working on' meant; drugs. Glossing over it in his mind, he kept focus on the case at hand. "What do the boy's foster parents say?"

"Middle-aged heterosexual couple. They're fine. I met the husband. Of course, I always show my Child Protection Services blue card. We're social workers, right? But I think they want to get rid of him anyway." Jeremy peered closer at Chas with concern. "You seem a little worried by it. You need to toughen up. These cases are commonplace."

The need to continually guide Chas was becoming irksome. Time for a reality check. "I'll tell you something. Before surrogacy was fully legalised in Australia and the market opened up, couples had to travel overseas to some third world country. Much lower demand back then of course, mostly heterosexual couples unable to conceive. But unwanted children were abandoned in squalid orphanages, left to perish. Now, in this country, they can go on a Social Security benefit. No doubt about it, marriage equality for same-sex has been a boom. Great for us, especially since the change of government. Opportunity abounds." He sat back, eyeing Chas with a mixture of amusement and distrust.

Gordon was staying interested, sharing Jeremy's amusement but wary. "If you're going to the boy's home, I suggest you take a Robin. This is better capability now." He lowered his voice, indicating Brent nearly within earshot. "Pity we can't control him with a handset. We've had enough situations lately. This could be a volatile scene you're going into."

"Yes, agreed." Jeremy stood, ready to proceed. "We'll take a Flasher too. Just in case. Never know how these things develop." He reached for the shoulder bag, then moved to the Robins and activated RobinB.

Still early evening as Jeremy, Chas and RobinB arrived at the house. Approaching the front door, they could hear shouting from inside. A boy's voice raised in anger. Jeremy pressed the door buzzer. The wife answered.

"Oh yes, come in. Jake told me you're coming." A diminutive woman with a kindly face, but a look of strain evidence enough of the domestic battleground endured every day.

"I hope you can do something. Manny is a very difficult boy." She grimaced as another yelling spree emanated from the next room. "I'm sorry. We haven't had him long, but it's always like this." She ushered them into the lounge.

Manny was standing at the kitchen entry, hurling obscenities. An average height boy of skinny build, shock of stringy black hair shoulder-length. Loose-fitting clothes didn't help a dishevelled appearance.

"You can't make me go!" he continued to shout in a loud, truculent voice. "You're not my father! I don't have a father! I don't need any piece of crap telling me what to do!"

A man's voice sounded from the kitchen. "All boys your age go to school. The new term starts Monday. You've missed too much. You will go, as long as you're staying in this house." Jake was trying to remain calm, but losing patience with the constant barrage of insults coming his way.

"What's so special about this house!? I've been in lots of houses! This one's crap! I don't have to be here!" Manny turned abruptly, suddenly aware of Jeremy's presence. His slim face was sweating profusely, mouth caught in an ugly snarl.

"Hello, Manny," Jeremy greeted, giving him a broad smile. "We met the other night, remember?"

Manny made no reply, regarding Jeremy and company with suspicion.

Jake emerged from the kitchen. "Jeremy, glad you could come." He moved forward to shake hands. Tired-looking, he was of humble nature, together with his wife doing their best to make a contribution in today's troubled society through their chosen field of foster parenting. But it was taking its toll. He'd lost weight recently, his normally solid frame looking a little fragile. Running a hand through thinning, wispy grey hair, he added, "Perhaps you can help with our situation."

Jeremy showed his credentials, then introduced Chas as a fellow social worker. "And you may know about the Robin robots assisting in many walks of life now." He indicated RobinB, which stood by passively, its senses taking in every action.

"Yes, we've seen them in the community." Unperturbed, Jake gestured towards the lounge chairs. "Please, take a seat."

Jeremy obliged, keen to spirit new recruit Manny away, but always aware he must invest time on the social front. "We can offer Manny participation in programmes that help young people. There's one on tonight. With your blessing, we can take him there." He refrained from flashing a smile, the situation presenting as sensitive.

"That sounds good." Jake cast a sidelong glance at his boy seated beside him. "Would you like to do that, Manny?"

"What do you know?" Manny snapped back, uncompromising in the incessant rejection of his guardian.

Jake stood. "Perhaps you should talk directly. I'll be in the kitchen if you need me." Remaining hopeful, he left them. His wife joined him, happy to keep well clear.

Chas, sitting next to Jeremy, suddenly decided he should be involved. "Do you like being with boys or girls?" he asked boldly, maintaining a steady gaze at Manny.

Jeremy cringed, not expecting Chas to interfere. The question was out of whack with preferred protocol.

Manny reacted with predictable belligerence, his upper lip curling in contempt as he picked up on Chas' sexuality. "What are you? Some kind of queer?" An ancient term he dredged up from something he'd heard in his endless wanderings. He blew a pout depicting ridicule, the closest to a laugh he could manage.

"Now now, don't be like that," Jeremy intervened with a quick smile, trying to smooth the way, at the same time seeking to restrain a now upset Chas. The boy was a handful, derailed and unloved but not stupid. Streetwise.

"You're one too! Hah!" Manny leapt to his feet, jerking his finger at Jeremy in an obscene gesture. He headed towards the kitchen, set to berate his provider once more. "Hey, craphead, you want a couple of queers to take me out!? You go out with them!"

An infuriated Chas, over-sensitised to any derogatory reference concerning his sexuality, jumped up and strode after the boy. Losing his cool, he began shouting a retort. Alarmed as a debacle loomed, Jeremy rushed over, irate at Chas for escalating it.

For the first time, an incensed Jake snapped. He appeared from the kitchen to fire a verbal lashing at Manny, his voice raised shrill and threatening, waving a long knife in the air he'd been using. His wife hung back, quivering with fright.

Then, the unimaginable. In a flash, RobinB was there, its memory accessed by recognisable input, computing to release relevant output. It snatched the knife, plunging it into Jake's chest, three times. His wife screamed, clawing at the creature. Again, the knife plunged into her, three times.

Both victims let out blood-curdling shrieks, crumpling life-less to the floor.

A shocked silence took over. Action frozen in time. Manny was the first to move. Suddenly galvanised, he swung away, heading for his room. A quick recovery, not unused to trau-matic events in his life. Moments later, he reappeared with bag slung over one shoulder and took off out the back door.

Jeremy and Chas were slower, but then a sense of urgency kicked in. "Let's get out of here," Jeremy uttered, backing away. His mind working again, he noted the knife next to the bodies, where RobinB had dropped it. Only Jake's fingerprints on it. Not wishing to be caught at the scene, he hastened to exit the front door. Chas and RobinB followed.

As Jeremy drove away, they could hear the faint sound of a siren, growing louder. Police called by a neighbour? Jeremy turned a corner and they sped away.

Back in the sanctuary of the Cave, Jeremy talked quietly with Gordon. "We have to get rid of him," he concluded, having related the further crisis. Still unnerved, he cast a quick glance at Chas now occupied at his computer next to Brent.

Gordon nodded, alarmed by another disaster clearly initiated then escalated by Chas. "That's too many times. He's a jinx. But he knows too much. What do we do with him? Bottom of the harbour?"

Jeremy hesitated, trying to settle himself down. "That's a bit messy. Maybe we get a Robin to do a job on him. Another good test for stage one Robust."

Gordon gave a grunt of consent. But the idea highlighted another concern. "The behaviour of Robin is a worry," he observed pointedly. "I take it you didn't enact it, rather it decided its own action. From the memory, when it saw the knife being waved around."

"Yes indeed. I thought Chongwe had that under control. We'll ask him. He and Mingsu should be here soon."

When their two Chinese partners arrived, the four men sat at the fold-down table. Chas was not invited to join them.

Jeremy began by describing earlier events of the evening. "We're concerned why RobinB took its own action, obviously learned from previous experience. Could this happen every time a Robin sees a knife? We thought your upgrades would ensure we maintain control." He looked at Chongwe enquiringly.

Chongwe, always sensitive to any hint of his expertise being criticised, sat up quickly with a sense of indignation. "Control by handset. I make other two Robins have Robin3 capable also. Agreed for Robust stage one. Different application have different signal from handset. Maybe you push button for RobinB action." Satisfied to have deflected criticism, he shared a furtive look with Mingsu, who remained poker-faced.

"No, I didn't touch my handset," Jeremy replied, a little irritated at Chongwe's subtle shift of blame. "RobinB acted by itself. I never took the handset out of my shoulder bag." Suddenly, a horrible realisation. "Oh, damn! I left the shoulder bag at the house! On the lounge chair." Again he cursed, angry at himself. "We left in such a hurry, before the police arrived." He glanced at Gordon, feeling sick. "A Flasher's in the bag too. Damn, damn!"

"You see, accident easy to happen," Chongwe responded. He gave Mingsu another meaningful sidelong glance. Then back to Jeremy. "Maybe you touch handset button by accident too."

"I know someone in Homicide Squad," Gordon cut in, hugely worried now. "That house will be closed off, a crime scene. But we have to get the bag back, if possible." A more pressing focus. Concern about RobinB's behaviour lapsed.

"We come to discuss Robust," Chongwe reminded them, after a lengthy pause. "I have upgrade. Prepare for stage two." He placed his carry bag on the table and extricated his computer.

"Wait, wait." Jeremy was uncertain, struck with a sense of losing grip on the whole operation. He caught the eye of Gordon, who was equally uncertain. "What does this upgrade do?"

"We discuss before." Chongwe seemed surprised. "Handset have green laser for target person. Three Robin now. For choose which Robin to action, use laser same way. Need to install upgrade for that." He put a hand on his computer and inclined his head towards the three Robins standing deactivated adjacent.

"Right. We did discuss that." Jeremy paused, at a point of decision which way to go. "I don't think we're ready for stage two yet. Stage one has gone well up till this evening. But now, we need to know why RobinB took its own action tonight, why your previous upgrade didn't control that." A refocus on their earlier point of discord.

Chongwe again appeared indignant. Mingsu stepped in, speaking for the first time. "We will check previous upgrade software and make sure control workable." He spoke in a bland, matter-of-fact manner, humourless and business-like. Abruptly, he stood, indicating to Chongwe it was time to leave. Chongwe packed away his computer and the pair departed.

Jeremy and Gordon were left in no doubt who was the senior of the two in the Chinese hierarchy. "Well, what do you make of that?" Gordon muttered.

Jeremy was thoughtful for a long moment, caught in a personal conundrum. Eventually, he replied, "You know, Chongwe and I have been together many years, dating back to the advent of marriage equality. A marriage of convenience in many ways, but it always worked because we had separate fields of expertise, overlapping enough so we were useful to each other. Only most recently have those fields merged for a common purpose. That has changed the dynamics." Another long pause. "To be honest, I've never been a hundred percent certain about him, always some reservations. Probably because of our different backgrounds. My involvement with his Hong Kong contacts has been superficial only. He doesn't divulge much, other than for operational purposes."

"Yes, I can see that." Gordon was listening intently, respecting the insider position his colleague held. "Why do you suppose he was hedging about RobinB taking its own action?"

"Good question. But that's typical of Chongwe. Any questioning of his expertise, even the slightest suggestion of failure, and he reacts way out of proportion. He's always been like that."

"A state of denial, would you say? But that doesn't answer the question why his upgrade didn't work. Total failure, in fact. If, and I believe what you say, you didn't touch the handset. RobinB saw the knife, boom, action just like that!" Gordon snapped his fingers to emphasise. "Almost as though Chongwe hasn't installed that control at all!"

They stared at each other in dismay, both smitten by the implications. Did Chongwe and Mingsu have their own agenda?

"That would explain why he jumped onto such a lame excuse as me accidentally working the handset," Jeremy surmised. "Diverting attention."

"Yes, but he must know that wouldn't stick, surely. You'd have to choose the application, then point the laser at intended target. Hard to do that accidentally, it's designed to be deliberate. Why would you murder that innocent couple anyway? Doesn't make sense."

"Very true." Jeremy took another long moment to ponder. "Maybe it's not so surprising. Again, typical of him. Chongwe might be brilliant in the highly complex world of technical expertise, but in dealing with people he's totally simplistic, always has been. Probably that's his arrogance. He knows he's brilliant, so he thinks everyone else is stupid, doesn't give much thought to what he says, just expects people to believe him." Jeremy put on a derisive smirk. "Besides, what possible advantage could he gain by deliberately not installing that control? I can't think of anything. Maybe it is just a failure to work properly, which he didn't want to own."

Gordon nodded. "Maybe. We can only wait and see, keep a close watch on everything. Mingsu said they'll check the software, so let's wait for that."

Jeremy agreed. "It's late. We'll take it up again tomorrow."

"What did you do with that girl? You know, the one with Chas' boy?"

"Lara. Don't worry, we've dealt with her. She can't talk to anyone."

Gordon looked relieved. "I don't care what you do with her, just keep her away from our operations. No way we want any chance she sees Brent, her so-called father." He grimaced at the thought.

"For sure. Pity we've just cut back to local only. We could have sent her on the next shipment out. She's got some class, would fetch a good price."

Gordon's mobile suddenly sounded. A message. "It's from Karl. What does he want at this hour?" Gordon read it out loud. "TOO ROBUST. PUT ON HOLD. K."

"What does that mean?"

"I think it means he's heard about the further disaster tonight with a Robin. Hah! I bet he doesn't want to put on hold the piece I'm supposed to be arranging for him." Gordon pulled a face in disdain, unimpressed.

With that, they summoned Chas and Brent and all departed the Cave.

Next day, a news item announced a sudden escalation of the government crackdown on private use of drones. The Science Minister, on interview, stated, "This is following up on the promises we've made to the people about privacy concerns. From today, an application must be made to the

Department of Services from anyone wishing to deploy a drone. Such application, required for all private use including by media outlets, must state the day, period of time, locality and reasons for the deployment. The information will be kept confidential by the Department, whose decision will be final, not subject to appeal. Exempted will be public use, by the Police and DP. They will continue maintaining safety, law and order, and identifying discriminatory influences in our society we are determined to stamp out. This is what we have promised and we are delivering."

The interviewer asked further questions, the Minister giving generalised answers that offered no relief from the severe restrictions imposed at short notice. Effective from today was a major surprise, providing no time for adjustment to plans any private user may have. Almost of emergency-type proportions.

"We've heard nothing of this!" Gordon exclaimed, stunned in disbelief. "Sure, we've talked about it, but why wouldn't we be included in the decision-making? Such a relevant issue. Karl would know. But his text message last night, short and abrupt, no mention of this."

Jeremy was equally as flabbergasted. "Does this mean we can't use our drones either?" He glanced at the row of them sitting idly on the bench. "We certainly wouldn't be making application!"

"That's not the worry. We're not using them much anymore, especially with Robust underway. The worry has always been others using drones, particularly the media."

"So these new restrictions are good for us. The DP are exempt. That helps us."

"Yes. And yet, Karl's text tells us to put a hold on Robust! That doesn't make sense. It should be the opposite, the way made clearer for us." Gordon looked perplexed, trying to reconcile the inconsistency. "I have to speak with Karl, find out what's going on."

For the rest of the day, Gordon tried to contact Karl, without success. Karl was not answering.

Chapter 18

The near darkness was oppressive. No power connected meant reliance on faint moonlight that barely reached them through one side window. Bars across eliminated the window as an escape route. Its outlook over tall scrubland precluded attracting the attention of anyone outside. As did any noise made, hardly discernible through the building's solid cement walls. As Lara had previously seen with Jude, the warehouse down a disused driveway beyond the end of a cul-de-sac was not conducive to chance discovery. Resigned to waiting, Lara sat slumped against a side wall, close to where a cell-like wall of bars began its stretch to the opposite side, locked gate midway across. It kept the captives well back from the building's front and only entry point.

The enclosed space was barren and unkempt, no furniture, the cement floor dirty. Lara shared it with nine others, all around her age if not younger. Two were the boys she and Jude saw abducted from the Valley. The others were four more boys and three girls. Two boys were in poor health, thin emaciated drug-ridden bodies sweating heavily. They looked like cases Lara had seen at the clinic suffering New AIDS. The stench of body odour completed a scene of morbid degradation.

There was no conversation, each buried in their own desperation. Lara had several times talked briefly with the two boys she recognised, Simon and Oscar, both presenting as of good character. But mostly her head was down, staring at the floor, suffering the misery in silence. Staying with her was the horror transpiring yesterday afternoon, two DP officers ripping her out from Dulcie's place, temporary incarceration with the others somewhere out of town, late night transfer to the warehouse. Since then, the day had passed slowly, hour after interminable hour in hot conditions, dominated by silent fear of what might happen next. A man visited periodically to check on them, bringing food and drink.

Memories of being traumatised at the Cave plagued Lara. She knew what Jeremy and Gordon were capable of. No abuse yet, but what was to come? She longed to be in Jude's arms again. Her mobile taken heightened the crushing isolation. Dreading her fate, she sobbed quietly, running fingers through her tacky hair, struggling to remain positive.

Feeling grubby, she headed for the toilet/washroom at the rear, stepping past the others sprawled in various poses around the floor as they tried to sleep. Thankfully, water was connected, the only service. After freshening, she returned to lie propped against the wall. No bedding or blankets. She couldn't sleep. Mid-evening now, the eerie quiet of little comfort.

Suddenly, the sound of vehicles pulling up outside. Soon the entrance door opened, voices, lights approaching from hand-held lamps. Lara jumped to her feet, alarmed.

"What's going to happen to us?" Oscar's voice was a quivering whisper. His body trembled, hands fiercely gripping the bars as they stood with the other frightened souls.

Lara had no answer, struck with a fearful premonition of detrimental action pending. Nowhere to run. She could only watch in trepidation as a dark figure headed towards them. In the half-light, four more men approached. She caught her breath in shock as several Robins appeared. Compliant, they followed the men, who chatted excitedly as if in anticipation. Too many, no chance to escape whatever fate lay ahead.

Then, a realisation. The men were Chinese, speaking Mandarin. Had Jeremy sent them? Lara focussed on the Robins. Five of them, each with ID branded on the forehead, different from ID tag she'd seen to date. Instinctively, she sensed this was not a Jeremy Gordon initiative.

As if to confirm, the leading man had no key for the gate. The lock was electronic. Two-way, unlike at the Cave. He had special equipment, two thin wires and a small black box. Similar to the equipment Jude had used and shown her.

Before long, the gate was open. Two Robins stood as sentinels while one by one, each captive was examined then ushered outside to one of two large vans waiting. Amidst verbal threats, they were bundled in through the rear double doors. Constantly shadowed by Robins, no chance of making a break for freedom. The two sick-looking boys were left, locked behind the gate again, rejected for whatever awaited the others.

Inside the van, bench seats lined each side. Lara took her spot at the front end. Four each side were joined by two Chinese men and three Robins guarding the rear exit doors. Feeling powerless, Lara sat quietly, trying to remain inconspicuous.

The vans backed out, then headed away through the deserted industrial complex.

"I sense trouble." Jeremy had a stern look, agitated. "I intended having it out with Chongwe tonight. But he wasn't there when Chas and I got home. I called him but he didn't reply and hasn't called back. His behaviour here last night, which you witnessed, and the developments today are unusual. Why is he avoiding me? So I asked you back here, even though it's late. We need contingency plans. Urgently."

Gordon nodded in agreement. "I've been thinking the same. Still no contact from Karl, after I left several messages. That's very unusual. What about today's surprise announcement by the Science Minister about drones? Too much coincidence. Everything going anti, all at the same time."

"Okay, so let's work out something." Jeremy drew a deep breath. "We have to build on our strength." He gestured towards the three Robins standing in inert mode by the drones. "All Robin three capable now. The problem is, we've been relying on Chongwe to go the next step. Somehow, we have to get around that."

Suddenly, Jeremy's mobile sounded. He glanced at the screen. "That's Partik. Our man at the warehouse. Why would he be calling me?" Moments after answering it, the alarm bells were ringing. "What!" Jeremy caught his breath in dismay. "Where were you?" He listened further. "Stay by your phone. I'll call you back."

"What's wrong?" Gordon shared his alarm.

"Those kids we returned to the warehouse. They've been taken!" Jeremy was aghast, turning a sickly pale. "Partik went for his nightly check and found only two boys there! They told him a bunch of Chinese men had just been, took the others, four boys four girls. And, wait for it, they had Robins helping them!"

"Robins! No way! How could that be!?"

"Chongwe. Only he could do that. From the AI factory, plenty of Robins stored there ready to deploy. Probably he's installed his latest upgrade in them too!"

Gordon cursed, furious. "Just what we suspected. A take-over! You were right not to trust him. And that slimy Mingsu, never know what he's thinking. His triad is too powerful!" Again he cursed, more vehemently. "What about Karl!? No wonder he hasn't returned my calls. That sleaze ball, what I've done for him! Feeding his fetishes and perversions, supplying him with boys and videos! For what! Nothing!" His anger exploding, he began pacing the floor, uncompre-hending. Loss of control was unprecedented.

"Not only Karl, the Science Minister too! And probably others. Maybe all down the chain. The DP? How long has this been planned?" Jeremy was incredulous, the decep-tion irreconcilable.

Both fell silent, caught in a stupor of disbelief.

Jeremy tried to rationalise. "How did they know about the warehouse anyway? Very few people know about that, or what we had there. Only you, me, Partik, a couple of DP officers. Not even Karl. I deliberately didn't tell Chongwe, trying to keep something for ourselves. Someone else must have told him!"

"Chas!" Gordon spat out the name, treating it like poison. "He was with you when you took those boys out there from the Valley, wasn't he?"

"Yes, he was. And when we transferred them all back there too. He's close to Chongwe. Both living in my house!"

Jeremy leapt to his feet, infuriated. "We have to deal with him. Now! Before he does any more damage."

"Let's go." Gordon was suddenly focussed, action available on one front at least. He indicated the Robins. "Bring all three."

Jeremy gathered relevant items in a bag, activated the three Robins and all exited the Cave.

At Jeremy's house, Chas had not yet retired to bed and Chongwe was still not back, despite the late hour. On seeing the Robins and Gordon accompanying Jeremy home, Chas was immediately alerted to a problem.

"What's happening?" he asked, emerging from the kitchen. Trying to be nonchalant but wracked with nervous tension. He backed away defensively into the lounge area.

"You tell us," Jeremy responded, eyeing Chas with cold contempt. "Did you tell Chongwe about the warehouse where we took those kids?"

Chas' eyes widened in genuine surprise. "No! I've hardly seen him. Except tonight, he just left actually. He's taking his stuff, moving out of here. What's going on?" He shook his head in bewilderment, feigning innocent bystander.

Gordon sidled up alongside him. "We don't believe you. Someone has been to the warehouse tonight. Hardly anyone knows about it, outside of us." He leered into Chas' face aggressively.

"In any case, it doesn't matter," Jeremy went on. "You've messed up too many times. Two more deaths with a knife, because of you. We've decided to terminate your services." With an evil smirk, he brought forward the Robin nearest to him; Robin2. He pulled a handset from his bag and quickly accessed the 'Attack' application.

With a shriek of terror, Chas turned to flee. Gordon grappled with him. Jeremy aimed the handset, the green laser dot landed on Chas' midriff. But before Robin2 could strike, RobinB shot past, reaching the pair first. Incredibly, it ripped Gordon away, grabbed his arm, twisting it. A sharp crack sounded. Gordon screamed in pain. RobinB released him and he fell to the floor, clutching his broken arm, crying out in anguish.

Robin2 stopped abruptly, its signalled output aborted by alternative corrupting input. Robins were not programmed to combat each other. RobinB, outputting its 'Security' set task activated for the Brett/Chas household, was intent on protecting Chas. Having dealt with the threat, it stood quietly by Chas as a loyal bodyguard.

All seemed frozen in time, a shocked silence save for Gordon's agonised moans. He lay hunched over on the floor. Jeremy and Chas were each rooted to the spot, struck dumb. But the Robins hadn't finished. Robin2 began glowing at the chest, flashing intermittently as a transmission installed to its black box. RobinB's dark eyes held it in a steady gaze. Moments later, RobinB's chest was glowing then flashing. Return response from Robin2. Sharing memory? Complementing programmed applications? Robin3 joined in, the same exchanges, chests glowing and flashing. Their bizarre communications over, the three Robins stood passive once more.

Jeremy roused himself from inertia. No one else moving, it was up to him. He still held the handset. Suddenly galvanised, he aimed it at RobinB and punched deactivation. Nothing happened. RobinB unaffected!

"Damn! What's gone wrong!?" Growing frantic, he slapped the handset, punching the buttons, more frenziedly as RobinB refused to deactivate. He aimed at the other Robins. Same result. They were uncontrollable! Horrified, he backed away, overwhelmed by a fearful sense of powerlessness.

Just then, a noise at the front door. Chongwe entered. Accompanied by two mountainous Chinese henchmen and a Robin, he sauntered into the lounge. Abruptly, he halted as the dramatic scene presented.

"What happen here?" He skirted around, assessing the forces in play.

Jeremy now saw him as a hostile adversary. After their many years together, he knew how to get at him. "The Robins are out of control, taking their own actions. Your programming is ineffective. The handset is useless." Far from crowing about it, he nevertheless relished the chance to needle his long-time partner.

Affronted, Chongwe reacted with predictable indignation. "You know nothing." He pursed his lips contemptuously, exuding an air of arrogant superiority. "I show you. I have upgrade here." Gleefully, he held up his mobile. "I will install. But only I know code to action." He touched his shirt pocket, where a handset slightly protruded. "Your handset never work now." With a self-endearing grin, he worked his mobile, targeting RobinB first.

Nothing happened. RobinB's chest did not glow, transmission not received. Chongwe let out a vile oath, disbelieving. He repeated the signal. Nothing. "What you do!?" He rounded on Jeremy, incensed. "You damage Robin!

What you do!?" He was shouting, convinced Jeremy was to blame.

"You see? Exactly as I told you." Jeremy gave a derisive snort, not displeased to see Chongwe rattled.

Enraged, Chongwe tried Robin3. Again, transmission rejected. Then Robin2, the same. "You do something to Robins!" He stormed towards Jeremy, challenging him face to face, inches apart. "How you do that!? Who help you!?" Becoming unhinged, his wild accusations were personal, carrying no logic.

Then, in an instant, RobinB moved. It turned slightly to fix its penetrating eyes on the Robin Chongwe had brought in. The fourth Robin's chest glowed, flashing. Return response followed. Another one added to the fold. A series of flashes ensued between all the Robins, resembling a bizarre light show. The effect was haunting, reducing the human presence in the room to frightening insignificance. All done in seconds.

Even Chongwe was shocked. But before he could react, the Robins were on the move. Three of them, quickly departing the scene as one, oblivious to their former commanders. They exited the front door. RobinB remained, standing resolute beside Chas.

Chongwe reeled back from Jeremy, his mind thrown into turmoil. The situation untenable, he looked for his companions. The two heavies had collected Chongwe's remaining possessions from the bedroom, two large boxes, and were standing by, impassive. Without another word, Chongwe gestured to them and strode towards the exit. In moments, they were gone.

Jeremy helped a depleted Gordon to his feet and they followed the others out, heading for the hospital. Chas, aware his presence in the house was no longer appropriate, made for his room to pack his bags.

Next day, Saturday, all hell broke loose in the news media. The crackdown on drones would severely curtail surveillance operations, a blight on investigative powers and press freedom long held to be sacrosanct. The media circus was swinging into full attack mode, demanding justification from government, highlighting hypocrisy in view of the contrary increased DP and Police powers. And fiercely seeking any whiff of corruption or a scandal. Not hard to pinpoint, as already exposed were MPs and DP involved in the cache a boat recently smuggled into Cairns. Merely the tip of the iceberg, according to informed sources.

State Minister Karl had been implicated. He was under close watch, along with others including the Federal Science, Police and Defence Ministers, even gunning for the Prime Minister himself. The Treasurer was prominent in media scrutiny, the Budget less than a month away.

Coln's Shadow Prime Minister was hot on the trail, seizing the opportunity to gain political mileage. Intent on furthering his already high media profile, he challenged the PM to more one-on-one public debates. The PM found reason to refuse, citing their busy agenda while belittling the Coln influence as socially irrelevant in today's world.

Social media was firing on all platforms. As always, a wide variety of views flowed. Popular opinion was fast trending towards resurgent cynicism, resurrecting disillusionment. Corruption intolerable to many, the honeymoon period for new Labour was well and truly over. The social media blitz resembled a continuous opinion poll, suiting Coln's renowned consensus philosophy.

With government woes rapidly escalating, the discrimination and equality versus progress and development divide was generating greater scrutiny. One, represented by Coln, promised future direction, the other promised direction-less politics. Was the cycle turning again? Prominent in the public forum was AI, many postings enthusiastically embracing the hundred-Robin trial, flying in the face of the factory's near closure. The promise of future life enhancement manifesting beyond current infancy was highly attractive. Encouraged by Coln, numerous postings suggested all kinds of tasks for Robin that would greatly benefit people. Exactly what the trial was set up to ascertain.

Of popular interest, repeatedly posted, were tasks relevant in the area of child care. Many parents keen to delegate responsibility and return to the workforce. Wide-ranging aspects being addressed, from baby care including bottle-feeding, diaper-changing, to general child-minding, facilitating play, early learning. Whatever takes the burden off parents and guardians, covering a comprehensive checklist of practical child-rearing. Only a few questioned psychological impact. Reliance on robots incapable of emotion or imparting love, just cold input and output. Consequences?

The combination of social and conventional media left little to be imagined, privacy of least concern as breaking news items frequented. One of these, already out there for a day, was the murder of a middle-aged husband and wife, each stabbed three times in their own home. The murder weapon, a kitchen knife left at the scene, revealed smeared fingerprints only, inconclusive. Their foster son, known as a rebellious young teenager, was prime suspect.

Further information just breaking shed new light on the case. Homicide detectives had examined a bag discovered lying on a lounge chair. It contained two items of particular interest, a video stick and a handset used to control Robins. The video instantly set off alarm bells. A series of short excerpts depicting sexually explicit and paedophile activity. Found with the handset heightened the alarm, indicating the involvement of a Robin in some way. But the victims had not been allocated a Robin under the trial. Neighbours described seeing a vehicle speed away from the house shortly after hearing screams from inside. Too dark for anyone to identify, but someone said one occupant looked like could be a Robin. Investigations were ongoing.

Social media reaction was immediate. A Robin implicated in another violent this time double murder, and paedophilia! Why would it be present and who was controlling it? Major shock and consternation quickly went viral. So many trial Robins injected into the community, envisaged for future advancement! Postings advocating child-care application took a radical turn against.

Another breaking news item was coming through. An example of Faketing exposed, through a tip-off to the media. It related to the murder of a father, extensively reported on already. Video evidence captured by a Robin had condemned the son, who'd been charged and was currently held in custody. But the tip-off alleged the victim's same-sex partner, in cahoots with a computer-clever work colleague at the AI factory, had falsified the video by Faketing, to divert culpability from himself. A second expert, called in to reassess the video, had detected minute traces of the authentic original. Police were hunting down both protagonists.

Again, social media platforms were inundated with inflamed reaction, bordering on hysterical. Faketing, responsible years back for severely corrupting the internet and a dirty word ever since, was unheard-of nowadays. Or did Faketing still happen, going undetected or unreported!? The near hysteria was heightened by the double murder just reported bearing a striking resemblance, use of a knife and again the presence of a Robin. Was a trend emerging involving Robins? People wanted answers.

At the Cave, Jeremy and Gordon were taking closer than usual heed of media activity. Vulnerable as never before, suddenly isolated by horrific change of fortune.

As the latest item played out on screen, Jeremy eased back in his chair. "Well, at least our leak got through to the right outlet," he proclaimed, grim-faced. "That should take care of Chas. Hopefully, Chongwe too. Except he'll probably go into hiding, protected by his Hong Kong mates. I wonder if Karl's still in their corner, the dirty two-timing rat! Probably he'll lie low, cut ties. While the heat's on."

"That's what we have to do now," Gordon responded. He looked pale, recovering from having his left arm re-set, now cradled in a sling. "Close it down, get rid of evidence, don't attract attention. Robust is dead. When my arm's right, I might go back to a bit of private eye work. You can continue being a dutiful Child Protection officer for the Department." He gave a quick smirk, the irony of it appealing. "We can start up again when everything settles down."

Jeremy sounded a grunt of endorsement, but was worried. "There are many in the network. Let's hope no self-serving do-gooder decides to turn whistle-blower." Then, another concern. "What about him?" He gestured towards Brent absorbed as usual at the end of the bench.

"Yes. He's a problem. I think ----"

Still watching the screen, their attention was caught by another news item of relevance. The parents of the two boys abducted from the Valley were being interviewed, irate and frustrated by lack of information, their boys still missing. A police spokesperson came on screen to offer an assurance they were doing everything possible to track down the boys. What had happened to them after release from DP detention?

"That can come back on us too," Jeremy observed, unusually pensive. "We had the young fellow Jude nailed with that one as well. But now, the way things are going, I've no idea."

"I'll give it some thought," Gordon replied. "We might be able to firm it up." He stood. "In the meantime, let's get on with our task here."

Another morning slowly going by, his third in this bleak, soulless place. No windows meant absolute isolation from the outside world, meal deliveries the only orientation as to time of day. Or lights out evening, on again morning. Adjacent inmates came and went, mostly non-talkative. A no hassle atmosphere, yet the dearth of meaningful contact with people was depressing. The warders were disinterested in him, entrenched in mundane routine.

Dulcie was visiting regularly, his only relief from boredom, his sole connection to the real world. He anticipated each visit, with hope Lara would be with her or for any positive news. But always Dulcie was alone and glum, nothing heard or seen of Lara. She helped keep his spirits up, but her visits were short, unable to talk candidly under monitored conditions.

Sitting on the edge of the bed, head bowed, Jude contemplated the prospects. Lara was uppermost in his mind, constantly. Arrest by the DP would normally be brief, citation issued then release. This was different. Now Saturday, second day of no news or trace of her. The Jeremy Gordon network fulfilling their threat? Could only be a dark outcome for Lara. Jude stared at the floor, choking back the lump of emotion in his throat.

His own situation was unchanging, frustratingly in limbo. The additional charges promised, allegedly supported by a new video clip, were yet to eventuate. No bail hearing either. But he knew it was all just a ruse orchestrated by Jeremy, likely to prolong indefinitely as long as they considered him a threat. He shook his head disconsolately, tortured by the stifling confinement closing him down.

Lunch was delivered. He ate a little, too churned up to be hungry. The afternoon drifted by. He lay on the bed, staring at the ceiling, waiting for Dulcie's next visit.

The warder came. Surprisingly, he led Jude not to the visitor's but to the administration front counter. An officer handed him a box carrying his personal effects.

"The charges have been dropped. You're free to go. Please sign this release form." The officer slid the form across the counter.

Astonished and elated, Jude signed the form, took his belongings and left the building. Unbelievably, he was free! A surreal feeling. Quickly he re-orientated. His mobile epitomised re-connection to the world and reality. Suddenly motivated, he checked it. No messages from Lara. Not surprised, nevertheless he was hit with a familiar sinking sensation in the pit of his stomach. A sense of urgency kicked in. Total focus now on finding Lara!

He called Dulcie. Soon she arrived, thrilled, and drove him to the factory. Thankfully, his bike was still parked there, untouched. Afternoon light was fading into early evening as they reached home.

Jude quickly came up to date with events occurring during his isolation, helped by media sources and Dulcie, able to talk freely now. Many postings flowing, about the Faketing, another murder by knife involving a Robin, much conjecture about Robins into the future, the crackdown on private drones and media reaction to it, heightened awareness of government corruption. All had ramped up hugely in his absence. Mind-boggling.

The reason for his release and charges dropped was now clear. Faketing exposed, what a blessing! How did that happen? What did it mean for Chas? And Chongwe? Not hard to envisage a big rift in their associations with the Jeremy Gordon regime and its powerful influences. Jude resolved to find out. But none of it shed any light on the fate of Lara. If anything, more obscure than ever. Gritting his teeth, he refocussed on priority one.

Well into the evening, he rode to Lara's mothers' place. Doris and Glenice welcomed him joyfully, but disappointed Lara wasn't with him. They had no information and were anxious. The longest time between Lara's visits and uncontactable by phone. Jude explained the circumstances, sparing unnecessary detail, leaving them with an assurance he wouldn't rest until he found her.

The night was getting late. Next was the Cave. He'd brought his lock-picking equipment. Soon he was inside, his heart beating faster as he played the torch beam down the long bench. No computers, all gone! He checked every drawer, none locked, all empty. On the other side, the drones were gone. The ensuite, bereft of any items. No sign of life in the adjacent room, the door not locked, nothing but the mattress on the floor where he'd found Lara last time. He wandered to the far end of the place. Double bed with canopy still there, but bare mattress only, no pillows. Camera and stand, the paraphernalia, trapeze all gone, just the hooks left in the ceiling. The Cave had been abandoned. Perplexed, Jude exited. The entry door clicked shut with a note of finality. More questions asked than answered.

What now? On a hunch, he headed for the edge of town, to the deserted industrial complex. At the derelict warehouse, he picked the entrance lock and stepped inside.

The torch beam cut through near total darkness, playing across a cell-like wall of bars. A shuffling sound from further back. Two figures emerged from the gloom, coming to the gate. Startled but suddenly with hope, Jude hurried to them. But no Lara. Both were young boys, thin haggard faces peering at him with looks of desperation. The smell of body odour was overwhelming.

"Any others here?" Jude asked anxiously. "A girl, with blonde hair? Her name's Lara."

"She was here," one boy replied in a croaky voice. "With others. Chinese men took them away last night. They had those robots."

"What! Robins!? Chinese!?" Jude's mind went into a spin. What did that mean? "Where were they taking them?"

The boy shrugged his shoulders. "Dunno. Can you let us out of here?"

Frustrated, Jude realised they had no more to tell. He picked the gate lock and released them. The boys took off out the exit. Jude slammed the gate shut, feeling better for one good deed at least.

Returning home, he grappled with the further evidence of major change. A group of Chinese with Robins! Surely a Chongwe initiative. Was it part of, separate from or supplanting Jeremy Gordon? The abandoned Cave suggested the latter. But he was still no closer to Lara. At least he knew she was alive, or was last night. Who was the most important player now; Jeremy or Chongwe? The question tore at him.

Chapter 19

Social agendas, never far from prominence in public debate, were enjoying a surge as the pressure on government mounted. The evidence of corrupt practices by several Ministers, even the leadership, was great incentive for people to test political resolve, especially on issues of equality, prejudice, discrimination so heralded in election doctrine. Hypocrisy, always a hated commodity.

The resurgence represented natural progression from earlier decision-making. Process of evolution. Social pundits likened it to the climate existing for cultural institutional change historically, citing contraception and the sexual revolution of late twentieth century, burgeoning computer technology expediting into social media, change in marriage laws institutionalising same-sex unions. All with consequences.

Politically in Australia, the 2024 election of Coln had installed a 'can do will do' government. Pragmatic Coln held scant regard for socially trendy labels such as discrimination and the like. When finally new Labour came to power, many issues jumped off the back-burner, interest groups encouraged to take advantage. Now, politically motivated, they were surging.

One interest group, the LGBT society, was intent on refocussing their further agenda. Following advent of same-sex marriage, natural progression early on had opened up sperm and egg donorship free markets plus full legalisation of surrogacy. Further progression had ushered in de facto relationships, indulging the relentless crusade for equality with the heterosexual world that for decades had trended against marriage. Couples living together unmarried had the same status in law as marriage, why not for same-sex couples? Bringing into the fold related provisions such as family benefits, property settlement under separation, single parent allowances and so on. At the time unsupported by Coln, nevertheless the High Court had ruled in favour. Another victory for the anti-discrimination sect, de facto acceptance further widening the potential for claimants on the Social Security budget. Consequences?

Such decision-making, by natural progression, was fuelling current debate. Social activists were pushing to lower the age of marriage, at present eighteen in Australia, to sixteen, in line with the age of consent in most States. But did age of marriage even have relevance anymore? Anomalous with sexual activity legal at sixteen and a couple living as de facto granted the same status anyway. Parental consent for marriage was less relevant nowadays in an environment embracing rights of the individual, particularly in same-sex families where always one or more parent was non-biological and more often than not distant.

The push, part of the surge feeding off growing political discord, was prominent on social media. And expanding to address further agendas, some new, some previously mooted but lapsing until a more receptive political climate prevailed. That time was now.

Abortion was one such agenda. Historically a highly emotive and divisive issue never really leaving the lime-light. Same-sex marriage gave it a greater focus. Advocates questioned why a surrogate mother who was not egg donor should have right of choice, given she was merely a vehicle with no biological connection. Right-to-choose purists, always adamant a woman's rights over her body was paramount, steadfastly refused to shift their position. The perennial battle with pro-life activists now a three-cornered contest, the prospects for resolution were more confused than ever.

The pro-lifers were continually campaigning for stricter regulations. Too commonly, surrogacy agreements included a clause to terminate if the future parents were dissatis-fied with the prognosis, such as incorrect gender, a health concern, sometimes no reason even need be given. Often tested in court, but a decision could go either way depen-dent on extenuating circumstances. Political will was needed to deem such clauses invalid. Coln had been disin-terested, leaving it for people to decide for themselves. The current government was vacillating, unclear on who was being discriminated against one way or another.

The marriage age debate was further escalating. A movement was gathering momentum to lower the age of consent. Lobbyists coining a new term, 'age of maturity', claiming children were developing more quickly at an earlier age than ever before. Sexual activity was common-place amongst younger teenagers, so why criminalise them by maintaining an unrealistic legal age? Again, numerous points of view proliferating on social media. A highly controversial topic.

Dissent within the LGBT community was becoming evident. The various factions, each with their own particular interests inside the broad generality of the movement, had through the years experienced friction due to those differences, but largely kept under wraps by the overriding fight for legitimacy in the world. Now, factional self-interest was rising, exposed amidst the heightened public debate.

The 'G' faction was largest. Covering the widest scope, it tended to dominate the same-sex agenda. They strongly supported moves to lower ages of marriage and consent. A minority group in the heterosexual world was also in favour, but without wanting to join a dynamic crusade. The 'G's, going further, advocated to scrap the concept of marriage altogether, arguing it was superfluous in today's world of de facto recognition, and lauding freedom of association rights. Fiercely upholding all aspects in the struggle to eradicate equality/ discrimination violations from society.

The 'L' faction had a different focus. Their main agenda concerned the having and rearing of children, from pre-birth to early childhood in particular. Not so obviously wrapped up in wider social implications or politically-based manoeuvrings. Yet they had deeper motivations. Little disclosed in public was a push to explore alternative options, to reduce or even eliminate the male input necessary to conceive life. Sperm donorship, forcing dependence on the opposite sex, was hitherto an unavoidable reality fraught with trouble and negative social repercussions. Their attention was drawn towards cloning as potential means to an end for female same-sex marriages.

The 'B' faction had an agenda of their own. They wanted recognition for bisexual people to have equal rights in relationships with male and female. Therefore the laws of bigamy should be amended to legitimise dual marriage, permitted simultaneously. All rights reserved in terms of children from potentially multiple parents, including Social Security entitlements. They supported the moves afoot regarding age or to remove marriage as an institution. Under the latter, bigamy would be an obsolete concept anyway. Although with a different agenda, they were mostly in harmony with the 'G' faction, since many 'G' members were undeclared bisexual.

The 'T' faction was probably the most disgruntled. Relatively small in numbers, they felt their concerns were not given due attention by LGBT. They wanted to lobby government for special funding consideration as to sex-change operations and related medical issues. And they were against any move to denigrate the institution of marriage, seen as the most secure medium for supporting their cause. Ratification, difficult to attain, was an obsessive driving force for them. A breakaway movement threatened.

Despite their differences, the factions would always be united in the eternally greater quest to maintain and build on their hard-fought legitimacy in society. Most issues were of overlapping interest. A steadily growing phenomenon, now commonly enacted, was for same-sex marriages male and female to combine resources, sperm and egg donors and surrogacy provided for each other. Keeping it all in the LGBT family. Resulting children as per normal, except with minimum four parents, subject to the relationship vagaries of two separate otherwise unconnected entities. And a further burden on Social Security. Burgeoning consequences.

The biggest uniting incentive was to seek greater impact and empowerment in the political arena. During Coln's long tenure, LGBT tried to infiltrate, riding on the back of Independents popularity by putting up candidates in electorates perceived to be favourable. But the consensus system worked against them. Insufficient public support compared to other Independent candidates equated to no Lower House members over successive elections, just a single one finally successful at last year's ballot. They had better success in the Senate, sharing in a balance of power position along with other minor interest groups.

Having failed to infiltrate Coln, they had switched their efforts to aligning with the Labour Opposition, who were more amenable on social issues. After helping Labour to power, their influence was now the greatest they'd ever enjoyed. The government's focus, radically departing from the Coln legacy, created a suitable and exploitable environment.

Coln's Shadow Prime Minister, attuned to public sentiment, at last succeeded in having the PM agree to an additional forum. In deference to the inflammatory issues currently raging on social media, the national broadcaster invited the Lib/Nat alternative Opposition Leader and the lone LGBT member to join in.

Sunday afternoon, the four protagonists sat around the studio table, except the PM at the last minute sent the

Treasurer to represent him. The large screen, in full view of everyone, was already receiving postings from the public.

Sharon opened proceedings. "Thank you for coming, gentlemen. We look forward to a full and informative discussion." She gave each a welcoming smile. "Treasurer, if I may start with you. Today's forum is to focus on the social issues worrying people of late, but before we get to that, could you give us a brief pre-Budget update?"

"Yes, thank you, Sharon." The Treasurer leaned forward, keen to make a strong showing. In his late thirties, a handsome-looking entrepreneur who'd risen rapidly through the political ranks. His lack of long experience in politics, however, caught him out at times. "The Budget is on track to deliver our objectives and provide the social reforms we've promised. I think people know what to expect from us, perhaps one or two pleasant surprises but you'll just have to wait for Budget night." He looked pleased with himself.

"Sharon, can I respond to that?" When Sharon indicated consent, the Coln Leader took it up. "We await Treasury figures with interest, but in the meantime we've had independent auditors do an appraisal. The results have come in and are quite alarming. It appears the Budget is about to dive deeply into deficit, contrary to the government's claims of a small surplus. This on the back of the very large surplus they inherited from us!" He held the Treasurer in a steady gaze, challenging him.

The Treasurer returned a look of indignation. "That's not true. Obviously, the auditors you use have accessed incorrect information."

The Lib/Nat Leader spoke. "Excuse me, Sharon, I can add something to that. We also have done an audit, anticipating Budget figures. And I confirm the large deficit. We've been investigating further. The reasons for it are very disturbing. If we have time, Sharon, I think this would be a good occasion to expose something of what's been going on." He was a cool operator, an older man with long experience in politics from two decades back when part of government the last time they were in power.

Sharon was a little surprised. "Perhaps we'll come back to it later." She hesitated, conscious of the postings coming in thick and fast. A few moments to assess. Most were highly critical, condemning of the political process, demanding disclosure and accountability. "We definitely will return to this. But first, I want to bring in our LGBT member." Under pressure to stay on course, she turned to the remaining participant. "Kris, there's been a lot of conjecture lately amongst the wider public as to just what the LGBT agenda is these days. Can you enlighten us?"

"Thank you, Sharon." Kris drew a deep breath. Waiting patiently, he was ready to deliver a prepared response to a question predicted. "I'm sure we would all agree it is important to keep pace with how life is evolving. To this end, we believe social values should reflect the changes in human development the modern era and advancing technology bring about. We must avoid dogmatic adherence to ageing traditions that no longer represent the realities of a progressive world. I expect you're all aware of the talk on social media right now, about the future of marriage, age of consent and other such matters. People are moving forward with the times, our children maturing earlier, so we propose introducing legislation to bring appropriate changes they want." He looked around the faces at the table, as if to seek acknowledgement of taking the moral high ground.

A stony silence ensued, the issues too sensitive for immediate commitment. All surveyed the postings flooding in. As usual, a wide variety of public opinion covering the entire spectrum from one extreme to another. Collectively, a state of confusion seemed to prevail.

Kris seized on the reticence around the table as a further opportunity. He focussed on the Treasurer. "The government has shown its determination to advance people's rights and freedoms, to stamp out discrimination. The basis on which you were elected. I understand, Treasurer, you will support the legislation we propose?" He exuded confidence, as though expecting confirmation of a fait accompli.

Unperturbed by looming controversy, the Treasurer lapped it up. "Yes, we do support modernisation, in line as you say with earlier maturing these days and the way human development is evolving. Social values must keep pace. We will work with you on this, so together we can ensure getting the balance right."

The Lib/Nat Leader was listening with growing alarm, irked by the Treasurer seemingly echoing the LGBT member's words as if they'd prepared a script beforehand. He'd been silent long enough. "We totally oppose lowering the age of consent. As for marriage, I think you should be ashamed for being a party to denigrating an institution originally devised as a fundamental cornerstone of human interaction lasting the test of time over centuries if not thousands of years." He glared at the Treasurer then LGBT member in turn. "You use the social change of a comparatively few short years to arrogantly ride roughshod over marriage, pretending to embrace modern values but actually following your own self-interest and of those you purport to represent. Shame on you for even imagining you have that right." Becoming steadily more angry as the wider implications crystallised.

He continued. "You talk of keeping pace with the evolution of life, as if this justifies your agenda. In fact, reality is the reverse. Evolution follows decision-making, a natural progression from whatever course we chart. But it can be ten, twenty years or more before our society feels the real effects, how changing our values manifests in practice over time. Our responsibility is to envisage that before making socially defining decisions."

Being from the older generation, he had memories of life prior to the advent of same-sex marriage, when the LGBT member was a young boy. Although heterosexual, he'd voted 'Yes' at the time, along with most of his government colleagues, captured by the irresistible political forces at play. But now, twenty-three years after the event, he'd seen enough to change his perspective. Consequences.

Another stunned silence fell. Sharon allowed time to peruse the postings. Many supportive of the Lib/Nat Leader's stance, suspicion of the Treasurer and Kris rife, amidst plenty of speculation over scandal already surrounding government Ministers.

She turned to the Coln Leader. "Shadow Prime Minister, would you like to comment?"

"Yes, I would." The Shadow PM sat forward, keen to take his turn after letting the others hang themselves first. He glanced at the Lib/Nat Leader. "I agree with you, Colin. We at Coln are also opposed to any tampering with the age of consent or the vital institution of marriage. But I disagree we'd have to wait twenty years to feel the evolutionary impact. That would be immediate!" He hesitated, giving a knowing half-smile as he fixed a penetrating stare at the LGBT member. "Kris, you want to lower the age of consent. To what? Fifteen? Fourteen? Lower?"

"Oh no." Kris was startled, put on the spot. "I think ---"

"You think? Who are you?" His stare deepened. "According to you, the only criterion worth considering is about earlier maturing of our children. But children mature at all different ages, younger or older. So who decides? You and your people?" He sat back, his voice turning sarcastic. "Maybe a psychologist, to assess every child individually for their maturity." He couldn't help a snort of derision.

"You exaggerate and mock the concept." Kris was fuming, not appreciating being humiliated. "People express their wishes and you disrespect them. You dwell in a past era, when inequality was fostered by prejudiced attitudes such as yours. That's the discrimination this government has rightly set out to eradicate from our society. We support them and we condemn your lack of respect. Both of you." He turned to include the Lib/Nat Leader in his tirade.

"You talk of respect," the Coln Leader retorted, remaining calm and unfazed. "Yet you would ambush our most precious institution that mankind has held fundamentally dear throughout the millennia. As if you have a god-like calling to suddenly know better. That is beyond disrespect, it is the ultimate in arrogance."

"Gentlemen, please," Sharon cut in, anxious to keep control of proceedings. "Please try to stay on track with the issues."

Another lull, another chance to peruse the postings flooding in at a furious rate. Too many to stay on screen long. Sharon slowed the scrolling. Strong support for the Coln and Lib/Nat Leaders now, seemingly a groundswell detecting dishonesty in the other two.

Encouraged, the Coln Leader was determined not to let it pass. "Sharon, to stay on track, we need to understand what's really going on here." He fixed another steely glare at the Treasurer. Then to the LGBT member, "Kris, we have a name for people who interfere with under-age children." Maintaining a steadfast resolve, he waited, giving Kris the opportunity to fill in the blank. But no response. "Do you want to tell us?" he prompted.

Kris was hesitant. "Tell you what?" He feigned indignation. "You're talking in riddles."

"No, just answer the question. Child abuse is what we're talking about. That's not a riddle. What name do we give people indulging in the sexual exploitation of children? Come on, let's see if you can say the word."

"I ----. You ----." Kris searched for firmer ground. "We know ----"

"You can't say it, can you? You can't say the word 'Paedophile'. Why is that? Why can't you make a simple honest statement of your intentions?" A harsh edge to his voice now. The Coln Leader indicated the screen, where postings continued strongly in his favour. He spread his hands in an expansive gesture. "Where are the people's wishes you claim to be respecting?"

"Sharon, can you please control our Coln friend?" The Treasurer breaking his lengthy silence, increasingly concerned at the exchanges trending the wrong way. "He puts his own twisted spin on some very good social reforms that people want." He paused, flinging an arm towards the screen dismissively. "Let's not get carried away with a few short-term responses inflamed by our friend's clever rhetoric. He seems to forget we were elected for our promise of social reform. Maybe that rankles with him, I'm not sure. But we should focus on the measures we, the people's government, are taking to honour the mandate bestowed on us."

The Lib/Nat Leader was next to speak. "Treasurer, logic would suggest lowering the age of consent and/or marriage must lead to having children at a lower age. Having them legally, that is. Does the expression 'kids having kids' make any impression on you? Already a problem in our society." When no immediate response followed, he gave an insipid half-smile then added, "I'll leave you to ponder on that one. In the meantime, yes why don't we focus on the measures you're taking, as you suggest? Perhaps we can return to the Budget woes now, as agreed we would. Sharon?"

"Yes, okay." Suddenly, Sharon put a hand to her earpiece. "Just a minute ----." A message coming through. "Yes ---- Really! ---- Thank you." A little stunned, she addressed the others. "Breaking news. Two separate incidents this afternoon, of Robin robots attacking people. One person killed with a broken neck, another stabbed to death with a knife! Details are sketchy at this stage, we're trying to find out more."

No one spoke for some moments, all thrown into a state of bewilderment. Eventually, the Lib/Nat Leader broke the tense silence. "That's devastating. I feel for the victims' families." Sombre, he paused to gather his thoughts, wrestling with the implications. "I'm afraid this looks like another blight on the AI industry. We know the factory has all but closed down, after previous incidents just like this latest news. So who is controlling these creatures now? How can this happen? More questions for your government to answer, Treasurer." He cast a meaningful glance at his political opponent.

"Yes. My commiserations to all those affected." The Treasurer drew a deep breath, buying a little time. "The problems at the factory go back a fair way, beginning before our time in office." He made a half-gesture towards the Coln Leader. "We were unable to turn that around, so had to put the factory on hold and now await the results of an enquiry. In the meantime, we'll investigate today's incidents and identify who is responsible."

The Coln Leader leaned forward. "Sharon, I want to offer my condolences to friends and family of the deceased. This is terrible what's happened." A brief pause, then he eyed the Treasurer sternly. "Instead of starting a blame game, we need to decide on a positive action plan. The government should immediately reopen the AI factory, restore its funding to a genuine level and reinstate the workforce. We can only hope the cutting edge world-renowned expertise we painstakingly developed over years has not already dissipated to other callings." He hesitated, letting his words sink in. "You know, when you withdraw support, for anything, and demonstrate lack of honest commitment, the inevitable result is loss of efficiency and control. Because you disappoint those dedicated to success. This is what has happened."

"Well, who's creating the blame game?" the Treasurer responded angrily. "This highlights just how far apart we are in our basic philosophies."

"Yes, it certainly does. Perhaps if you committed the same resources to it as you do towards your abstract, inward-looking ideologies like so-called equality, as if such a thing is even feasible, and discrimination, then the outcomes might be a lot different. Instead, you appeal to populism, hiding your self-gratification behind the mask of political correct-ness. Maybe the confusion you create suits your underlying agenda." Incisive, the Coln Leader held nothing back.

"You have no respect for people's rights!"

"Oh? Well, thank you Treasurer, for finally admitting to your hypocrisy. You're so strong on people's rights, then in the next breath you want to scrap marriage and lower the age of consent!"

Sharon cut in. "Gentlemen, please, we're getting personal again." She turned to the Lib/Nat Leader. "Colin, you were about to speak on Budget matters. Can you take it up from here?"

"Thank you, Sharon." The Lib/Nat Leader cleared his throat, roused from amusement over the last exchanges. "As I mentioned earlier, we have identified a number of factors about to send the Budget plummeting into heavy deficit. It paints a dark picture, I'm afraid." He noted the faces watching him intently from around the table. The postings had even slowed noticeably. Everyone waiting with bated breath.

"Some issues we know about already. The balance of payments has worsened significantly. Although savings occur through withdrawing funding from projects, these are far outweighed by resulting reduced royalties and lower tax receipts. Unemployment has shot up, adversely affecting benefit payments including for disabilities. As a result, the Social Security bill has blown out, exacerbated by many more single parent payments compared to this time last year. The social overtones, I might say, are rather relevant to the climate this government is enabling." He gave the Treasurer a hard look, then similar to the LGBT member. Both returned murmurs of dissent.

Colin continued. "The Health budget has skyrocketed. Some of this is expected. The scourge of New AIDS, which Coln was unable to overcome through their tenure, but is certainly worsening rapidly under Labour. Running in parallel is the perennial fight against superbugs and viruses, as yet no silver bullet to follow antibiotics becoming redundant some years back. Hospital beds are overflowing with cases, rates of infection rapidly worsening." He paused, gratified his points seemed to be striking the right note. Postings flowing in steadily were heavily supportive. "We only need another pandemic to erupt, then who knows the outcome. Could be anything."

"But other factors are not so expected. Mental Health is a huge burden on the Budget now, very clearly spiking sharply since last year. Especially in the young, with teenagers easily the highest rate of increase. Very disturbing. Not hard to see a connection to issues of social relevance we've been talking about. And to drugs. I'm no Coln supporter, but I did come to appreciate the Rehabilitation Centres they set up. Labour quickly disbanded them, and since then the drugs problem has spiralled up exponentially. Hospital facilities can't cope, let alone the contribution to Mental Health blowout. Why has it all gone this way? Well ---- I'm coming to that."

As a short break ensued, the Treasurer jumped in. "Sharon, do we get the opportunity to respond to some of this?" Increasingly, the weight of antipathy was becoming intolerable, social media postings damaging.

"Sharon, it is important I put everything on the table," Colin countered forcefully. "Then we can be in no doubt what we're confronted with here. If I may?"

"Please, proceed." Sharon held up a hand to restrain the Treasurer.

The Lib/Nat Leader resumed. "We're still investigating, but the evidence we have to date is compelling. I think it's well known the close association between Labour and the LGBT hierarchy, going back a long way. Their politics developed into a firmer partnership after Coln came to office. Political donations aplenty, LGBT Independent candidates contesting strategic electorates attempting to split the Coln vote, Preference deals, mutually beneficial promotions and advertising. None of this is a surprise. But of course, all with the promise of payoff when Labour finally returned to power. A frustrating wait through five Coln terms. What a huge build-up of payoff expectation! No wonder the LGBT agenda is so prominent this past year!" He paused to take stock. Only the Coln Leader seemed to be enjoying his presentation. The postings continued strongly in favour. He drew a deep breath, ready to move in for the kill, having circled his prey enough.

"Now, what is not well known is the further association with organised crime and the underworld. Going on just as long, we believe, deeply entrenched with at least one Asian triad group. The association includes a paedophile ring, drug smuggling, arms shipments, human sex trafficking. And who knows what else. We all know about the luxury launch and its cargo seized in Cairns recently, just one example. The Federal MP and State Minister involved have been named. I could name others, but refrain from doing so until we have a full and comprehensive list confirmed."

"These are outlandish accusations!" the Treasurer suddenly shouted. Animated, he leapt to his feet, glowering furiously at the Lib/Nat Leader. "You should withdraw them immediately or face the full weight of defamation law. You are not under Parliamentary privilege here, I remind you."

"Furthermore," Colin went on, ignoring him, "we've been hunting down the money trail. Soon after taking office, the government set up a slush fund, under the guise of social compensation. Many transactions from it are obscured by a convoluted network of financial conduits and overseas havens, but we've traced enough to confirm recipients consistent with the associations I just mentioned. Other transactions, to so-called compensation beneficiaries, are simple and unobscured, presumably to portray the fund as an authentic arm of our Social Security system. No wonder the cost blowout and pending dive into Budget deficit! Treasurer, this is your patch. Perhaps you can enlighten us further about your slush fund activities." Satisfied, he sat back and waited for the Treasurer to implode. A brief glance at the postings revealed numerous shocked responses, a public outcry gathering pace.

The Treasurer, seated again, struggled to contain his rage. Not helped by the disastrous postings flowing in. "You've made some very serious and outrageous allegations. I don't propose to give them any credence by discussing them here. I'll refer them to the Attorney-General for appropriate action." He cast a sour look at the Lib/Nat Leader.

Continuing on, "About what you call a slush fund, yes we do have a fund to compensate victims of social injustice, those not covered under existing benefits. Certainly, many in the LGBT community qualify. For instance, you spoke of single parent payments, of course increasing, since dissolution of same-sex marriages must have the same entitlement as heterosexual. There are children effectively orphaned by reneging would-be parents. Transgender people deserve assistance for their often difficult medical issues. I could go on with more. But how can I convince someone who deliberately sets out to slur our well-known and accepted association with LGBT? Perhaps your long time as an Opposition party is cause for resentment?" Pleased to feel he'd hit back with some effect, he offered the LGBT member a look of reassurance.

The Lib/Nat Leader was unmoved. "Sharon, I stand by everything I've brought to people's attention today. We'll have more to say as further information comes in."

A pause in proceedings. Postings continued unabated, little changing from a heavy bias condemning government for corruption and hypocrisy. The Treasurer's attempts to appease were seen as diversionary, failing to face the reality of Ministers already implicated in scandal seemingly aligned with the Lib/Nat Leader's allegations.

The Coln Leader, inwardly applauding his fellow Opposition leader's efforts, spoke next. "Sharon, I'd like to endorse the revelations our learned friend has exposed today." He nodded acknowledgement to the Lib/Nat Leader. "We also have been investigating, independently. Our findings to date closely match. The Treasurer heaps scorn on Lib/Nat's long period in Opposition. A frustration I can well understand, by the way." He allowed himself a quick self-indulgent chuckle.

"But he might well be describing Labour's own motivation. The obsessive focus on discrimination, prejudice, equality, these supposedly vital issues of our time, we believe is all just a scam. Really it's the LGBT agenda. Playing into the do-goodism pervading our society, the surest bet for a return to power. In partnership, they eventually managed to manipulate an election successfully, at the fifth attempt." Again he surveyed the faces around the table, letting out another knowing chuckle. "Then came the payoff. Which you so clearly alluded to, Colin. That's what we see now, decimating the nation's Budget."

Before his opponents could respond, he continued on quickly. "Unfortunately, the Budget is not the only decimation. Pity, since money troubles are generally recoverable. But loss of society's values and eroding our most precious institutions are not. The groups associated with, identified by Colin, have been systematically embraced and enabled by Labour. Closing down the drug Rehab Centres, paving the way to feed organised crime operations and a paedophile ring. Police and DP officers in cahoots, not sure how extensive but must be significant to be entrusted with increased drone surveillance powers. At the same time banning the private use of drones, media scrutiny too threatening. All but closing the AI factory. What are they afraid of?" Again he paused, conscious of how important were perceptions and to keep it balanced. "To be fair, we don't know how many MPs and Ministers are complicit. This is the task now, to find out."

A deathly hush descended. Neither the Treasurer nor LGBT member felt inclined to exacerbate a now calamitous forum by further arguing, with postings hotly adverse. "I'll refer your comments to the Attorney-General. You can expect there to be repercussions," the Treasurer finally concluded. "I have nothing further to add at this point. Perhaps we're at a close now, Sharon?"

"Yes, thank you all for participating," Sharon agreed, signalling an end to proceedings.

Chapter 20

Public reaction to the fiery clash between political leaders was intense. Widespread shock at the extent of corruption allegations dominated social and conventional media. No one waiting for proof, previous revelations about Ministers enough to arouse full condemnation of the Labour government. Other than diehard do-gooders driven by Labour's social agenda, everyone else wanted them kicked out of office, as immediately as possible.

People wanted Coln back. While on the surface, Coln had seemed deficient on social matters, in fact their impressive achievements in pushing projects through and resolving difficult or festering issues by direct practical action had, by natural progression, done more to alleviate people's perceived social ills than any amount of preoccupation with examining human rights and the like. A tenure lasting fifteen years evidence enough. But in less than one year of Labour, regression back to the pre-Coln days of sensitivities too easily offended, incessant over-analysis, paralysis by political correctness, opportunistic game-playing politics, now suddenly overlain by dramatic exposure of horrific scandal, was an abhorrent realisation mobilising the normally apathetic silent majority.

Coln appreciated, although hardly lacked, the impetus prompted by public outrage. Barely after leaving the studio, the Coln and Lib/Nat Leaders agreed to table in Parliament a Vote of No Confidence against the government. Unfortunately, next scheduled sitting was two weeks away, just before Budget night. The Coln Leader resolved to identify any provision in the Constitution to force an emergency sitting under these extreme circumstances. Agreed also was to sharply ramp up investigation of Police and DP involvement.

Keeping close to his mobile, Jude followed every moment of the afternoon's political stoush. Had the community arrived at a defining juncture? He was aware of much already. But the breaking news of two more Robin killings set his mind abuzz. Chongwe in control now, what was his agenda? Today's revelations about links to the underworld, a triad group! How senior a figure was Chongwe? An army of Robins available from the hundred-strong trial and stored at the factory! He shuddered, fearful of ultimate intent.

Late afternoon. Still no movement at Jeremy's house. Hiding within the old bus shelter, he'd kept vigil all day. The most likely source of detecting a lead to Lara's whereabouts. Chongwe was the prime focus, probably responsible for the last known action that removed Lara and others from the derelict warehouse. Taken to where? There was no clue.

Jeremy had left and returned several times during the day, each time on his own. Jude followed him once, keeping safe distance. To and from the Child Protection offices, of no help. But no Chongwe was the outstanding conclusion he was reaching. Not a surprise, consistent with all evidence pointing to a rift between them. Probably Chongwe was staying with his underworld contacts. Very difficult to track him down. And dangerous. Jude shook his head in frustration. What was the way forward? How to find Lara? Fear for her ate at him constantly.

His mind turned to Chas. No sign of him either. Probably he'd moved out too, another rift with Jeremy. Maybe re-arrested for Brett's murder? Certainly he should be, following Faketing exposed. Uncertain, Jude continued to watch Jeremy's house, determined to be as sure as possible before leaving.

The light was fading, early evening approaching. His mobile was continually active, regular breaking news items. More Robin incidents coming through. People being accosted in the streets, without apparent reason or warning. Reports of forced abduction, unaccountable aggression turning violent if resisted. Eyewitnesses were posting descriptions and pictures depicting arm-twisting and related actions. Jude recognised the enabling he'd been a party to testing. No further fatalities, but a growing sense of alarm was spreading quickly.

Watching in dismay, he tried to disseminate between postings, many seemingly repeat coverage of the same incidents. Yet, adding to previous suggested more than isolated examples now. Start of a concerted, organised operation? What did Chongwe and his group think they could achieve!?

Reports gave no indication of who was controlling the Robins. Not one mention of anyone, Chinese or other, with a handset targeting a victim. Had Chongwe installed additional capability? Sending them out with pre-determined intent? Jude shook his head, dumbfounded.

Another incident was posted, of similar action. A conventional news report informing the public, then a State Minister urging everyone community-wide not to panic, best to stay indoors, extra police resources being deployed. Federal Ministers were sought for interview, but none contactable including the PM. Especially calling for the Science Minister, but he couldn't be found. Furthering the impression of a government in disarray.

Eventually, the AI factory's Implementation Chief, Francis, was tracked down. He tried to project a calm persona but was clearly agitated. Unable to offer a satisfactory explanation, he instead gave a reassurance they had control of the Robins, these actions merely the result of a recalcitrant employee.

"We're confident we know who is responsible," he affirmed, sounding more assured than he felt. "He's been missing from the factory for some days and we're doing our best to locate him." He hesitated, knowing it was inadequate, more was expected of him. "Three Robins, with advanced capability, disappeared recently from secure storage at the factory. We believe these are being used in the attacks we're seeing today. I don't want to unduly alarm anyone, but we think it likely other Robins currently out there in the community under our trial programme are being rounded up and drawn into it. Therefore, we ask everyone who has a trial Robin, please deactivate it and keep it hidden, indoors or whatever. Tomorrow Monday, we will be coming to collect all trial Robins and return them to the factory for safe keeping.

This will minimise the potential for a worsening problem. Containment first, then police and security services can do their job. Thanks for your understanding and cooperation."

The Chief's obvious reference to Chongwe was hardly a surprise to Jude. Confirmation the evil schemer had probably gone underground with his criminal accomplices. More items were coming on screen, the Coln Leader with a critical assessment. Public reaction to the factory Chief's unconvincing assurances was largely negative, a level of panic setting in. Plus further anti-government sentiment, no input from that source only heightening the perception of complicity. More fuel to stoke the Coln fire.

Darkness had fallen. Nothing more to gain watching Jeremy's place. Jude left, another idea in mind. He rode to his long-time home. Still a cordoned-off crime scene. In stealth, he pushed past the barrier at the front. From the side, he could see a light emanating at the rear. Was his hunch right; Chas?

Unafraid of his would-be father now and realising he had just as much right, he returned and entered by the front door. Chas was in the lounge. And close by, RobinB, standing passive but activated. Its cold dark eyes fixed on Jude, recognising him. A familiar look, the scene reminiscent of their time living here together.

Chas reacted sharply, coming forward to confront him. "What do you want? Why do you come back here?"

"This is my home too," Jude responded, unfazed. "I need some things from my room." He held Chas in a steady gaze. Then he indicated RobinB. "Have you heard? The Robins are attacking people in the community. This is one of three causing it, according to a report from Francis at the factory. Where's Chongwe?"

With a smug half-smile, Chas moved next to RobinB, putting his arm around it possessively. "He protects me. Programmed for Security set task, remember?" He let out a self-endearing chortle. "The Robins out there are acting on their own. No one can control them, including Chongwe. I don't know where he is." In a sick way, the latest adversity seemed to please him. "Handsets are useless now."

Reality suddenly hit. Although distrusting Chas, his words had the ring of truth about them, consistent with the evidence. The AI factory's stated goal was to create a robot capable of learning, able to build further on its programming. Input via the senses to memory, repeat circumstance presents, output chosen from memory. Jude had seen enough examples already. Had it gone too far? No longer controllable! Aghast, he stared at RobinB with a new respect born out of fear.

His priority concern was flooding back. "Do you know what's happened to Lara?"

Chas shook his head, his upper lip curling in contempt. "No idea. Nothing to do with me." Still unsupportive, too selfish to respect Jude's alternative sexuality.

Jude hadn't expected a positive reply, but the unbending attitude irked him. "She was taken while I was stuck in jail. I'm sure you know about that! Taking the rap for you when someone corrupted the video evidence! But you must have dropped out of favour with Jeremy, so they reversed it, right? The police will arrest you again. I'm surprised they haven't already." He felt better for rubbing in the truth.

"Hah!" Chas retorted with derision. "Two DPs already tried. They got broken arms for their trouble." Again he held RobinB close, affectionately. "You see? I'm safe with him."

A waste of time, Jude decided. He swung away, to his room and picked up a couple of items. Heading for the front door, another surprise. RobinB followed behind him, accompanied by a shout of anger from Chas. As Jude reached his bike with the creature alongside, Chas flew out the door in near hysteria.

"Wait! Come back! Don't leave me!" He rushed to RobinB, clutching onto its arm.

Jude took off. RobinB pulled away from Chas, leaving him screaming in vain. It ran along easily beside the bike, all the way to Dulcie's place.

Amazed and thrilled at the sudden turn of events, Jude nevertheless could only wonder what next with the Robins? The 'Security' set task protected him and Chas equally. Did the 'Surveillance' set task, activated by his fathers to have him followed, give him preference over Chas? Further evidence of a crude ability in RobinB to make reasoned choices? Backfiring on Chas, the irony of it not lost on Jude.

Monday dawned, first day of the new school term. Jude had no intention of attending, far too much else to deal with. In sombre mood, he wasn't much company for Dulcie at the breakfast table. The spectre of Lara's fate hung like a morbid cloud over them.

First port of call was the factory. Although that probably meant losing the protection of RobinB, which had stood in the lounge keeping station loyally throughout the night, he felt an obligation to heed the call of Francis and return it there.

Still possessing his factory ID, he had no problem clearing entrance security. With RobinB at his side, no questions asked. He went straight to the offices. Francis wasn't there, neither were any senior management staff. The Computer Centre was deserted. He found Marcel wandering the factory floor checking on the skeleton staff left to carry out basic maintenance. Security was the largest group in attendance now.

He was about to greet Marcel when suddenly, RobinB left his side and dashed a short distance to the bay where rows of completed Robins were stored. The nearest Robin began glowing at the chest, flashing. Transmission done, it moved off heading for the factory exit. Then the next in line, same sequence.

Marcel reacted with a shout of consternation. "What goes on!?" He swung round to face Jude. "You brought RobinB back! What's it doing!? What are you playing at!?"

Initially shocked but now stung by the veiled accusation, Jude leapt forward. "Stop!" he cried, grabbing RobinB by the arm. "Stop doing this!"

To no avail. Unmoved, RobinB continued activating the horde of statue-like Robins. One by one, the flashing glow of a chest, upgrade communicated, the dark eyes with deepened awareness, swift departure. RobinB emitted a brief flash each time on completion, its loyalty to Jude in abeyance to tend a greater calling. Jude stood back, helpless.

Marcel aimed his handset, furiously punching the buttons. But no effect. Unable to deactivate a Robin, he threw the handset to the floor, splintering it into pieces. Enraged, he called for Security. Officers tried closing the factory doors, but the next Robin flung them open, injuring an officer in the process.

Robin by Robin, row by row, the bay steadily diminished until eventually it was empty. An army deployed, upgraded with state-of-the-art Robin3-level capability. Only RobinB remained, its task complete.

Intent on assigning blame, Marcel gave a signal. Two officers moved in and gripped Jude in informal arrest. Moments later, both were screaming with broken arms as RobinB reverted to protecting Jude. Everyone watching backed away in fright. A pall of finality settled over the empty storage bay and grossly depleted factory floor.

Feeling alienated, Jude eased away from Marcel. A sense of the factory now enemy territory kicked in. Galvanised, he quickly made for the exit. RobinB followed at his side. No one tried to stop them.

Once clear of the factory, the enormity of what just took place hit him. He cursed, angry at himself for bringing RobinB back. But the outcome was inevitable. The issues ran far deeper. To create a robot with self-sufficiency, learn and enhance capability mirroring human development, was an irresistible temptation of progress and ambition that took no account of non-technological vagaries. Yet Jude was thankful the original programming was further empowered not superseded, supporting RobinB's activated 'Security' and 'Surveillance' set tasks that protected him. For how long? There were no guarantees.

He decided to ride the streets and observe, safe as long as RobinB stayed with him. Robins roaming the walkways and open spaces were aplenty. Mostly they meandered along, not obviously seeking anything or to engage anyone, nor each other. Except their senses were sharp, surveying everything. That much Jude knew for certain. Every person a Robin passed was given obvious attention, as if weighing the option of engagement. Fewer people than normal were on the streets, fewer vehicles on the road. A sure sign of fear already gripping the community. And breaking news not even through yet about the factory breakout!

To Jude, the random scene epitomised every Robin consigned to an aimless existence, divorced from the life-enhancing advancement envisaged by and for their human creators. Cold input and output had no long-term purpose, vision or ambition. Would that be learned over time?

Suddenly, a skirmish ahead. Jude slowed. A Robin had intercepted a woman and her son. The mother screamed, the teenage boy was yelling, his arm twisted behind his back as the Robin marched him up the road. They turned a corner to disappear behind a building, the distraught mother tearing after them frantically.

A police vehicle moved slowly down the road. It passed several Robins before coasting to a stop. Two DP officers alighted, the driver remaining with the vehicle. Assigned the task of recapturing or regaining control, the two approached a single Robin that stood idly close by. Although seemingly in a state of limbo, it was watching. The merest hint of an aggressive move was enough. It dashed forward. A resounding crack was clearly audible as one officer's neck snapped to an incongruous angle. His lifeless body toppled to the pavement. The second officer yelled an oath, but had no time to flee, his neck grasped, another crack, another casualty.

Horrified, the vehicle driver backed away quickly. The Robin made to follow, then appeared to change its mind. The vehicle sped off.

Aghast, Jude watched from a distance. Robin behaviour was unpredictable, yet the attack was selective, other people passing not attacked. It was all about perceived provocation. But on a hair-trigger. No one could know whether a simple innocent moment, movement or act might signal the wrong perception. The path from input to output was too direct and simplistic, bereft of lateral thinking, moral or social checks and balances. No emotion-based judgement. Life's demands, complex for humans, were simple to a Robin. No chemistry, no feelings. Just input and output. Realistically, could a robot ever be expected to safely substitute for human endeavour? Consequences.

He was about to head away when another police vehicle appeared up the road. Followed by another, and another, a convoy. Some were vans, a mixture of Police and DP. A dramatically escalated operation underway after the spectacularly failed initial foray. In fear of what was unfolding, Jude cringed back, finding a shop entrance recess that afforded a measure of concealment.

Officers were disembarking. They carried weapons, heavy batons, handguns, some heavier firearms. With clear intent to round up Robins and herd them into vans for repatriation, they moved to where several were milling about in a cluster.

It all happened in a blur of action. Detecting aggression, the Robins attacked. Shouting of instructions quickly turned to screams as officers' bodies with broken necks began falling to the pavement. Initially they outnumbered the Robins, and more arriving, yet it was a mismatch of speed and agility. Robins flocked to the scene from further afield, including RobinB which suddenly darted away, leaving Jude frightened and cowering into the far corner of the recess.

A shot rang out. And another. Officers were re-grouping into combat formation, firearms pointing to pick off targets. The frenetic barking of instructions, a volley of shots fired from heavier weaponry. A Robin fell to ground. But only one. Others were swarming. Too fast, too precise, they swamped their foe, defying the sporadic gunfire.

The horror scene raged rapidly to a climax then subsided just as quickly. Suddenly, no more gunfire. Just the sounds of residual shouting and yelling as a few fear-struck officers managed an escape to their vehicles and departed. Like a pall of damnation, an eerie quiet descended over the carnage.

The bodies of slain Police and DP littered the road and pavement. Amongst them, a few Robins had succumbed to the firepower, but many presided over the aftermath. They filled the street, returning to former meanderings. RobinB re-joined Jude, who remained pressed into the recess in shock.

Eventually, he emerged to stand with his robotic companion, amazed by its return to dutiful station as if nothing had happened. He noticed two sizeable bullet holes in RobinB's skin, at lower abdomen and shoulder. Seemingly not affecting its capabilities, missing the chest area, the black box untouched. Struggling to settle his ragged nerves, he retrieved his bike and headed away. RobinB ran alongside.

At home, he joined Dulcie in front of the big screen. She'd watched it all, through social media beamed from a couple of DP officers remaining in their vehicles. It was going viral, worldwide. Postings portrayed major panic gripping the local community, people terrified to venture outdoors. Outrage over government inertia was skyrocketing.

After repeated failings of Ministers and leadership to answer media calls, the Prime Minister at last fronted the cameras. Under duress, he clearly showed the strain. "Anyone following media will be aware of what happened in Queensland a short time ago," he began cautiously. "This is terrible and I offer my sincere sympathy to the families of police officers who have fallen victim to the actions of Robin robots. These heroic members of our Police and DP work tirelessly to make life safe for us all. We can only admire their selfless courage and dedication to duty in tackling the Robins, committed to maintaining order on our streets." He paused to take a deep breath, glad to have got dutiful compassion correctly out of the way.

"We are working around the clock to ascertain why Robins have turned rogue. Management at the AI factory, especially the highly acclaimed computer staff there, are spending every waking hour devising a suitable response to bring our partners of the future back in line. Of course, a Robin operates under programmed computer-based control. So be assured, we will find an electronic solution." Again he paused, gratified to have portrayed himself as having answers.

"In the meantime, I urge everyone to continue normally with daily life, steer well clear if you see a Robin, but no need to panic. A Robin will only attack if it perceives an action as threatening, enough to trigger an output response. Thanks for your attention." He offered a reassuring smile, but it came across unconvincing.

The interviewer was quick to step in with further questions, but the PM maintained a steadfast adherence to prepared script. He would not be drawn into commenting on the inadequate performance of his Ministers.

Dulcie looked at Jude anxiously. Having experienced minimal contact with Robins, she was confused. And nervous of RobinB's presence, even though it stood passively to one side apparently unthreatening. "What did he mean by only attack if they perceive a threat? Those Robins were attacking every officer." She hesitated, indicating RobinB. "What about this one? Is it safe?"

"The PM was right about that, actually," Jude assured her, while far from certain about the reliability of Robin behaviour. "The trouble is, that perception can be from the most minor of acts, which a person might not even realise they're doing!" He was concerned for Dulcie. "This one had Security activated to protect our household. That means Chas too. It should include you, because you're close to me. But just in case, best don't do anything it might take the wrong way." Hardly a resounding confidence boost for his mother, he realised.

Opting to worry her no further, Jude kept quiet about the PM's other comments. Robins perceiving a threat were the only words of truth the PM spoke. The rest was a mixture of self-serving political correctness and down-right lies. Embellishing the Police and DP in the wake of their slaughter with words like 'heroic, courage, dedication', knowing full well the complicity of many in corruption and scandal. As for staff at the factory 'working around the clock' and 'spending every waking hour', he'd found the offices and computer centre deserted this morning! Their principle computer genius, Chongwe, was long gone.

The Coln Leader came on screen. He proceeded to castigate the government for its uncaring ineptitude and abdication of duty. Repeating his relentless call to discard socially trendy policies and adopt Coln-style action, he urged the PM to accept an offer of bipartisanship, emergency measures desperately needed before disaster turns to catastrophe.

Through it all, social media continued to project public outrage and fear. Calls to sack the government and bring back Coln were growing at frenetic pace. While not contributing, Jude identified with the frenzy, envisaging hundreds of Robins running wild all over town, with no known strategy to control or restrain them. Learning all the time, the use of firearms now inputted to memory! How and where would it end!?

Chapter 21

Options were few. As leads, Jeremy, Chas and Chongwe had all dried up or disappeared. One possibility remained; Gordon. No one else was left with connection to the forces stealing Lara away. But Gordon's whereabouts was a blank, his residence unknown, the Cave defunct.

Tired of viewing repetitive social media activity that led nowhere, Jude went to his room. Remembering the information Lara had gleaned online, he searched the Sex Offenders Register and found her father's details, address a mandatory inclusion. He printed off a copy. Brent would lead him to Gordon.

Then another thought. "Yes, I wonder. Could be useful," he murmured to himself.

Mid-afternoon now. He told Dulcie he might be a while, then left. Again, RobinB ran alongside the bike.

Doris and Glenice were pleased to see him, except Lara not with him. They'd heard nothing further. Both looked stressed out. Not only about Lara, the Robin attacks also.

Jude reassured them RobinB was safe, then put his idea. "I know you're very much against any contact with Lara's father," he began tactfully. "But this might be the only avenue left. I've followed up every other lead, and the trail is stone cold."

Both mums looked startled, not expecting pressure from that quarter. Doris took it up hesitantly. "We have good reason to reject him. He's a bad man, doing bad things." She glanced at Glenice, who was shifting feet nervously. Reluctantly, she asked Jude, "What did you have in mind?"

"I'm wondering if you have documentation proving his sperm donorship to you, maybe original agreement? With photos would be good. And also, do you have a recent photo showing you and Lara together?" He paused, concerned to respect their feelings. "I'm not sure if you know, but he's seen Lara recently, without knowing she's his daughter. An unfortunate encounter, not Lara's fault. Brent is associated with people I'm sure are responsible for her abduction. He might know where she's been taken, or can find out. If I can convince him that he's her father, then he might want to rescue her."

Doris stared at him a long moment, struggling to reconcile unexpected revelations. "No, we didn't know that. We knew Lara was interested in locating him, against our will." A hard set to her face, another glance at her partner. Sceptical, she went on, "I don't think you understand what sort of man he is. It's likely he won't want to know, might even react the other way and harm her."

Jude indicated RobinB. "This Robin is programmed to protect me and anyone close to me. It already knows Lara. I won't take this further unless I'm sure it's safe and we're protected."

"Can you give us a few minutes?" Doris replied, still sceptical. She turned to Glenice and they moved away.

After a private animated discussion, Doris peeled off and went to the bedroom, leaving Glenice visibly distraught. Soon Doris returned, with papers. She handed them to Jude.

"We don't have a sperm donorship agreement. It was all a bit rushed at the time." She grimaced, displaying a degree of cynicism. "But that's a copy of Lara's birth certificate. It shows all details, dates, even thumbnail photos of me and Brent. The Department was more reputable than most agencies back then." She hesitated, giving Jude a serious look. "The other one is a recent picture of me and Lara. We don't like this, but if you feel it is the last resort, then we have no choice but to take the risk."

Jude assured them he would play it cautiously. He thanked them, shared an expression of hope, then departed with RobinB.

Still daylight left in the afternoon. He checked his printout. Not far to Brent's address. He made his way there. An older suburb in a poorer part of town, many houses lacking maintenance. Brent's place, halfway along a cul-de-sac, looked neglected, grass high at the front. Jude passed slowly by, but couldn't see if anyone was home.

The cul-de-sac had no convenient hiding-place. He took up a bench seat at the end, prepared to watch and wait from a distance. The presence of RobinB was hardly conducive to remaining inconspicuous, but its loyal protection emboldened him. The occasional vehicle and a few people wandering up and down helped obscure him. They kept well clear at the sight of a Robin.

Nearly an hour passed, dusk approaching. Then at last, a late-model vehicle, too flashy for these dour environs, pulled up outside Brent's place. Brent emerged from his house, climbed in beside the driver, the vehicle did a U-turn and headed away.

Buoyed with anticipation, Jude followed, keeping safe separation. A short trip later, they came to a middle-class suburb, coasting down a mildly busy street. Jude stayed well back as the vehicle ahead stopped outside a modern-looking home. Gordon, one arm in a sling, and Brent alighted. They strode purposefully to the front door.

A woman answered. An altercation ensued. It quickly escalated. A flurry of action, the woman screamed. A man appeared. The small group spilled into the open, Brent attacking the pair ferociously. They were no match for his immense strength. When Gordon, standing to one side, called a halt, both lay writhing on the ground, crying and moaning, faces battered and bleeding. Gordon stepped forward, leaning over them to mouth a few harsh words, then swung away, leaving them to fend for themselves.

Jude watched from behind a vehicle on the other side, dismayed once more by a Gordon activity. A debt-collecting exercise? Alternative string to Gordon's bow, having closed down the Cave.

Quickly on the move again, they passed through another suburb, reaching a tree-lined avenue in a leafy district area. An affluent part of town. Gordon pulled in against the kerb. Keeping well back, Jude and RobinB settled behind a large tree ideal as an observation post. Darkness had fallen, but the streetlighting was ample.

Gordon and Brent stayed in their vehicle. With side window down, Gordon set up a small camera on the sill, aimed at a large upmarket dwelling across the road. They waited. Not long later, a sporty-looking vehicle backed out of the driveway, driven by a young man. He gave a quick wave and accelerated away. Gordon had the camera rolling.

From two doors down, another young man left home and walked to the house of interest. He was let in at the front door by someone unseen. After appropriate time elapsed, Gordon unhooked the camera, stepped out then hurried across the road with Brent. They disappeared down the side to the rear of the property.

Before long, shouting and yelling suddenly from within. The man's stay was short-lived, as he came running up the side pathway, naked above the waist, stumbling as he struggled to pull up his trousers. Hyped-up and cursing, he escaped back to his house. Gordon and Brent appeared, laughing together as they ambled back to their vehicle.

Watching spellbound, Jude wondered if the resident was a woman or man, heterosexual or same-sex relationship being violated. Not that it mattered. A small addition to statistics either way.

Gordon doing private detective work, seemingly with a mandate for direct action, was hardly a surprise. But closing down their paedophile activities, at least temporarily, only made it harder to track down Lara.

It dawned on Jude there was hardly a better time for confrontation if ever he was to gain information about Lara's whereabouts. RobinB would thwart any adverse reaction. Even, he expected, able to deal with Brent, strong as he was. Feeling bold and committed, Jude stepped out from behind the tree, in full view near a streetlight as the vehicle completed a U-turn and approached.

Gordon slowed and stopped alongside. He jumped out. Brent joined him. "Well, well!" Gordon exclaimed. "Jude, isn't it? I had a feeling we were being followed. What's your game?" He eyed RobinB warily, knowing enough to refrain from any aggression.

"I want to talk to you," Jude responded, determined to be forthright. "Lara has been taken, I'm sure you know. Can you tell me where I can find her?" He remained calm, preferring not to sound too demanding.

Gordon gave an insipid half-smile. "If I knew, why would I tell you? You're both a danger to us. You know too much." Always, he aimed to take control.

Undeterred, Jude changed tack. "I'm sure you're aware of the turmoil the Robins are causing right now. Especially the government in chaos. I doubt anyone would be interested in listening to me, even if I wanted to say something, which I don't. I just want to find Lara, that's all. Please." He stopped short of open pleading, trying to stay conciliatory.

Gordon let out a quick laugh. "You're right. But the turmoil will die down eventually. Then what?" His last words hung in the air, carrying a myriad of implications. "Tell you what, I'll be honest with you. I do know where she was taken to. But since then, she and others have been taken elsewhere, by another party. I don't know to where."

Jude hesitated, distrusting. But the comments squared with his knowledge to date. "What other party? Chongwe?"

Gordon shrugged his shoulders. "Maybe."

Jude eyed him with suspicion, struggling to restrain a growing anger churning at his insides. His last resort option loomed large. Putting everything on the line, he decided to go for it. "What about your partner here?" He indicated Brent. "I think you know he's Lara's father. Does he know? Do you think he might want to find and save his daughter?" He held Gordon in a steely glare.

Gordon stepped back a pace, clearly rattled. He looked at Brent anxiously. "Don't believe what he says. He's bluffing." His voice slightly shaky betrayed unusual uncertainty, bordering on fear. Highly uncharacteristic of a man normally the master manipulator.

Brent was mildly agitated. "What did he mean, Boss? I don't have any daughter. Why did he say that?" His eyes darted about a little crazily.

The defensive reactions surprised Jude. Not the menacing threats he was expecting. Perhaps RobinB a factor? Encouraged, he pulled the papers from his back pocket and held them out to Gordon. "Here, I have proof."

Quickly reassessing, Gordon waved the papers away, nervous of RobinB should Brent exceed his tolerance threshold. "Listen, I can help you to this extent. If you believe Chongwe is responsible, you could probably track him down at Old Chinatown, next to the Valley. But overtly or covertly, either way it's dangerous." He glanced at Brent, relieved to avert an imminent behavioural spiral downwards.

Jude wavered, momentarily daunted by the challenging logistics of Gordon's suggestion. But it was a lead, the only one. Most likely, neither Gordon nor Brent knew anything further regarding Lara. He put the papers back in his pocket. "Okay, I'll try that."

Back in control, Gordon's mind was ever calculating. He inclined his head towards RobinB. "How did you manage to gain the allegiance of this fellow? This particular Robin was protecting Chas."

Jude could see no harm in reinforcing a position of strength. "It was assigned to our household in the trial. The Security set task was activated to protect us."

"Yes, I know." Gordon let out a quick chuckle. "But now, it's with you only. That leaves Chas on his own." With an insidious smile, he again glanced at Brent. Then back to Jude. "If there's nothing more, we'll leave you to it." He swung away, signalling Brent to follow.

Pensive, Jude watched their vehicle head up the road and disappear around the corner. He felt uplifted by the further prospect in his search for Lara. But highly dangerous. Gordon was certainly right about that. With a fatalistic sense of destiny, he returned to his bike and departed the scene.

Nearing home, a horrible premonition suddenly struck him. Gordon's words were ringing alarm bells in his head. He stopped abruptly, turned then started back. Reaching the street he knew so well, the sight of Gordon's vehicle parked outside his old home was confirmation enough. An unaccountable fear for Chas gripped him.

Entering familiar territory, RobinB dashed ahead. Seeking Chas, it disappeared inside the house, Jude unable to keep up. In moments, a commotion erupted. Brent came staggering out, clutching his head in anguish, bellowing with the roar of a wounded bull. He stumbled haphazardly across the front yard, slammed into the fence and collapsed to the ground, the bellow reducing to a tortured whimper. A spectacular reversal from the all-powerful aura pervading when he terrorised others.

Incredulous, Jude moved closer, uncertain about offering help. The man's swollen neck was turning a purplish hue, evidence of whiplash. Yet he'd survived. Withstanding the Robin killing system, testament to his superhuman-like strength.

RobinB emerged. With cold deliberateness, it took station beside Jude, remaining passive despite Brent being unfinished business. Symptomatic of one-off output uncomplicated by lateral thinking as to outcome.

No one else emerged. With a mounting sense of peril, Jude went inside. At first, nothing. No sounds. Reaching the lounge, he saw a form on the floor. It was Gordon, not moving. His neck was skewed to a crazy angle, one eye dilated staring unblinking at the ceiling. Another unfortunate perishing at the hands of a Robin, another statistic.

Jude felt no remorse for him. But where was Chas? Not in the kitchen, or bathroom. At the bedroom door, Jude froze in shock. Chas was hanging mid-air, a cord around his neck tied to the ceiling fan. Head bowed forward, face bloated and red, eyes bulging like spotted balloons, swollen tongue lolling from one corner of his mouth. The foul smell of excrement poisoned the air. Gutted, Jude doubled over as a wave of nausea swept through his stomach.

He recovered a little composure. What to do? Try to get Chas down? By the legs, he lifted him, but couldn't reach up to release the cord. RobinB was there. In a moment, it inputted Jude's attempt and had Chas down, dropping him onto the bed. Done with typical coldness. No sign of a reaction, having failed to protect Chas under Security set task. Nothing resembling regret, guilt, sorrow. Could emotion be learned?

Jude stood rigid, staring at Chas's body. The upturned face was gruesome. Cuts and bruises evidenced treatment meted out prior to final demise. He gave a sickly groan, again nauseous as he comprehended the execution-style retribution administered by Gordon and Brent. Opportunistic in RobinB's absence. He turned away, his mind choked, jumbled emotions in chaos.

A noise in the lounge room. Brent had re-entered. Somewhat recovered but wobbly on his feet, he staggered forward. Spying Gordon lying prone on the floor, he rushed over and dropped to his knees. "Boss, Boss!" he cried urgently. His soft whining voice belied the cruel nature, starkly contrasting the bellowing roar emitted a short time ago. He gently touched Gordon's cheek. "Boss." He seemed bewildered.

Then, as he stood, something snapped in his brain. Another deafening roar burst from his throat, as if expending the last breath from his lungs. His body shook violently, muscles rippling as a massive adrenalin rush took hold. Stumbling away, arms flailing, he crashed into a cabinet, obliterating the front in a shower of glass. Then he went berserk. Careering aimlessly around the room, he smashed anything in reach. Furniture flying, lounge chair hurled through side window, every loose item, adornment, household possession swept to the four corners, holes punched in walls. All amidst a cacophony of grunting and bellowing, giving vent to the raging grief-driven fury that crazed him.

He stormed out to the front yard. Jude's bike was there. He smashed it against the wall, then threw it aside as a crumpled piece of scrap. Ripping the pathway gate off its hinges, he flung it through the front window in a splintering crash. Three vehicles parked at the kerb, one Gordon's one a small truck, were no match for his violent rage and enormous strength. He tossed each on its side, one on its roof, windscreens shattering. A rubbish bin at kerbside was sent hurtling through the neighbour's front window, spilling rubbish across the lawn. Finally, with no further items nearby to attack, he let out another horrendous bellow and began a weaving stagger heading away.

With extreme caution, Jude crept out from the bedroom as Brent left the house. A quick survey of the carnage, then he hurried to the front door just as the gate came crashing through the window. RobinB followed, remarkably without an output response throughout Brent's rampage. Only property threatened not people. But always it was inputting to memory.

He saw his broken bike and witnessed the trashing of vehicles, the rubbish bin. At last, the human beast was finished and departing. Jude set out on foot to follow the shuffling figure, keeping well back.

Watching the rear view of a vile hitman meandering morosely up the road, Jude couldn't help seeing him now as a forlorn lonely misfit. Incongruous with the man's intrinsic role in evil. The normally specifically targeted violence was this time wild and indiscriminate, fuelled by grief. Where did the sudden loss of long-time mentor and sponsor, the man he fondly called 'Boss', leave Brent now? No prospects, no favour with authority, no friends, no alternative life. Just a devastated loose cannon, a chemically castrated direction-less dinosaur.

Pre-empting any danger of feeling pity for a wounded monster, Jude reminded himself of the cruel fate dealt Chas. Yet, in stark contrast to the outpourings just witnessed, he felt no such grief for his would-be father. His two fathers had chosen the path through life for their family, each dying by the sword lived by. Consequences.

The ironic twist to Chas' demise gave him a moment of remorse. RobinB, leaving Chas on his own to favour protecting himself, had left the way open for Gordon to take advantage. And if he'd not been late in following the execu-tioners, RobinB would have been in time to thwart their evil intent. He should feel guilty, but he didn't, the moment of remorse passing quickly. The end of Chas was fated to be.

Following Brent's erratically wavering tracks seemed a pointless exercise. But Jude was curious, the route clearly not towards the man's home. Desolate confusion a residual effect? The constant menace of loose Robins roaming the streets was a factor, no telling what Brent might do at any juncture to trigger an output. Everyone rode that knife-edge now. Near deserted streets was evidence of that. They passed a couple of Robins without incident. Brent not inputting as a threat for the moment.

Jude suddenly recognised where Brent was heading. Jeremy's place. Of course. The only soul left in the world for Brent. Jeremy answered the front door. From across the road, Jude observed them together. The conversation seemed muted, the body language not particularly animated considering the circumstances.

Jeremy spied him. He broke off from Brent and signalled him over. Hesitant, Jude crossed the road to join them. He was wary, but had RobinB by his side.

"Come inside," Jeremy invited. Neither welcoming nor commanding, a matter of convenience only. They sat at the coffee table. He looked serious, without the usual arrogance. "A lot has happened lately. Brent just told me about Gordon." He barely paused, just a fleeting moment of acknowledgement, as if their association meant nothing more than business. "You know too much, seen too much. I want to know what your intentions are." His tone was flat, pointedly non-aggressive. Very conscious of RobinB.

To Jude, Jeremy's focus on self was a repeat of the scene with Gordon. "Did Brent tell you what he did to Chas?"

Jeremy glanced enquiringly at Brent, who was standing apart, sweating profusely and unusually nervous. RobinB was his first ever experience of a power matching if not exceeding his own. "I took care of him, Boss. Like you wanted."

New 'Boss', Jude noted. Brent slipping back into familiar mode? How wrong to see him as lonely! He didn't have the mentality for that, as long as there was someone to call 'Boss'. But Jeremy was different from Gordon. Would it work? He returned attention to Jeremy. "My intentions are only to find Lara. That's all I want. Maybe you can help me with that. Then I can help you, sharing the protection." He indicated RobinB.

The concept of siding with Jeremy seemed preposterous, yet mutual benefit was always a powerful motivation. Recent events left Jeremy in a weakened state. Jude himself had no appetite for tackling Chongwe and company alone, even with RobinB's help.

Jeremy cracked a quick smile and chuckled. Signs of the old Jeremy. "Why would I help you? Lara knows as much as you about us." But he wasn't dismissing the idea. To get back at Chongwe was a burning incentive. And the prospect of gaining control over a Robin appealed.

Jude was quick to reply. "You've closed down the Cave. Gordon's gone. How would we find evidence against you? Even if we wanted to, which we don't. We just want to be together and get on with our lives, no hassles."

An imperceptible nod as Jeremy comprehended. "How do you imagine I can help you anyway? Lara was taken by others, I don't know where to." He spread his hands, feigning innocence.

"Yes. Gordon told me. Chongwe's comrades took her, with other captives. I'm sure you know that." Jude paused, noting Jeremy offered no dissent. "Gordon also told me where to find Chongwe. At Old Chinatown."

Jeremy gave a knowing grunt. "That's right. But you wouldn't want to enter that minefield. Things happen there you have no concept of." He looked away, becoming distant.

Jude caught his breath in consternation. "I hope they didn't take Lara there!" The thought made him frantic.

"Who knows." Jeremy spoke distractedly, his mind focussed elsewhere. A hard set came onto his face, something stirring from deeper within. Unusual for Jeremy.

A lengthy silence fell. When finally he refocussed, he was as serious as Jude had ever seen him. "I can't guarantee we'll find Lara. But Chongwe is the one. You must leave him to me and Brent. We have a score to settle. Your Robin will be important though. Together, we might just have enough power to get us through." He nailed Jude with a penetrating stare. "Do you understand what I'm saying? Chongwe is the focus, maybe leading to Lara, maybe not. This is the only way I'll do it."

Jude could hardly imagine the gravity of the task. But he was committed. "Okay, agreed. What's this score you have to settle?" He sensed more to their history than evident to date.

"Ah." Another long pause, seemingly making up his mind, as if weighing up how much to confide in Jude. "We've been together a long time, Chongwe and I. Met around 2018, just when same-sex marriage came in." He allowed himself a quick smirk, but it was without humour. "You see, he's straight-out gay. I'm bi." His eyes bulged as he leaned forward, needing to emphasise the point.

"I had the perfect life at the time," he went on, his tone sceptical now. "Married to a good woman, eight year-old daughter we loved dearly, me with a good job in Child Protection Services. Only a junior position back then, but I was young and ambitious. Out to prove something to my father." A stronger tone of cynicism accompanied the last comment. "Too ambitious. There were one or two bad eggs in the Department even then. Before the days of Coln, that was. The Department wanted to push same-sex initiatives. Sign of the times. State and Federal Labour were like hand in glove, as they are again today. Politics, you can't beat it."

Another pause, another humourless smirk. "All the talk now is about discrimination. In those days, reverse discrimination was rife, driven by political correctness. But it suited me, especially when Chongwe turned up. He knew someone there. We made exciting crazy plans together, great expectations with his computer genius and the future of AI beckoning. I met Gordon then too, with his political contacts. The rest is history." He shifted his eyes to stare into space, genuinely affected.

"Wow." Jude was listening enthralled, amazed at the different side of Jeremy presenting. Like floodgates opening for the first time. Soul-searching after the recent split with Chongwe? But was there more? Such a deeply felt change in Jeremy's entire demeanour suggested so. "What happened to your wife and daughter?" he asked on a hunch.

Jeremy continued to stare, letting the question hang in the air. He seemed oddly calm, beyond emotion. Eventually he responded. "Yes, quite. What happened. My marriage was history too then. But I didn't care, I was flying with Chongwe and Gordon. And I still saw my family in regular visits. But Chongwe didn't like it. Not out of jealousy, rather branding them a threat he couldn't control." The merest hint of emotion showed briefly, before Jeremy jammed it back under wraps.

He continued, "My wife hated him with a passion. I think she tried to do something. Then one day, my wife and daughter were gone. Found lying in a ditch, each with a bullet through the head." Intense and fighting himself, he fell silent once more. But only briefly. "I hardened up after that, knew what I was involved in, what the underworld was capable of. When you're in that deep, you stay in or die. So I channelled it, made sure if anyone was to be hurt, I'd be the one giving not receiving it. And so it went on." Projecting an air of fatalistic inevitability, he stood abruptly and began pacing the floor.

Jude was agog, trying to digest the extraordinary revelations. Unbelievable Jeremy would confide in him this way, given the uncompromised perpetrating of evil to date. Everyone had their background, no one was born evil.

As if reading Jude's thoughts, Jeremy re-took his seat, intense once more. "I tell you everything so you know why I agree to help you. But doing it my way, for my own benefit. After all I've sacrificed for Chongwe, now he duds me. Well okay, that's how it is, the way we operate. But he must pay. That's also the way it is. If not for Chongwe, I'd have a grown-up daughter and a couple of grandchildren. Instead ----?" He spread his hands, palms up as if to emphasise the emptiness. "He must pay." Grim-faced, he sat back, gratified in the moment.

Comprehending the tough logic of the underworld, Jude turned his mind to practicality. He indicated Brent, who was hovering nearby as the loyal enforcer. "What about him? Gordon's prodigy. Can you handle him? I just saw him trash our place, off his head. Losing Gordon has hit him hard."

"Sure, don't worry about that. They had a special bond, no doubt." Jeremy nodded reflectively. "Gordon was a private man, no one else he was close to at a personal level really, even me. He was bisexual, like me. Two marriages, both not lasting long. No children." He paused, the characteristic smirk returning. "His interests were wherever lay the best return, business-wise. That's Gordon. Nothing was out-of-bounds. Very attractive to some politicians." The cynicism back again.

A lull in conversation ensued, both reflecting on what may lie ahead. They discussed the logistics, exchanged mobile contacts, then Jude departed for home. The night hour was late. A long day, much happening, a lot to reconcile.

Chapter 22

M id-morning, Jude and RobinB arrived at the Valley carpark, using Lara's bike. He eased into a spare space next to Jeremy and Brent here already.

"Right on time. Very good," Jeremy commended.

"Hoverbike more versatile?" Jude remarked, noting their alternative choice of transport.

"In case we need a fast getaway." Jeremy reverted attention to a portable screen clipped on top of the handlebars. A birds-eye image was showing, a network of narrow alleyways weaving between rows of old two-storey buildings. A labyrinth of obscure intrigue by any assessment. Access was unsuitable for vehicles wider than a bike. Much in shadow, a few people were discernible in the gloomy light, wandering around, in and out of building entry points or sitting impassive outside. Remnants of a bygone age, when once vibrant work and shop outlets with accommodation atop thrived, many now disused or abandoned.

"Old Chinatown?" Jude presumed, peering keenly at the screen. "How do you get these images?"

Jeremy pointed to the sky. "See the black speck up there?" He focussed back on the screen and a set of controls attached. Levering a joystick one way then another caused the screen image to shift correspondingly, bringing into view other parts of the area.

Jude looked skywards, seeing nothing at first, then just able to pick out a small black dot that shifted in sync with the joystick. He glanced amusedly at Jeremy. "Private use of drones is illegal now, unless you obtain a permit."

"Indeed it is." Jeremy smiled condescendingly. "Who's going to stop us? The DP I know wouldn't care, the rest are running around trying to catch Robins. I keep it high elevation, hard to detect with the naked eye. We're away from aircraft flight paths."

He worked another control. The drone's camera zoomed in, picking out an old Chinaman sitting hunched against a building wall. Viewing was invasively close, enough to identify his features, unshaven appearance, butt of a cigarette hanging from his mouth.

"Just a demo," Jeremy quipped. He zoomed back out, then repeated the sequence at other targets. Satisfied, he settled on a suitable zoom height. "No Chongwe in sight. But if he comes or goes, we won't miss him." He traced his finger down an alleyway, to where it intersected a wider road. "That's the only way in or out. From the Valley."

Jude watched, intrigued. But impatient for something more certain. "So, what do we do now? Wait for Chongwe to appear? Or can we go in and find him? Maybe Lara's in there somewhere."

"For now, we wait and learn more. Chongwe will appear at some stage. We can go in, but first I want to know if he has control over Robins again. He only needs one to neutralise our Robin, then we're in trouble. This is his territory. He has plenty of henchmen. Heavies who can deal with Brent." Serious, he cast Jude a stern sidelong glance. Then shrugged his shoulders, more casual. "Lara is either there or some-where else. Who knows? We can't decide an action for that."

Jude was a little perturbed by Jeremy's dismissive atti-tude towards Lara. But it was as agreed, no choice. A bizarre conundrum, an arrangement at odds with their history to date. And so, they waited.

"Okay, here's something," Jeremy suddenly declared, breaking the impasse.

Three hoverbikes had left an innocuous-looking building to move slowly down an alleyway. Jeremy zoomed in the camera image. Each bike was loaded with white canvas bags strapped to pillion seat. He zoomed in closer. "That's Chongwe! Riding the leading bike." Galvanised, he pointed out the figure to Jude.

The bikes wound down another alleyway, negotiating the maze. Reaching the Valley road, they accelerated away. But for only a short distance. Slowing, they turned up a lesser side street, then to a minor road lined with warehouses petering out to a dead-end. Bordering the outer boundary, a dividing road separating Old and New Chinatown. They swung in at a warehouse near the end.

Jeremy shifted the drone across to gain a better viewing angle. Inside the warehouse, with roller door raised, the rear end of a large truck was visible, its double doors open to receive goods. Chongwe and his two comrades began transferring the canvas bags.

"This is our chance!" Jeremy exclaimed vociferously. He leapt onto his bike, signalling Brent and Jude to action.

"Quick, while they're isolated! Only three of them, no Robins! We can handle that!" Brent took the pillion seat. With a fierce look depicting a steadfast resolve, Jeremy backed out then took off fast, urging Jude to follow.

Startled and bemused, Jude headed after them, RobinB alongside as usual. Onto the Valley road, a short hop only to the minor road and warehouse ahead. But in that time, reality struck home. In a flash, Jude realised Jeremy had not changed. Self-interest was the man's sole motivator, to take out Chongwe, satisfying personal aggrievement. But Chongwe was the only lead to Lara! Was that about to be terminated? As they reached the warehouse, Jude sorely regretted getting sucked into Jeremy's plan and exploitative use of RobinB.

Chongwe and his helpers were loading the last bags as Jeremy's bike skidded to a halt beside theirs. Immediately, confrontation loomed large. Chongwe sauntered up to Jeremy. "What you want here? How you find us?" Angrily, he summoned his support forward. Two huge Chinamen, hand-picked by Chongwe to inflict the heaviest of heavy hitting when required.

The attitude changed abruptly when Jude pulled in. A Robin involved. Chagrined, Chongwe backed away, signalling restraint on his heavies. A compromised position, highlighting the loss of control over Robins this brilliant genius was yet to rectify.

Jeremy took it up, seizing the opportunity for advantage. "You left unfinished business behind." The arrogance was back. He glanced pointedly at RobinB, then at Brent standing close by awaiting action. "We're here to finish it."

Chongwe remained cool, weighing his options. He had full confidence in his henchmen and their capability hitherto unrivalled. One on one with Brent was winnable, but the other had no chance with a Robin. He felt out-manoeuvred. "What business you mean?" Playing for time.

"Ah." Jeremy's eyes gleamed, the adrenalin flowing. "Selective memory, is it? We had a pact, remember? Going back through all the years. But finally when it suits, you reneg on it. Your power play didn't work though, did it. The Robins themselves have control, not you." He gave an insidious laugh, brimming with pent-up resentment. When Chongwe, becoming agitated, made no reply, Jeremy was spurred on. "All that I sacrificed for you. All the promise of great things. You took my family from me! For what!? Now you spit on me, you dare to trash my long years of commitment!" His voice rose steadily, his body beginning to shake as an alarming depth of hatred manifested. "You must pay!"

"Wait!" Jude stepped forward quickly, noticing for the first time a bulging shape hidden beneath Jeremy's shirt. The outline of a knife pouch? Jeremy's hand was moving to it. Disaster imminent. The scene was tense, the air electric. Surely close to triggering a Robin output reaction. Decimation the only outcome, especially should a knife be deployed!

Suddenly, he felt no affinity with self-serving Jeremy. Nor with Chongwe, except no Chongwe meant no lead to Lara! Desperate, he made a snap and fateful decision. "This has nothing to do with me," he announced boldly. "I'm out of here." He turned away, frantic to remove RobinB from the mix.

On the point of serious action but unexpectedly blind-sided, Jeremy was irate. "You can't leave! We have a mission we agreed on!"

But Jude was already on his bike and away, relieved to escape with RobinB in tow. He didn't look back. The sound of Jeremy's shouted oaths quickly faded as he rounded the street corner, completing a clean breakaway. Leaving Jeremy in a precarious bind, but Jude felt nothing for him. The evil schemer deserved whatever fate had in store.

Reaching the entry point from the Valley road, Jude had one thought in mind. If Lara was held in Old Chinatown, he would find her! He headed slowly up the narrow alleyway, observing. People were scarce, those he passed mostly old men wandering aimlessly, sitting or squatting against a building wall, wiling away their final years. No enterprise evident here. The perfect front for Chongwe and his group.

Retracing the path Chongwe's small convoy had tracked down, he came to their starting point. A building no different from others, but a good place to begin his search. With his small bag of tools in hand, he passed through the entrance of an old shop. RobinB followed.

The remnants of once better times were dirty, unkempt, abandoned. Jude didn't hesitate, starting straight up a wooden staircase, disbelieving anyone would reside here but grimly determined to find out. A short landing at the top serviced two doorways to rooms beyond. But the extraordinary eye-opener was at each end, where large openings had been roughly punched through the common walls to adjoining abodes, crudely linking into one long access

377

corridor. Signs suggesting collective interaction of more than usual numbers of people.

The air was musty and stale, smoke-filled. At the first doorway, he saw why. A circle of people sat cross-legged on the bare timber floor. Each held a long thin pipe connected to a large glass jar centrally placed and filled with dark brown fluid. A small flame beneath kept the fluid bubbling. The participants, mostly elderly men and women but several younger, all sucked on their pipe regularly, sending plumes of smoke into the hot stuffy airspace. A morbid silence presided.

Jude reeled back, choked in a bout of coughing as the sting of passive smoking clawed at his nose and throat. He began sweating profusely, a headache setting in. No one in the room acknowledged him, or showed any concern at the sight of a Robin. Disgusted, he veered away.

Coming to the second doorway, his head cleared a little as the air quality improved marginally. This room was as bereft as the first, save for a small cabinet, rickety table and two wooden chairs. No floor coverings, paint peeling off the walls. A small window provided gloomy illumination. In the far corner, an alcove housed toilet and a dirty washbasin, where a young man stood bent over. An unpleasant smell hung in the air, competing with the drifting smoke.

The Chinese youth straightened and emerged into the room. Eyeing Jude without emotion, he dropped on the table a syringe he'd just finished using. Old needles were scattered across the tabletop. He seemed unperturbed by RobinB. His appearance reeked of low self-esteem, clothes dishevelled, no shoes. But his face told the real story. Sunken cheeks, pale complexion and the eyes, bloodshot, dilated, red-rimmed. Windows to a quiet hell. A soul without expectation or hope.

"You want some?" he offered Jude in a bland tone of voice.

Sickened, Jude backed away, then hesitated. "Have you seen a blonde girl?" He traced the rough shape of Lara's hair with his hands. "You know? Blonde? Her name's Lara."

The response was an unlikely positive. "Next door." An arm outstretched, pointing the way.

With a gasp of excitement, Jude rushed out the door. Through the crudely formed opening to the adjoining abode, then he was standing in the next doorway. What he saw shocked him to the core.

Inside, three figures were slumped in various poses across a mattress on the floor. Young women, clad only in torn skimpy tops, otherwise naked. But the shock was the blood splatter smeared everywhere on body, clothes, mattress. Arms were worst, covered in blood oozing from numerous cuts. Even as Jude stared in horror, the silent ritual continued as one girl passed their shared razor to another.

A sick feeling of revulsion hit Jude in the guts. Yet he had eyes only for the shoulder-length blonde hair hiding a downturned face. "Lara! Lara!" he cried, charging across to her. "What happened to you!?" He fell to his knees, clutching at her.

She lifted her head, meeting him with a blank stare. The spaced-out look of a drug-crazed soul far gone, face gaunt, body emaciated. It was not Lara.

Jude fell backwards, appalled. A horrible moment of doubt struck, but quickly passed. He was certain. Even allowing for change imposed by drugs, he knew Lara's features well enough. This girl was a long way down the road to hell. Months if not years of systematic debasement.

The other two girls were no better. Mind-blowing. The pungent smell of body odour and blood was suddenly over-powering. Frantic to get away, Jude staggered to his feet and lurched towards the exit. Unseeing, he banged into the young addict he'd met next door.

"You like the blonde," the lad drooled. "I take that one." He shuffled forward, shedding his clothes. Naked, he squatted beside the darkest-haired girl. His thin body with ribs protruding was a repugnant sight.

Further repulsed, Jude stumbled out, gasping for breath as he strove to leave the horror scene behind. Slamming against the corridor wall, he was smitten with a wave of nausea. Retching, he vomited the contents of his stomach onto the floor. Feeling a little better, he moved on, to the last doorway before the end wall.

Several people were in this room. An elderly man and woman, male couple younger and a henchman of the type accompanying Chongwe. Old mattresses on the floor, basic furniture, rudimentary kitchen and toilet alcove represented their all-purpose living quarters. All but the henchman were smoking, the air again putrid. As one, they turned their eyes to Jude, but no one offered a greeting, just a collective stare, like a silent vigil. Unnerving.

Jude steeled himself, determined not to lose sight of his mission. "I'm looking for a girl called Lara," he explained,

justifying the intrusion. "With blonde hair. About this tall."
He raised one arm to indicate.

Still silence, no one moving, just staring. Eventually, one of
the younger males came forward. Expressionless, he stood
tall, quietly plying an unspoken leadership role. "Blonde girl
next door." His head inclined towards where Jude had just
been.

The elderly woman, seated at a wooden table where a
Chinese board game was in play with her partner, let out a
short cackle. "You want blonde. Hundred dollar." She broke
into a toothless grin.

Jude's stomach churned once more. Unable to fathom an
exploitative mentality worse than uncaring, he murmured an
apology and swung away, intent only on distancing himself
from another den of iniquity.

He quickly returned the way he'd come, pointedly avoiding
a look into the adjacent room. Back to where he started, the
oppressive smoke haze catching his throat in another coughing
fit. He stepped through the other punched-out opening in
common wall, reaching the first of two more rooms.

A door, with lockable handle, barred the way. No one
in sight. He was about to extricate his lock-picking equipment from the bag, but realised the door wasn't locked.
Emboldened by RobinB protection, he passed on through.
No one inside. The room presented as living quarters, in
relatively good condition. A full set of furniture included
three-tier bunk beds with mattresses and blankets. But the
place was bare of personal possessions. Someone recently
vacating? If Chongwe's, he was still around. Curious, Jude
retreated back out.

The second door also was not locked. Inside, the room appeared unused, bereft of furniture or any large items. His eyes widened in surprise, fixing on a low stack of folded bags in one corner. The same style bag Chongwe and his helpers were transferring to the warehouse a short time ago. Confirmation enough linking Chongwe to these premises?

Frustrated, he returned to the corridor. Close to end wall, nothing further to see. He felt certain this was Chongwe's patch. But no Lara, no clue from anyone who might have seen her. Was it a blessing? The relief when the blonde girl wasn't Lara was palpable. Lara in that state, what a horrifying prospect! He'd heard of self-harming, but only as a label until seeing the heinous reality. Lara herself once described it to him, a regular ill she'd seen while doing her community service at the clinic. According to the medic there, cases were on a rapid increase. People with low sense of self-worth, in despair seeking diversion from their greater pain. Another sign of the times? Drugs a major catalyst.

With heavy heart, he made his way downstairs and exited the building. He could only wonder at the world of extremes Chongwe operated in. Obscene profits of the underworld benefited the elite, but what about tossing a few crumbs to those Chongwe shared premises with? No empathy, just a place of temporary convenience after splitting with Jeremy.

The task of searching all Old Chinatown's dark nooks and alleys was hopeless. Could RobinB, knowing Lara, dash in and out of every building? It stood passive, had been uninvolved throughout the exercise, no lateral thinking to comprehend his quest. Learning ability did not stretch that far. How to instruct it? No means for that. Not feasible. He must revert to previous tactics. Weaving slowly back to the Valley road, he refocussed on how to repair the angst with Jeremy. Turning into the minor road, he knew in an instant it had all gone wrong.

Rounding the corner, he nearly ran into Brent. The man was stumbling about in a state of exhaustion, barely able to keep his feet. Clothes ripped, sweating heavily, he was a mess. Grunting incoherently, he fell to his knees as Jude swerved to avoid him. He stayed down, head to the road surface, panting with the effort of violent exertion.

"What happened?" Jude skidded to a halt. Then he saw.

The entire street was like a war zone. Everything in sight smashed, damaged, upended, scattered. Warehouse roller doors were buckled or ripped from their runners, windows smashed. Light poles, feeling their age, were bent to incongruous angles, a couple uprooted to lie across the road. The street was deserted, two vehicles only at kerbside, both flipped over pointing underbelly to the sky, windows and windscreens shattered. All warehouses being infrequently visited storage facilities, no one was available as witness. A deathly pall of devastation hung over the aftermath of Brent's rampage.

Dismayed, Jude surveyed the carnage. Clearly, Brent had thrown everything he had into it, expending all his great power, depleting him physically to the point of collapse. Must have been a frightening spectacle to behold.

Steering clear of the beast, Jude continued down the road. Nearing Chongwe's warehouse, another shock. A figure lay prone on the ground. He slowed, coming closer. It was Jeremy! Jude leapt off his bike and rushed to him. But it was too late. Jeremy's head was unmoving, mouth open but no breath coming out, one upturned eye unblinking and dilated. A pool of blood seeped out from under his body. Next to it, a wicked-looking blood-smeared knife lay discarded, damning evidence of the violence perpetrated.

Jude stepped back, horrified. Three figures were standing idly by the warehouse entrance. His eyes met Chongwe's, a silent exchange without warmth. The two heavies watched him, impassive. Both showed the effects of heavy exertion, one with blood splatter on his clothes. Mountainous, brutal enforcers. Jeremy stood no chance. Nor Brent, even with his until now unequalled strength. The fight must have been titanic! Or did they merely contain him then let him go? Interested only in nailing Jeremy? Certainly they cared nothing for property on a wider scale decimated by Brent. Chongwe's was the only warehouse undamaged.

Struggling to deal with the vivid images, Jude remounted his bike and reversed back from Jeremy's body. As with Gordon's demise, he felt no remorse for Jeremy, no guilt over removing RobinB protection, just a sense that fate had again dealt an ironic justice. He stared at the knife. Jeremy's own? Used against himself! RobinB suddenly worried him, its history on sighting a knife not good. But it was staying passive. No input action, no output reaction. Nevertheless, another reason to get out of there. Turning quickly, he headed off.

He didn't get far, encountering Brent staggering towards him with arms waving erratically. Fear-struck, Jude made to speed away from new danger. But Brent's demeanour was non-aggressive. He reached out when Jude stopped, as if seeking help.

"You my boss now," he croaked meekly, swaying on his feet in front of the bike. "I take care of things for you. What do we do, Boss?"

Astonished, Jude gave him a long hard look. The mouth still crooked, eyes still wide as if startled, no different from previously. Yet unimaginably, the hint of an underlying vulnerability was there. Physically, he was supreme. But mentally, he needed someone to guide him, make decisions for him, legitimise him. Without that stability, he was directionless, easily turning psychotic with devastating results. Loss of Gordon then Jeremy had triggered exactly that. Hardly an excusable rationale! The fiendish hitman had no moral compass, a social misfit committing numerous serious crimes. Due to association with his long-time mentors? No doubt.

Jude was in two minds, nervous to accept the responsibility thrust upon him. Did Brent have no one else in the world? Probably he did unknowingly, from the many sperm donorships enacted within a morally loose system. Lara was one! Reminded of that spurious unrecognised relationship, Jude resolved he would lay it all open at the right time. Incentivised with thoughts returning to Lara, he made a decision.

"Okay." Thinking ahead now, he indicated Chongwe's warehouse. "How about you pick up Jeremy's bike. Then we go."

"Yes good, Boss." Brent set off towards the warehouse.

The bike was retrieved without incident, Chongwe and the other two having moved inside out of sight. Jude noticed the screen and drone controls missing off the handlebars. Chongwe undoubtedly aware of their significance.

They returned to the carpark. No drone now. Jude found an observation post offering direct line of sight to the Valley road intersection. No other way back, Chongwe must reappear. They settled down to wait.

Conversation between them was near non-existent. The silence suited Jude. He had no idea how to relate to Brent at a personal level. There was no humour, no lighter side to him. A convicted paedophile, with violence, never rehabilitated, devoid of remorse. As metronomic from input to output as a Robin. Except when personal security was under threat. Then, a catastrophic outpouring of emotion and fury. The man operated at one extreme or the other, nothing in between. Stealing a sneaky look at the hard-chiselled profile of his face, Jude couldn't help a moment of amusement mixed with awe, utterly at odds with the record of evil. But one thing was clear. Brent was a monster, yet devoted total loyalty and dedication to whoever he called 'Boss'. A rare commodity in today's prevailing culture of opportunism, insincerity, political correctness.

The wait was a chance to catch up on the latest social media. Local postings were full of hysteria, panic-stricken accounts of Robin encounters with wide-ranging outcomes from minor injury to fatal. It continued to go viral worldwide, along with ever-deepening outrage over government inadequacy. Military action by the armed forces was mooted as an option. But the Robins were too scattered, decentralised, impossible to round up. A Robin could turn up anywhere, unpredictable. And all the time, they were learning.

Jude gave himself a shake, suddenly aware his focus was drifting. He didn't want to miss Chongwe.

"Boss." Brent pointed towards the intersection.

A truck was turning onto the Valley road. Jude could just make out three figures in the cab. Chongwe's truck, evidenced by the canopy and rear double doors visible as it accelerated away from Old Chinatown.

"Come on, we follow," Jude urged, jumping back on his bike.

They tracked the truck through the urban sprawl, keeping safe distance back. Jude preferred reverting to a covert strategy, despite the confidence boost of adding Brent's considerable muscle to the reliable power of RobinB in the event of confrontation. The absence of a Robin in Chongwe's latest activities encouraged a further sense of advantage. Yet he knew not to underestimate Chongwe. Anytime, the computer wizard might front up with a new upgrade and recapture control of all the Robins dispersed around town. The only surprise was he hadn't managed to already. Then he'd be all-powerful, with no authority yet successful in restraining the Robins let alone influencing their behaviour.

Self-autonomy was clearly evident, Robins wandering the streets, but mostly without particular intent or purpose, harmless unless someone inadvertently or otherwise provided the wrong input. Impossible to conceive how they would further evolve, under their own autonomy. What if Chongwe was the last hope of wresting back control!? That sudden thought came as a shock. Jude could imagine no counter to either force. He only hoped RobinB, for now running faithfully beside his bike, would remain loyal. Far from certain.

The truck reached a quieter part of town, turning into a minor road within a light industrial area. Another warehouse was the venue. Jude stopped at a suitably obscure spot from which they could observe.

A few people were about, no one at Chongwe's warehouse. Chongwe unlocked and lifted the front roller door. While he manoeuvred the truck to back in, his two helpers carried out a long rectangular sturdy-looking wooden container, using handles each end. It was heavy, a strong effort required. Loading continued a while, further viewing blocked by the truck's opened rear doors. A glimpse was possible of recognisable white canvas bags thrown in last as the doors were being closed. Roller door lowered and locked, the three climbed into the cab and the truck eased away. Jude could only speculate as to the contents inside the heavy containers. Arms cache perhaps? Would be consistent with knowledge to date.

Again they followed well back from the truck. Returning through residential environs, they arrived at a middle-class suburb. Chongwe parked in a quiet side street. From the rear, one henchman lifted down a hoverbike, then straddled the pillion seat as Chongwe took the driver position. The pair headed off, leaving the other henchman with the truck.

Through a couple of intersections, turning down a leafy tree-lined avenue, then Chongwe pulled in at an expensive-looking property. Security gates barred further progress. Chongwe worked his mobile. A short wait before the gates partially opened, enough to facilitate entry. At the same time, a man appeared at the residence front door. He stepped out onto the porch, his manner welcoming. A burly individual, paunchy, clearly overweight.

"That's Karl," Brent uttered in a flat tone, showing neither surprise nor concern, but a rare willingness to speak without being prompted. "Jeremy's boss."

"Right, right. Minister of Child Protection Services." Jude couldn't recall seeing him in the media recently, despite the topical issues and scandals of late. He gave a wry smile. Hardly a revelation seeing him connecting with Chongwe, no doubt about to learn of Jeremy's fate.

"He comes to the Cave often," Brent added. "To get videos and arrange for boys. I did good for him a couple of times."

They continued to observe from a precarious position behind a large tree. Chongwe and Karl were engaged in what seemed a serious conversation. Suddenly, Chongwe's off-sider made a swift movement, a gun to Karl's temple. A loud pop sounded, Karl toppled over, his lifeless body hitting the deck with a thump. All over in a split second.

Chongwe and his hitman swung away abruptly. Mission accomplished, they hastened out the gates, jumped on their bike and sped off.

Shocked again, Jude cringed back behind the tree, relieved to avoid detection as the enforcers shot past intent on a fast getaway. Once more, the workings of the underworld were chillingly apparent, the callous elimination of a superfluous but threatening inconvenience execution-style.

By the time Jude and Brent retrieved their bikes parked behind another tree, Chongwe was gone. They hurried back, Jude anxious not to lose contact. The truck appeared, turning onto the busier road to head in the opposite direction. Pursuit resumed.

Moving to the northside now. Another warehouse visited, goods similar to previous loaded. Further on, they came to a popular truck stop near the northern outskirts of town. Chongwe took a spot amongst other trucks at the generous parking area. He and his two heavies made for the food outlet.

Jude, Brent and RobinB pulled into a nature park on the other side of the road. A set of sheltered table and bench seats was inconspicuous while offering clear view of activity opposite. Jude settled back, prepared to wait.

Late afternoon, darkness not far off. The truck stop had basic accommodation. Whether Chongwe intended staying the night, meeting somebody or merely a brief stop before continuing on, Jude resolved to maintain the vigil for as long and far as it took him. The only certainty was the significance the substantial quantity of goods collected through the afternoon represented. Surely about to be delivered, distributed or exchanged in some way with someone.

The three figures of interest exited the building with their food and headed for the accommodation huts. They disappeared from sight. Feeling hungry, Jude purchased food for himself and Brent, made use of the amenities to freshen up, then returned to the park shelter. A long night likely in store.

Chapter 23

dle time was opportunity for a more in-depth look at the media and social media. Jude was soon rueful he'd not been more attentive to it over the last couple of days. The focus locally on Robin incidents, the hysteria, reaction and advice from authorities, condemnation of government, Coln and Lib/Nat Leaders stepping into the breach, all ongoing. The PM offering no answers, Treasurer with crushing Budget woes, both more concerned with political damage control. Still no Science Minister fronting. Another Federal Minister implicated in underworld activity. None of it was a surprise anymore. But the big news was of a major scandal breaking.

Exhaustive undercover investigations by media, spanning more than two years but greatly ramped up by recent events, had exposed a secret racket involving the Deputy Prime Minister, LGBT sole Lower House and their Senate MPs, and an arm of the Medical fraternity. In one corner of a major hospital, mostly given over to research, a facility was engaged in cloning humans. Starting years back, when Coln was in power but unbeknown to them, it was set up by the rogue ambition of research personnel in league with LGBT agenda, drawing in the then Labour Opposition through political deal-making. The 'L' faction with dreams of producing children for female same-sex unions through a process not requiring male sperm donorship.

A steep rise in funding to LGBT since last year was clearly payback for the years of their political manoeu-vrings, Preference deals, promotional machinations that eventually attained ascendency for Labour over Coln and Lib/Nat at the ballot box. Awarded under guise of the recently revealed Social Security slush fund for supposed disadvantaged. The hospital in question, not for the first time embroiled in scandal, benefitted, a large chunk traced to the cloning setup. Further contributing to cost blowout about to send the Budget crashing into deficit, let alone the moral and ethical issues. Identified also were secret payouts to the MPs involved, part recycled indirectly via the slush fund, part directly from same-sex couples paying for the service.

The Deputy PM, a heterosexual woman married with no children, as Foreign Minister hardly involved in recent scandal until now, had the media in hot pursuit, but was not answering calls, currently overseas. Speculation was rife she'd been trapped under LGBT threat of revelations over past political favour, which at best had been subversive if not criminal. The mysterious death of a popular but anti-gay Coln candidate just prior to one election was a cold case suddenly attracting renewed attention. Kris, the lone Lower House MP, had been similarly coerced, being of the male 'G' faction sometimes at odds with the 'L' faction. Political pressure at the highest level included manipulating the balance of power LGBT Senate members held.

Further investigations were ongoing. Particularly diffi-cult was to ascertain the number of children been created through cloning, since cases were simply absorbed seam-lessly into sperm/egg/surrogacy records. Three were confirmed, others suspected. Health problems were showing already in the oldest, a four year-old boy. A suspicion of premature ageing and a condition resembling autism but different, under testing, from any previously known case. Lack of emotional expression was apparent, as if soulless.

Jude stared wide-eyed at the small screen. "Of course, why wouldn't it be so?" he muttered to himself. "Cold process, cold outcome."

Postings abounded, reflecting further public outrage. Fuel for even greater condemnation of government now totally discredited. Was there any Minister who could be trusted?

A news flash was coming through. The State Minister of Child Protection Services discovered murdered outside his home, a single bullet through the head. No gun found at the scene precluded the notion of suicide. A short critique was a damning indictment of his activities, including links to the underworld and a paedophile ring. His closeness to Federal counterparts and the PM was highlighted, with contacts in America's National Rifle Association. Past controversy, when Labour accepted politically motivated donations from the influential NRA, seemed likely to resurface.

Again Jude stared incredulous at the screen, where an image of the NRA lingered. In his mind, the picture of a long wooden box, possible arms shipment, being loaded aboard the truck replayed vividly. An already dark impression of the underworld just became darker.

Feeling daunted by the forces at play, he looked for any sign of Chongwe across the road. Nothing yet. Apprehensive about his prospects, he watched Brent pacing slowly back and forth in limbo. Still unsure whether he'd inherited an asset or liability.

Darkness was falling. The nature park was deserted, traffic steady along the arterial route north. Another truck pulled in opposite. Chongwe's still clearly in view, but no one returning to it suggested Chongwe was not here to meet anyone and do business.

Suddenly, the wait was over. Chongwe and his heavies appeared, striding towards the truck.

Jude signalled to Brent. "Looks like we're on the move again." The stop a brief interlude only, perhaps seeking the cover of dark?

A familiar pattern quickly resumed, Jude and Brent following comfortably back from the truck, RobinB trotting easily alongside Jude. Travelling north into the rural countryside. An hour went by. No deviation off the main highway, no stopping at townships, no meeting anyone, seemingly clear intent to reach a particular destination at all speed.

Another hour going by, no change. Slipping into a stupor-like reverie, his mind began playing tricks with wild crazy thoughts. What if the Robins could never be contained? Learning too fast! Could they replenish nano-power eventually lapsing? What if arms shipments were for promoting terrorism or a war? Was drug smuggling expediting ruination of the nation's youth? No political will to combat it, only pretence and complicity hidden behind a façade of privacy concerns and political correctness. What if Chongwe was trafficking clone babies?

"No, no, cut it out!" Jude admonished himself. "That's too sick!" He shook his mind clear, refocussing on the truck's tail lights ahead. They had a mesmerising effect. A pair of beacons breaking through the black night. No moonlight to assist, opposing traffic not heavy, somewhere in no-mans-land. Concerned, he dropped further back, their own headlights potentially a giveaway.

Over four hours now. He had no idea where they were, except further north. Without warning, the truck slowed, braking. It turned right, onto a lesser road. Reaching the turn, Jude flicked off his headlight, signalling Brent to do the same.

Confident of remaining undetected, he concentrated on not running off the road, the blackness of night friend and enemy alike. Another hour passing. Absence of lights was sign of a remote area uninhabited. Of comfort was RobinB's glowing green eyes keeping loyal station adjacent, affording the creature superior night vision.

The road changed abruptly, a cloud of dust throwing up from the truck as they hit a gravel surface. Jude was forced to fall back again. Descending now, the road windy, dropping down an escarpment. He had to be careful, nearly sliding off the edge. It seemed an eternity, but at last they levelled out. The way ahead narrowed to barely a track. Lights from a building were away to the left, the first since the main road. Excited, he sensed they'd reached destination. As remote a spot as could be imagined. Surely few people came here.

Jude kept back, needing a place of concealment in a hurry. A little further on, the building lights relinquished vague outlines of ghostly shapes, a small hill at the base of the escarpment. They slipped in behind it, hiding the bikes. Kneeling down, they could peer over the top in relative safety, the building just a short distance away. Relieved, Jude quickly reassessed.

They'd arrived at the coast, a light sea breeze freshening the air, gentle swish of small waves lapping the shoreline in jagged lines of whiteness. The truck, instead of continuing to the building, veered right. It travelled a few meters further then stopped. Suddenly, the area lit up, from floodlights along a jetty protruding out from the water's edge. Chongwe backed the truck up to the jetty entry point.

Jude's attention switched to the building. Perched on an elevated rocky outcrop, it was palatial. White-painted stone walls, ornate fascia, a pair of tall majestic pillars fronting wide decorative entrance doors. Around the eaves ran a line of red-painted dragons. Chinese influence. An imposing structure, dominating the small cove it overlooked. Amazed, he wondered why anyone would construct a residence of such magnitude and expense way out here, or who would want to live at such an outlandish location. Movement at the entrance. They were about to find out.

The doors flung open and two men appeared. They started along a pebbled path that wound its way down the outcrop.

"That's Mingsu," Brent observed in his usual bland manner. "Chongwe's boss. He comes to the Cave sometimes."

The other man was non-Chinese. Jude recognised him instantly. "The Science Minister! Wow! What's going on here?" He let out a low whistle, stunned.

The two men reached the flat and headed for the jetty, just as several more appeared at the top and began down the pathway. Two of five were non-Chinese. Jude thought he recognised one. Another government Minister, but not sure of his portfolio. Maybe the other also, or a DP officer? He was recalling the officials recently implicated in the media. Whatever the case, gravitating here, a wild unlikely outpost, clearly evidenced something of major significance underway. More than just to escape invasive media scrutiny. Breath-taking! He watched with heightened anticipation, the adrenalin kicking in again.

The participants congregated at the jetty, each greeting Chongwe. There was movement on the water. A boat, good-sized runabout, emerged through the far reaches of flood-light influence, motoring towards the jetty. It slowed, glided in and berthed, the pilot slinging a rope over a bollard. Bringing in more contraband to load on the truck? Spellbound, Jude looked further out to sea. Through the gloomy residual light, the faint outline of a large luxury launch anchored offshore was at the limit of vision, completing the elements of clandestine activity. Its size, defined by single park lights at bow and stern, was of a small ship. Ocean-going? Obviously. No further confirmation of purpose needed.

Then, a surprise. Chongwe's two heavies were unloading from the truck. Long wooden boxes and white canvas bags were soon stacked on the ground. Someone was opening them, showing contents to the interested party, the politicians present especially engaged. Military weapons being demonstrated, boxes of ammunition, amidst playful exchanges, plenty of laughter and animated chatter. Large horde of drugs also. A business-like air quickly returned. All items re-packed, boxes sealed up, the heavies began ferrying it along the jetty on a cart. Goods leaving the shores, not more coming in!? Totally unexpected. Jude was perplexed, forced to do a re-think.

When all boxes and bags were loaded, the runabout pulled away, heading back out to mother launch. A diffused blur fading into the gloom. At the launch, the transfer of goods was vaguely visible, lifted aboard using a hydraulic platform. The runabout returned to the jetty, empty of cargo.

Chongwe slammed the truck rear doors shut. The Science Minister and two colleagues made their way back up the pathway. They disappeared inside the house. A short while later, they reappeared, with three others. Two wives and a same-sex partner. Each person carried a bag or wheeled a larger trunk, weighed down with personal possessions. At the jetty, all gear was loaded on the runabout, which made its second trip to the launch. Again, it returned empty.

Jude now comprehended the scenario playing out. It had all become too hard in Australia. Triad leader Mingsu was pulling the plug. Chongwe and his cronies had lost control; of the Robins, the AI factory, the politics, the DP, the media, everything. Not that they couldn't get away with anything or beat the system. Quite the reverse had been proven. Was it too many people with personal agenda, convoluting operations, making it too difficult to profit efficiently? But mostly it was the Robins, Jude believed. Throwing the entire community into disarray. And the politics, the discredited Labour government causing similar effect. For Chongwe and company, better to get out and reset elsewhere. Taking with them the Science Minister and a couple of others on the run who were still useful. Not so Karl, a State Minister only, deeply involved but obviously had become a liability, of lesser worth than Federal figures. Jude could see it all as he watched the protagonists, wives, partners in crime all milling about the jetty entry, ready for departure.

Chongwe headed up the pathway. He was inside the house not long before reappearing. And behind him, Robins!

Jude caught his breath in a shocked gasp. Robins! That changed everything. He counted five of them. Controlled by Chongwe, they followed their master to the jetty, joining the party mix hovering expectantly. All awaiting deliverance to a new life.

The altered dynamics unexpectedly imposed were galling to Jude, but not without logic. Of course, Robins commandeered before RobinB released all from the factory. Precisely as expected from Chongwe. Why had he not taken all the Robins? Was that his intention, but RobinB did it first? Undercutting an overconfident Chongwe. The irony of it! Jude shook his head in wonder, owning his own part in enabling it. But which was the lesser evil? Self-autonomous Robins now terrorising the community? Or if the same had eventuated under Chongwe control?

Then, in a flash, he visualised a derelict warehouse. Were these the Robins he'd been told transferred Lara and other captives!? His eyes snapped back to the house. Fear-struck, he suddenly saw not an impressive-looking mansion but a towering monument of evil. Lara! Was she here!? Had he found her!? With a strangled cry, he made to leap forward as a wave of euphoria swept through him. But it lasted a moment only. He cringed back as a big hit of reality struck. What could he do?

He felt hopelessly impotent, as powerless to thwart sex trafficking as the other underworld drugs and arms activity. What treatment and abuse had Lara suffered!? Had she been violated repeatedly? A desperate urge to act welled up inside him. How to make a difference? But nothing was certain. Just because he saw Robins didn't mean Lara was here. She could have been traded elsewhere. Anywhere! Was she on the launch already, about to be whisked away for delivery to whatever exploitation awaited? He stared at the vague shape offshore, the latent threat lying menacingly and tantalisingly at arms-length away. Yet the possibilities were endless.

Chongwe having uncorrupted Robins without self-autonomy was huge. No doubt he had upgraded their software. These Robins could pose a challenge different from other Robins, unique. Could RobinB influence them, corrupt them as it had the others? It was the only hope.

Jude knew he must do something. Once Chongwe and company left these shores, any chance of tracking down Lara, wherever she might be, would be lost. And taking all that illegal contraband to promote human misery in another location, with a few Robins to establish a new power base uncontested. In an inspirational moment, Jude made a decision. All or nothing, everything on the line here at this place, whatever the cost!

Turning to Brent, he put to him a plan of action. When finished, Brent acknowledged with a short grunt. "I'll do a good job, Boss."

People were standing around, seemingly hesitant to enter the jetty. Waiting on a signal? Time was running out, final transfer about to happen. Trusting to fate, Jude started forward. But suddenly, a distraction. From up the road, a set of headlights was moving towards them. Behind, a second set. Everyone's attention was riveted, as two vehicles pulled up adjacent. Signalling restraint on Brent, Jude stayed back, thrown into uncertainty. Had the authorities, DP or Police, finally caught up with the action?

Six people alighted, four adults with two children of teenage years. They had bags and travel gear, obviously intent on joining not spoiling the party.

Disappointed, Jude recognised two of the male adults. Federal Minister of Defence, and of Police and Correctional Services. He'd seen both in the media recently. The other adults, one male one female their partners, he presumed. Not lost on Jude was the relevance of both Ministers' portfolios to Mingsu Chongwe operations. Suspicion surrounding them was afoot, but no particular scandal incriminating them currently. Perhaps about to break?

Mingsu and Chongwe emerged to confront them. An altercation quickly developed. Clearly, the new arrivals were neither expected nor wanted.

Changing perspective, Jude suddenly saw the diversion as the best opportunity likely to present. Committed, he motioned Brent and RobinB forward.

Chongwe was shouting at the two Ministers. "We not do it anymore. You not come with us. You go back. Fix politics." In the next instant, he became conscious of a new presence. Startled, he swung round, coming face to face with Jude. He staggered back a step, momentarily flummoxed. But his anger remained. "What you do here!? Where you come from!?" Then he saw RobinB. His manner changed, aware of danger for the first time. He pulled back further, less aggressive to avoid an output reaction.

Time seemed to stand still in the next moments. A deathly quiet fell, the wider group of people held in thrall as a standoff unfolded. The floodlit area, contrasting the black backdrop of night, was a narrowed down pool of intrigue.

But Chongwe was thinking fast. He held up a handset. Coming forward, he pointed it into Jude's face. "You think your Robin have control. I control!" With an evil grin, he waved the handset in the air, then worked the buttons.

Jude shifted aside, giving RobinB clear passage as Chongwe's Robins galloped across to join the fray. They stood ready to enact Chongwe's next command. This was the moment. Everything depended on next action. Jude was expecting this moment, putting all on the line. Who had greater powers; RobinB or Chongwe?

But then, another distraction. Movement again at the house, more people exiting to start down the pathway. A group of eight, herded by two Chinese minders. Jude's heart leapt as one captured his attention. A blonde head of hair and figure he knew well. Lara! It was her!

A surge of adrenalin pulsed through him, a tremendous urge to rush over and rescue her. But just as quickly, the futility of challenging Chongwe's superior forces numbed him. Frozen to immobility, one of the gathered participants waiting, he along with all eyes followed the eight being marched to the jetty. The two minders, not the heavy hitting type Chongwe employed personally, but they carried heavy batons and seemed ready to use them. Jude was aghast, fearful. The captives were submissive, no one resisting. Had they had it beaten out of them!?

Despite her positive view of life, Lara had begun to despair of ever escaping her captors and seeing Jude again. Treatment had been harsh, but she knew far worse was in store, well aware of the sex trade and inexorable abuse pending when they reached final destination. Approaching the jetty was like a death sentence being unavoidably executed. Desperate for a last window of hope, she flung a look around the gathering. People watching, ready to follow them out. The Robins. Then she saw him. Jude! Was it him!? Her step faltered, she turned towards him, the thrill of sudden hope flooding in. He was signalling to her! Could he do something? But before she could respond, a baton dug into her ribs, shoving her forward to the jetty entrance. Contact lost, despair again. No one could beat the Robins.

Jude saw the moment when she noticed him. Frantic to bridge the gap, he held an arm up, sending her a message of hope. The moment carried a powerful exchange cementing their bond, then contact was snuffed out. Rough treatment by a minder made his blood boil. He looked at RobinB, his only chance to make a difference.

Chongwe was observing with amusement. "Lady friend gone," he crowed arrogantly. "You not see her again.

We get good price for her. Maybe she learn new tricks."
Unashamedly brazen, he was without moral fibre. But the
presence of RobinB was of greater concern. "Now I show
you new trick." Confident, he again waved his handset in
the air. Intense, he worked the buttons.

Pre-empting reaction, RobinB fixed its eyes on the fellow
creations. One by one, each Robin glowed at the chest.
They remained stationery, no longer heeding Chongwe. He
was irate, yelling at them. Furiously, he worked the buttons
again. Each glowed at the chest again. But still they didn't
move. Flying into a rage, he kept plying his handset, with
same result. Throughout, RobinB maintained its penetrating eye contact. Chests continued to glow, on and
off. RobinB's also, return response. A bizarre light show,
accompanied by Chongwe's screams of fury. Failure was
incomprehensible to him.

Initially, Jude was ecstatic. RobinB doing the same as
at the factory, his hope rewarded! But something was
not the same. The glowing was not flashing. Transmission
received but blocked, not taking effect. Chongwe's
upgrade, RobinB corrupting, nullifying each other, power
struggle inconclusive. An impasse set in, all Robins
neutralised, as if choked with confusion. Jude was agog,
anxious to break the spell and regain RobinB protection.
But unlike Chongwe, he had no means of instructing his
Robin.

Yet in that moment, as if a divine intervention was
transcending all the evil, he realised this was the opportunity presenting. The chance he craved! Robins incapac-
itated, Chongwe self-absorbed, others struck with inertia.

Trance-like, he fixed his eyes on the target. He nudged Brent. "Come on! Now!" They ran.

It all unfolded as if in slow motion, but every second a crucial godsend. With single-minded focus, they shouldered through the gathering. No one stopped them. They sprinted hard, reaching the jetty. From halfway down, Lara saw them coming. Jude screamed at her, throwing his arm out to signal ahead. "Go!" he yelled frenetically. "To the boat!"

Galvanised, Lara broke from the group, flying now. Fired up, the other captives followed. Shouts and screams filled the air, the jetty a scene of mad action. It happened fast. Two minders lashing out with their batons, Brent collaring them, flinging them with impunity into the water. He hardly broke stride, making it to the runabout first, jumping in, tossing the unsuspecting pilot overboard. Leading the frenzied escape, Lara threw herself off the jetty, landing sprawled across the boat's stern. She scrambled in. Others made it aboard. Hyped to fever pitch, Jude flung the rope off the bollard, leapt in, grabbed the controls and opened the throttle. He swung away, putting precious water between boat and jetty. Barely a moment later, the Robins arrived.

Once able to break the impasse, RobinB ran at speed to the jetty, intent on following Jude to keep dutiful station. The other five were close behind. With no experience of water, RobinB kept going, off the jetty and plunging in as it tried to reach Jude. Two other Robins with it. But Robin software included no ability to walk on water, or swim. Thrashing arms and legs, the water boiling, but the struggle didn't last long. Unable to float, the creatures sank slowly beneath the surface and disappeared. The remaining three, a stride behind, inputted the demise, computed alternative output and stayed on the jetty. Four captives, unable to board the runabout in time, stood stranded with them.

With the boat idling from safe distance, Jude and Lara clasped each other in a heartfelt embrace. But reunion was cut short as they witnessed Robin capitulation. Losing RobinB before his eyes hit Jude hard. Unaccountably. It was only a robot! Yet it had been dedicated and utterly loyal to him, to the point of its downfall. Better than he'd come to expect from most humans. Stunned, he stared at the patch of water swallowing his companion, his saviour.

Chongwe was running along the jetty, yelling and gesticulating at them, incensed. Vaguely amused, Jude punched the air, rubbing in the change of fortune, enjoying the sight of an evil-doer losing power and control.

Lara joined in, arms held aloft, exulting in their triumphant reversal. "Go back to your computer!" she hurled across the divide. "Try something that works!" Released from the trauma of recent days, she felt exhilarated. Two of her fellow escapees, Oscar and Simon, let out a huge cheer in support.

Aware danger was still too close, Jude engaged gear, turned the boat in a circle and sped away.

Looming large through the half-light, the launch impressed as a sleek luxurious piece of grandeur. But that was hardly of interest to Jude. With a deftly judged broadside, he washed alongside the loading platform. Brent jumped off. He worked the hydraulic controls, raising himself to deck level then clambered aboard.

Immediately, shouting and yelling, turmoil. The captain and his mate appeared at the rail, trying to fight off Brent.

Their efforts were futile, the contest brief. Brent grabbed the captain, flinging him over the rail into the sea. Then the other.

A lull ensued, Brent disappearing from view. The launch began rocking side to side, sounds of crashing and splintering emanating from the bowels. He reappeared, descended on the platform and jumped aboard the runabout. Jude opened the throttle and pulled away.

Keeping well clear, they stopped to watch. The launch was lower in the water. Slowly, it went down in a bubbling froth of turbulence, giving off a series of gurgling groans until the last piece of superstructure submerged. The vessel, complete with illegal cargo, began its long fall to the bottom.

Again, a loud cheer went up from the escapees. Justice had been served.

Lara shared in their celebrations. With the furore and relief of gaining freedom dying down, she was returning to normal self. Focussed on Brent now. Her father! More than impressed by his efforts, but confused as to the extraordinary turnaround in allegiance, she leaned close against Jude and whispered, "Have you told him? About me?"

Jude smiled knowingly. "I did tell him, but I don't think he believed it. He doesn't talk much, hard to know what he's thinking." He hesitated, then added, "There's a lot I have to tell you. Gordon and Jeremy are dead. Chas too."

Shocked, Lara made to reply, but Brent had moved closer. "Did I do a good job, Boss?" he uttered, emotionless.

Jude and Lara shared a bemused look. To Brent, he replied, "You did a good job."

With a final sense of gratification, Jude swung the runabout away as the last remnants of disturbed water settled, leaving no trace of what lay beneath. He motored quietly towards the shoreline. Coming into view was a scene of devastation onshore.

Bodies lay on the sand, and ground adjacent the vehicles. None were moving. Two people, Chongwe and Mingsu, were left standing along with the three Robins. Clearly, the Robins had acted. Whether corrupted by RobinB or instructed by Chongwe was open to speculation. Had Chongwe gone crazy? Striking out in wild retribution? Or Robin reaction to violent threat? The only certainty was the final demise of several MPs, partners and associates, for whatever reason. Consequences.

THE END

Epilogue

F ederal Labour went into total collapse once news spread of horrific scenes at a remote cove in North Queensland. Public distrust of politicians and disillusionment over the system electing them had returned to the all-time high of two decades ago when the absence of genuine vision led to the Coln phenomenon. After a Vote of No Confidence passed in Parliament, a fresh election was held and the people voted Coln back into power. The Lib/Nats became the official Opposition, Labour decimated to a minor party role.

Coln set out to reinstate projects and renew impetus for initiatives underway prior to being thrown out of office. Nearly a year of ineptitude and inaction to surmount, damage control required early to counter political fallout, not too difficult then to regain forward momentum. Except for the hundreds of Robins spreading terror through communities far and wide. Overcoming this menace was paramount, before the people's support could be harnessed and progress happen.

Two Robin features opened the way for exploiting a vulnerability in them. Their reaction to any threat was simple and decisive, the uncomplicated path from input through memory to output near instantaneous, the learning process expanding memory but with minimal change to a narrow band of predictable outcomes. And they remained individualistic, with no tendency for collective action or relating to each other, self-contained once receiving Robin3 maximum upgrade. No emotion, no feelings of attachment. The appearance of acting for each other had accompanied decimation of the Police convoy the day of release from the AI factory, but it was individual, each with the same output reaction to a threat and so many present at that time and place. Subsequently, they dispersed, attacks usually from one acting alone, over time rare to even see more than one at a time.

First response by Coln was to engage the Armed Services. Equipped with military weaponry, they could easily take out Robins, if able to catch up with one. They employed drones to track them down, but success was limited. The Robins had learned about guns from the day one encounter with Police. And they were fast. Targeting one had to be quick. Either they were too elusive and disappeared or reacted aggressively. As many servicemen were casualties with broken necks as Robins were eradicated. A very inefficient operation, tying up military personnel, one Robin at a time if they were lucky, disaster if unlucky. A better method was needed.

When Jude and Lara escaped the cove, they held station offshore in the runabout and contacted the authorities by mobile. By the time Police arrived, Chongwe and Mingsu with their three Robins had long since gone. A search went out, but they would never be seen again in Australia.

RobinB, in its demise, was spectacular for its simple unwavering output from 'Security' set task, mirrored by Chongwe's two Robins with their output reaction. The ignorance about water impressed as the better method for eradicating Robins. Entice Robin to a suitable body of water before provoking aggressive output from the safety of a boat, pointing a gun usually sufficient, clear out quickly to put a gap of water between. By and large, it worked well, if a Robin was close to water. A severe limiting factor, with many having wandered inland. Strict precision was essential, could easily go wrong. Great pains were taken each time to ensure no other Robin was around to witness and learn avoidance of water. An exploitable advantage out of their individualistic existence.

The process was laborious and dangerous, more casualties incurred, rate of success slow. Then, a third Robin feature was discovered. When RobinB activated and released the horde of Robins from the AI factory, it had imparted its own upgraded state to each and every one. Also to Robin2 and Robin3 in their interactions, subsequently transmitted to all other Robins out there under the trial programme. Every Robin had RobinB's 'Security' set task activated, specific to protecting Jude.

A chance discovery, when a Robin spied Jude and attached itself to him just as RobinB had done. Jude easily led it a considerable distance to its watery grave, no need for threatening it to provoke an output reaction. He became principal Robin-catcher, using assistance from tracking by drone. It was hugely time-consuming, but rewarding despite the callous indifference he was forced to adopt in administering their fate. Not coming naturally to him, but he understood it was all the consequences of over-reaching ambition.

Gradually, Robin by Robin, their numbers depleted until eventually, Robin sightings became an infrequent occurrence. One could appear anywhere anytime, however. Even years later, giving rise to speculation they'd acquired the means to replenish nano-power. Jude was ever wary of Chongwe. Would the evil genius reappear one day with his three Robins to again wreak havoc? No doubt applying further upgrades! Or had he escaped to set up in another country?

Coln allowed the enquiry to run its course, mindful of appearances and public perception. But they didn't wait for its recommendations, immediately returning the AI factory to former standing, full funding reallocated as part of a renewed boost to Research and Development. Most of the factory's expertise was still available. No Chongwe, but computer wizardry was not his alone, others well capable of resuming Robin and drone development. And nanotechnology. The serious issues were not about capability, rather about ambition and control, the less tangible forces at play. After a short period of reassessment and unperturbed by the huge wasted funding banished to watery depths, they soon had Robin4 on the way. Jude was highly dubious. The ever-motivating quest for greater achievement in the name of progress would always drive the agenda, but had the lessons of over-indulgence been learnt? Would over-reach be containable next time?

Also with immediacy, Coln consigned Labour's social agenda to the scrapyard of history. Legislation pending was thrown out of Parliament, including tightening control of private drone deployment, oppressive furthering of anti-vilification laws aimed at regulating people's behaviour, associated tinkering with privacy, discrimination, victim compensation provisions, draft Bills to change marriage and age of consent, all scrapped in their entirety. The secret slush fund hidden within Social Security was closed down, funding to LGBT drastically slashed amidst howls of protest from diehard social pundits claiming prejudice and peddling equality guilt trips. Coln was determined to tear down the mindless cloak of political correctness instrumental in the original rise of Independents now re-elected by a vastly more matured not so apathetic silent majority. Social media, frenetic as always, was highly supportive.

With urgency, Coln's focus returned to projects of primary significance in progressing the country forward. Stage three of the grand water scheme ready for construction to deliver far north floodwaters, the reafforestation programme, more clean Energy resources to come onstream from the nation's still much untapped potential, the Canberra to Melbourne Very Fast Train promising another regional town real estate boom with businesses to relocate as well as refugees of Climate Change and sea level rise. And more, all underpinned by promoting R and D to the forefront of endeavour, reopening the pathway to advancement, supporting enterprise over entitlement.

Budget woes would take time to turn around. Heavy initial costs were investment in greater productivity to meet ever more demanding challenges into the future, mitigating the effects of Climate Change. Seen by Coln as opportunity not burden, swinging the Budget back into surplus. They recognised worldwide pressures particularly relevant to Australia, two fundamentals of life increasingly dominant as defining priorities; Water and Energy.

The Health sector would continue to heavily impact the Budget. Wide-ranging, constantly changing with advances in technology, strongly supported by Coln through R and D. Urgency was compounding in the quest for new remedies to combat superbugs and out of control New Aids.

An immediate priority was to resurrect Rehabilitation Centres for drug users. Refurbishing buildings used previously, re-staffing and stocking, in recognition of a perennial ill facing the nation having rapidly regressed since Centres were closed nearly a year ago. More Centres planned, with intent to ease the pressure on hospitals and Mental institutions. No time to waste, the DP straightaway converted back to the Drugs Police. A short sharp period of purging eradicated the bad elements and obvious corruption, clearing the way for renewed confidence in DP actions. Enhanced surveillance and drone capability, one of the few measures of Labour to be retained, was embraced and pushed through by Coln. All trending back in the right direction once more.

Along with providing the solution to rid the community of Robins, alerting the authorities and divulging information about the Mingsu group and paedophile ring led to remarkable public notoriety for Jude and Lara. They neither sought nor desired the attention, at times overbearing as media regularly pestered them for interviews. And, of course, the social media frenzy. Both preferred a quiet return to school life, possible for Lara but Jude was often absent in the greater calling to pursue Robins. Their peers revered them now, in stark contrast, particularly for Jude, to the disconnect he'd always felt. An endearing experience, nevertheless.

What to do with Brent was a burning problem. Chemical castration had supposedly cured him of sexual predatory behaviour, and certainly he was docile as long as stable circumstances prevailed. Stable seemingly provided by someone he could call "Boss". Legitimising him, demanding no leadership or taking of responsibility. Could he successfully live an independent life? Was he really cured? Jude and Lara had to know. But when they confronted him with the evidence of being Lara's father, he quickly spiralled steeply downwards into a tailspin, trashing his own place in a blind rage. He could not handle responsibility, especially of an emotional kind.

Police arrested him, requiring a tranquiliser dart to subdue him. Identified for his recent outbursts against people and property, he was returned directly to jail. And there he would remain indefinitely. No trial, a court order merely invoking special provisions in law unique to convicted sex offenders, able to renew or extend a previous term if repeat offending. Supporting the widely accepted view that sex offenders too often could never be truly rehabilitated.

Brent's final demise upset Lara for a time. But she was philosophical, realising it was the life he knew. To take on official guardianship of him was untenable. Her mums were happy. On all counts, thrilled Lara was back, her ebullient personality relatively unchanged by traumatic events.

Jude maintained his association with the AI factory. Management greatly appreciated his involvement to date and mature insight well beyond his youthful years, an invaluable asset. On graduating from school, he joined the hierarchy in a newly created role specially aimed at addressing the moral and social ramifications now recognised as intrinsic to future development. A role he would cherish. Bringing him in close connection to Coln, direct contact with a new Science Minister.

Operating as a one-person consultancy, Jude soon expanded his horizons to a community-wide people-oriented focus. A profound calling growing in him for years, generated out of family dynamics, ramping up hugely in recent times. Lara assisted, part-time until finishing her final school year, then they formed a partnership. The remainder of her community service at the clinic was waived, however she continued a close association with Barbara and Tony as the building was converted back to a Rehab Centre. Lauded in high acclaim and impressing Coln, she and Jude were given what now ceased to be the safe injecting room to set up office. The large room next door they'd known as the 'Cave' was renovated to resume its former use as a dormitory for detained drug users. Ten beds only and the one ensuite. Not a large Centre, conditions basic, but a functional going concern in the wider scheme of things.

Jude and Lara, sharing the office space with disciplines across a spectrum of psychological and practical renown, offered a counselling service. Jude steadfastly avoided use of such a label that carried formal restrictive connotations, since he listened with equal enthusiasm to advising, blessed with a great propensity for drawing people out of themselves. Lara's natural positiveness was in similar vein. Together, they developed a reputation that greatly attracted people in need. With reservations, they kept open social media channels. Involving more people was better on balance than the often distorting influence.

They did have a specialty. Children of same-sex marriages. With their own experiences to call on, few scenarios presenting were of any surprise. And there were many. Demonstrable with spectacular repetitiveness were the repercussions of three or more parents and at least one non-biological. Time and again, a child of same-sex marriage would present with deep-seated troubles traceable to fundamental causes of problematic parenting. Indoctrination from birth tough to overcome, a generation growing up often with confused values yet to be understood by the rest of society. And becoming old enough to themselves have children, married or de facto. Domestic violence was a common ingredient. Jude and Lara received many as drug detainee cases. They tried their best, never condemning, always open-minded in seeking a way forward. Fraught with frustration, but these were the consequences.

Their efforts gelled with Coln's determination to reverse the social trending branded as unhealthy that had regenerated under Labour. The consensus approach refreshed, social media revealed the stirrings of a new trend that opposing pundits were quick to counter-brand with their own label of unhealthy. A growing intolerance of self-serving attitudes in certain quarters of society with personal agenda. Advocating severe culling of over-generous Social Security entitlements, citing single parent payments, slamming LGBT for narcissistic selfishness. A groundswell developing of surprising fortitude. Or long-time harboured within a patient silent majority? Emerging from the clutches of political correctness? Society values beginning a new cycle?

Evolving values, progressing out of decisions enacted, would always bear the responsibility. Whether from social revolution such as same-sex marriage, life-enhancing AI or anything else, the politics was defining. Self-interest too often hidden behind standardised rhetoric, propaganda, deal-making and the peddling of power. Coln could never hope to transcend that, despite being 'can do will do' people drawn from all walks of life, few from traditional non-creative non-productive professions that should be the tools not leaders of government. But Coln's direct action to develop the nation's potential, to insulate against the worsening effects of Climate Change went some way to appease the scourge of disillusionment. A dawning realisation that politics had proven to be a destructive force in the world not a constructive force. It all impressed on Jude a philosophy about the evolution of life that was irrespective of political, social, business-related or whatever. Every action, every decision has a consequence.

Jude had no interest in joining politics, despite pressure from Coln. Nor Lara. But they appreciated the Coln way, contributing through their partnership, dedicated to addressing the social ills pervading the community. From his second office at the AI factory, Jude maintained a close watch on the development of Robin4. The failings of Robin3 were dissected, more failsafe provisions programmed, awareness of water incorporated. Testing underway again, the swiftness of pushing it through disturbing to Jude. More consequences imminent?

Nanotechnology was a special fascination. He kept in contact with technicians Luke and Natasha at the small laboratory. Rapid progress was happening, new compounds created. One day, a breakthrough. Natasha succeeded in altering cells, converting them into a completely different product by rearranging atoms and manipulating the molecular structure. A stunning achievement. Opening an entirely new path into the future, the potential to render viruses and cancer cells benign, to enter a new world of disease and medical treatment. Why had nanotechnology not been gloriously embraced when first enabled decades ago!? But how would the ability to change the structure of matter further manifest over time? Moral questions, as always, lagged behind technology.

Jude and Lara had a new focus. Lara was pregnant. A joyous time, shared by Dulcie, Glenice and Doris. Uncomplicated consequences.

Author Bio

Vaughan was born in New Zealand, attended Takapuna Grammar School and graduated with a civil engineering degree from Auckland University. During the 1970s and '80s, Vaughan worked on large dam and water supply projects, was Resident Engineer on hydroelectric construction and spent two-and-a-half years in Papua New Guinea as Chief Engineer for the National Housing Commission. In 1987 he migrated to Australia. Vaughan was part of an aid group to Swaziland in 1989, developing a water resources computer model. On return to Australia in 1992 he left civil engineering to own and run a squash centre in Mackay, Queensland with his wife, Bernadetha. In 2006 they moved to Brisbane, running management rights unit and townhouse complexes until 2018. Now semi-retired, Vaughan has indulged his love for writing to present his third novel Consequences.

OTHER VAUGHAN
WHITLOCK TITLES

can be found at www.vaughanwhitlock.com

HUMAN STOCK

As the world spirals towards total war, the Australian government builds a survival shelter for a lucky few. The world they re-emerge into is bleak, empty and devastated. Angered by the damage wrought by men, society is soon dominated by women. They use genetic engineering to create a sub-race of obedient clones, and strictly control the fertility of the population. Led by one man who arises from oppression, a handful dare to resist, and to uncover the diabolical secret at the heart of the new society! There is horror, love, hate, loss, discovery and failure, but simmering beneath is the lust for power and control.

*"**Human Stock** delivers a powerful story and one that will keep the reader thinking well past the last word."*

Robert N Stephenson (*Altair Magazine*)

"A gripping doomsday scenario … will this be our future? A challenging first novel, playing sleight of hand with social convention."

Kurt von Trojan
(*author of* 'Mars in Scorpio' *and* 'The Transing Syndrome')

"… thought-provoking … gives the reader a frightening insight into what could happen to the world as we know it."

John Morrow's Pick of the Week.

2030 THE INNER LIMITS

In a bleak, dry world unable to recover from total war 20 years before, a crazed megalomaniac uses his computer genius to control an army of indestructible combat machines and lord power over surviving communities.
In southern China, an ambitious research doctor studies the human brain. The clash of technologies drives Artificial Intelligence across the threshold, and the machines take over.
One man, attaining special powers of insight from a near-death experience and motivated within a euphoric but abuse-founded love triangle, leads a small resistance group. Can he succeed? What does he ultimately discover!?

… sequel to the highly-acclaimed novel, **Human Stock**

www.ingramcontent.com/pod-product-compliance
Lightning Source LLC
Chambersburg PA
CBHW070156120726
47909CB00001B/139